SOMEWHERE BETWEEN LIGHT AND TIME

AIDEN LEMAN

Prologue

The signal on the heart monitor quivered and slowly faded into a flat line. Suddenly, Lana was hovering out of her body and watching the doctors as they battled to resuscitate her. An ethereal light was glowing under the ceiling, and her spirit gravitated toward it. She soared into an otherworldly tunnel, from where she was drawn into an even brighter, more magnificent radiance. There stood her mother, who greeted her on the Other Side, and now came her grandparents, all welcoming her to this supernal place. Here were so many souls Lana had known before she had even been incarnated on earth. Some of them were still waiting to start their lives as humans, while Lana had already returned. This realm of light had been her home long before.

Now her mother was speaking to her again, more loudly this time. 'It is not your time yet,' she heard, and eventually, she found herself back in her physical body. It was a cold night in January 2020, and she was in England. Her head was still throbbing from the meningitis fever that had sent her into cardiac arrest, but she was alive.

Her near-death experience had called to mind hidden recollections of the Other Side, memories from before she was born, but Lana also felt she had been sent back here because her work was not complete yet. She gripped on to the old abolitionist medallion that was dangling from her neck, and she immediately thought of her good friends Elias and Henry, for suddenly, everything made sense. The history of this century-old medallion was deeply entwined with the story of Elias and Henry, two very special people to her. And from the moment Lana had first seen them together, she'd sensed something about the two she was not able to articulate. Until now. Throughout the last few months, she'd been given so many clues to the puzzle, but now she finally grasped the bigger picture.

Like a tapestry that had been woven in a bygone time, all their encounters and experiences in history had somehow unravelled into the present era and produced a story that Lana now understood in a different light. The story of Elias and Henry was one that had begun almost one hundred and seventy years before.

Part I

A Journey Through Time and
Witnessing Four Human Miracles in
The Course of History

Strange New World

Tuesday, 7 June 1853, began as a clear, star-filled night over North America while the effulgent Milky Way illuminated the sky of Maryland. Fresh rural air swept across the fields south of Greensboro. This place lay on an internal border of a new country that had only been created some seventy years before and named the United States of America. Almost complete silence filled the misty pastures, save for the hustle of seven fugitives who'd been rescued from a Southern plantation that night. They were dark-skinned men and women who'd all been born into slavery, and they were dressed in tattered clothes, trudging along, thirsty and exhausted.

As they came out of some dense bushes, one of them was trembling and looking all around himself as if death could snatch him from any corner. He was part of a group of slaves who were following a short, dark-haired woman walking slightly in front of the seven. They called her Harriet, and she was leading the way. Among this group also trudged along a young woman, who had a broken arm and was holding hands with her eleven-year-old daughter, Anna.

It was a scene not too rare in this country that had

grappled with slavery since its foundation; an incident slave catchers had long reckoned on, and an occurrence well anticipated in those border regions; except that those men and women were being watched by two ghosts hovering along on this solitary trek, unseen by their human companions. One day, in a different century, they would be born as human beings themselves and named Elias and Henry, and this was the first time they had found themselves thrust into an observatory visit from the Other Side. It was a strange experience, being in the pool of souls one moment and here the very next, for their human lives had not even begun yet. Their own time in this dimension still lay ahead of them, but they knew whatever happened in the past would ripple through to the future… It almost felt as though some higher power was showing them a few human beings whose legacies might interweave with their own journeys as humans, whenever that time would be.

Soaring alongside the train of people, the two eternal brothers were stung with pangs of emotions they had never been acquainted with. Fear, doubt, horror, thirst… every one of these people radiated their own thoughts. Elias and Henry could hear them all; they followed every word, and yet, they had no power of their own. For they were only observers in a world that wasn't theirs yet. This place was like a foreign universe to them.

Clandestinely, the fugitives approached the border town of Greensboro, one of the last towns in the South, and stopped by a forlorn stone well in front of it. It lacked a bucket, and the rope looked feeble and rather unstable, but just strong enough to hold a light person. Harriet, the leader of the group, threw a few small rocks into the well and listened out for their resonance. She noticed the centre was deep, but the rough, rocky interior almost had enough grip for someone to climb on. Going down this well would be risky, but the dehydration of a man called for action to be taken swiftly, for he wouldn't last much longer.

Anna being the lightest, she was wrapped within the rope and handed two water flasks made from fine pinewood. Harriet had brought them for the mission. Cautiously, she and Anna's mother lowered the little girl into the well. When the child was halfway into the hollow, she looked up at the adults with fearful eyes and began to shake her head ominously.

'It will all go well, child,' her mother Magdalene said.

'Just hold on to the rope!' Harriet added.

The next thing Harriet knew, two gunshots were fired from nearby, shots that came from revolvers, about half a mile behind the group. Slave catchers! These brutes were roaming the state for fugitive workers at night. Immediately two of the group screamed in horror and then covered their mouths with their hands. Too late now, Harriet feared, for it was exactly the noise those slave catchers must have wanted to provoke. She saw Magdalene instantly place her hands on her chest, as if propelled by shock, turning her head to the side. But the second she looked back at her daughter, her mouth gaped open in disbelief, for she had already let go of her child's rope. Anna was now dangling in the water. Only Harriet was still holding on.

'Quickly, into the bushes!' she commanded. 'Get inside those bushes, everyone!' she ordered again, pointing towards a set of short trees that demarcated the forest.

The fugitives did as they were told. The dehydrated

man glanced down at the trembling child, half-immersed in water, and then back at Harriet.

'We'll get her out,' she reassured him. 'Hide and tell the others to duck. Don't make any noise.'

He nodded and dashed away to join the other four.

Left on their own now, Harriet and Magdalene were scrambling to hold on and pull up the feeble rope. It was so disheartening; every time it seemed to be working, the child slipped from the protruding rocks again and tumbled straight back into the water. Maybe Anna feared the slave catchers were close by, and she was intentionally trying to stay inside the well, Harriet started to wonder. Maybe she did *not* want to come out after all. The child was shaking and speechless, her eyes filled with terror as she looked up at Harriet and her mother, seemingly paralysed with shock.

'Please, Anna. If you don't climb at all, we can't get you up. Grip the stone under your feet!' pleaded her mother. 'Don't let go!'

Harriet noticed the rope was looking weaker the longer the hoisting dragged on, for the friction on the metal bar was wearing out the fibres and threatening to break the cord. They could not afford much more chafing on this rope; the girl had to put in some effort herself now.

'Anna, please, all you have to do is cling on and climb with your feet.' Harriet's voice echoed in the well. 'Will you do this for us, please?'

Anna remained silent and nodded tentatively.

'Thank you!' Harriet's relieved words reverberated inside the stone structure. She took a deep breath and summoned up the force to yank the little girl towards herself, aided by her despairing mother. Anna had already come halfway up the well, panting, her eyes fixed on the adults; then the fabric of the rope started to give way. The fibres began to untangle from each other, and like a loosening spiral, they separated out until the cord snapped. Immediately Anna tumbled back into the stone well and splashed into the water. Her body was immersed to her waist, and she looked up at the two adults, her eyes filled with tears of horror. Then her feet must have slipped from the shallow margin, because in the very next second, she was dragged into the deeper centre of the circle, exhaling precious oxygen as she went.

'Anna can't swim!' Magdalene cried out, seemingly oblivious to the slave catchers nearby.

Harriet held her hand over her mouth and watched Magdalene jump into the well, diving under in search of her little daughter.

Every second, hope dwindled a little further. The mother and child had been underwater for over ten seconds when Harriet suddenly noticed she was no longer standing alone. Behind her towered a tall, imposing figure. In fact, now the figure was approaching her, the grass swishing under their feet. Adrenaline overcame Harriet. The moment she turned to face the figure, they put their finger to their own lips and hushed her.

'Shh! We mean you no harm. Do not worry,' whispered the stranger. It was a young woman with long hair and gentle blue eyes. Dressed in a nightgown, she was carrying a rope twisted into a tight coil. 'We were watching you from the window,' she said. 'How long have they been gone for? How long have they…?'

A sudden gasping of air emanated from inside the well along with the splashing of water: Magdalene was re-emerging above the surface, carrying her coughing daughter in her arms. She was struggling to get a grip on the rough inner edges of the well. By now, the slave catchers couldn't have been more than four hundred yards afield, and they were probably fast approaching on horseback.

Swiftly, the tall woman swung her rope around the metal bar and sank it into the hollow space below. Carrying her daughter on her back, Magdalene stretched for the sturdy line and began to climb up the well. She pushed against the protruding rocks under her feet while Harriet and the woman scrambled to haul out the pair. Harriet grasped Magdalene's arm as they reached the top, then the mother collapsed to the soft ground, nearly dropping her little girl from her shoulders. They lay there coughing but could only allow themselves a few seconds' respite. Harriet nudged them on, for she knew the bounty hunters were swiftly advancing and about to close in at any moment.

'This way! Quickly!' said the young woman.

By now, the remaining five slaves were being ushered into the woman's house by a shorter, less imposing man, who was rushing them along the misty pasture. He had a meek appearance with neat, ginger hair, and Elias and Henry immediately sensed they were standing in the presence of the couple whose timeline on earth would be intertwined with theirs. There was free will, of course, and nothing could have been set in stone yet, but they both felt it was the legacy, or perhaps the lineage, of this particular family that was likely to interweave with their own journeys as humans, whenever that would be. Tonight was the first time they were ghosting this strange physical dimension, but they were already confronted with the brutalities of this world. Down here, it seemed as though souls punished each other simply for the identities they took on in this realm. It was all like a lottery of birth, and those who won this lottery became the masters over the slaves that lost. Then there was gravity—this strange, invisible force that tied all matter to the ground. All this grappling with the forces of mechanics was as strange as visiting a foreign universe.

'My house is not far,' said the tall woman, who motioned Harriet to hurry.

Rushing to follow her towards a small timber cottage, Harriet carried Anna in her arms as Magdalene staggered behind them. Once inside, the woman double-locked the entrance and hid the fugitives in the coal cellar below.

'Stay silent and remain in here, whatever happens,' she warned the slaves, and then she firmly closed the trapdoor to the underground room.

Save for the lambent light that filtered through the timber boards of the cellar ceiling, darkness dominated this crowded, small space. Harriet and the adults had to crouch down to fit in.

Up on the ground floor, the woman hauled the couch over the trapdoor and shut the curtains before she extinguished every candle in her home. She padded back to bed with her husband and tucked herself under the duvet. Silence gripped the house.

From the nearby field gradually emerged the sound of horse hooves; they grew louder as they approached, until they seemed to stop just outside their home. One of the horses let out a distressed neigh, and grinding footsteps now made their way to the cottage. Then five quiet but ominous knocks sounded from the wooden door.

The husband immediately jumped forward with a jolt, seemingly overcome with fright, and looked to his wife. She hushed him and gestured that he should lie still, that he should not make a sound, and that those men would eventually give up on them and move on.

She was wrong, and the faint knocking only became louder and more aggressive until it seemed as if the hunters were trying to break in by force.

'Open the door! We know you're in!' one of them suddenly shouted, giving the timber a furious kick.

'I'll go. You stay in bed, Seamus,' whispered the woman. She rose from her bed and slowly approached the timber entrance with a light shakiness in her legs. She was about to turn the key and open the door; then she intuitively held back for a second and reached for a little medallion she was wearing around her neck. After giving it a quick glance, she removed it and swiftly hid it in her nightgown pocket.

'Open this damn door!' another voice suddenly shouted, and a fist was rammed against the wooden slats.

Slowly, the woman turned the lock and then feigned an expression of fatigue and nocturnal exhaustion as she beheld the two brutes in front of her. One was carrying a pistol, the other one, a bright oil lamp. The two men sized up the lady in front of them and immediately softened their gazes a little, as though they were attracted to her. Still standing by the entrance, they seemed to shift their view further into the open bedroom and now looked at her husband, who was still lying in bed, as if speechless with fear.

'What are you looking for at this time of night?' the woman asked.

'Slaves,' responded the apparent leader of the two. He

was the one carrying the pistol, and he spoke in a deep, authoritative chest voice. 'Runaway slaves, seven or eight of them. Have you seen them? Them bastards ran away from their owners. They're trying to head north to Canada.'

The woman shook her head. 'We've been in bed since ten. Nobody ever comes here at this time.'

'Interesting. So how do you explain those drops of water on the floor, ma'am, and the fact that we saw candles burning in your house a minute ago?'

The young woman hesitated before she responded. 'I just went to the toilet and got my feet wet in the bathroom. That's all.'

The apparent leader of the slave catchers shifted his gaze from her face and looked down at her feet, immediately raising his eyebrows. The young woman glanced down at herself and then saw it too: her feet were completely dry, but some grains of soil were stuck between her toes. She had obviously been outside on the field very recently.

'What is your name, ma'am?' asked the man with the gun.

'Rachel.'

'Rachel what?'

'Rachel Jones.'

'How old are you?'

'Twenty-seven.'

'Where are you from?'

'Worcester.'

'You're from Massachusetts, then?'

'No. Worcester, England.'

'You are from Great Britain?'

'Yes, England.'

'That dumb man over there, your husband?'

'No. That's just a random beggar I picked up on the street last night. Well, of course he's my husband! What do you assume?'

'Do not mock us, ma'am, or you will regret it, and your random beggar too!' responded the apparent leader. He asserted his right under the 1850 Fugitive Slave Act to enter their private abode, and along with his assistant, he barged into her property. They seemed hell-bent on finding the runaway slaves and returning them to their legal owners.

Swiftly, all the candles were lit once again as the bounty hunters rummaged through the cottage and shifted every piece of furniture on the way. Eventually, they settled their gazes on the inconspicuous cellar door in the sitting room when they looked across from the bedroom door. At once, the apparent leader reached for his pistol and drew it from its holster.

'Ma'am, what are you hiding in there?' he asked, pointing at the trapdoor.

'In where?' replied Rachel.

'You *have* heard me, ma'am. What do you have in there?'

She wavered a moment and then stuttered, 'The door doesn't open. There's nothing in there,' quickly hiding her hand inside her nightgown.

With wide-open eyes, the two slave catchers glanced at each other in obvious disbelief, then began marching towards the cellar door, armed with their pistol.

Harriet and the seven had noticed the commotion that was emanating from the ground floor—after all, candlelight shimmered through the timber boards again while a pair of stern masculine voices rumbled from above. It was fear-inspiring, and if young Anna were to lose her nerve, it would all be over, and they would all be sent back to the plantation. Magdalene and Harriet were holding and caressing the young girl. Then two pairs of leather boots began to thud towards their hiding place.

It was the first time Elias and Henry had felt stirred to act in this world, but they knew whatever they did would be futile, for they had never touched anything in this three-dimensional world before. They were powerless observers on a day when they were not meant to partake in mankind's timeline yet, and as far as people in 1853 were concerned, these ghosts did not even exist.

'Pull the trapdoor shut!' Elias shouted a few times. But there was no reaction whatsoever to his inaudible ghostly voice.

'Pull the handle towards yourselves!' Henry repeatedly shouted into Harriet's ear, but still, he effected no reaction in this physical world.

The slave catchers had now reached the cellar door and stretched for the metal handle from above. Imminently, the slaves would be found. For only a brief moment, it seemed as though young Anna intuited the presence of these two spirits, looking around herself as if sensing someone else was hiding with them. Henry quickly laid his hand upon her shoulder and whispered in her ear, 'Please, tell your mother to hold the handle. Quick!'

The very next second saw a sudden change in Anna's demeanour. Elias and Henry would never find out why she acted the way she did, whether it was the intuition of a young child who had sensed the urgency of the moment or whether she had genuinely heard the voice of a spirit yet to be born.

Suddenly she lifted her soaked arms towards the near-invisible handle, and as if by common accord, the adults instinctively followed. Magdalene and two of the men pulled the handle down towards themselves, almost dangling off the ground as they kept the cellar door shut.

'This damn thing is jammed!' cursed the leader above. 'Come on, let's give it one more pull.' He scrambled to yank up the wooden flap with the other bounty hunter, but on this particular trapdoor, their efforts were wasted.

'You see. I told you people, that door doesn't open,' said Rachel. She felt her face relax into a beaming smile. The armed brute dropped his face in disappointment and finally let go of the handle, giving the timber floor one furious thump with his fist.

'Let's get out of here!' he commanded his colleague, rising to his feet with a livid sigh.

While her husband was still observing the scene from bed, Rachel ushered the dejected slave catchers out of their modest cottage and shut the door. The moment she locked it, her little medallion slipped out of her nightgown pocket and dropped onto the floor, clinking as it hit the wooden boards by the entrance.

Instinctively, the two spirits took a closer look at this object below. It was a circular medallion, slightly over two inches in diameter. The centre of it depicted a black man in a loincloth, kneeling in chains and facing to the right. Over him were embossed the words AM I NOT A MAN AND A BROTHER? The solid metal was shiny and smooth. It seemed such a powerful image, and it so brilliantly encapsulated the shackled human condition viewed from the Other Side. It was an abolitionist medallion, and that must have been why Rachel had concealed it from the sight of those slave catchers. Henry stretched out his hand to touch it, but the moment his ghostly hand reached the pedant, it went right through, reminding him that he and his eternal brother were still observers, and that their time to shape the history of humanity had not come yet. Now Rachel was reaching for the medallion herself, and for a single second, she suddenly held back, as though she could sense the presence of Henry's hand.

That night, Rachel and her Irish husband treated their guests to a late welcome dinner and a strawberry dessert. The leader of the fugitive group eventually introduced herself as Harriet Tubman.

'Harriet Tubman? Are you the abolitionist who escaped from slavery and later became a conductor on the Underground Railroad?' Rachel asked.

Harriet nodded.

'We heard about you, and how you risk everything to save other slaves.'

'It's been four years now since I escaped,' Harriet recalled. 'I still remember that day in 1849… and I felt like I was in heaven. But I knew I had to return and help those that were still living in bondage.'

Rachel told her all about the abolition efforts that had borne fruit in Great Britain, how William Wilberforce and the Clapham Sect had brought down that barbaric institution from which so many greedy people had profited, and how the House of Commons had eventually passed the Slave Trade Act of 1807 and the Slavery Abolition Act of 1833. 'One day, slavery will also come to an end in America. I know this will happen. America will live up to its promise of liberty and equality. One day, in the very distant future, there might even be a black president running the United States.'

Harriet and the seven stayed for the following day, but after dusk set in, it was time to travel further north again, for they had to reach Canada to escape their fugitive status, and all travelling had to happen at night. It had just gone ten o'clock, and the cicadas were chirping on the grass when the group was about to set off. Rachel opened the door to another starry night and gave each of the former slaves a goodbye hug. She stopped at Harriet, sensing that she was standing in the presence of someone who would go down in history as a celebrated hero. Rachel wanted to give her something very special along the way and produced the abolitionist medallion.

'Where did you get this from?' asked Harriet. 'It's beautiful.'

'Josiah Wedgwood made these in England.'

'Who's Josiah Wedgwood?'

'He was an abolitionist, like Wilberforce and my grandparents. People wore these medallions in the Clapham Sect and during the abolition efforts until slavery came to an end in Great Britain. I want to give it to you for good luck, Harriet, because here the struggle still continues.' Suddenly Rachel took Harriet's hand. 'I'm pregnant now. I hope when my child grows up, there won't be this cruelty anymore. All humans are born free.'

Harriet held the medallion in her hands, looking at the metal with a soft glow around her eyes, but then declined the gift. 'You keep it, Rachel,' she said. 'They are likelier to catch me if I wear a medallion like this. Pass it on to *your* children, so they can remember this episode in history.'

Rachel wavered for a few seconds before she cupped her hand over the medallion and put it back around her own neck, tucking it under her dress. She exchanged the gift for a flask heavy enough to fetch water from the pulley of a well.

'How do you even know where you are going? Do you ever get lost in the dark?' Seamus asked just as they were about to part.

Harriet looked up into the night sky and pointed to a group of seven stars that formed the constellation of the Big Dipper. 'Do you see those two stars at the edge of the rectangle?' she asked.

Rachel and her husband nodded.

'If you picture a straight line between those two, and then draw the same line further, it will hit that bright star there, the North Star. All other stars can move, but the North Star will always point towards the North Pole. From here, it will only be a couple of miles to the free state of Delaware. From there, we will continue north until we reach Canada. And freedom.'

Rachel gave Harriet, Anna and Magdalene one last hug. Then the train of eight parted and drew towards Polaris. Seamus and Rachel lingered outside their house until the group was almost out of sight, giving them a final wave just before they disappeared into the distance. Silence had returned to their home.

'Why did you tell those slave catchers your real name?' Seamus challenged his wife.

'Because they were about to search the house; they would've seen our names on all the letters from England or demanded to see our passports,' Rachel replied. Then she suddenly frowned. For a couple of seconds, she felt as though they were being watched by a neighbour standing on a back porch maybe eighty yards from their cottage. She looked across, but now there was nobody to be seen, although an oil lamp was still brightly flickering outside.

Not everybody in this area was part of the

Underground Railroad, and Rachel knew they'd better be extra careful from now on, for anyone could send a telegram and report sightings of fugitive workers in this area. The penalty for Rachel and Seamus would be imprisonment and a fine of one thousand dollars. Still, the struggle had to be continued until slavery itself was abolished. In this belief, Rachel held firm.

The next second, Elias and Henry found themselves back on the Other Side again, away from the confines of earthly time. It had all felt like a taster of the human life they would embark upon, probably in another epoch. This journey had been like a glimpse of history, a quick peek into the lives of a few people whose legacy or lineage they sensed might reach into theirs one day. They communicated telepathically, speaking without words or names.

'Do you think… that's what life will be like for us?' Elias silently asked Henry.

'I don't know,' his eternal brother replied. 'Perhaps those people, or maybe their timeline, might be significant for us one day.'

'The world will have changed by then.'

'It seems as though life is all shaped by where you're born,' said Henry. 'Becoming human is like a lottery of birth.'

Indeed, earth had been a very strange and brutal place to visit. But however bleak this place was, it also abounded with courageous people who swam against the current and took history into their own hands. In a dimension where souls were bound by gravity and could kill each other with a single bullet, the bravery they had beheld that night shone like a genuine miracle. It was from then on that Elias and Henry would repeatedly find themselves thrust into observatory trips from the Other Side. The world was evolving slowly. Technological advances came incrementally. The population was growing steadily, and yet every time they emerged on earth, it was always this particular family they found themselves with: Rachel and Seamus's naturalisation plan did not bear fruit, and they were deported to Great Britain after neighbours alerted the police about their involvement in abetting fugitive slaves. Though their descendants would continue the family's legacy, their own relationship ended six months later, for Seamus found his strong-willed wife too stubborn and too dominant after they returned to England, and he left her the following year. He accepted a post at a British trade mission in East Prussia, where he married a second time in 1856, becoming a father to three more children. Because the laws of the time precluded any formal divorce from his first wife in the United Kingdom, all these children were Prussian citizens through their mother.

Seamus remained in Königsberg until his death in 1911. He was outlived by Rachel, who spent the remainder of her life running an orphanage in Herefordshire, where she died the following year, a grandmother of five children. The two had never spoken to each other again while on earth.

Early Twentieth Century

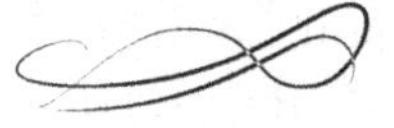

There was a narrow strip of land that belonged to nobody. A graveyard where people did not dare to venture. It was a place where dead bodies lay strewn and left to moulder. A site where instant death awaited innocent humans, and where grenades and gunfire separated souls from their bodies. It was also a place that, decades later, historians would write about as the site of a spontaneous, rare miracle in the midst of a dark age—one of very few human wonders Elias and Henry would witness as observers.

Today was Thursday, 24 December 1914, two years after Rachel's death. European countries had been connected in such rigid alliances that the assassination of a single person in Sarajevo had sparked an outbreak of conflict that would soon engulf thirty-two states. Every day, more troops were exterminated in artillery and grenade attacks, while gunfire and shelling would claim ever more lives, many of which belonged to teenagers, conscripted and turned into fighters after leaving school. One of those war sites was a narrow, forlorn strip of land in Belgium. Here, along the Western Front near Ypres, fighting between Great Britain and Germany was stalling, and the warring parties had dug long, narrow trenches to protect themselves from enemy fire, seeking shelter and warmth at night. The clouds of the last few days had given way to a clear, moonlit sky, which lit up the ice crystals on this deadly field between the two opposing trench lines. A glowing, frosty mist was hovering over this place as two ghosts descended upon no-man's-land. It was the sixth time Elias and Henry had found themselves spontaneously ghosting this dense gravity-dominated dimension. And it was always the same when they stood near humans: they could hear every thought, sense every feeling, and still marvelled at the way people behaved. The two recognised one of the soldiers inside the British trench, for he was Rachel's great-grandson, Private James Adam. They soared into the trench and hovered over Rachel's descendant. A tall eighteen-year-old, he was dressed in a heavy winter coat and thick leather boots. The young man ate the last forkful of his beef stew and moved the candle closer to his copy of the *Daily Telegraph*. The newspaper was opened on page five, where the headline read TITANIC DISASTER: MORE THAN TWO YEARS ON, ONLY 330 BODIES RECOVERED FROM SEA.

He rose from his makeshift chair and narrowly squeezed past fellow soldiers as he trudged back to position twenty-five. Through his binoculars, he dutifully observed the opposing trench line. The atmosphere on the German side had been strange all day. There had been no shootings and no grenades for hours; in fact, it was an eerie calm that lay over the place tonight—calm except for the frosty wind that blew about his cheeks as it howled like a raging wolf. Then the wind suddenly stopped. James looked all around himself as he was visited by an uncanny, and yet, benign sensation as though someone invisible were hovering over him. He shook his head and continued to watch the German brutes through his field glasses.

Something strange started to unfold now, something unusual that James had not seen before, and that was so unlike German soldiers. One by one, a whole row of conifer trees emerged on the opposing trench line, until there must have been at least a dozen. Was this some kind of attack? They looked like evergreen fir trees, and now glimmering lights appeared on them, as though somebody was lighting a series of candles. The next minute, the whole enemy front line glowed in a festive radiance that was both beautiful and also very worrying.

'Sergeant… Sergeant, we have a problem,' shouted James, saluting his superior as he approached.

'What's the matter now? Are the Krauts preparing to attack on Christmas Eve?' replied the sergeant.

James shrugged his shoulders and passed the binoculars over. 'I don't know, but they've lit up their trench with candles and trees and all that. Look!'

The lambent, flickering candlelight could now be seen in the distance with the naked eye, and at least two dozen of James's comrades were trying to make out more details with their field glasses. Suddenly a faint humming commenced in the nocturnal silence of no-man's-land, quiet at first, then growing louder as more enemies joined in. The humming now became singing in German, emanating across from this strip of death. It was a little haunting but also bizarrely beautiful, for the words of the song were unknown to James, but the tune was familiar. It rekindled memories of childhood, family, safety, and then even brotherhood. '*Stille Nacht*', or 'Silent Night', was being repeatedly sung out from the enemy trench.

James noticed a few of his battalion had begun to hum along impromptu. Then the humming gradually turned into singing. Now the same melody was being chanted in German and English. Whether it was intentional or not, James could not tell, but gradually, a strange musical harmony was setting in on both sides of the choir. Some crazy lads suddenly rose from their German trench, waving with candlelit fir trees. Could they be drunk? James wondered. They took a few steps towards the British and then stopped.

'*Es ist Weihnachten!*' one of them shouted over, and '*Kommt doch mal rüber, Ihr Engländer!*' *It's Christmas. Come over here, you English!*

James glanced over to his sergeant for reassurance, but all he did was make a gesture of ignorance, shrugging his uniformed shoulders. They were in a war, after all, and all this could be a ruse.

Still, the German lads continued to wave with their candlelit fir trees, gesturing to the English to step over. Nobody took the bait. Suddenly, at the very far end of the trench, one British soldier appeared to accept the invitation and hopped out of the pit, his hand firmly gripping his Lee–Enfield rifle. The sergeant immediately raised his hand and paced towards him. Then, for some reason, he held back and let the private march on.

'*Kommt doch mal rüber, Ihr Engländer!*' the Germans shouted again.

Another two, then three on the British side followed suit, gingerly approaching those German soldiers in no-man's-land.

More people followed on both sides. If so many of them could do it, and they were all surviving, maybe he could take the risk too, James mused. His rifle was fully loaded and ready over his shoulder. For a second, he closed his eyes. Then he rose to full height with his chest jutted out, and the next second, he was standing on the forbidden, frosty graveyard. It might as well have been a foreign world to him, an unknown reality. All that time, they'd only been a mere two hundred and fifty yards away from each other, and now they were approaching the heartless brutes that had massacred hundreds of their men. *Always keep your eyes on their hands*, James kept reminding himself. Suddenly he spotted a German soldier who was stealthily sliding his fingers towards his Mauser, as though he was preparing to attack. Immediately, James froze on the spot and reached for his own rifle. *This was all a trap!* Swiftly, he swung around his weapon, ready to shoot the advancing Germans. For a single second, he hesitated, watching. Now, his opponent's hand slowly moved past the pistol and concealed itself inside a pocket. Maybe he was just freezing on this chilly night, James started to hope. Still, vigilance had to be maintained throughout the crossing. He spotted a much meeker soldier, with cringing, fearful eyes, whose frowning face betrayed a very reassuring war anxiety, and James intuitively trudged towards him. The man was clutching a small candlelit fir tree in his left hand. They fixed their gazes and gingerly approached one another. James did not understand what it was, but he felt this strange sensation, as though somehow a spirit or two were guiding him towards this particular man.

Then, on a patch of frosty white ground in the middle of no-man's-land, he was one of around forty soldiers who met from two belligerent battalions. Spontaneously, they saluted each other and then even shook hands. '*Frohe Weihnachten*,' the Germans kept saying to their enemies. Most of them showed rather tense expressions on their faces, but gradually they appeared to drop their guard just a little as they released the strain from their cheeks. James stretched out his arm and shook hands with the man he'd intuitively walked towards. He introduced himself as Jens Altmann.

Elias and Henry had known all these souls from the Other Side. Two decades ago, they'd all ventured from one common home, but here on earth, they resided inside the bodies of two belligerent nations, like the property of earthly masters who had moulded them into mortal enemies. It was a curious spectacle to understand, for souls were no longer kidnapped and exported as slaves from abroad. The slave trade had ended for good. But if a government could force its own passport upon a soul, if a government could claim a person belonged to its country, anything could be done to them. They could be torn out of higher education, conscripted, turned into warriors, and sent to their deaths en masse. But that night, these war-locked troops spontaneously put down their deadly roles.

James and Jens lowered themselves onto a cold patch of grass and warmed their hands by the glowing candles on Jens's small fir tree—the Germans called it a Christmas tree.

'Why are you guys fighting us?' James eventually dared to ask.

'We are fighting for freedom and for Kaiser Wilhelm,' Jens replied.

'Is that really what the kaiser made you all believe?' James responded, a little miffed. 'How can you be fighting for freedom if *we* are fighting for freedom?'

'I don't want to fight anybody anymore. I just want this war to be over.'

'Didn't you *choose* to join the army? Didn't you *choose* to fight yourself?'

'Of course not! Why would anyone fight for this kaiser? *I* know they're just using us here.'

'I didn't volunteer either. I was going to study Biology at Aberystwyth. Then the call-up papers came.'

'For me, it was medicine. Heidelberg University. I was there one semester; then I got conscripted. These people think they own us. They think they can do anything they like with us.'

'Do you hate us?'

'Hate? I hate those who've pushed us into this war. I hate those who think they can use us however they like.'

There was a tiny tinge of an English or maybe an Irish accent in those last words, and James stared into Jens's eyes with curiosity.

'Your English is very good,' he remarked. 'Have you ever lived in Britain?'

'No, but my great-grandfather was Irish. I learned English from him. He only died a few years ago.'

'Well, *my* great-grandfather was also Irish, but he was a loser, I tell you. I don't even know when he died.' It was a strange thing to confide to a war opponent, but these two men would probably never see each other again… James could tell him whatever was on his mind.

'A loser? Why would you say that?' Jens asked.

'Because he deserted our great-grandma. They had a child together, and then he made off and never came back. That was in 1854.'

'Where did he go?'

'Königsberg, Prussia.'

'Hmm… that is where *my* Irish great-grandfather moved to in 1854,' Jens said pensively. 'That's where I'm from.'

'Really? But…'

Jens looked at James for a moment as though he

shared the same improbable thought, then he glanced forward to the glimmering candles on the Christmas tree. Some frost particles were twirling around it as a frigid gust started to sweep over the trenches again. The very idea that these two might be distant cousins fighting each other in the same war was frightening, but at the same time… *Gosh, this is such a small world*, James thought. People could all be related somehow, and yet different governments were commanding their allegiance.

'My great-grandfather's name was Seamus,' said Jens. 'He lived in America for a while, in a little town called Greensboro. What was your great-grandfather's name?'

'I don't know his name,' James admitted, 'but yes, he also lived in America. He lived in Maryland before he moved back to England. Then he just left for Prussia and never returned.'

'He never wrote home again?'

'My great-grandparents didn't get on, so they stopped all contact. We always suspected that he had started a new family, but we never knew.'

'Family. *Familie*,' Jens muttered to himself. 'Perhaps they will call an end to the hostilities after tonight, or perhaps they will call a truce until New Year. Or do you think we will fight again tomorrow?'

'Maybe… maybe not. But even if the peace lasts a little longer, sooner or later, it'll all start again.'

'I guess none of our leaders will want to give up.'

A few moments of silence lingered between the two as they watched others exchanging food, chocolate, and even wine. The whole atmosphere was so surreal that they might as well have been on a foreign continent where war did not exist. Nobody genuinely wanted to fight this war, and gradually there was a sense that there would never have been a war in this December 1914 if it hadn't been for a handful of leaders that possessed over hundreds of thousands of young men.

Before midnight, the soldiers started to stroll back to their home trenches, although none of them seemed to be in a hurry, James noticed. He briefly held off and tugged the German soldier's sleeve.

'*Was ist lost?*' Jens asked. *What's going on?*

James fumbled in his coat pocket and produced a few cigars, staring at them with a feeling of surrender before he handed them over to his distant cousin. 'In case we don't see each other again, a little Christmas gift from me,' he said. 'Cigars from the King. Take them!'

Jens baulked a little and looked all around himself, as if he worried what his superiors might say to such a present. But then, some others were doing exactly the same, and today nobody seemed to bat an eyelid. Jens appeared somewhat reassured and slowly reached for the gift. He fumbled inside his own pocket, from which he produced a thin brass handle that was connected to a shiny metal cone. It reflected the white moonlight like a precious crystal.

'What is it?' asked James.

'It's a *Kerzenlöscher*. Sorry—I don't know the word in English, but it's like…'

'What do you do with it?'

'I don't know what you call it in English,' Jens repeated. 'You put it on a candle, and the fire goes out. Maybe you can take it as a souvenir from tonight.' He held the metal over one of the candles and waited until the flame disappeared underneath it.

James stretched out his arm and gave the shiny brass a feel with his hand. He could not think of any use for such an item, the British side having no Christmas trees in their trenches. But perhaps he could hold on to it, and if he survived the war, it would become a reminder that spontaneous miracles could occur any day, like a token of hope. At this, the two soldiers bade farewell to each other and retreated to their trenches with their presents. James was hoping he would never face this man in battle, for the same unlikely thought still lingered in his mind. Deep down, he now knew his great-grandfather really had founded another family lineage in Prussia, though he also sensed this would be the only time he spoke to his distant cousin.

He marched back to his customary position in the trench, where he leaned onto a buffer of sandbags and gazed up at the night sky. James thought of his pregnant wife, their unborn child and his parents and slowly sensed he'd partaken in a moment of history that night. Then he had that strange feeling again, this eerie sensation as though a spirit or two were standing around him. It was the same feeling that had guided him towards Jens Altmann, and now this feeling was nudging him to write back to family and record this significant moment. Just then, a few snowflakes started to fall into the trench, and they softly landed on James's leg. He lit an oil lamp, dug out a piece of paper and wrote:

Dear Dad,

A little miracle took place in the trenches near Ypres today. You will never believe what happed to our division this night. I think it was about half past ten or so. I was on watch duty, and suddenly the trenches opposite filled with fir trees…

The letter was posted the following day and addressed to the chapel where James's dad worked as a vicar. But the author would never read his response, for he was killed in Belgium just after New Year.

Out of Elias and Henry's observatory jaunts to earth, this was the only time when Rachel's and Seamus's diverging lineages had met. Their legacy was continuing, though, and James Adam's descendants would go on to become doctors and nurses, working in county hospitals around central England and even for the Red Cross.

Mid-Twentieth Century

When t the Great War finally ended, the cost to human life was more than twenty million, with a further twenty million injured. The following decade saw an episode of hyperinflation cripple the economy of Germany and plunge the country into recession. When the nation was further hit by the Great Depression of the 1930s, the seeds were sown for a leader who would soon steer mankind's timeline into some of its darkest years. This leader spared nobody who'd lost the lottery of birth. By the early 1940s, millions of people had already been killed in the war Hitler had commenced, while whole communities of Jews were housed in ghettos, used as slave labour, and eventually gassed to death.

One of these places was the Kraków Ghetto, and it was here that Elias and Henry found themselves ghosting earth on their eighth observatory jaunt. Today was Tuesday, 2 February 1943.

By eleven o'clock on this snowy night, a dense fog had descended upon this Jewish ghetto and spread into every street and alleyway, making the ramshackle stone buildings appear like haunted apparitions. Some rusty old lanterns lent a little light to this sombre place while water dripped from the gutters. The only other sound that intruded into the silence of this curfewed district was the distant barking of one or two German shepherds, a few hundred metres away. The barking was becoming more aggressive as a teenage girl with long hair glanced behind herself and dashed away into a narrow passageway. She was dressed in torn trousers and a tattered fleece, on which was sewn the Star of David, which marked her as a Jew. She ripped it off and pushed the little piece of fabric into the snow.

This orphaned girl was Alona Garfunkel, a member of the Akiva resistance, and right now, she was being chased by the German Abwehr. Two others from the group had already been detained that evening, and now they were after her. Unaware was Alona that two ghosts, or unborn spirits, were also accompanying her.

By now, Elias and Henry were accustomed to being powerless observers in a foreign world, but human behaviour intrigued them, especially when people acted courageously or wrote history.

The mercury dropped below freezing, and the girl tightly rubbed her hands together as her teeth chattered and she bit on her lips. Every time she exhaled into the frigid air, vapour emanated from her airways, giving away her scent to the police dogs behind. The barking sounds became even more ferocious, and the girl started to sprint towards the end of the alley, her torn shoes squishing into the thick snow. At the end of the passage, she turned right into an even narrower pathway and charged through the heavy fog. She could hear the sound of the German language behind her, muttered by two or three young men. When the girl finally saw through the fog, she realised she'd gone into a dead end, and now there was nowhere else to run or hide.

'*Stehen bleiben! Bleib stehen, Mädel!*' someone was shouting from behind, followed by aggressive growling.

They couldn't have been more than sixty metres behind when Alona reached the deserted house at the end of this narrow backstreet. A broken waste container stood against the dilapidated building, and the girl quickly took a look. Inside, it was filled to the brim with smelly rubbish; below, there was not enough space to conceal a human. And surely, the German shepherds would instantly sniff out her whereabouts and betray her to the savages from the Abwehr. If only Elias and Henry could alert the girl to the old fire ladder on the corner of this passage, she might still stand a chance of escape.

Maybe it was an instant of telepathy, for no sooner had they projected their thoughts than Alona glanced to her left and sized up this rickety structure, but then she shook her head. Certainly, it would crumble under her weight and collapse to the ground, she concluded. The girl looked about herself frantically, trying to make out anything at all she could use to escape or protect herself. She could not see it then, for the fog was obscuring her view, but the two German shepherds were already in the alleyway now, and they started to charge towards her.

She heard the crunching of snow under racing paws and quickly turned her head. Out of the fog emerged two pairs of twinkling eyes and the sharp canines of police hounds, dashing towards her ferociously. Alona had no more time to think. She instinctively grabbed the rickety fire ladder, the first three rungs breaking immediately under her weight. Adrenaline surged in her veins but helped her focus on the thirty-metre climb. The girl was unaware of the two observing spirits that soared on either side of her, but she *was* conscious of the two Germans that had now arrived below and were trying to clamber up. No sooner had she reached the frosty slanted rooftop than the lower half of the ladder collapsed for good and crashed to the ground.

Cursing in German immediately roared up from below, followed by one warning shot in the air. Alona was hiding behind the chimney, trembling, and now looked down over the other side of the building. It was a sheer thirty-metre drop to the street, but this side had to lead out of the ghetto, she remembered. Alona spotted another old fire ladder and swiftly made her way towards it. She was about to turn backwards and clamber down the rungs, but out of the dense fog emerged another climber in the dark, mounting the steps towards her on this side.

Elias and Henry knew this man was Manfred Altmann, son of Jens Altmann and great-great-grandson of Seamus. He now worked for the Nazi Abwehr in Poland.

Alona had nowhere else to turn, so she instinctively climbed into the sooty chimney, scrambling to shuffle down. The shaft was narrow and suffocating, always conveying the impression she would reach a dead end or remain stuck forever. Then there was a diagonal drop, almost like a metal slide, and the girl emerged from a dead fireplace, coughing and covered in soot. The fireplace stood in some kind of disused warehouse, maybe an old jewellery or pin factory that had been shut down after the occupying forces had invaded this area. This was why the building had been equipped with escape ladders, she concluded.

Except for the little light from the nebulous street, darkness prevailed over this chamber, in which work tools and old debris lay strewn across the broken floor. Alona cracked open the decrepit door and peeped over the unlit stairwell that wound itself around the deep, disused vestibule. Suddenly, a crashing bang sounded from below, as though someone had broken through the front door of this old factory, and footsteps started to race upwards. It had to be the two Nazis with the dogs. They began to shout again, as the snarling of their German shepherds echoed up the hollow vestibule of the factory.

Instinctively, Alona dashed back into the workshop and attempted to lock herself inside. She frantically twisted the broken key, but the lock appeared to be jammed, and she was unable to thrust the bolt into the hole. The sniffer dogs would surely find her here in no time. Turning back, she sprinted towards the window and looked outside while aggressive footsteps made their way up towards this room. Alona sighted no escape ladder this time, and if she jumped from here, she would certainly fracture her legs, or worse.

Suddenly a rustling sound emanated from the chimney, and ash fell into the fireplace. It had to be the other man from the Abwehr, the one who'd mounted the building from the city side. Any moment now, he would tumble down and arrest her.

Alona trailed her gaze along all the factory equipment until she intuitively settled on an old wooden cabinet, not much taller than a young child, sitting right by the wall. Someone was now sliding down the fireplace, and without any hesitation, Alona darted towards the little cupboard and locked herself inside. Attempting to restrain her breathing, she tried to lean back against the wood when she realised some of her hair was still stuck outside, and now it would be too late to open the cabinet one last time.

Still, the sniffer dogs seemed to have missed her, their barks becoming more distant as they led the Nazis into the neighbouring workshop. Alona uttered one quiet sigh of relief; then she felt a tug on her hair as the cupboard was opened by a tall, balding man, armed with a handgun and a radio device. (It was Manfred Altmann in the course of his duties.)

Alona let out a short, high-pitched screech. Then this brute kicked her further into the cabinet just when the other Nazis stormed the obscure workshop, spurred on by their beastly companions.

'*Has du sie gesehen, Manfred? Wo ist sie?*' one of them shouted.

Manfred pointed out towards the winding, hollow stairwell. '*Da drüben! Da drüben läuft sie! Hinterher. Nach oben!*'

Alona did not understand what this man was shouting, but whatever it was he said, now the other two Nazis were running back onto the winding stairwell. Of course—this man had kicked her further *into* the cabinet, as if to conceal her, she now realised. Alona watched as he stepped towards the stairway but then gingerly retreated back into the workshop, gesturing for her to hush and keep on hiding in the cabinet. Then he marched out of the room and shouted a few things to the other Nazis in German.

She was alone now, and yet this workshop had never felt completely empty; she always had this strange sense as though a benign entity was with her: By now, the more bravery Elias and Henry sighted, the stronger grew their own desire to become human themselves. The whole sense of being human and making a contribution to humanity's timeline now loomed like an adventure they both looked forward to.

The workshop door suddenly creaked again, and footsteps marched in Alona's direction. The cabinet was yanked open by the same man that had concealed her a couple of minutes ago, and now he gently pulled her towards the entrance. The balding man pointed down towards the ground, as if to tell her that the way was clear and she should make a run for it.

'*Lauf runter, Mädchen. Lauf,*' he whispered to her. *Run down, girl. Run.*

He handed Alona a small piece of paper with a name and an address on it, as though he was urging her to seek refuge there. Within the chamber, it was too dark to read the whole card, but she could make out part of the address, Deutsche Emailwarenfabrik, and the name on top, Oskar Schindler.

'This man will help you. Now go quietly,' he whispered to her in Polish.

Alona blessed him with a quick glance of gratitude and a single touch on his arm. Now, the commotion from the other Nazis was emanating from a workshop above, and the girl swiftly made off down the dark stairwell.

'*Manfred, hast du das Weib gefunden?*' one of the other Nazis shouted, his voice echoing down the hollow vestibule. *Manfred, have you found the lass?*

'*Sie hat sich irgendwo versteckt!*' Manfred roared up. *She's hidden herself somewhere!* He felt good in his own conscience, although he knew what he had just done was punishable by death. An old door suddenly creaked downstairs, and seconds later, a heavy grinding sounded from below, as though someone had opened up a decrepit window to the outside.

'*Das Mädchen ist unten!*' one of the other Nazis screamed down, his hand gripping his pistol. *The girl is below!*

Immediately, all three thudded to the ground floor of the vestibule and sprinted into the disused shop floor from which the noise had emanated. It was facing the inner city, away from the ghetto, and now the girl had managed to escape through one of the tall windows. The three Nazis climbed out onto the nebulous street and looked about themselves, still accompanied by their ferocious German shepherds. This time, they would not take any lead by themselves but remained still, close to their human owners. The girl could have gone anywhere now.

'I think we've lost her, Manfred,' the mission leader muttered resignedly. They spoke German among themselves.

'We'll get those traitors next time,' Manfred replied with vigour. 'Those bastards have no escape; we'll find them eventually.' Then he withdrew from the ghetto along with the other two Nazis, whose mission he'd just sabotaged.

It was the moment Elias and Henry found themselves back on the Other Side again, but somehow this visit had felt different from the others.

'Tonight was one of the darkest times we have seen in this dimension,' Henry silently said.

'Yes… but things always get better again. All this darkness only makes human courage more luminous,'

Elias telepathically replied.

Indeed, if anyone had ever caught a glimpse of the two ghosts, they would probably have called it a miracle, but to Elias and Henry, the real miracle was watching mortal human beings risking their own lives to help others survive.

It was not the last trip the two eternal brothers found themselves on before the end of the war: Alona had been lucky that night and had found shelter at the mysterious factory the following day. Until the end of the war, she would be protected by the man on the card—Oskar Schindler, the owner of Deutsche Emailwarenfabrik. He would place her on a special list along with over a thousand other Jews, and take her to a new place of refuge in Czechoslovakia.

For Manfred Altmann, the hunting of Alona Garfunkel was the final straw in his time with the Abwehr. It was such a treacherous and brutal circle he worked for day in, day out, and the only way he could reconcile his job with his conscience was by spying for the Soviets, helping them liberate the country until Germany's unconditional surrender in 1945. His hometown, Königsberg, was ceded to the Soviet Union and eventually renamed Kaliningrad, while ethnic Germans were used as slave labour and then expelled from East Prussia. Because Manfred had spied for the Russians, he was allowed to stay on, provided he learned Russian and took on Soviet citizenship. He declined the offer, wishing to settle down in occupied Germany instead, but then he fell in love with a Russian woman the same month. Manfred remained in this new country and founded a family of his own in the north of Murmansk Oblast.

Last Observatory Jaunt to Earth

The period immediately following the war was an interesting one to observe. A gradual reconciliation between European countries displaced the usual balance-of-power alliances on the continent while numerous international institutions were formed around the globe. But in tandem with this development evolved an Iron Curtain, which soon divided the world into two ideological camps, led by two cold-warring superpowers. The country whose Nazi movement had committed atrocities during the first half of the twentieth century was now split along that curtain, and so was its former capital, in which a callous brick wall brutally divided its families into East and West.

Also affected by this Cold War division was a place five and a half thousand miles south-east: Vietnam. It was a country where the retreating colonial power left a split along the 17th parallel that would soon embroil the nation in decade-long warfare. It was also the country where Elias and Henry found themselves upon their twelfth, and what would turn out to be, their most heart-warming, observatory jaunt as visitors. Today was Sunday, 23 March 1975, and the two eternal brothers were standing in the company of James Adam's grandchild Karen Chapman. She had followed in the footsteps of her father and was working as a doctor in war-torn Vietnam. Together with her husband, John Chapman, another British physician, she'd now lived in Phú Lộc for almost five years.

Being so close to the 17th parallel, Phú Lộc was of strategic importance to both North and South Vietnam. In one of the numerous villages around the district resided Karen and John as unofficial guardians of an orphaned teenage girl, named Anh Nguyen. From the waist down, she had been paralysed by a grenade attack, in which she'd lost both of her parents three years before. Since then, John and Karen had taken care of her to fulfil a promise they'd made to her biological parents. They homeschooled her, teaching her English, and they always reminded her that when this war was over, they would take her to the United Kingdom, and she would start a new life and make a success of it. They would always encourage her to study and find out new things by herself, always reminding her that advances in neuroscience meant doctors in Britain would be able to repair her spine one day. Almost every month, they kept saying, 'There will come a time soon when scientists will collaborate globally, and each time a candle is lit in one place, a wave of knowledge will ripple through like a chain of connected lights.'

It was the morning of 23 March 1975, a hot, sunny day, the mercury climbing up to thirty-one degrees. At eight o'clock, John and Karen left for another day's work and commenced their drive towards Da Nang. They did not know it then, but North Vietnamese soldiers had already attacked northern Phú Lộc and were now heading towards their village. Nor did they know that the North Vietnamese had intelligence of an orphaned girl who was bonding with Western capitalists and that the soldiers were preparing to teach her a lesson that day.

Elias and Henry followed the British doctors towards Da Nang but then changed course and soared back to the farming village when they sensed the troops approach. The atmosphere was still tranquil here. A few peasants were tending to the rice paddies around the village, while chickens clucked in the street at the sight of stray cats. None of them sensed what two unborn spirits saw coming from a distance.

Anh was sitting inside her thatched cottage, playing a round of Vietnamese cards with two friends from the village, Kue and Dat. Kue had just lost the last match to Dat, who was smiling to himself blissfully as he rubbed his hands and shuffled the deck to deal out a new round. Suddenly, bullets were fired outside. First one, then two, then a whole magazine. Screaming immediately followed. Someone had just been killed.

Kue froze on the spot, then hid under the table, a sensation of cold expanding in her body. From there, she watched all the cards dropping to the floor and Dat racing for the window to look out.

'Tank! Tank!' he shouted, covering his frightened face with his hands. Swiftly, he glanced under the table and briefly locked eyes with Kue before he turned around and barrelled forth towards the rear bedroom.

Kue braced her head in her hands and closed her tearful eyes for a few seconds. She could feel her body trembling. Cautiously, she re-emerged from below and looked about herself. Dat had vanished from the front room, while Anh was sitting in her wheelchair, shaking speechlessly. She always reacted like this whenever there were banging noises or small explosions.

Outside, people were being rounded up and yelled at. Then one of them was shot. Any moment now, the soldiers could march into *this* cottage. Kue had to run and join Dat hiding in the rear bedroom, and she had to move quickly.

The girl turned her back on Anh and started to run. Then she suddenly halted herself and glanced back at her friend. Anh looked so defenceless and vulnerable, but her heavy wheelchair seemed too hard to push. Screams were flooding in from outside. Kue had to run for herself now, before it was too late. For a moment, she locked eyes with Anh, who was frozen in shell-shock, and then changed her mind. She hastened towards her friend and trundled her into the very back of the cottage, tears running down her cheeks.

In a tiny cupboard, the three children concealed themselves while Kue attempted to shut the wooden door. 'It's not closing!' she kept lamenting, for the wheelchair was taking up too much space. The three children yanked the door towards themselves, but however hard they tried, the size of the wheelchair precluded any success.

'Anh, you have to get out of this chair!' Kue eventually concluded, looking at Dat for help. He nodded tentatively and yet did not move a single inch, his body quivering.

Kue gently unloaded Anh from her metal chair and lowered her onto the floor. She pushed out the wheelchair, and the three children pulled the door towards themselves with one tug. This time, it finally shut.

'Thank you so much!' Anh whispered to her friends. 'I will never forget your help.'

For a couple of minutes, the kids hid inside the cupboard, clasping each other's hands. Suddenly Kue whispered, 'Oh no! We should've hidden the wheelchair.' It was such an obvious tip-off, standing right next to this closet, and if the soldiers marched in now, they would find them immediately. Was there still time to do something? she wondered. She could feel her lips quivering, and her hands were covered in sweat. Then she took a deep breath and forced herself out of the closet one more time, wheeling the chair towards the front entrance.

'Kue, be careful!' Anh whispered behind her.

Elias and Henry followed the girl into the front room, aware there was very little time left. Kue looked all around herself, trying to find a hiding spot. There just had to be somewhere to conceal the wheelchair.

Suddenly, there was an angry banging on the frail timber door. Kue turned around frantically and then realised she'd knocked off a porcelain plate, which dropped from the table and shattered on the wooden floor. Immediately, she covered her mouth in shock, dropping her chin and her gaze towards the floor. The girl had just let down the other two children, and she felt guilty. It was all her fault. Now the banging on the entrance grew ever more intense.

The next thing she knew, the cottage door had been prised open by a man in his mid-forties, who headed straight for the trembling child. He was dressed in full military uniform, brandished a large pistol, and was accompanied by another, slightly older soldier.

'Are you Anh Nguyen?' he demanded. 'Are you the traitor child?'

Kue opened her mouth but felt unable to utter a single sound.

'She can't be,' remarked the other soldier. 'The traitor girl can't walk.'

'Where is the traitor girl?' shouted the first officer. He slapped the girl across the cheek.

'I don't know! Really! I am alone!' she cried. The younger officer grabbed the wailing child by the ear and dragged her along to the next room. Under the bed, the bamboo table, inside the wardrobe, the soldiers all looked, but it was the small brown closet on the wall that seemed to catch their attention. Kue could hear it too: Breathing noises came from within.

Elias and Henry had been so much exposed to human behaviour that they emulated it now as they tried to block the way toward the cupboard. They knew, of course, their efforts would bear no effect in this three-dimensional world, for, in 1975 they were still souls without human bodies. Through the two spirits strode the troopers, and they reached the little closet in no time. Without any more warning, they yanked open the feeble door and dealt each of the weeping children a kick in the stomach.

'Come out of there!' commanded the older one. His companion yanked out the teenagers, swore them to silence, and then evicted Anh's friends from the cottage. But Anh herself had to be taught a lesson. Anh had acted as a traitor to the nation by letting herself be brainwashed by a pack of foreign wolves, and she would receive the appropriate punishment. To that, the two soldiers would see.

It was now six o'clock in the evening. A red sun was setting over the rutilant horizon, and the invading forces had retreated from the area. John and Karen were finally able to sneak back into the village, but the place no longer felt the same. The atmosphere around it was sinister, almost deadly. It was as if people were under some kind of curfew, barred from leaving their cottages, or maybe scared to do so. Were there still snipers around? they wondered anxiously. This village was no longer a safe place to be; they had to get back to Britain as quickly as possible, and they had to take Anh with them.

John and Karen were unable to have children of their own, but they had always lavished the same kind of love on Anh as they would have on their own daughter. They were determined that she would have a bright future back in the United Kingdom and that she would be able to walk again.

John inserted the key into the lock but then realised that it no longer fitted, that somehow it had been tampered with and their cottage had been targeted. He did not know it, but the military commander had inadvertently jammed the mechanism when he'd prised the timber open that morning.

Inside the cottage, Anh was sat on the wooden floor, her arms tied behind her to a heavy couch. Her mouth was duct-taped, and she was looking at the front entrance, which was now booby-trapped to kill the two British doctors. A loose metal rod had been placed by the door, and as soon as it moved inwards, it would prod a detonator that would set off a bomb affixed to the door. An additional grenade had been laid on top of the inner door frame, and this would probably fall on the victims in case they were still alive. It did not have a linchpin; in fact, it looked more like an improvised impact grenade. Those soldiers obviously wanted her to witness the full gore of a killing and teach her a lesson.

Anh heard the wrenching of a key inside the front door and knew it was her foster parents trying to get back in. The bolt seemed to be jammed, but if her foster parents continued to force the key, the lock would eventually give way, and she would lose another pair of parents this day. With all her strength, she started to scream through the duct tape, warning her foster parents to stay out.

'Something's happened to Anh!' her mother uttered outside.

Her dad began to shout. '*Bạn ổn chứ? Bạn có nghe thấy chúng tôi không?* Are you all right? Can you hear us?'

The more Anh shouted to stay out, the more desperate her parents seemed to become, and the more vigorously they tried.

Anh was still able to move her arms, and perhaps she could try to free herself from the heavy couch, she pondered. The teenager pulled her arms, but the harder she yanked, the deeper the constricting rope cut into her skin. She felt blood trickling down her hands. Yet, the very thought that these kind human beings would be blown away the next minute propelled her on. With the palm of her hands on the floor, she pushed herself forward, dragging the couch along on her broken back. Maybe she could move the rod with the bottom of her foot simply by pushing herself with her hands, and the bomb would never go off. The couch was so exhausting to haul, but it was just about manageable.

While her father continued to unjam the lock, Anh kept dragging herself forward until she finally reached the rod. It lay right next to her foot, and all she had to do was thrust herself sideways a little. She nudged herself along the floor, but she didn't move. It seemed as though one of the couch legs had snagged in a small groove and she was trapped, unable to move in any direction. She screamed through the duct tape, but her foster parents just scrambled more desperately to force the lock. If only they could just smash the windows, Anh hoped—But it was such a frightful, distressing scene that this thought must be eluding them, she realised, for her foster parents were entirely focused on her tortured voice behind the door.

All options were exhausted now, and it seemed futile for her to try any further. Elias and Henry had never touched any physical matter before, and neither did they succeed this time in moving a rod but a single millimetre. Their time had not come yet.

For a short moment, Anh gave up; then a sudden stroke of intuition flared up in her. Perhaps, just *perhaps*, if Anh tried hard enough, she might be able to move her paralysed leg one last time, she felt. It seemed the only possibility left, and Anh was determined not to lose another pair of parents to this war. She stared at her paralysed toes and visualised moving the bottom of her foot, as though she was projecting her intention from within. Naturally, it did not work, not even for a single millimetre, for her lower spine lacked any pathway to her brain. Still, she persevered as hard as she could.

The next thing she knew, all the rattling on the door

caused the impact grenade to drop from the door frame, and it settled itself between Anh's useless leg and the untouchable rod. Immediately, the girl held back; the grenade hadn't exploded yet, but if it was subjected to any more disturbance, it could. Adrenaline froze her on the spot while all the traumatic memories of that grenade from three years ago were flooding her brain again.

It was in the next ten seconds that Elias and Henry saw something they had never witnessed before, nor had they known humans were capable of it. They knew Anh's soul was confined inside her paralysed body, but it appeared as if this unwavering selflessness almost propelled her spirit beyond her corporal vessel. With all her might and projected intention, she strove to move her left foot towards the grenade. It was as though she projected her will so relentlessly and indefatigably that for a fraction of a second, the universe just blinked and allowed Anh to thrust her paralysed foot one last time. Instantly, the grenade exploded as the rod finally shifted from the detonator, taking the girl from this world.

The blast blew a hole into the side wall, severed the ignition cable from the blasting cap, but somehow spared the entrance, in front of which Karen and John recoiled in terror. They knew Anh was no longer alive but were unaware their foster daughter had just sacrificed herself for them.

For a few seconds, silence and horror dominated the village lane. Then an ethereal white light glowed up beside the ruptured cottage, shining with a brilliance that was indescribable in human language. Such a rarity was it for any living human to see this light from another dimension, but it was as if their foster child wanted to speak to them one last time as her soul emerged in front of them, looking perfect, radiant and whole. It was more a telepathic message of gratitude: 'Thank you, Mum and Dad, for the last three years. I am fine, and I'm going home now. You must try to have a child of your own. I love you, and I will see you again in a few decades.' Then she was drawn into this wonderful light that seemingly carried her forth from this world.

There was something else both Karen and John had seen, even though neither of them understood what it was. Two human silhouettes of light had stood next to their foster daughter, showing neither gender nor ethnicity, and yet they had felt so very familiar. They had slowly faded into nothingness as the ethereal light gradually vanished from this dimension.

It was the only time Elias and Henry had ever been visible to humans while they were still spirits. Very soon now, it would be their time to descend humanly.

John and Karen left for London the following day, where they would set up the Anh Nguyen Foundation for Neural Research and devote the next three decades to spinal cord injury. Every few years, they would return to the spot where they had seen this light and say a prayer or two in memory of their daughter. They did eventually manage to have a child of their own.

Anh Nguyen was the final miracle Elias and Henry witnessed as observers, for they never found themselves thrust into another observatory trip again. Since 1853, they had witnessed the transformation of this curious place on a dozen trips, in which they had followed the timeline of six generations. Earth was such a strange and illogical dimension to observe. Every soul who descended to the physical world would lose their equality and find themselves shackled to arbitrary wealth and geographical boundaries. Eternal brothers and sisters sundered into warring countries and cities, and like a lottery of birth, these human shackles would shape the entire timeline of a soul on earth. Those who won the lottery of birth would keep their place in this hierarchy and strive to keep the losers at bay. The brothers and sisters that lost had found themselves imported as human goods and slaves from the west of Africa, only to feed the wealth of the winners, and now they faced being shut off at the borders of richer nations.

But there was also something on earth that souls could never attain in this perfect home of the Other Side, something that attached meaning to earthly existence and made the journey to this dimension an adventure to look forward to: every soul who incarnated humanly was able to leave their own imprint of progress on humanity's timeline. And whether those moments were small acts of love or major rewrites of human history, they would always loosen the earthly shackles a little and light the way to a more perfect world. Each generation had faced its own challenges, but each generation also manifested its own little miracles and heroes.

Elias and Henry had so much to live up to. Ever since they'd found themselves thrown into their first observatory trip in 1853, they had sensed that their own lives would somehow be intertwined with the legacy of Rachel and Seamus, this large family they had been accompanying for over a hundred years. Nothing was ever set in stone, but there had to be a reason why they were shown those people and those moments in history. They knew, of course, by the time they found out more, they would no longer retain any recollections from the Other Side.

At last, a farewell ceremony was held to bid the two souls goodbye for a human lifetime. Fellow souls reminded the two that they would be visiting them as observers, just as Henry and Elias had observed those who'd gone before them. Hugs were exchanged; well wishes were given; encouragement was lavished upon them, for it was the greatest journey a soul could embark on, and everyone had such respect for it.

A final light-hearted moment took place when a playfully mischievous soul soared up and clung on to Henry's back, then whispered to him telepathically. 'Bring us back some of those funny-looking Spanish grapes! I'd like to taste one here.'

Henry turned around and nodded in amusement, imitating human behaviour.

Then the two souls bade farewell to their companions and, finally, to each other. They had made it their mission to follow in the footsteps of those role models that had so inspired them and to continue in their ways of kindness and self-sacrifice.

If only they had known the challenges that were awaiting them now.

The two souls departed from this realm of light that manifested as a stream of virtually timeless eternity, and they were conveyed into the physical world, which was bound in a more tangible kind of time—like a journey between light and time. They were born on 7 June 1996 and were named Elias and Henry.

Part II

Early Childhood and Youth

Childhood

Somewhere inside the Arctic Circle, about twenty degrees from the North Pole and less than one hundred miles from the Barents Sea, there lies a little village near the Kola Peninsula where the aurora borealis illuminates the night sky above and shines upon the frost below. Waterfowl and skuas soar over the land; wolverines, moose and Arctic foxes roam the area freely, but people do *not*. For somewhere through this territory runs an international border between three neighbouring countries: Norway, Finland and Russia. It was here, on the Russian side, that Elias was born, in the little village of Rayakoski. And it was here that he had his first memories as a human.

If anyone had asked him about his earliest childhood recollections, he would probably have cited the mysterious aurora borealis, the Northern Lights, that so majestically illuminated the sky above. Though he had no knowledge of physics, he sensed that there had to be something very powerful or miraculous about an entity that could light up on its own and so freely move across a dividing line that even as a child he was told never to cross, lest he face dire consequences from Russian officials—what his parents would call 'Santa Claus with military batons'. Although Elias had always been told about his mixed northern European heritage, the citizenship of his generation was Russian, and the country tightly controlled who entered and exited the land.

He spent the first few years of his life in the border village of Rayakoski, where he lived in a two-bedroom apartment with his parents and elder brother, Mikhail. The children were homeschooled, and they grew up bilingual, speaking both Russian and Norwegian at home. And it was here, on 30 October 2003, that Elias had one of his earliest formative memories.

A brown-haired seven-year-old with blue eyes and a distinct pale face, Elias was clad in a heavy winter coat and thermal trousers. For footwear, he wore snow boots that went up to his lower calves and complemented his purple gloves.

It was five o'clock in the afternoon, and the sun had already set over this Arctic region, bringing in a cold wave that left residents cowering by their stoves. Not so for Elias, who'd persuaded his parents to let him play in the snow with the neighbours' daughter. She was called Sophia, and she lived on the floor below. Roughly the same age as Elias and a little taller, she had long blonde hair, green eyes and a fair complexion. She was dressed in insulated trousers and a thermal jacket to which a little hood was attached. Like Elias, she wore winter boots that covered most of her lower legs.

'Don't venture out too far, kids! Stay around here!' shouted Elias's father. He gave them a thoughtful wave and stepped back into the warm, cosy house.

'Yes, of course!' replied Elias. He watched his father disappear into the stone-clad building and then felt his face relax into a smile that was appreciative of parentless freedom. Immediately, he turned to Sophia.

'What shall we do today?' she asked. '*The Lion King* is on. Shall we just go back and watch it? Let's just stay in this time.'

'I'd rather not,' replied Elias. He took a few steps away from the apartment block and stretched out his hand towards Sophia. But on this particular afternoon, she did not seem eager to follow. Normally, she didn't mind the snow, but today it was unusually deep for the time of year, even Elias noticed.

'Aren't you freezing, Eli? My feet are so cold,' Sophia said.

Elias began to play around with a film camera, which his parents had recently gifted him, and he looked north towards the aurora borealis, stretching his finger towards this majestic green-blue radiance that flowed like weightless water. He edged a little closer to Sophia again and tugged her by the sleeve. 'Let's go and follow this. Come on!'

'But Mum and Dad said to stay around here,' Sophia protested.

'Don't worry. We won't go far. I just want to get a little closer, just a little bit,' Elias reassured her.

Sophia still seemed reluctant, shrugging her shoulders and citing the merciless temperatures of the day, but then finally, she gave in. Elias took her by the hand and started to lead the way, happily smiling because she had relented.

Gradually, a few steps turned into a few metres; a few metres turned into a few hundred metres, and a few hundred metres turned into half a mile. Before they knew it, they had ventured into dense woodland and found themselves in close proximity to the international land border. The further they wandered, the tauter Sophia's face became and the more she lagged behind, as though she sensed something Elias was not yet aware of. Still, she did not say a single word.

'What's wrong?' Elias eventually asked.

'Where are we? Do you remember the way home?' Sophia replied.

But Elias's curious gaze was entirely focused on an Arctic fox that seemed to be on the stealthy hunt for a little rabbit. 'Look at this,' he whispered inquisitively. 'A white fox. I want to take a picture. Get down.'

'And I want to go home, please,' Sophia whispered, tugging her friend by the jacket.

But all Elias could think of was their luck in walking into this hunting game as he prepared his camera for a good shot of the scene.

Suddenly the young rabbit seemed to sense the Arctic fox, and it quickly made a dash for some bushes. Almost instantly, the hungry fox leapt into the air and started to chase after the rabbit at incredible speed. Jumping to his feet himself, Elias had to capture a photo of this spectacle, but before he realised it, his right foot slipped and became stuck in a snow hole. His left foot swiftly followed, and before he had any time to react, he had been swallowed by the snow up to his knees.

At once, he felt his body going limp as he froze in shock. *This wasn't supposed to happen!* shot through his mind. He began to sob as he struggled to free himself from the powerful grip of the tight hole, then he looked up to Sophia. 'Help me, please. Help me, Sophia!' he uttered, stretching his hands towards her.

Sophia rushed to his aid and gripped his arms, scrambling to raise him up from this treacherous place; it seemed almost impossible. Suddenly she stopped and appeared to freeze on the spot. She let go of his arms as her features became all tense again. There was something out here that seemed to terrify her, and Sophia took a few steps away from her friend.

'What is it?' asked Elias, crying. 'Come back, please!' He listened out, and then he could hear it too: sounds from the distance, maybe a few hundred metres away. Those were the howls of the volkosobs, the wolfdogs of the Russian border guards, who appeared to be closing in on them.

'Can you hear that?' asked his friend. 'It's the volkosobs. We must be on the border. They must be coming to pick us up!'

'Then help me out of here! Please!' Elias wailed frantically. Suddenly he was overcome with a sensation he'd never been acquainted with. It was he who'd dragged Sophia into these woods, being the great adventurer, and now he was demanding she rescue him. He did not know what to call this sensation, but it made him feel weak and very little.

Sophia locked her frightened eyes with her neighbour's. She appeared to think for a few seconds and then stepped a little closer once more, straining to pull Elias by the arms. And again, it seemed virtually impossible, for Elias was barely helping himself. He could feel the stabbing pain in his foot but did not know he had a sprained ankle from twisting it when he had fallen into the hole. He panted in exhaustion as Sophia strained to lift him out of the snow.

'Elias, climb, please!' she said, still pulling on him.

'I *am* climbing. I am!'

'No, you are not! You have to try harder. Come on, Eli. Hold on to my hand.'

The next moment, Sophia's attention was gripped once again by the wolfdogs in the distance. This time, they were emitting an even higher-pitched snarling sound, baying frantically for the two humans who had erred into the Arctic wilderness. It was truly fear-inspiring, and Sophia let go of Elias's arms once more. She looked at her friend with an expression of guilt, cringing, and moved her hands behind her waist. Sophia conceded. 'I'm going to get Mum and Dad. I am sorry, Elias. I will send for help.' And she turned her back to him.

'No, wait, Sophia! Please stay!' wailed Elias, his voice cracking as tears ran down his snow-covered face.

Elias was now in the woods on his own, his jaw dropping towards the freezing ground. The hole wasn't very deep at all, but every time he jerked his foot, it swamped his brain with more pain. He tried to think of a prayer but could recall none. Within just a few seconds, he had gone from having a wondrous, innocent adventure to experiencing the most frightening event of his life. Absolutely nothing could have prepared him for such a sudden turn of events. It was as scary below as the aurora borealis was glorious above. He remembered that at the edge of this forest, there was a river that marked the border with Norway, but a small strip of woodland on this side also belonged to that country, and now he must be within such close proximity to the dividing line.

Gradually, his breathing became slower and shallower

the longer he trembled in the snow. His head began to feel very light, and he gently lowered his eyelids as he slowly drifted towards sleep.

Then, suddenly, the howling of those wolfdogs again! They were drawing past on the other side of the bushes, swishing through the thick snow. Could this really be happening? he wondered. Could they really be passing him by without taking note of him? He did not know it, but it was the white fox that had diverted the attention of the wolfdogs while it was still consuming its fresh meal.

Now the guards' chatter became louder and more formidable until they drew past on the other side of the shrubs. Elias exhaled a sigh of relief and then became aware of the chattering sound of his teeth. What if the dogs could somehow sense it and returned? he feared.

The next thing he knew, snow-crunching footsteps were approaching from the dense thickets behind him, sending a shudder through his spine like ice on his skin. He turned his head around as a dark figure stepped out of the shrubs and stared at his frozen body. At once, Elias looked away and covered his eyes under his palms. *This is it. This must be the end!* There could be no way out of this one.

'Elias, it's me,' whispered the soft voice next to him. 'Don't be scared. It's only me.'

Elias opened his eyes and sighed in relief at the sight of Sophia. 'You came back for me,' he whispered.

'I didn't want to leave you alone.'

'I thought you were going to get your mum and dad.'

'I changed my mind. Let's get out of here,' she said. The girl took off her gloves and rubbed her hands against Elias's cold face and neck to warm him. 'Are you all right?'

'Thank you, Sophia!' he responded, blinking away some of his tears.

'Please, let's get out this time,' said his companion, who handed him a small tree branch to grip on to. On the count of three, she pulled with all her strength while Elias thrust against the snow, and Sophia almost tumbled onto her back when she finally dragged him out of that monstrous trap.

Elias let himself drop to the ground with a loud sigh, but then immediately regretted his actions, for the wolfdogs must have heard this expression of relief, and they started howling once more. Immediately, someone blew a whistle, which Elias knew commanded the fierce volkosobs to return and resume the hunt.

Distraught, the two children leapt to their feet and attempted to flee, but Elias was still numb from the cold, and his ankle hurt with every step he took.

'Faster, Elias! Come on!' cried Sophia as she pulled him by the sleeve of his thick down jacket.

'I can't run,' replied Elias, limping forward clumsily while the predators surged through the woods behind them. He stretched out his arm, and the pallid girl grabbed it, dragging the injured child with her like a brother in arms on the battlefield. Along the snow-covered taiga, she pulled her friend forward; then a hidden branch emerged out of the snow and tripped the girl to her knees, taking Elias down with her to the ground. She swiftly pushed Elias into a small bush in front of them, where they hid and cowered.

Instinctively, Elias tried to stop himself from shivering. But the very thought of the sharp fangs of at least two wolfdogs inspired more fear in Elias than he'd ever felt before, and it brought his whole body to a tremble.

Looking into her friend's eyes, Sophia stretched out her quivering hand and placed it on Elias's ever so calmly. It was the first time someone had shown him so much care outside his own family, and he instantly felt his heartbeat steadying, reassured by the presence of another human being so close beside him.

They did not know it, but by now, the volkosobs were a mere twenty metres from their shrubs, sniffing for the scent of humans. Here the two wolfdogs split up and snuffled along in different directions. The male wandered off, seeking the smell of the ravaged rabbit, whose remains the Arctic fox had carried away. His companion, a slightly younger female, had somehow missed the presence of the children and was about to pass right by the two fugitives. Then she froze. There was something. She gauged the scent of human adrenaline and turned her head to face the brush.

A clawing sound emanated from the ground, and then the beast became visible to the children. Her gait was predatory and stealthy while she gingerly prowled towards the little shrub as her paws sank into the deep snow below. She stuck her head into the bush and glared at the two fugitives with glowing eyes, snarling from her clenched maw. Her jaws opened, and she exposed her pointed canines to the two kids, who shivered as they held hands and then hugged. They sensed they had to maintain eye contact with this beast and never show their backs. But an attack was imminent.

Then Sophia did something that Elias could not

understand. It must have been pure instinct, but the girl let go of Elias's quivering hand, gently stretched out her own and began to caress the ears of the beast. Suddenly the tense look on the volkosob softened, as though she had never been shown any sort of affection before, or maybe it was an emotional reaction she had long suppressed. Closing her jaws again, she gave Sophia a nudge with her head and let out a single whine. Then she slowly skulked her way out of the brush and strode backwards into the open forest.

Now it was high time to make a run for it once and for all, and Elias slowly rose from the shrubs. He lifted his body through the thin twigs, but then felt Sophia tugging him down by the hand.

'Wait, Eli,' she whispered to him. 'Wait till the guards have passed.'

Indeed, the border guards became audible again, and Elias ducked back into the bushes. They sounded like men in their early twenties, but they spoke with deep, fear-inspiring voices that grated with every word. The louder they became, the more Elias felt the irresistible urge to jump to his feet and run, but his friend continued to press him down. Now she was using both arms.

'Elias, please. If you run now, they will see us,' she whispered. 'Please. It's almost over.' Laying her hand on Elias's snow-covered knee, she gave it a few strokes.

The two border guards passed them by on the other side of the shrubs, chattering in those angry, grumbling voices. Sophia loosened her grip on Elias and put her index finger to her lips. Her friend nodded to signal that he'd understood, and he remained silent. Very soon now, it would all be over.

It wasn't clear whether the two wolfdogs had spotted a prey animal or whether they had run into the Arctic fox with its rabbit carcass once again, but less than two minutes later, they suddenly burst into a chorus of high-pitched howling that reverberated across the border forest.

This time, Elias was finally pushed over the brink and lost his nerve. 'I can't take this anymore,' he uttered. Pushing Sophia's hands away, he leapt to his feet and began to run out of the bushes, only to remember his hurting ankle a few seconds later. Still, he had committed to fleeing the scene now, and to this purpose he would stick. Once again, a guard blew the whistle that must send the volkosobs back to the chase.

Sophia rose from the taiga shrubs and sprinted after the injured boy, then clasped his hand. Behind them, two sets of paws ferociously pounded the deep snow, accompanied by savage growling. An instant later, the pair of wolfdogs leapt from the coniferous trees and paced towards the children. The female one, the beast they'd met earlier, appeared to hold back at the sight of the kids, but the other wolfdog hastened towards the two fugitives with a ferociousness that no longer allowed the thought of taming.

With her trembling hand, Sophia quickly picked up a small branch from the taiga soil, which she threw across to the male hound. She probably wanted to activate his playful fetch instincts, but the dog must have interpreted the throw as an attack. And with all his strength and beastly anger, he pounced upon the little girl, who dropped to the ground, and then sank his canine teeth into her thick down sleeve. Her wails of pain reverberated across the Arctic forest like the howling of an injured animal.

It must have been her young voice that alerted the border guards to the fact that they were merely dealing with children, for one of them immediately blew a lower-pitched tune on his whistle, and the male wolfdog abruptly stopped. He took a few steps away from Sophia, turned around, and backed off.

When the two young guards finally caught up with their canine companions, Elias was hovering over a bleeding Sophia, who was lying on the ground and still wailing from the ferocious bites. Her down jacket had absorbed most of the piercing force, but still those relentless teeth had penetrated the skin on her right arm and left her with deep open wounds and contusions.

The two young border guards came running towards the children. They looked worried, perhaps even a tad friendly. Then the senior of them patted his colleague on the back, and both appeared to stiffen up, scowling with flinty stares. The older one shook his head and said nonchalantly, 'Jesus, all this fuss for just two stupid children. Why did you not tell us you were kids, huh?'

'We thought you were angry because we are at the border,' Sophia said through her pain, trying to rise from the snow-covered ground. The guards started to laugh.

'We are looking for a draft dodger in this area, not silly kids!' said the younger of the two. 'Next time, you don't play here, or if you must come, tell us you are just stupid children, so we don't have to set the dogs on you! Is that understood?'

Elias nodded and was again overcome with this sensation that made him feel weak and so little.

The border guards demanded the telephone number of Sophia's parents and ordered her mum and dad to come and pick her up from the border forest. The junior guard attempted to wipe the blood off Sophia's right arm and apply a little pressure to stem the bleeding.

'Do you know what a draft dodger is, young man?' he asked Elias.

The young boy shook his head.

'One day, when you grow into a real man, you'll find out.'

When Sophia's parents arrived to collect them, the world as Elias had known it was no longer the same. The stunning magic of the aurora borealis belied the grim harshness that life could so randomly throw even at children. He was nothing like the strong, brave role model he'd always liked to imagine himself as. In fact, he'd been acquainted with a sensation that left him feeling sluggish and contritely humiliated. He'd led his neighbour into an adventure he'd thought he'd been commanding, and it had been his friend who'd ended up rescuing him. And now she bore possibly lifelong scars because of his silly actions.

But there was another powerful awareness that had been enkindled in him that day, something Sophia had shown him and that he'd hitherto been unaware of and felt unable to describe even to himself. There was a kind of heroic bravery and brotherly compassion that he'd seen in movies but had never known could exist in real life. It was a love, almost like a force, that he'd witnessed in Sophia and now deeply admired. In fact, he wanted to be like her. At a certain level, it was as magical a force as the stunning aurora borealis, if not far more miraculous. It was something he would start to look out for from now on but would mostly find only in moderation. This day would remain one of his earliest formative memories.

Clear, fresh water fills the basin of an old, disused quarry, while ancient wells and monasteries stand on the green land and hark back to times long gone by. A century-old castle overlooks a pleasant lake in a green pasture. Sometimes people come here to swim or fish. Nearby, a herd of deer roam freely in a country park. Cattle and sheep graze on hilly grassland and shy away from occasional horse riders. Here a total of eight miles of rocky spine extends between Worcestershire and Herefordshire, hills whose fissures and fault lines have generated spring water since medieval times. In the early hours, crepuscular sunrays shine upon the morning mist that rises from the grassland and sweeps across the fresh rural air. These are the Malvern Hills, an Area of Outstanding Natural Beauty in the middle of Great Britain. And it was here that Henry was born, in the small village of Little Malvern, where he had his earliest childhood memories. He was the son of a local kiosk owner who ran a fish-and-chip shop in nearby Great Malvern, a small town of fewer than thirty thousand inhabitants.

As a child, Henry liked comic-book heroes and always aspired to be one. In fact, if anyone ever asked him, he would probably have recounted that his earliest memories all revolved around glittery toys and dolls. Superhero dolls were his favourite, and they far outranked the dull board games he found around his home. Almost on a daily basis, he would indulge in his own reveries, imagining he was flying over the redbrick buildings of London, or over the English Channel and into France.

Very often, he would play 'heroes and villains' with his fellow children, but only on the condition that he would be the superhero. And whenever they asked to switch roles, he would argue, cry or simply abandon the game.

One of his earliest formative memories occurred at Great Malvern Whitehawk School on 7 November 2003. It was a cold day on that particular November morning, for the clear sky the night before had laid ice crystals on the hills, and the family car had to be defrosted before Henry's dad was able to take him to school.

By half past twelve in the afternoon, some pupils in the lower years were still shivering as they sat at the lunch tables that stretched nearly the entire length of the canteen. It was a very tall, old dining hall, with paintings of famous academics hung up on a glistening wood-panelled wall underneath churchlike windows and above a disused marble fireplace. Among the children, there was a rumour that all these paintings were part of a national treasure and that the biggest treasure was still buried somewhere on the school grounds. Smartly dressed in a traditional English school uniform, they were finishing their lunch of chicken nuggets with roast potatoes when some of the kids started to yell across to their classmates on the neighbouring bench.

Near the far end of one of the benches sat a seven-year-old boy of medium height with a round pale face, eating his dessert of vanilla sponge cake. He had light blonde hair, green eyes and a few freckles on his cheeks. This young boy was Henry, sitting with his classmates Carl and Matthew, and right now, all he could think of was the maths homework he'd copied from another pupil and handed in as his own. If he got caught again, if he got into any trouble at school again, his dad would confiscate his Nintendo GameCube for a month.

'Why do you want to be the strongest superhero every time we play this game?' Carl asked him.

'Because… because I am clearly the bravest in our year,' Henry replied.

Carl and Matthew glanced at each other with soft sniggers and then turned back to Henry.

'No, you're not!' said Carl.

'Yes, I am!'

'Come on! You're scared of the dark. You're afraid to walk on your own. You're afraid of Mr Anders, and you're afraid to speak to girls.'

'Yes—but in real danger, I would be the bravest.'

'Prove it!'

'How can I prove that?'

Carl took his gaze off Henry and appeared to reflect on something. Suddenly he smiled to himself, all excited, and began to whisper something in Matthew's ear, covering the sound with his palms. Matthew gasped with a bright smile and punched the air before whispering something back to Carl. They both began to laugh, and Carl rubbed his hands together. 'We know how you can prove it,' he said to Henry.

'What do you want me to do?'

'You know the old treasure by the abandoned tree house?'

'There is no treasure. It's only a myth,' Henry replied.

'Are you saying you're afraid to go and dig for it?'

'No. Only that it's—'

'Then show us!' said Matthew. 'Go to the tree house all by yourself and look for it. Show us you're not afraid.'

'What if there is no treasure?'

'Then show us whatever you can find.'

'But we are not allowed around there. We can only go into the woods when we do cross-country. If they catch me——'

At this, Matthew suddenly turned to Carl. 'You see. I told you he's still afraid. He's always scared.'

'No, I am not!'

'So why won't you go into the woods, then?' Carl asked.

Henry sighed. 'How do I know if the treasure is buried underneath the tree house or inside it?'

'You have to look in both places and bring us whatever you can find,' Carl replied.

'Okay. I'll prove it to you guys. I'll go and look for the treasure.'

His two classmates fixed their gazes on each other again. Then Carl whispered something else to Matthew, who flinched back a little and nodded with a grin.

'Okay, but you have to wait until it's one o'clock,' said Carl.

'Why?'

'Just because! These are the rules.'

These two were obviously up to something, but by now, Henry had already agreed to this test of courage and had to go along. What did he have to lose now?

'Okay, I will wait until one,' he replied.

His two classmates hastily finished their desserts and started to clear up, leaving Henry with a clearer view of

Mr Anders, who was sitting on the bench behind. He was their grumpy, ever-so-cynical maths teacher, and right now, he was probably marking their homework from the day before. This teacher had a habit of getting Henry into trouble every few months, always calling his parents about little things here and there.

Henry returned his tray to the kitchen and gingerly sneaked past the grumpy man, taking a sneak peek at the work he was assessing. It didn't look like maths this time. Mr Anders was reading a newspaper, on which the headline said something Henry could not understand except for the words TONY BLAIR and IRAQ. He knew that Tony Blair was the prime minister, and whenever his parents were watching the news, every time he heard mention of Iraq, there would always be tanks of some sort. Mr Anders turned the page just as his head pivoted around, and Henry quickly made his way out of the dining hall.

He slunk into the school shed, where he borrowed a small shovel, and then strode towards the school woodland, hiding the tool inside his jacket. At the edge of the woods, he held back, feeling his pulse beating a bit more vigorously. It was only recently that he'd got into trouble for copying someone else's English homework, and if he was caught breaking rules again—it was a prospect that filled him with dread. Looking around himself, he found there were no teachers to stop him, and he slowly crept into the woods.

The soil was hard with glistening frost, while a steady but humid air welcomed him into the woodland. The further he wandered, the harder his stomach became and the slower he walked, until he remembered Mr Anders would be looking for him if he didn't return by the start of the next period. He speeded up again until he stood in front of an ominous fence, whereupon hung a rusty rectangular sign, warning people to KEEP OUT. When he'd first joined Great Malvern Whitehawk School, the area that was beyond this barrier had still been part of school grounds, but at some point, they had sold this section of land to a large adjoining property, whose mansion stood on the other side of it. There were so many rumours about why the new owners had put up a tree house only to let it fall into ruins, including that it marked the hiding spot of an old treasure. Some said it was buried right underneath, while others claimed it was hidden inside. Henry had always had his doubts about it, but now he slowly climbed over this forbidden fence and then sneaked his way towards the tree house. There was nobody about, so he quickly started digging away at the soil, only to find that it was so hard that the shovel would not sink in. He thrust, pushed and plunged, but the shovel simply refused to penetrate the earth by more than a few millimetres. He tried a different spot, but it was exactly the same there. *How will they even know that I actually came here?* he asked himself. Maybe he could just gather whatever he found in the woods and show it to Carl— after all, they weren't here to check on him.

Suddenly a fearful sensation of weightlessness expanded from his core. There had been a quiet whisper coming from the thickets, and for a second, Henry wondered if he was being watched. If the owners caught him trespassing, he would find himself in so much trouble, and instinctively Henry covered himself behind a tall tree, peeping around the trunk. He ducked and waited, hiding the shovel inside his blazer. However, there were no more whispers, and nobody came chasing after him.

What if the whisper had come from someone Carl had sent to witness that he had really come here? He realised he'd better make an effort to climb up to the creepy tree house as well. *Just go in and out.*

The wooden ladder lay flat on the ground, enshrouded in icy soil and dead plants. Henry propped it up against the tree house, whose base sat over three metres above the ground. He started to climb up, leaving the shovel back on the ground. The rungs were cold against his bare hands, and he kept reminding himself not to glance down.

The opening came into view as a pungent woody smell wafted from the place, and the next step Henry took brought him inside this uncanny, shabby structure. It was completely empty inside, save for some dormant spiders in the corners. Gingerly, he padded to the other end of the little house, and then heard a faint grinding sound emanating from where he'd climbed up. He walked back to the door, but now the ladder was no longer there. Instead, six pupils from his year were standing below, and as soon as he came into their view, they burst into collective laughter and immediately high-fived one other. They continued to smirk mockingly.

For a second, the shock of the missing ladder triggered a fear of heights in Henry he'd not known before, and he almost wobbled over before he quickly retracted his torso. Down below stood Carl and Matthew, as well as two other boys and two girls he all knew. They were still laughing at him.

'Fancy yourself a superhero? How're you gonna get down now, Henry?' Carl cried.

'Did you really think there was a treasure up there, you muppet?' Matthew yelled.

'What are you gonna tell the owners when they find you?' shouted Carl. 'What are you gonna say to your parents and Mr Anders when he comes looking for you, eh?'

Then one of the girls threw her vanilla sponge cake up at the tree house. It landed straight in Henry's face and sent him cowering back inside. Wiping the cake off himself, Henry realised how teary his face had become.

Carl had never been his direct enemy. In fact, very often they had been able to sit and play together, so Henry had no idea how much delight he took in bullying other people. Now a lot of the things Carl had done to other classmates suddenly made sense. Falling for this trap made him feel weak, and he intuitively crouched down in the furthest corner of the tree house where he vented his tears, holding his head in his palms. The embarrassment of it sent a strange, tingling, hot feeling into his face while he listened to the taunts from below. But the fear of being caught by the property owners was even greater.

Gradually, the voices became quieter, until they faded away, and Henry slowly crawled to the door to check on the bullies. None of them were there anymore, but neither was the frosty ladder to climb down. Henry retreated back into the far corner again, where he braced his head in his hands.

By now, it must have gone past one fifteen; the next period must have started. Mr Anders must have noticed his absence and sent people to look for him. What could he say to defend himself? Or worse, what if the landowners found him and accused him of trespassing? They would tell the school; the school would call his strict parents; they would give him a brutal roasting; then his dad would confiscate his Nintendo GameCube for a month and give him all sorts of punishments. The more he dwelled on it, the more he felt his hands moistening and tears trickling down his face.

Suddenly there was a strange tapping sound, as though there were another person inside the tree house. Footsteps followed. Somebody was clearly climbing up the ladder that had just been hidden from view. Henry waited.

'Mr Anders?' he said timidly.

Nobody responded.

He looked towards the little opening, and the next thing he knew, one of the bullies had climbed back up and was staring in his eyes. This girl was Naomi Watson, but everyone just called her by her middle name, Lana. She was the most mischievous child in their year, always playing pranks on schoolmates and even teachers, and always cracking jokes about her own friends. And now she'd suddenly come back.

'Hey. I am sorry we taunted you,' she said softly. 'Let me help you back down.'

For a second, there was a strange melting sensation in Henry's heart, which he'd never experienced before; he quickly hid his teary face in his hands as the girl slowly approached him. Lana might have been the biggest prankster in their year, but Henry knew she also had a large heart, and she was one of only a few children who'd share their snacks with others, and sometimes even let them copy her homework. He felt the girl's hand on his shoulder as he slowly turned his head towards her, and she looked at him the way his grandparents would if he had a paper cut, came down with flu, or had a high fever.

'Mr Anders will be looking for you if you don't come down with me,' she said softly, stretching out her arm towards him.

Henry took her hand and let himself be guided back towards the door. 'You mustn't tell Mr Anders I came up here,' he said.

'Why not?'

'He'll tell my parents. They'll shout at me. Please, Lana!'

The two had reached the little door, but when Henry glanced down at the ground, things no longer felt the same. It was as though the shock of the missing ladder resurfaced every time he dropped his gaze towards the frosty soil, even though it was clearly standing right in front of him now. He'd never been particularly comfortable with heights, but this new adrenaline rush made his legs shaky with fear.

'What's wrong?' Lana asked him.

'I can't climb down like this,' he replied.

There was a moment of quiet as Lana looked down towards the ground and then back at Henry's frightened face. She obviously sensed what was troubling him. 'I'll go down first and steady you,' she offered. Lana began to descend on the ladder and then reached out for his ankle, nudging him along. It was either now or never, so Henry slowly tilted his body backwards, then followed the girl towards the ground. Her feet were only two rungs or so away from his, her body virtually covering his, and he felt her gentle hand support him on the back. It suddenly occurred to Henry that if he fell now, he would take her down with him, but she had obviously accepted the risk.

As soon as they reached the ground, they bolted towards the classrooms, Lana leading Henry by the hand. A soft swishing sound emanated from their school blazers as they rubbed past autumn shrubs and climbed over the forbidden fence.

The next thing they saw was an agitated Mr Anders barrelling towards them, along with their form teacher. For a brief moment, Henry squeezed Lana's hand, and she returned the gesture with a little nod. Then they faced up to their teachers.

The trek back to the main school building was almost as frightening as Henry's time inside the tree house. 'How did you know we were in the woods?' he eventually asked.

'Because Joshua saw you walking in,' Mr Anders replied brusquely. 'You haven't answered my question yet. What were you two doing beyond that fence? You are in big trouble!'

A long silence followed.

'It was all my fault,' Lana suddenly volunteered. 'I wanted to see inside the tree house but then couldn't get down. Henry climbed over the fence to help me.'

'Is that so?' their maths teacher asked.

Henry nodded and suddenly felt all the tension drain out of his muscles at once. He was overcome with relief and gratitude… but there was also shame. Something stirred up inside him. How could Lana be so brave? She obviously regretted joining in with the bullies, but now she'd gone so far to make up for it.

Subconsciously, this was the moment when he learned love could be shared outside his own family.

It was not Henry's first recollection of his childhood, but it was definitely one of his earliest formative memories. That day, he had become acquainted with some powerful emotions.

Youth Events

Time passed, and it was now early 2012. While the United States was governed by the first black president in its history, Vladimir Putin was running for a third presidential term in Russia, seeking to take back control from Dmitry Medvedev. The country had seen a series of economic reforms that had increased gross domestic income and wealth. Purchasing power had increased significantly, and yet the number of emigrants from Russia had not declined. Elias's family had relocated to Nikel, another Arctic border town near Norway, where his parents had found employment at an urban smelting plant. They were living in a humble two-bedroom apartment on the outskirts, working away on a modest but steady income.

Today was Wednesday, 15 February 2012, one of the most significant days in Elias' youth. It had gone five thirty in the afternoon; the sun had barely risen at all over the Arctic Circle, leaving this northern border town in near pitch-darkness. Elias was crouching by the window of the children's bedroom, where he looked across to the forlorn suburban park. Today, there flowed no northern lights, and the winterly branches had been covered in thick snow by a howling blizzard that was raging about the town. Another hour of this, and it would be hard to get out at all, he thought. Like his brother Mikhail, Elias was dressed in a thick woollen jumper and thermal fleece trousers. Two pairs of socks and a soft pair of cotton slippers lent warmth to their feet, for though the rooms were heated with tiled coal stoves, the Arctic temperatures of the long winter months never allowed the flat to go above seventeen degrees Celsius.

Elias turned from the window, warmed his hands on the ceramic stove and helped his brother pack a waterproof rucksack, for Mikhail needed to flee the country that very day and not return for a long time. He'd just come back on the Arktika train from St Petersburg University, where he was studying for his degree in neuroscience. Initially, Mikhail had been granted a deferral for his military service, but the armed conflict in Chechnya had been ongoing since 1994, and the government was growing weary of undergraduates dodging their national service. Now they were stepping up their fight against those cowardly draft dodgers that had put education before national duty. Too much blood had been spilled already for the government to backtrack on Chechnya now; the fight against independence had to be won, even with the blood of undergraduates. When Mikhail's parents had received the official cancellation of his deferral, they had told him to return to Nikel straight away. Now they were preparing his escape across the border to Norway.

'Really? All of them have been sent to Chechnya already?' Elias asked.

'Yuri was drafted at Christmas; he got sent to

Chechnya in January. Levi was conscripted last month; he'll be in Chechnya by March. Five people in my class—they all got deferrals—are now going to Chechnya. The state needs all these recruits,' his brother replied, shoving his bristle hairbrush in the rucksack.

Elias paused to reflect on the fate of those poor people. There was something outrageously unjust and merciless about these practices that left him with a churning sensation in his stomach and a feeling of being imprisoned in this country. 'Well, if they need more people to fight and die for them,' he said, 'maybe they should just put up salaries for professional soldiers or something. We are not their slaves. We don't even feel Russian! They're punishing us simply for our nationality. We didn't choose to be born here, did we? They can't do this to us.'

'They can, and they do,' said his elder brother. 'They have been doing this for three centuries.'

'I wish Grandad had never left Norway. I wish he'd stayed in Stavanger, so we could also be Norwegian and not face this crap here,' said Elias. The rucksack was finally packed, and the two brothers strained to close the zip of this overloaded backpack.

'Is Dad driving you all the way to the border?' Elias asked.

'Dad's driving me to the river. He'll drop me off close to Bjørnsund, and I'll cross alone.'

'You'll swim across in this weather? The water is almost ice!'

'It's a five-hundred metre crossing. Don't worry. I can make it. Nobody's expecting anyone to swim cross in February.'

'Will Dad equip you with a wetsuit?'

'There were none in stock. We have no time to wait. I have to flee tonight. And once I am in Norway, I'll head to Uncle Harry, in Bjørnevatn, and apply for asylum.'

'Oh my God!' Elias uttered. His brother's plan sounded strenuous but simple—so simple, in fact, that Elias suddenly had an ominous hunch that the journey to safety would turn out a lot bumpier.

Just then, there was a single knock on the bedroom door, and their dad entered.

'Dinner's ready,' he said, gesturing for his children to accompany him to the dining room. 'Are you done packing?'

His sons nodded, and Mikhail pointed at the overfilled waterproof backpack.

Their dad gave it a feel with his hands and said, 'Come on, kids. This might be our last dinner together for a long time. Then we have to say goodbye.'

Dutifully, the children followed him into the dining area, where he and their mum had prepared traditional Norwegian soup with Bombay potatoes. In here, the air was a lot warmer, and more pleasant too, for the boiling of the soup had heated up the room and permeated the air with a savoury, appetising scent.

When the children took their seats at the dining table, their mum had a safe box on it and was counting a small stack of bills that did not look like Russian roubles. 'Six hundred, seven hundred, seven hundred and fifty, eight hundred, two thousand eight hundred Norwegian kroner,' she said. Mother slipped the bills neatly into a brown envelope before sealing it with a strip of adhesive tape. 'That should be more than enough to pay Uncle Harry.'

'Pay him?' asked Mikhail.

'For hospitality,' replied mother. 'We don't want to make him feel ill-used,' she added. Rising from her seat, mother put on a pair of oven gloves and carried over a pot of hot fish soup to the decrepit dinner table. Elias leaned forward over the pot and relished the delicious fumes that rose from the liquid. They brought back memories from early childhood and visits from his Scandinavian relatives, for every time they called on them in winter, a hot bowl of Norwegian fish soup was prepared for all to share.

As the Alexandersen family dug into the delicious soup, the adults discussed their plans to help Mikhail gain a place at the University of Oslo sometime this year. Hopefully, he could have some sanctuary at Harry's place until the summer, maybe borrow some books from the Bjørnevatn library, do a bit of self-educating and then apply for admission for the August term.

Mikhail told his parents all about a newly discovered extracellular matrix powder, which scientists were hoping might hold the secret to regenerating destroyed body tissue. 'Eventually, we'll be able to regrow anything,' he said. 'Lost limbs, broken spines, we could cure blindness, deafness—everything.'

Mum and dad nodded at each other and smiled glowingly. Elias knew they were smiles of pride, for he and Mikhail had always been top of the class, and now his brother would utilise his intelligence to contribute to such scientific advances. His brother would not join some senseless war and throw grenades at innocent people or conscripts from other jurisdictions. His brother would use his skills to *heal* people.

Right then, the doorbell suddenly rang, and Mikhail

looked up from the table as if a bucket of ice had been thrown on his back, freezing on the chair.

'Ah, don't worry!' Dad said nonchalantly. 'It's probably just Mr Patel. I lent him the tyre pump this morning.'

He rose from his seat and casually strolled towards the front entrance, walking through the cold of the narrow corridor, away from the delicious soup. He was about to open the door, then he intuitively stopped and stole a glance through the peephole. Three men in their mid-thirties had congregated on the doorstep, armed with pistols and a Taser, waiting to be let in.

Adrenaline swamped Mr Alexandersen's body, for he knew from his own time in the army that these men worked for the Internal Troops. He covered his mouth in shock and tried to weigh up all possible options. None of them looked particularly fruitful from this point.

The soldiers rang the doorbell again while one of them began to fumble around with his gun. Quietly, Mr Alexandersen hastened back to the dining table and motioned his family to hush.

'What's the matter?' asked his wife. 'Who is out there?'

His younger son rose to his feet and stared into the fearful, frozen eyes of his elder brother, as though they could both sense it.

'Sit back down. Pretend nothing is happening,' whispered Mr Alexandersen, and then he turned to his wife. 'Get Mikhail away. It's the army. They know he's home. Quick! Quick! I'll talk to them. Hurry!'

Repeated vigorous bangs were being made on the

front door, more reminiscent of burglars or thugs than state authorities.

Mrs Alexandersen leapt from her chair and grabbed their firstborn son by the jumper. She led him to the hidden mezzanine loft at the back of the flat, where she concealed him along with his overfilled backpack. 'Elias, you stay where you are. Pretend nothing has happened and you haven't seen your brother,' she whispered.

Then Mr Alerxandersen quietly padded back to the entrance and looked through the peephole again. More aggressive bangs thudded on the door. 'Sorry… just a second! Who is out there?' he asked. 'We're having dinner.'

'Open the door at once! It's the Internal Troops!' shouted one of the soldiers. His voice sounded abrupt and angry, if not completely overbearing. 'Open the door, I ordered!'

Mr Alexandersen quickly glanced over at his wife, who signalled that it was safe to let them in. He gently opened the entrance as he feigned an expression of surprise and ignorance. The man in the middle wore a bulging golden stripe on each shoulder and therefore had to be the sergeant, the leader of this mission. Mr Alexandersen pulled off the military salute that he'd been taught in his own army time, and the two soldiers flanking the sergeant returned the greeting. But the leader himself remained stiff and cast an aggressive glare into the suburban flat.

'Sergeant,' Mr Alexandersen said. 'What brings you here? My family is having dinner now.'

'Your son,' replied the sergeant. 'And don't pretend you don't know this.' Along with the other two soldiers, he marched into the humbly heated property and began to survey it, shaking his head at the flat's interior, and all the while, they dragged their snow-covered boots over the carpet.

'Our son? Elias?' Mr Alexandersen repeated.

'Oh, come on, stop pretending. Your other son, Mikhail,' came the sergeant's reply. 'Did you not receive the order papers? Mikhail was supposed to report for duty this week. But he did not turn up.'

'Well,' replied Mr Alexandersen in a quivering voice, 'we are indeed expecting him tonight. He's coming back from uni today, so…'

'Sergeant, can I offer you something? Would you like some soup?' interjected Mrs Alexandersen, who now emerged from the dining area, pointing at the old table with her palm.

'Er, sorry,' Mr Alexandersen said to the sergeant. 'Let me introduce you to my wife. This is Marjorie, the mother of our two boys.'

'How do you do?' said Marjorie in a light-hearted voice that did not match the tension in her face.

The sergeant seemed to pick up on this straight away, and he immediately marched towards Mikhail's empty seat.

'Now, look at this! What do we have here?' he remarked in his sly and supercilious tone. 'We spoke to your son's university, and they said he took the afternoon train from St Petersburg *yesterday*. He should have arrived here long before now. Why else would there be a hot bowl of soup at an empty but very warm chair, and why is your younger son shaking as if you're concealing the truth from us?' He strode towards Elias and placed his hand firmly on the boy's trembling shoulder. 'Tell us, young man, are your parents lying to us? Are your parents being deceitful?

Is your cowardly brother here?' he demanded.

A spine-chilling dizziness came over Elias as he felt his pulse racing. He stole a glance at his motionless parents, waiting for some kind of clue, some kind of instruction. But none came this time, for obviously neither of them was prepared to see their son interrogated thus. Elias caught a glimpse of his mother's shaking hand before she gingerly folded her arms behind her back. Then he felt the soldier tightening his grip on his shoulder before he shouted, 'Search the bloody flat! Find the bastard and bring him here!' At the snap of his fingers, his two assistants dispersed and commenced the hunt, like dogs obeying their master, heading for the bedrooms.

Within a few minutes, the three officers had virtually uprooted the family flat in their search for their lost property. Such was the chaos caused by the men that no shelf was untouched, no cupboard was left alone; nothing was spared. All clothes, books and personal effects were ruthlessly pitched onto the carpet, as if all the belongings of this disgraced family had now become state property.

'Where is the coward? Where is the bastard?' one of the soldiers kept muttering to himself while he rummaged through the flat for evidence of Mikhail's return.

The only interesting object they were able to find was an old medal, a military honour they used to bestow on people who demonstrated courage in service to the state. It was attached to a worn but still-colourful ribbon, on which were sewn the initials *M.A.* The sergeant stared at this military antique as though he spitefully coveted it, and then he turned to dad. 'Who is M.A.? Does this belong to you?' he asked sternly.

But it was Mum who shook her head and quietly replied, 'M.A. stands for Manfred Altmann. He was my German grandfather. He spied for the Soviets during the last war.'

The sergeant curled his fingers around the heirloom while he glared at mum with envious, tightening eyes. Then his attention was suddenly caught by a metallic clanking noise that emerged from the far end of the flat. 'What was that?' he asked. His face tensed up, and he instinctively slid his hand closer to his pistol holster.

'We've searched everything,' replied the private by his side. 'There is nobody else here. We've looked in every nook and cranny.'

'So what was that sound, then?' demanded the sergeant again. He was getting very irritated now. The military team leader marched to the far end of the corridor and signalled to one of the privates to follow. The other one remained and kept a close eye on the Alexandersen family as they watched the two soldiers from the dining area.

'Look, it was just his ladder that collapsed,' said the private, pointing into the children's bedroom.

His superior did not seem convinced. 'Why would they even keep a ladder?' he muttered ominously. He looked about him suspiciously and inspected every centimetre around him. Finally, his scrutinising gaze stilled, and he pointed at a partially-hidden hatch on the corridor ceiling, near the parents' bedroom. 'Does that door up there open at all?' he demanded.

'Yes, it does, Sergeant,' replied Dad after a moment's hesitation. 'But you wouldn't be able to fit anyone up there. It's only for the pipes and the water.' His voice cracked on the last three words, and for the first time, the sergeant began to smile.

'So you wouldn't mind, then, if I put a bullet through this door, would you? I mean, just to prove you're telling the truth, of course,' he replied. The sergeant gripped his gun and drew it from the holster, then pointed it towards with ceiling hatch with a malignant sneer.

It was too difficult to gauge whether this monster was being serious or whether he was merely bluffing and enjoying the entertainment of catching a whole family entangled in their own lies. Elias looked at his unreactive parents, both pallid, with chins trembling and their breathing sounding more strained. The young boy felt as though someone had just added the last drop of water into his overflowing vessel, and he was about to explode from within—his own brother was about to be shot, and there was nothing they could do to save him.

'No!' he suddenly screamed, bolting into the corridor. He made a rapid dash towards the evil sergeant and rammed his body into him.

'Elias!' he heard his parents shout from behind.

The next thing he knew, the alarmed sergeant had trapped him in his powerful grip, struck him on the head and wrestled him to the floor. Almost immediately, he felt a powerful surge of electricity lancing through his back as his entire body spasmed. For a second, he let out an unearthly scream. Then he found himself paralysed and rendered speechless by the shock of the Taser. Lying still on the floor, he became aware of his inability to rise or even move.

'Stop! Stop this!' shouted his distressed mother, who rushed towards her motionless son.

His dad tried to follow suit but was immediately subdued by the second private, who jostled him to the floor and placed his hand around his neck in a stranglehold. The soldier noticed Mom dropping an envelope from her apron, and he motioned his comrade to pick it up.

'Right, that's enough!' bellowed the sergeant, panting in consternation. 'That's enough, everyone! What a wild and unruly family we have here! It's disgraceful!' He ordered the first private to climb up to the loft and detain the fugitive on the spot.

By the time Elias had regained his capacity for movement, his brother was handcuffed in thick metal shackles and ready to be led away. They were about to part, but then something brought a twinkle of joy to the sergeant's eyes.

'Pay attention now!' he started lecturing. 'You all know that you've been abetting a fugitive by hiding a conscript in your flat, despite clear order papers. And don't you pretend you didn't know about this. We know you did. You also know that we could arrest all of you as accomplices if we wanted to. But luckily for you, we're a very reasonable bunch here, aren't we?'

At this, his two assistants nodded with a beholden smile.

'Yes, we are a very reasonable bunch. We will leave you in peace, and as a token of your gratitude, we are happy to accept this gift of over two thousand kroner.' He sealed the envelope again and hid it away in his pocket, along with Manfred Altmann's medal of honour.

The soldiers looked so much happier by the end of this mission than when they had first stepped in. The merciful sergeant graciously permitted the family to give Mikhail one last hug. And then, like a lost-and-found pawn, like a piece of state property, they led him away into the army car. Elias leaned his head out the window and watched the vehicle slowly disappear into the Arctic snow fog as it drove away towards the barracks of Murmansk.

Indeed, it was a night of shattered dreams for the entire family, and a day that would forever brand itself on Elias's subconscious. He'd learned something very important about the state: if the government needed you, they would take you. In fact, they *owned* you. Your ownership of your own destiny, your own soul, mattered nothing.

And thus, as the night progressed and the upheaval of this setback gradually sank in a little more, this was the moment when Elias learned not even adults were immune from tears. Lying awake in his bed, unable to sleep, he overheard his parents weeping. Quietly, he padded across the corridor and placed himself outside their bedroom, trying to listen in.

'No,' said Mother, 'this cannot happen again. I won't be able to bear it another time.'

'We'll send Elias abroad before his order papers come,' replied Dad.

'Abroad? They took all our savings!'

'We can save up again. Or maybe we can send Elias to study in Norway,' Dad mused, 'and he won't even have to come back until he's past the conscription age.'

'If we had more money, I would send him to Britain.'

'Why Britain? Do you know how hard it is to get into the UK?'

'It's all too early to decide now. Let's see what happens in the next few years. There might not even be any conscription here when Elias turns eighteen.'

'You don't believe that, do you?' replied dad. 'They'll still be conscripting children here at the end of the century.'

'Do you think so? Let's see what happens. We have to worry about Mikhail first.'

Suddenly Elias heard quiet footsteps coming in his direction, and he took a step back. One of his parents was probably heading for the toilet, and he'd better withdraw to his own bedroom, anyway.

It was a night that had changed the family forever, and Elias had learned a valuable lesson: individuals were the property of the state. They existed to serve the government but did not exercise any ownership of their own fate or soul. Even after all those stories of progress they were taught at school—the abolition of slavery, the prohibition of servitude—if the government recognised a person as its own citizen, that person was still its property.

Elias suddenly had a rather vague and yet powerful moment of déjà vu, as though history had just repeated itself. Somewhere in his hidden recollections flickered a scene in which fugitive slaves hid beneath a trapdoor, concealing themselves from state authorities. He probed his memory, trying to recall events that could fit this scene somehow, but found none. At least, not on that night.

Opinions: society and the media shape them; pivotal experiences trigger them. Some are imparted by parents, while others evolve over time.

Today was 13 June 2012, and the annual cross-country run of Great Malvern Whitehawk School—a pivotal day in Henry's youth. The mercury reached twenty-eight degrees in the morning, and the clear, sunny sky saw some locals taking a dip in the lakes around the hills.

The competition itself always involved two laps around the school campus and totalled nearly one and a half miles. The annual game was meant to boost pupils' morale and help them keep fit, but what interested students the most was always who won. And in the last four years, the top honour had always gone to Henry, for he was the most athletically capable student, and other pupils set a lot of store by his physical talents. Today it was once again time for the teenage boy to bask in this glory. And this time, his competitive father had even agreed to attend and film the awards ceremony so Henry would remember those moments in years to come.

It was almost one o'clock in the afternoon when Henry strolled out of the canteen, dressed in brand-new Adidas trainers and a white T-shirt. He ambled over the green school meadow, sauntering past the nineteenth-century campus chapel and the stone shed until he reached a round duck pond. Here he leaned against one of the wooden benches and started a series of leg stretches while mallards quacked in the still water. In front of him sailed a grey heron, seemingly on course for the towering hills. Behind him, there was nonchalant chatter from school-mates of all years.

The chapel bell chimed one o'clock, and a hand suddenly placed itself on Henry's shoulder. He turned around and looked into the eyes of his friend Emmanuel, dressed in traditional summer uniform.

'All right, mate? Getting ready for the race, I see,' he said.

'I was born ready,' Henry joked. 'What about you, mate? Are you not running today?'

'No, not this time. I got a note from the doctor— pulled a muscle in my thigh. It needs to heal. No sports for me until the end of the month.'

'Ouch, sounds painful.'

'It's all right for me. But I heard there's competition for you this year.'

'There's competition every year, but this year, I had *better* win. My dad wants to film the thing at the end.'

'You mean the awards ceremony?'

'Yeah, that's the one.'

'Daddy's boy!' Emmanuel teased him.

'Hey, my parents are very competitive people!' Henry declared. He stretched his legs onto the bench again and continued his warm-ups. 'So, who is this new competition you're talking about?' he eventually asked.

'Have you not met Jeremy this term?'

'You mean the South African boy in 11D?'

'That's the one.'

'We've played football before. He's a strong lad, has a lot of skill, but the one time he tried to snatch the ball from me in the finals, I outran him.'

'Well, just watch out for him if you want to come top again this year, mate,' Emmanuel advised.

Privately, Henry admitted that part of him felt nervous about being filmed, because he worried the pressure of having to win might distract him and tilt him towards second place this time. Emmanuel wished Henry good luck and assured him he would be cheering for him near the finishing line.

A little later, the chapel bell chimed half past the

hour, and the runners were gradually gathering for the race of the year. Henry made his way towards the other competitors, trying to secure a spot as close to the front as possible. *It would be such a pity to miss first place by just a few seconds.* He edged his way past the other participants as far as the queue allowed him to and then projected his view back at all the competitors behind him. He caught a glimpse of Emily, the first girl he'd ever dated, which was back in Year 10. She lifted her arm to give him a friendly wave, and Henry waved back just as he caught sight of his current girlfriend, Jill. She was a tall brunette with a somewhat tanned face, dressed in sturdy Nike trainers and even wearing the golden bracelet Henry had recently gifted her. Not far behind her stood Lana, with her perpetual smile, but unlike the others, she did not have any shoes on at all, as if her feet were made from leather or she didn't care about hurting herself. Lana was always so chilled and down to earth, as if nothing in the world could ever worry her. Out of all the people in his school, she was the one he admired the most—there was such a carefree attitude in her that he'd never seen in anyone else.

The referee was lifting the starting gun to signal the beginning of the annual race, and Henry looked forward to fix his gaze on the Malvern Hills. The starting pistol was now above the referee's head; there were only a few more seconds to wait... *Bang!* With a single blast, the entire GCSE group was set into motion.

Lifting his body to full height and kicking the ground with his rubber soles, Henry immediately overtook Jeremy and every single participant in the race. Once again, he was heading for certain victory. He visualised himself as a superhero who had just shed his human attire and was now on a mission to save the school. The woodland was a touch muddy under his sturdy trainers, but Henry had learned throughout the years to reserve a good amount of energy for this stretch. He ran past the spot where the old tree house had once stood, now long demolished, and then emerged out of the woods.

Gradually, the finishing line of the first lap came into view, and crowds of teachers, pupils and parents were cheering on their children as they approached. Henry squinted over at the spectators, but for some reason, his father had simply not turned up. At least, Emmanuel was still cheering for him, as he'd promised, clapping jubilantly when Henry was about to draw past.

'Where is Dad? Have you seen Dad?' Henry mimed to him.

His friend pulled an expression of confusion with his arms, then suddenly shouted, 'Watch out!'

Very briefly, Henry had lost focus on the race, and the next thing he knew, he had tripped onto a patch of uneven earth. He thumped the ground with his clenched fist and attempted to lift himself up as swiftly as he could. But as soon as he looked ahead, he realised in disbelief that he'd already been overtaken in those few seconds. A fellow GCSE pupil from his own class, Aaron, was now running ahead of him and seemingly heading for first place. *That's impossible! This just can't be real!* Henry fumed. He summoned up all his energy reserves and tried to accelerate.

The second lap saw a tight race between Henry and Aaron. Henry certainly had the stamina and speed to gain first place, but the more he thought about his dad's mysterious no-show, the more he felt his energy being sapped, and the more he lagged behind.

Now, by no means would he call himself a daddy's boy. In fact, he and his parents had a turbulent relationship at times, but because the race meant so much to him, a broken promise from his own dad did hurt and confuse him. *Dad is just running a little late*, he told himself. *By the end of the race, not only will he be standing there, but he might even be filming me crossing the finishing line.* And just like that, he zipped towards Aaron with a renewed sense of purpose. Deep down, he knew he was only deluding himself.

Gradually, Henry was approaching the finishing line again, and he turned his head towards the spectators. By now, he'd expended so much energy that he was determined to overtake Aaron regardless of his father. He visualised propelling himself forward with a renewed supply of fuel and was about sixty metres from the finishing line when he set one foot ahead of his rival and finally overtook him. At last, he was heading for first place once again.

Suddenly a crude voice was shouting at him from the audience. Henry squinted to the left and immediately sighted Carl, his arch-enemy since their primary years. Scrunching up a disdainful face full of glee and mockery, Carl shouted, 'Daddy's boy, eh? Where is your beloved daddy now? He ain't coming, because he knew you'd lose this time!' He raised his hands high and clapped in gloating amusement.

By this stage, Henry had already overtaken Aaron and was about to win, but those distracting comments were just too hurtful to ignore. He stared at the vile spectator and imagined lunging at him with a leap. For a second time, he had lost focus on this all-important race. Snapping out of it, he swiftly faced the front, but the next thing he knew, he'd been outrun once again, this time by another, much taller and even faster boy, who was now heading for first place. It was Jeremy, the South African kid, as other students called him; he seemed virtually unstoppable now.

Henry's sobering realisation that he could no longer win the race drained the remaining energy out of him, and the moment he slowed down to content himself with second place, he was overtaken a third time. Aaron sped past him like a cheetah and placed himself between Jeremy and Henry in the last five seconds of the lap. By the end of the race, Henry had been relegated from undefeated champion to a mere third place. And still, his dad was nowhere to be seen.

The bell chimed quarter past two when the winners lined up on the podium in the foreground of the green hills, ready to receive their awards. For the first time in four years, Henry was not awarded gold. Or silver, in fact. No, this time, it was all different. This time, the top prize went to a newcomer, an outsider, a foreigner, someone who'd only been on the premises for a term and had managed to steal all his glory. The three of them were still basking in a prolonged round of applause when Henry's mum suddenly turned up unexpectedly, having joined the other onlookers, and gave her child two thumbs-up. It was all too late now, and Henry was still dwelling on his father's no-show as he gazed into the crowd.

Then his line of vision crossed Carl once more. The

vile pig was sneering so obnoxiously and full of contempt that Henry imagined throwing his bronze medal at the boy. When his enemy's eyes finally snapped onto his, Carl's gleeful, sneering face descended into such joy and schadenfreude that Henry was no longer able to bear it, and finally, he gave in to a darker side. *I should've slapped that bastard. He will be punished.*

Henry felt his cheeks redden with anger, and a split second later, he stepped off the podium, barging towards his enemy with a clenched jaw and two clenched fists. 'You will pay for this!' he bellowed at the boy.

Carl appeared to be backing off a little, but he was soon cornered by his much stronger opponent and was now standing with his back against a wire fence.

'Did you hear me? You will pay for what you did, you son of a bitch!' Henry shouted again. His darker instincts eventually took over and brought his blood to a boil. He began to shove Carl against the metal fence, swearing at him as he did.

Hold on! This doesn't feel right. I am not normally a brutal person! shot through Henry's mind. His hands began to quiver, and he swiftly recoiled from such violence, as though a string were pulling him back and reining him in. Too late now, he found, for his actions had been duly noted by the headmaster, who came to grab him by the arm like a security guard. He yanked Henry away from his enemy as his mother stood and watched, flabbergasted, her jaw dropping at this rare sight.

The next thing Henry knew, he was sitting in the headmaster's office and wishing he had the power to turn back time. It was a carpeted, oak-panelled room with a stone fireplace on one side and a Union Jack between some tall shelves filled with maths and history books. The headmaster's lecture was dragging on.

'We operate zero tolerance for violence, and you know that, Henry. What Carl did might've been uncalled for, but that does not give you the right to push him. Do you understand?' he demanded.

'I am sorry, sir. It happened in the heat of the moment.'

'You must learn to control the heat of the moment.'

'Yes, sir.'

'Is that all you have to say?'

'I am sorry, sir. It will not happen again. I promise.'

A long moment of silence passed. Then Henry repeated himself. 'I am sorry, sir. I promise.'

At this, his headmaster glanced away and examined the school reports in Henry's file. He looked up and remarked solemnly, 'Look, Henry, you are a young man now. Almost ten years ago, when I was your maths teacher, I caught you skiving off in the woodland.'

Henry recalled this episode all too vividly and looked up in surprise.

'I only found out a lot later that Carl had bullied you into it, and Lana had made up a lie to protect you. When I realised this, she surpassed all my expectations, and I was very much hoping she would also inspire in you—how can I put it? A sense of solidarity or at least forbearance… but from what I saw today, you still have a long way to go, and—'

'I didn't mean to do it! I acted on impulse! Don't you understand?' Henry interjected.

'I am not finished yet, so please don't interrupt me,' Mr Anders responded solemnly. 'From what I saw today, you still have a long way to go, but you still have time.

You're still young, Henry, and you still have two years with us. A lot can happen in that time.' The headmaster eyed Henry's bronze medal, which was still dangling on his chest, and quietly asked, 'Will you please hand back that medal to me?'

'What?'

'You'll have to hand back the medal. On school grounds, we operate a completely violence-free zone. So, I must make an example of you after this incident today.'

Are you telling me I get cheated out of gold, then I get cheated out of silver, and now I've got to hand in this last bit of consolation? Henry bit his tongue. Reluctantly, he removed the medallion from his neck and handed it back to Mr Anders, who deposited the prize in an ornamented blackwood drawer. 'Thank you, Henry'.

'Can I go now, please?' Henry asked. He inhaled a lungful and was ready to run outside and maybe scream.

'Please remain seated. Actually, there's one more thing I wanted to tell you, young man,' said Mr Anders. Then he broke the news of his decision to cancel Henry's nomination for prefect for the following academic year.

'What? You can't be serious, sir!'

'We take violence *extremely* seriously. And I must make it clear that if you show any such behaviour, then you won't be put in charge of other pupils. It's as simple as that.'

Curious, Henry enquired who would take his position instead, noting that the number of prefects had always been fixed. 'You won't pick Jeremy, will you?' he asked.

'That will be my concern,' replied the headmaster. 'Your concern should be to rein in your temper.'

'Jesus. He's only been here for, like, five minutes—'

'He's been here since January, and in that time, he's demonstrated honesty and hard work.'

Henry felt a tightening sensation in his stomach as his mouth gaped wide open.

Finally, Mr Anders dismissed the pupil for the day and asked to speak to his mother.

'Are you still going to New Zealand this summer?' Mr Anders asked just as Henry was about to step out of the office.

Henry turned around and nodded. He'd actually completely forgotten about his trip coming up in the summer.

'Well, that's certainly something to look forward to this year,' said Mr Anders. 'Some quality time with Mum and Dad.'

At those words, Henry strode out of the office as his mum was invited in for a private chat. As he sat in the corridor outside, he was overcome with a sense of shame that extinguished the light at the end of the tunnel. A chain of events could turn so quickly. One second, he had been heading for first place; the next, he had lost everything. There was just no order in this sphere of reality. Every action was just like a spin of a roulette wheel.

What could Mum and the headmaster possibly have been discussing for over five minutes now?

Almost out of nowhere, his girlfriend suddenly appeared, heading for the girls' bathroom. Henry smiled at her, but even he knew his expression must have come across as artificial and rather strained, and this time, Jill did not smile back.

'Jill, what's the matter?' asked Henry, stretching his

hand out to her. He was feeling the need for some consolation on a day like this.

As Jill passed him with sad, puffy eyes, she removed the bracelet from her wrist, which she returned into Henry's outstretched hand.

'Jill, what are you doing? This was my gift to you.'

'I'm sorry, Henry. I don't want to be associated with someone who beats up others, and—'

'I didn't beat up Carl. I just pushed him a little. He deserved it. Do you know what he said to me? Come on, Jill, please!'

'I'm sorry, Henry. We can still be friends and say hello and stuff, but you were really mean to Carl today. I'll see you around.' And just like that, she walked off.

In the evening, a dinner of mashed potatoes and haddock fillets was served, and Henry finally learned the reason his father had failed to show up at the event. The family were sitting in their dining area, at the rear of their rectangular bungalow. The back door was wide open to let in the cooler air. Henry learned his father's fish-and-chips kiosk had gone bankrupt that week, and his father had been negotiating a new loan at the bank. They had not got it this time.

'Couldn't you have told me a little earlier?' Henry scolded his dad, lifting his hands from the dinner table.

'We didn't know I'd be in there for so long. When I knew I wouldn't make it in time, I texted Mum straight away.'

'I don't understand this,' Henry mused. 'The shop was still running really well at Christmas... How can it just go bust from one day to the next?'

'Well, things just change, son; nothing ever stays the same. Things always change,' Dad responded. 'How is your dinner?'

Suddenly, a thought pierced Henry's mind like a poisoned thorn, and he put his hand over his mouth. 'Oh my God. Please don't tell me it's that gyro stand that put us out of business—the Greek one that opened in January—because they also sell fish and chips, right?'

At this, his parents regarded each other in silence. Then his dad turned to Henry and nodded. 'Please don't feel bitter. The second you feel bitter about competition, in any business, you fail. We'll get ourselves out of this, I promise.'

Thereupon, Henry let out a sarcastic sigh and attempted to give them an artificial smile. Well, at least they still had the New Zealand holiday to look forward to. Yes, that was certainly something to hold on to in these moments of dread.

'And by the way, Henry, we're so sorry, but we also had to cancel the holiday to New Zealand,' his mum then confessed.

Henry was feeling as though someone had just deprived him of his faculty of speech, gaping at his parents with an open mouth. 'Are you guys kidding me? What kind of a nightmare is this?'

'I'm afraid, son, you'll have to find something else to do this summer,' said Dad.

Slowly, a hardening sensation was creeping into Henry's stomach, and he found himself beginning to pant. *Must remain calm. Must remain composed,* he kept telling himself. 'Well, what about Vietnam?' he muttered.

'What do you mean, Vietnam?' replied mum.

'I could join Grandma and Grandad on their pilgrimage to Vietnam this year, right?'

'Grandma and Grandad aren't going to Phú Lộc this year. Besides, they already took you with them last time,' Dad said.

'There are loads of things you can do around here,' mum considered. 'You could work at that fruit farm with… what's her name again?… Naomi?'

'You mean Lana?' Henry replied.

'That's the one. Doesn't her uncle run a fruit farm near here? They're always looking for labour in the summer.'

Dad nodded. 'She's right. You are sixteen now. It's time for you to do some proper work for a change. I'm gonna call and ask if they can give you a job over the summer. You're a practical kind of guy, aren't you? Then show it! Rather than just sitting here, feeling sorry for yourself!'

'How do you feel about this idea?' asked Mum.

Reminding himself to stay collected, Henry noticed how heavy his breathing had become. A train of thought was paralysing his mind, for there came a realisation today that settled on him like fog descending over his home, and for the first time in Henry's life, the word *foreigner* aroused a connotation he had not discerned before. In a deep, slow voice, he vented, 'They come into our land. They steal our jobs…'

'Right, that's enough! Just watch what you say!' commanded Father, but his son continued nonetheless.

'They come into our land. They take our jobs. They go straight to the head of the queue…'

'Which queue, son?' asked his dad. 'Stop this!'

Henry's mum cut in. 'But, Richard, our son *does* have a point. I've said that before, so many times. There really are too many foreigners here.'

A powerful sense of validation comforted Henry and propelled him on. 'They come to our lands. They take everything, and still, they are not content. They take our jobs, and now they're taking our holidays.'

'That's enough!' shouted Dad, hushing his son with his index finger. 'As long as you live under this roof, there will be no such language. Do you understand?'

'So what language do you want to hear, then?' cried Henry, rising from his seat. 'Do you want to hear Greek and Turkish everywhere and lose your next business too, you loser? You're nothing but a huge failure!'

Dismayed, Henry's mum rose from her seat, tears welling in her eyes. She stretched out her hand towards her teenage child, but Henry dashed into his bedroom and slammed the door shut behind him, flinging himself onto his mattress. To cope with a day like this, he needed to be alone.

Life could be so arbitrary and ruthless at times. Anything could happen, and there was nowhere to hide from the messy reality of the adult life he was about to enter. Beyond his bedroom door, his parents were trying to calm him down, reassuring him that everything would be all right, and that they were trying to get him a job at Lana's uncle's farm. Henry's mind, however, was elsewhere that evening. He had to make sure he ring-fenced his own slice of the pie in life, protected it and shielded it, whatever that slice may be.

Part III

Of Light and Miracles

Reunion after Twenty-Three Years

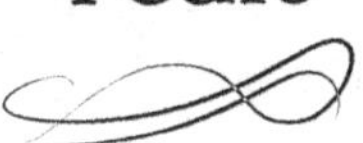

Coincidence: some people call it luck; some call it chance; yet other people like to invoke the notion of destiny or fate. Some philosophers would probably struggle to reconcile the idea of predetermined destiny with a world of autonomy and free will. Random coincidences, they might argue, can happen at any time. After all, according to the mathematical law of truly large numbers, the probability of outrageously unlikely events occurring in a world of over seven billion samples significantly outweighs the chances of extreme coincidences *not* materialising daily. And yet, so many people will go through life and remember the odd event here and there with a lingering feeling that there was more to it than pure chance…

Little did an individual soul on the A57 service know that this particular train from Oxford was taking him on a direct rendezvous with fate. It was Friday, 2 August 2019.

The carriage was packed with summer holidaymakers heading for rural England or the beaches on the west coast. Tourists from Japan and the United States were chatting away as a young vendor rolled his trolley through the railway coach, selling the occasional refreshment to passengers. Right now, the train was passing through Worcestershire and slowly approaching Great Malvern station. It gradually slowed down to a crawl, as though it was waiting for another service in front of it to pick up. To the left of the tracks extended a range of solemn green hills that stretched northwards and led past old stone cottages and woodland. To the right lay vast fields of grassland and the occasional livestock farm. It was quite an idyllic part of Great Britain, but it was also one that carried a somewhat forlorn, mystical vibe, opined a young man looking out the train window. A twenty-three-year-old postgraduate in neuroscience, he was reading a book on stem cell dedifferentiation and annotating lines of text. The young man was of medium height, with brown hair and blue eyes. His complexion was quite pale, and he was dressed in a short-sleeved lumberjack shirt and black jeans. From his shirt pocket protruded a blue travel document pursuant to the UN's 1951 Refugee Convention—it had been issued by the Home Office and gave him the right of abode on this island. On his feet, he wore simple grey plimsolls. This young man was Elias Alexandersen, who'd been living and studying in Britain for the last three years.

An announcement came over the speakers in the carriage. 'This is the Western Railway service to Aberystwyth. The next station is Great Malvern. Please remember to take all your personal belongings with you. Great Malvern will be our next stop.'

There was chatter in Elias's seating cluster, and the young man looked up from his book. In front of him sat two men in their mid-thirties, speaking in strong Texan accents. One of them was sturdily built and boasted a beard, while his companion appeared a little shorter and much shyer. They were both reading copies of the *Daily Mirror*.

'They got a new Prime Minister here,' said the shorter one. 'His name is Boris Johnson. I think he previously served as foreign secretary. Do you think he will agree to a second Brexit referendum?'

Brexit! Ever since Elias had arrived in the UK, Brexit had been the most debated topic everywhere. He focused back on his book and listened on quietly.

'No, do you know what a second referendum would look like?' asked the bearded travel companion.

'Like what?'

'Well, it would be a bit like saying, "Hey, we don't like the result of the first—let's get a different one." I mean, no general election is ever rerun. That would be absurd.'

'Oh, yes, they are,' his shyer-looking friend replied. 'Every four or five years, an election is rerun and people are asked, "Do you still agree with the choice you made a while ago?" Even Theresa May reran the election in 2017, because she wanted more MPs. Every few years, people are asked if they want to change their minds.'

'Yeah, but a referendum is very different.'

'How so?'

'In a referendum, people vote on an issue, not a government.'

'Every election is fought on issues. Every election is

like a referendum on a manifesto of different issues.'

'But if a government ignores a vote of such significance, don't you think it's like saying to everyone, "Hey, we don't really care what you think"?'

Elias's smartphone beeped, and he immediately looked down at his device. It was an encrypted incoming email from his mother, written in Norwegian.

Elias, I know you rang me yesterday, but I missed the call. Did everything work out in the end? Remember, you must stop these online campaigns and you must stop helping other conscripts defect for a while. We know somebody from Russia is trying to track you down. So you must stay away from Oxford until the end of the summer. If you can, you should tell the UK police and make them aware. Hide somewhere. Please respond encrypted.

As he typed the reply, Elias recalled all too vividly the political activism that had got him into trouble with authorities in Russia. Only very narrowly had he escaped his draft and his internment in a re-education camp.

Mum, who was it that tipped you off? Was it the council clerk that tipped us off before? Yes, I am leaving Oxford until the end of the summer, and I am going to work on a fruit farm in a place called Malvern Hills. It was advertised by another Oxford student, actually. Take care!

Elias sent the message encrypted while the Texan tourists were still engrossed in their Brexit talk. He calmly slipped the phone back into his pocket, but the very next second, he jolted from his seat as though a grenade had been pitched at him: A nearby man in his sixties had banged the table with his palm and now rose with a clenched fist. Striding forward towards the Texan tourists, he waved his index finger like a headmaster and then lectured them. 'Listen, you two! You can't just come to a foreign country and put your oar into our politics for all to hear. I wouldn't turn up in America and judge Donald Trump on the Amtrak. And I'm absolutely fed up, reading and hearing about this topic day in, day out. So do us all a favour, gentlemen, and be a little more courteous to the host. Got it?'

Somewhat flabbergasted and a little miffed, the young tourists silently glanced at each other as they were reduced to small nods. Then the man in his sixties pressed them again. 'Have you understood what I just said?'

In a seating cluster nearby, a girl in her mid-twenties suddenly rose and started to approach with long strides and a soft smile. She was a confident-looking blonde woman who had somehow retained her looks of innocence and youthful vulnerability. A pale girl, her wide aquamarine eyes radiated an aura that instantly caused heads to turn towards her. They emitted a bravery and a sense of compassion that seemed to shine from her heart and complemented her intelligence. Her hair hung down to her shoulders, and she was dressed in a plain short-sleeved T-shirt with blue jeans. For footwear, she wore bohemian suede ankle boots. Elias recognised her. During term time, this postgraduate worked as a librarian for St Anne's College.

'Excuse me, sir,' she said to the senior passenger. 'You were saying it's unkind to intrude on the politics of the host country, so may I ask how kind it is to raise one's voice to tourists to curtail their freedom of speech? And all the while, bellow a frightening roar into the carriage?'

Her elevated, crisp English accent contrasted with her youthful, hippy-like appearance and seemed to cause a second of confusion for the elderly man. He winced a little, then stared down the grinning girl in an irate silence.

'You stupid, naive millennials,' he eventually sighed. 'You just continue the way you are; you'll see what's coming your way.' He pointed at the girl's forehead with his raised index finger and presented her with a frown of disapproval on his angry, flinty face. The young woman pulled off an innocently mischievous smile at the senior, and without further ado, he retrieved his suitcase from the luggage rack and swiftly headed for the carriage door. At the junction between the two cars, he briefly stopped and looked back at the girl and the tourists. He beamed over one last stare of disapproval with his eyebrows raised, shaking his head in consternation, then wandered into the next carriage.

'Thank you, miss,' said the bearded man, stretching out his hand to her. The young woman shook it and gave the two tourists an infectious smile.

'That sure was unexpected,' commented the shyer-looking one. 'Thank you for sticking up for two strangers.'

'No worries. It was nothing, really. I hope this little experience hasn't spoiled your holiday.' She was speaking in the same friendly, open-hearted manner she always showed in the library.

'It certainly hasn't, after your intervention,' replied the sturdy one. 'Are you from around here?'

'I used to live here as a child. Where are you guys travelling to?'

'Porthchapel Beach,' replied the tourists in concert.

'We're changing trains in Worcester,' added the bearded man.

'Ah, Cornwall. You should definitely take a walk to Pedn Vounder Beach,' said the librarian. 'It's a little nudist beach just ten minutes from where you're heading. You might enjoy it in this heat.'

The sturdy, bearded man seemed flabbergasted and swiftly stole a glance at his travel companion before he started to blush. He looked back at the young librarian, who was showing her mischievously innocent smile again, giving the two men a thumbs-up. 'Well, anyway, I hope you enjoy your time in Cornwall,' she said.

The shorter man returned the gesture and stretched out his hand to her. 'My name is Stewart, by the way. It was nice to meet you.'

'Lana. Nice to meet you too. Enjoy your trip.' She was about to head back to her own seat when she glanced over at Elias and gave him a quick but very affectionate smile with a gleam in her eyes. Then she turned around and started to stroll back.

'Wait!' she heard the pale boy call from behind. He immediately rose from his seat and walked a little closer to her. 'Wait,' he said again. 'I am Elias Alexandersen. Are you Lana Watson, the one who advertised the farm job? I wanted to meet you at the station, but I was late. Almost missed the train.' He spoke perfect English that was virtually indistinguishable from that spoken by locals, save maybe for a tiny trace of a Scandinavian or Eastern European accent.

Lana blessed the young man with another heartfelt

smile and confirmed his intuition. He was right—she had actually recognised him, Elias being a frequent visitor to her library, but had no idea this handsome man was the one that had come to join her on the farm. She checked her phone again and now noticed two missed calls from him in the last hour.

Hastily, Elias retrieved his backpack from the rack and seated himself in her cluster. The train was still crawling forward at snail's speed, but it gave Lana some time to get acquainted with the newest harvest worker on her uncle's farm. She recalled they had seen each other on plenty of occasions at the Oxford Union, the university's debating society, and had probably spoken more than a dozen times in the library, although they had never introduced themselves in two years. Elias reminded her of the one occasion he had been late returning two science books and had worried about the fine he would incur, only to have Lana blink it off with a smile and let him go. Lana chuckled to herself at the recollection of that incident.

'So, it's neuroscience you're studying, right?' she asked.

'That's correct. What about you?'

'I did physics and philosophy for my bachelor's. Literary philosophy was my favourite, so I am doing my postgraduate in English literature.'

'Physics, philosophy, and English. Those are very diverse fields. Do you want to go into publishing or creative writing one day?'

Lana nodded. 'Preferably in magical realism. Once I get an idea for a novel, I'll start drafting. What about you? Are you planning to go into research after you're finished?'

Elias shook his head. 'You need a DPhil for that, but unfortunately, they've only offered me *self-funded* doctorates so far. Do you know how much they cost?' Elias explained all about his current studies into finding ways of reverting specialised cells into progenitor types or stem cells. That way, dedifferentiated cells could be used to repair broken tissue, just like stem cells, but without the controversy of killing unborn embryos.

'That sounds like a DPhil in its own right,' Lana remarked. 'It's a shame you can't continue your research, because I imagine those therapies could potentially cure a lot of diseases… So, do you think you'll be leaving Oxford sometime next year? Or are you thinking of going back to Russia?'

At the mention of Russia, Elias shook his head at once, almost as though he'd run away from that country. 'I'll see how things go,' he said. 'I might find another job at the university and end up staying in Oxford. It is such a nice city. But I take it you prefer the countryside, if you choose to work for your uncle every summer?'

'I don't really see it as *working* for him, to be honest. It's more like a summer pastime, to clear the mind. The farm is practically my home over the summer months.'

'You have a lot of harvest experience, then?'

'You could say that, yes. I'm the most seasoned harvest worker on the farm—along with one other guy, who you'll meet later. His name's Henry. I've known him since primary school.'

'Henry…' Elias muttered to himself pensively.

The train suddenly shook with a violent jolt, and for a few moments, Elias seemed deeply engrossed in thought, glancing out the window towards the hills before he solemnly moved his gaze back to Lana.

'He's one of the most hard-working harvesters, actually,' Lana said.

'Henry… that sounds like a very posh name,' Elias remarked. 'What's he like?'

It was a comment that made Lana smile. Having known Henry since the age of five, pretty much growing up with him and seeing him on good as well as bad days, Lana knew nobody could ever call him posh. But maybe for someone who'd never met Henry before, his name could invoke an upper-class connotation. 'He's a nice guy… funny. He works very hard. We like him a lot on the farm.' She wavered for a few seconds. *But* do *try to avoid him when he's drunk. He's a really friendly person, but after a few drinks, he turns into a different man*, Lana was about to say, but thought better of it. No, that wouldn't really be right. Elias and Henry had never met before, so it was only fair to let Elias form his own impression of her old schoolmate.

Just then, another train announcement suddenly sounded, interrupting the two postgraduates. 'The next station is Great Malvern. Please remember to take all your personal belongings with you. This is the Western Railway service to Aberystwyth. Great Malvern is our next stop.'

'That's us,' said Lana. 'Get your luggage. It's a tiny stop. We only have, like, thirty seconds to get off.' She retrieved her backpack from the luggage rack and helped Elias with his heavy, bulky rucksack from which his books stuck through the zip. She led the way to the exit. At that point, the train came to a complete halt, and the doors opened up.

It was one of the first times Elias had travelled to the English countryside, and he took an inquisitive look around at the platform. Great Malvern was a rural station that boasted the elegance of ragstone erected in refined Gothic architecture. It gave off such a different vibe from the urban train stations of Nikel or St Petersburg. When he and Lana then stepped out of the air-conditioned train, Elias was immediately struck by the full brunt of the August heat while the sun shone from the sky unimpeded. Lana led the way through the little town of Great Malvern until the pair were finally standing at the foot of the famous green hills. They seemed quite steep, and now they had to be traversed, for the fruit farm lay on the other side. On the slope to the beacon, Lana showed Elias a stone well from the early nineteenth century, where the two filled their bottles with cool spring water and then continued the climb.

On a day as hot as this, Elias wondered why Lana didn't just order a taxi or ask her uncle for a lift. He couldn't ask why, for Lana was his new boss now, and a question like that would make him sound all too lazy. But slowly, heat lethargy started to kick in, and sweat was dripping down his face, Elias being a child of the Arctic. He watched Lana wandering on so gracefully and already admired her: the further they hiked into nature, the more at ease she appeared to feel, leaning backwards with this relaxed meditative gaze while she inhaled the fresh air of the soaring pastures. She lowered herself onto the grass for a moment and even removed her heavy boots. Lana tied them to her backpack and continued the journey shoeless, treading on lush grass, rocks and pebbles.

While the two postgraduates slowly approached the orchard, the industrious harvest workers were in the final hours of their shift. This was Windmill Farm, an apple-and-hop field that occupied over a square mile and had been family-run for the last two and a half centuries. Temporary harvest workers lodged in a hopper hut, an old stone cottage built in the nineteenth century that once housed seasonal harvesters from London. These days, it mainly accommodated migrant workers from Eastern Europe, who slept on bunk beds lined up against the walls of an open rectangular room. The house also included two private chambers. One was always reserved for Lana, who even tended to keep her summer clothes and an array of accessories locked inside throughout the year.

The other private room was occupied by the second most seasoned harvester of the team, Henry Chapman. He had finished his shift a little earlier than the rest and was already on his first bottle of wine. For it was a Friday afternoon, and this young man was already pregaming for the pub visit in the evening. Together with Lana, he was unofficially considered a senior, or a foreman, on the farm. A blonde-haired young man, he was dressed in a lush-looking white shirt and smart black trousers. And even in the comfort of his own room, he preferred to be clad in smart-looking dark leather shoes. He'd put on John Williams's iconic *Superman* theme on repeat and was dancing away to it, pretending to fly. His right arm was lifted into the air, his fist outstretched towards the window, and with his eyes closed, he imagined flying across the Atlantic. He was on a mission to save the world.

In fact, so loud was the music, and so engrossed was he in his heroic reverie, that he did not even realise repeated knocks were being made on his door by someone trying to catch his attention. In his weightless, light-headed euphoria, Henry hummed along to the music and slowly spun his flying body around until he noticed a brunette girl was standing in the doorway and straining to bite her lip at this scene, smirking in apparent amusement. It was Sylvia, a seasonal worker from Kraków, who was in her second year of service. Swiftly, Henry retracted his arms as he felt the blood gushing up to his reddening cheeks. His whole head felt desperately hot, and he knew his face had to be the colour of a ripe Royal Gala now. He immediately turned off the music.

'Er, I'm just rehearsing for a gig—for the Hop Festival, you know… just rehearsing the steps and stuff,' Henry uttered clumsily.

Sylvia was still biting down on her lip when she let her hand drop from her mouth. 'Ah, yes, I can see that. I fully understand,' she said in her Polish accent. Then she appeared to crack at this rare sight and eventually gave vent to her giggles.

'You should really have knocked,' Henry griped.

'I am sorry. I knocked and you didn't answer.'

'Well, you should've knocked harder, then.'

'I shouted your name, but you didn't hear.'

'So, what do you need, then?'

'Rows eleven, twelve and thirteen are finished. We need the ladder from your room, the big ladder for the… how do you call them again, the type of tree?'

'I know the ones you mean. The Gravenstein trees. That's all right. Make sure you use the ladder in pairs, okay? One person climbs up, and the other one holds the ladder. Do you understand?'

'Of course.'

'Okay. Once you're done with those, please let me know, and I think we can call it a day, all right?'

'Yes, sure,' Sylvia replied with a playful giggle that reminded Henry of someone else.

Taking a deep breath, he asked, 'By the way, have you seen Lana around? She was supposed to get in today.' He immediately sensed his heart beating more heavily at the mention of Lana.

'No,' Sylvia replied. 'Why she didn't come at the beginning this week, like the others?'

'She had stuff to do at uni,'

From the front entrance of the hopper hut came a couple of workers from Sylvia's team, offering to help her carry the ladder. As soon as they stepped out of the little cottage, Henry slumped back into his upholstered desk chair and took another gulp of his delicious French wine, burping loudly.

This year was his eighth summer on the fruit farm, and even though he'd been offered a job at a rare exhibition event in Worcester, paying a far higher rate, he had chosen to come back to this place. The previous year, he and Lana had enjoyed some special moments together—or so *he* liked to think, and Henry was hoping they could take their relationship to the next level this time. And as far as he knew, Lana was still single. It would all have been different, of course, had he been awarded a place at university or had he finally landed a decent-paying permanent job. But his A-level grades had failed the entry requirements, and since then, he'd been drifting from one temporary role to the next. Whether it was due to his difficulty concentrating, his constant reveries and daydreaming, or his procrastinating attitude towards anything academic, so far, he'd never landed a single permanent post. Henry still remembered the first two job applications he'd made. Both of them had gone to classmates who were children of Polish immigrants, while one of them had even managed to secure a place at university a year later.

Elias and Lana had traversed the hills and were coming down on the western slope, ambling past dexter and shorthorn cattle on both sides. Lana kept glancing at her recruit from the Arctic Circle and noticed how he was grappling with extreme exhaustion as he dragged himself along beside her, sweat dripping down his face. She started to regret making him travel on foot, but Lana had wanted to show Elias this part of the country, which meant so much to her. Right now, they were strolling across a private spinach field at the foot of the hills, and the refreshing smell of nature and remote countryside triggered childhood memories, which ran in front of Lana like a movie of the past. Underneath her feet, she felt the soft texture of fertile soil, which curved up and down in little grooves and revealed the occasional pea gravel. To her, it was like meditation in motion, grounding herself in Mother Nature and the earth—being one with the environment. It was what she had always enjoyed the most.

'Are you all right?' she asked Elias, putting her hand on his shoulder.

'How much further is it?'

'Shouldn't be more than fifteen minutes or so now—
we are almost there. Just try to enjoy the countryside.'

Elias looked around himself to try and fathom what it was
that lent this whole place its somewhat mystical vibe.
There were miles of hilly grassland, imbued with a sense
of bucolic freedom. Everything here was completely off-
the-beaten path. With Lana lending a helping hand to
him, the pair climbed over a wooden fence and stepped
onto Dawson Road, a narrow but long and curvy country
lane lined with private properties and small livestock
farms. Elias had never seen anything quite like this in
Russia. The buildings around here all appeared as if they
hadn't been renovated in over half a century, but it was
exactly this derelict nature that filled the lane with a rustic
charm, as though the area harked back to a past era. To
the left of the pair was a small dairy farm, which must have
been in use since the late nineteenth century. Inside it
stood a wooden barn for its horses, which roamed freely
on the property, frolicking and grazing. To the right of
the pair was a small churchyard with a dozen graves
clustered around a spired stone sanctuary. It must have
been erected no later than the 1850s, as the Victorian
architecture contributed to its mystical but very
welcoming atmosphere. Towards the southern horizon,
Elias could make out another spired building—a little
brittle but radiating a somewhat frozen-in-time aura. It
was an abandoned chapel, Lana said, one whose
demolishment the council had kept postponing until they
passively kept it 'out of fear of losing a landmark'. The
thought of an abandoned chapel intrigued Elias's

imagination, and he already felt drawn to it. He definitely had to visit that place before he left at the end of the harvest. This whole route was like a journey to another epoch.

They entered an earthy riding path curving away from the private lane and hemmed in by a little woodland on each side. As it forked out, Lana led Elias through a small grove of aspen trees until they were approaching an iron gate at the centre of a white metal fence. Elias wiped his face with a soft tissue, gazing at the vintage door bell, just as a few surprised rabbits bolted past the couple to seek shelter inside shrubs and underground burrows. Just then, Lana suddenly looked up with wide-open eyes and immediately speeded up a little.

'What's wrong?' Elias asked.

'Do you see that animal in the fence over there?' Lana replied, pointing at a jerking rabbit that seemed to be entangled in the mesh fence in front of them. It looked as though it was writhing about in pain near the far end of the metal barrier. Elias nodded, and Lana tugged him by the arm. 'Poor little thing! Can you help me free it?' Immediately, she began to head for the creature.

'Are you sure it won't panic when humans come near it?' Elias asked.

'Somebody has to keep it calm. Can you just stroke it while I try to untangle it, please?'

'Okay.' Elias nodded somewhat passively as he followed his new boss towards the traumatised rabbit. The closer they came, the more it jerked about, as if in fright. It made Elias a tad shaky himself, as though the plight of this animal was repelling him like a similarly charged magnet. For even a scared rabbit, tame as it may seem, had teeth and bit in self-defence.

'Here. Just stroke it gently,' Lana said, and then she gave the rabbit a few pats on the back. She sounded ever so placid, as if nothing untoward could happen.

Cautiously, Elias reached out for the animal while Lana stretched her right hand into the mess of wire and began to unravel it.

'Hold on. We're almost there,' she said, twisting the sharp metal, which started to slice into her own skin. A single drop of blood fell from her hand. Then the cuts grew larger.

It was such a harrowing scene to watch—the girl was trying to free the animal so desperately that her injured hand became tightly trapped in the mesh alongside the rabbit's foot. Lana wrenched her arm, but now her bleeding hand was completely entangled in a sharp mess. The more she twisted, the more blood it drew, and the bigger the cuts grew. She did not say a single word, not flinching even once, but Elias became aware of the acute discomfort on her grimacing yet stoical face while her own struggle with the unforgiving metal dragged on. It was such a heart-rending sight to watch, and he instinctively reached out to lend her a helping hand.

'Careful. The wire is sharp; you might hurt yourself,' Lana calmly warned him, and she gently shoved away his hand. 'Keep stroking the animal. We'll get there eventually.'

Elias longed to help, but he held back, knowing his assistance would be refused again.

Twisting and flexing her trapped hand, Lana eventually managed to gain a little more space between her palm and the metal. She quickly gripped the fence and pulled it away from the rabbit, which must have felt the wire loosening, and prepared to make an escape. Elias noticed Lana's hand was about to get entangled once more, so he hastily reached for the coil by the rabbit, yanking it sideways with a twist. Instinctively, the rabbit retracted its foot from the space in the coil and hopped out. When it was finally free, it no longer seemed to be in a hurry to outrun the two humans. Under the soothing strokes of Elias, the little mammal lingered a few more seconds before its natural instincts kicked in. It briefly looked into the eyes of its two rescuers, almost as if to say thank you, then it scuttled back to its extended family in the spinach field.

'Thanks for that,' said Lana, her hands still bloody from the metal wire.

'Are you all right? You're bleeding.'

'Ah, that happens all the time when you live in the countryside. Thank you for your help.' She nonchalantly wiped her hand with a little tissue as though nothing could bother her. With her injured hand, she opened the old gate and pointed inside. 'Right, this is it. This is Windmill Farm.' And what a gigantic orchard this was. The place was certainly hard to get to and even harder to find, towered over by the Malvern Hills, and tucked away in the middle of nowhere. Lana gave Elias a tour. The front part of the farm contained the large apple orchards, where Lana showed him the Worcester Pearmains, Braeburns, Fujis, Early Harvests, Gravensteins and Royal Galas that her uncle grew on the field; most of those varieties were not ready for harvest yet. A quarter tonne of Cox apples was also produced, which the family sold to a cider brewery in the Cotswolds. There also stood a wooden shed, from which a single accountant did the paperwork for the enterprise and paid the wages to seasonal harvest workers.

At the southern end of the premises stood a two-storey barn, around which a few chickens were pecking for food. Close to this building was a deserted oast house from the late nineteenth century, which had once been used to process tonnes of hops. Lana's uncle Samuel and his wife had lived there for decades before they had relocated to the more luxurious windmill, leaving the place seemingly time-frozen as a reminder of centuries of harvest history.

To the rear of the property, there was a hop field of over eighty hectares. It resembled a small organised forest, even though those Humulus shoots didn't look quite ready for harvest yet. The crown jewel of the land stood right in the centre: the old windmill, which had once produced flour in the nineteenth century and now housed Lana's uncle Samuel and his wife. A solid hardwood base held the weatherboarded structure, which was crowned with four sails. From the ground, an exterior staircase zigzagged up to some mysterious storage chamber—even Lana had never caught a glimpse of the interior.

'Why's that?' asked Elias.

'I don't know. They've always kept that room locked for some reason, even from the inside.'

The two did, however, catch a glimpse of Barcelona, who darted off into the windmill through a cat flap. Barcelona was the family cat and had been thus named after a trip to Catalonia. She would access the windmill through a mini-chamber equipped with two cat flaps on either side, giving her free access to the windmill and the outdoors. When the couple were out, whichever harvest worker was on cat-feeding duty would open this back entrance and cater to her natural needs.

The pair were cheerfully greeted at the entrance of the windmill, where Samuel gave Elias a firm handshake. He seemed so happy to see Lana, but Lana herself appeared even more delighted when she introduced Elias to her uncle with a bright, enthusiastic smile, pointing towards him with her flat palm. It was the first time Lana had introduced him to someone else, but she was clearly proud to be seen around with him, Elias noticed. In fact, the more he reflected on it, the more he became aware of it: the girl was almost beaming with a love-at-first-sight look. She constantly glanced at him with a yearning, twinkling expression, as though she saw in him something extraordinary, even though Elias thought of himself as the shyest, most uptight boy, with nothing like the courage this girl had shown twice since they'd met today.

For a second, Lana clasped Elias's hand, then she led him inside the windmill. There were no rooms on the ground floor, as the space was filled with supporting structure for the building, but there was a narrow passage to the spiral staircase, which wound itself up in five loops inside the tower, leading into the living room upstairs. Just like the surroundings, everything inside looked very old, Elias quickly noticed. All the furniture had an antique appearance to it, adorned with carvings or decorated with lush metal engravings. Some of these depicted winged messengers, while others showed leaf patterns, but all of them harked back to the late nineteenth or early twentieth century. There was even a scent of the forest that permanently lingered in the air, which, along with dozens of glimmering scented candles, endowed the mill with a somewhat therapeutic, remedial quality. The two postgraduates stepped into Samuel's narrow study, Lana carefully treading over an exposed screw-top protruding from the floorboards.

'I see you're still walking around barefoot in summer,' Samuel said to his niece.

'For as long as the weather allows me to.'

'I still remember the first time you went without shoes for a whole month. One morning, your sandal fell apart, but you just never bothered to get a new pair until the end of the holiday.'

'That must have been, like, six or seven years ago now.'

'Maybe, and then you stepped on a bee, and everyone thought you'd finally be more careful. We offered you a spare pair, but you just put a plaster on your foot and continued as you were. You're still the free spirit you've always been. You haven't changed.'

Each of them had to sign a one-sided employment contract and hand in a photocopy of their passport, for relative or not, official procedures still had to be followed.

Elias took a sneak peek at Lana's passport copy as it came out of the photocopier. It read:

Surname: WATSON
Given names: NAOMI LANA
Nationality: BRITISH CITIZEN
Date of birth: 01 JUL 96
Place of birth: GREAT MALVERN

So, Lana was actually her middle name then.

Samuel placed the piece of paper underneath Elias's

copy, which, for some reason, he decided to read aloud, as though he'd never seen a Refugee Travel Document before. "'Alexandersen, Elias... Seventh of June 1996... Rayakoski, Russia... With right of abode and the right to work.'" He nodded to himself, intrigued. He was about to place both papers into a black binder when something seemed to catch his attention, and he stopped in his tracks.

'Seventh of June 1996,' Samuel uttered again, examining the passport copy of another harvest worker. 'This person here has exactly the same birthday as you.' He turned to his niece. 'Did you know Elias and Henry were born on the same day but thousands of miles apart?'

Lana shook her head as Elias intuitively stepped a little closer to Samuel to steal an inquisitive glance at Henry's passport. But as soon as he laid eyes on the piece of paper, a gust of rural air suddenly blew into the windmill and brought the whole file of paper copies to a flutter. Immediately, all the candles were extinguished, smoke rising from their wicks towards the ceiling. There was something strange about it, because it didn't look like the effect of the gust; the wind had stopped now, but the papers continued to flutter on for a few more seconds. It almost looked as though an invisible force were browsing through the thin folder while the papers seemingly flapped around of their own accord. Even Samuel seemed taken aback as he firmly placed his hands on the binder and then locked eyes with his niece. Elias had never seen anything like this before. It almost felt like an omen of some sort. He turned his head to Lana, but she casually shrugged her shoulders, as if to say, 'Well, sometimes strange things just happen.'

Her uncle filed those last copies into the binder,

which he locked away into a rosewood cabinet, continuing to shake his head at this rare occurrence.

Before long, it had gone past five in the afternoon, and Lana was leading Elias into the old stone cottage, the hopper hut that was going to be their home for the next couple of months. Elias was still dwelling on the strange gust of wind when they stepped inside, then his attention drifted elsewhere: a small patch of ryegrass upon soil was lying on the creaky floorboards by the entrance, while a little spider crawled past the pair and appeared to be dragging along a tiny leaf. Light goosebumps came all over Elias, making his skin feel as though it were crawling at this sight. Never had he stayed on a farm before, and he'd probably expected a little more cleanliness from a communal cottage, maybe even a bit more tidiness as well. But it was only going to be for seven weeks, he reminded himself. And it allowed him the chance to experience some authentic English countryside. Besides, it gave him the opportunity to be acquainted with a somewhat eccentric but enigmatically enchanting girl, though he still felt nervous around her; she was, after all, his boss. Most important of all, he was safe here until the end of the summer, safe from the Russians who were trying to track him down in Oxford. If he kept a low profile and got on with everyone, they were never going to find him here, on this farm tucked away in this rural area at the foot of these hills.

Elias still found the extradition threat a little strange, for Russian officials wouldn't normally come to England to kidnap people… unless it was all done under the radar or the kidnapper themself had a vested interest in him. Anyway, he was going to take a short nap now and recuperate from the journey.

Meanwhile, Lana was knocking on a private bedroom inside the cottage as she leaned her ear to the door and repeatedly called, 'Henry!' There were some very faint sounds coming through the door, as though the occupant was listening to loud music on their earphones but did not hear her. 'Henry!' Lana called out again. Eventually, she gave up. 'I'm going for a cross-country run on the soft soil,' she said to Elias.

Soon it was evening, and the cottage was bustling with the commotion of harvest workers returning from the local store. Some of them were cooking their dinner in the kitchenette, grilling chicken and trout on an old fireplace as the food crackled over the little fire. To an evocative smell of fresh country air, Elias awoke from his long nap and looked about himself, removing his foam earplugs. These were the people with whom he would spend his first rural English summer.

There was Nora, a pale, dark-haired girl from Valencia, in a long red top that hung down to her thighs and completely concealed her shorts. She was engrossed in her smartphone and would giggle to herself at incoming text messages. There was Gregorios, a young man from Greece, with blonde hair and a five o'clock shadow. He was dressed in a white vest and polyester shorts, and he had a humble, going-with-the-flow facial expression. There was Sylvia, from Kraków, a returnee from the previous year. She actually looked the most industrious of them all. And there was Ian, a very capable, sturdy young man with a kind facial expression and blonde hair.

Judging by his accent, he was probably a local worker. Maybe he lived nearby and was only visiting the hopper hut in the evening. Then there was Charlie, a man in his late fifties with a nasal Glaswegian accent. Elias was told this man was a distant relative of Samuel's and he lived in a caravan nearby. Elias tried not to judge, but from the way Charlie slurred his words and behaved, he thought he might be a drug addict. And then there was Lana, of course, the light and soul of the party, with a near-perpetual smile. Elias felt so privileged to be her special pick. But there was at least one other person he would meet that day.

'Did you have a nice nap?' Lana asked, bringing him a glass of tap water. They were both sitting in the communal living area, chilling on the old cabriole sofa.

'I am sorry I slept for so long.'

'No, *I* am sorry I made you walk all that distance today,' Lana replied.

Some people were chatting about a pub visit after dinner, and Lana suddenly remarked, 'Actually, this reminds me—I'd better get my passport, in case we go out later. I'm just gonna be five minutes. Just going to the windmill.' She gave Elias another pat on the shoulder and was about to head out.

At precisely this moment, Henry looked out the door from his private bedroom, having finally woken up from his own prolonged snooze. He was holding on to his second bottle of wine as a light dizziness was hanging over him, and he moved slowly. Henry beamed his gaze across the cottage, and there she stood: good old Lana, whom he hadn't seen in a year. Delighted, he raised his hand and was about to shout out to her. Then he intuitively held back and retracted his hand. Lana had obviously never made an effort to greet him and, in fact, did not even see him. Instead, now she was affectionately patting the shoulder of a worker he'd never seen before. Who was this man that Lana looked at with such an expression of tenderness?

'Just going to the windmill!' she said. Then she made a dash out the door.

'Lana,' Henry muttered dejectedly, dropping his gaze down at his leather shoes. He took a few steps into the communal area, where he placed himself like a fly on the wall, clutching his bottle of wine and watching as the newcomer introduced himself to Gregorios. His name was Elias, he heard. There was also a slight alien twang to his accent. This man was clearly another foreigner, and now this foreigner was telling Gregorios all about his time at Oxford, his job as an administrative assistant and how he'd met Lana at uni. This foreigner had gained a place and found a job at an elite English university, while Henry was running from one temporary role to the next.

Elias was whining about the 'hot English summer' and the state of 'this grimy cottage', and now the cheeky newcomer was even slagging off all the messy people in Britain. Or at least, that was what it sounded like. A churning sensation crept into Henry's stomach. This outsider showed complete disrespect for the host country that had accepted him, awarded him a place at one of its most prestigious universities—probably even at the expense of a native—and still he was complaining. This entitled foreigner embodied so much that Henry most detested.

Sorry, mate—you can't just wander into my country and expect everything to be done to your standards. It's just downright rude. If you don't like my country, then just clear off! Henry imagined saying to this foreigner. He suddenly remembered how much he'd already drunk that day and instinctively lowered the wine bottle to the timber floor. He was, after all, a farm senior and still had to force himself to act professionally, especially around new staff.

'Ah, Henry, come and meet Elias,' Gregorios shouted out to him. 'This is Elias, from Russia. He's Lana's friend.' Henry took a few steps towards the pair as Gregorios turned to Elias, asking, 'Have you two met before?'

When Elias turned his head around, it was the first time he had ever laid eyes on Henry. He was dressed very smartly, especially for a summer evening, almost as though he worked in some kind of corporate office. At first sight, he also appeared very confident, almost a touch overbearing. But he also gave off an expression of discontent on his flinty face. In fact, it was more than just a facial expression; it was almost like an energy that he carried with him while he glared at Elias with his stern, angry eyes.

'No. It's my first time here; we've never met before,' Elias replied to Gregorios. He gingerly stretched out his hand to this disgruntled-looking farm senior before a static charge jumped from Henry's body, and then, for the first time, Elias shook hands with Lana's old schoolmate.

'Nice to finally meet you, Henry,' Elias said. 'I've heard some good things about you.' The stranger opposite him still looked a little tense, with narrowing eyes on a pinched countenance, and Elias intuitively attempted to pull off a friendly smile, politely maintaining eye contact with his new supervisor.

'So, how are you finding it so far?' Henry eventually asked. 'Did you have a good trip over here?'

'It couldn't have been better. Lana showed me all around the area. She's absolutely fantastic.'

Elias noticed this flinching, pinched facial expression again as Henry jerked back and questioned. 'I see. Have you worked with her before, then?'

'No. It's my first time on this farm, actually. We have different jobs at St Anne's College.'

'So what brought you to *this* part of the country, then? We never get Oxford University students working on a hop farm. It's quite random, actually.'

Elias hesitated, for this was a question that had to be thought through carefully. 'I guess I just needed to get out of the city for a while… and get some fresh air for a change.' The man opposite him did not seem convinced, as a short but ominous silence lingered between the two. Suddenly Elias was overcome with a strange sensation, as though he'd met this very man before. It might have been a long time ago, but it almost felt as though he were speaking to a brother from another lifetime. It was a feeling Elias had never experienced around anybody else. 'Have we ever met before?' he cautiously asked. 'Have you been to Oxford lately, or maybe…?'

Tensing up in a sudden frown, the farm senior replied dejectedly. 'You're obviously a very smart kid, but not everybody is lucky enough to go to university, mate.'

'I wouldn't really say I am smart, to be honest. Maybe I was just lucky. I was in the right place at the right time.' Elias attempted to smile.

'I think you might be right,' Henry replied. 'Maybe you *were* just lucky, being in the right place at the right time, so remember that.'

Elias could not tell whether it was merely his perception of things, but he had an awkward hunch that this imposing man harboured strong reservations about him. The two had never met before—they had obviously come from completely different walks of life, but there was something in Elias that seemed to really incense Henry. Or was it just the alcohol that embittered this man? Elias wondered when a whiff of wine fell from Henry's mouth. Maybe on a normal day, he was a very easy-going chap, for why else would Lana consider him such a good friend?

Just at that moment, Lana ambled back into the old cottage, clutching her passport and driving licence. For a few seconds, her gaze vacillated between Elias and Henry, as though she sensed something she was unable to articulate, then her face relaxed into a warm, heartfelt smile the moment she locked eyes with her old school friend. Even Henry appeared to drop all that tension from his facial muscles. He and Lana shared an emotional embrace by the entrance. Then Henry led the way to his own room.

It felt so special to spend a few private moments with Lana, and Henry was ready to pour out his heart after one long and difficult year. 'I brought you something this time,' he said, opening his mini-fridge to produce an ornamented box of chocolate truffles. Lana's head jerked back a little, then she stretched her hands out to his present. Hopefully, she would like it. She turned over the box as her gaze wandered a little lower down until she spotted the price tag Henry had left on the packaging. For a moment, her eyes bulged, and her jaw loosened just a little.

'Henry, you really needn't have bought this for me.'

'But I wanted to. You're one of the only people I can speak to properly.'

The two exchanged all the recent gossip and town news, and Lana talked about progress on her postgraduate thesis. Henry told her all about the temping jobs he'd had in the last ten months, how somehow none of them had turned out to be permanent roles and how he was trying so hard to find a more secure job. He told Lana about his father, who had been diagnosed with bone marrow cancer a few months before and was not expected to live beyond Christmas. He spoke of how it was a constant worry on his mind, putting pressure on him to find a more permanent role to please his dad, for he could not allow his father to pass thinking he'd brought a failure into the world. Lana was really such a wonderful listener.

'If there is anything at all I can do for you or your family, let me know straight away,' she said. And then she granted him a few seconds of respectful silence. It was a quiet that was soon disrupted by chatter from the communal area as distinct voices filtered through to his bedroom.

'So, who's this other guy you brought to the farm?' Henry eventually asked. 'What's his name again?'

'You mean Elias?'

'Elias. That's the one. Are you friends with him?'

'We have spoken quite a few times at uni. He's a nice guy.'

'So what's he doing on your uncle's farm, then? He said he had a job in Oxford.' Henry noticed he sounded a tad harsher now that they'd moved on to another subject.

'Well, he works as an admit assistant at St Anne's College. But they always run on reduced staffing during the summer holidays. What's wrong with spending a few weeks in the countryside?'

'I don't know. I just didn't expect anyone to turn up from your uni. Why didn't he just apply for something part-time in Oxford? Don't you think it's a little random for an Oxford postgraduate from Russia to work on a farm for the summer?'

Lana appeared to think this one through, but the very next second, the pair were interrupted by roaring and bellowing from the communal area outside, which sounded as though civil war had broken out. Henry hastily opened the door to poke out his head. Bob, the general manager, had entered the cottage and was pulling on Charlie's collar, dragging him out of the hut.

'How many times do we have to warn you?' he thundered. 'You're a bad influence. You will stay out of this hut, and—'

'I wanted to meet the new people,' Charlie slurred, nearly tripping on a loose apple.

'You can say hi to people on the field. Now, go back to your caravan. You're a bad influence.'

'I just wanted to make some friends,' he protested on the way out.

It really was the same game with him year in, year out. Living in his self-contained caravan nearby, he'd occasionally take drugs and always find himself banned from the hopper hut. Henry himself had long stopped getting involved in the rows, even as a farm senior.

The rest of the evening passed quickly. Elias got to know the remaining fruit-pickers and enjoyed his dinner of roast lamb with mashed potatoes and peas. At half past eight, the harvest workers ventured out to the thatched country pub to enjoy some fresh pints of cider and cool beer. Elias knew a pub visit in the UK could go on late into the evening, but not this time, for Henry suffered from a rare kind of epilepsy, which could be triggered by flashes of bright light. And as soon as Gregorios snapped a picture on his film camera, the poor lad had a seizure and ended up being carried home on Lana's shoulders, accompanied by Elias. While the other harvest workers continued to revel in the country pub, Henry would rest for the remainder of the night.

Back on the farm, Lana and Elias were all by themselves now. And part of Elias felt nervous, being alone with his new boss, for he felt all too tipsy and had to pay too much attention to what he was saying.

'Right, Henry will be okay, I think. Shall we go back to the pub and join the others again?' he asked.

With somewhat puffed-out cheeks, Lana shook her head winsomely and reached out for his hand. 'Let's take a walk around the orchard,' she said. Even Lana sounded a tad tipsy.

Before long, it must have gone half past ten, and the two were still strolling around the orchards, Lana sometimes grabbing Elias's hand. Even though the sun had descended for the day, the heat of the brighter hours still lingered in the air, and Lana seemed unable to get enough of grounding herself on the soft soil of her uncle's farm. By now, stars were brightly shining in the sky, glowing celestial bodies that illuminated the apple orchard and the vast hop field below.

Elias was not a heavy drinker at all, and he could feel all too clearly the effects of the pub beer in his veins while he basked in a state of mild blissfulness. Ambling in the clean rural air of the Malvern Hills, he recalled his childhood memories of the mysterious Northern Lights as the Milky Way lit up the orchard like a spate of fulgent lanterns. The pair had done more than two laps around the farm when they reached a little spot right in front of the hop field, where Lana suddenly stopped and gently squeezed Elias's hand. She was acting a little like she'd known him for months already, a trait Elias found adorable, and eventually, he caught himself dropping his guard. Lana might be his boss, but she was a young twenty-three year old like himself, Elias reminded himself.

'Let's sit down for a bit, Elias,' Lana said softly, lowering herself onto the grass. She crossed her outstretched legs and pointed towards the western slope of the hills, underneath the Milky Way. Out here, it seemed a lot brighter than in urban Oxford. And apart from the occasional owl screech, a therapeutic silence lay over the place.

'How many stars do you think there are?' Elias asked.

'Over seventy billion trillion, including all the neutron stars and black holes.'

'You know the number by heart?'

'I did tell you I studied physics for my bachelor's.

There are more than two trillion galaxies, each containing millions to billions of stars.'

The two reclined further onto the field until they lay flat on their backs, viewing the peaceful night sky from the ground. Elias felt Lana's hand gently place itself on his. It caused a sudden weightless sensation in his stomach that spread outwards and brought his pulse to race. He turned his head towards her, and she blessed him with a dazzling smile, her friendly eyes twinkling.

'They say that when we look at the stars at the edge of the universe, we see the light that was emitted over forty billion years ago,' Lana said softly. Her calm voice had a strangely soothing quality for Elias. He was reverently regarding the distant Milky Way when a bright shooting star zapped across the sky, but the moment he settled his gaze on the flying spark, it evaporated somewhere between the mesosphere and the stratosphere. Elias shifted his eyes towards the hills, and his attention was caught by a particularly bright spot that sat halfway towards the horizon. It was much more luminous than the stars around it, and yet it did not twinkle like the other ones.

'What do you think is up with that star?' he asked. 'If you focus on it, it's a lot brighter, but it doesn't have that glint.'

'That is not a star; that's a planet. Planets don't twinkle. Only stars do. That one there is Venus. It doesn't twinkle, because it reflects the light of our sun and is a lot closer to us.'

'How do you know all this about planets and stars? Did you specialise in astrophysics?'

Lana shook her head. 'My favourite was quantum mechanics, actually. But Mum and I used to gaze at the stars all the time. Sometimes we used to climb to the summit of the hills around midnight just to view the night sky. Mum used to tease me that I turned out so full of mischief because I was born under the zodiac sign Cancer.'

'And you believe in those superstitions?'

'No, not really, to be honest. It wouldn't be very fair to us if the stars dictated our personalities. It would detract from everyone's uniqueness.'

'I've never bought into astrology myself,' Elias admitted.

'Take you and Henry, for example. You were born one thousand five hundred miles apart, but you are both Geminis. You are twins, born on the same day, under the same stars. And yet you've turned out to be very different people.'

'I had a really strange feeling today, as though somehow I've known him before,' Elias said. 'But I also got the feeling he really doesn't like me at all.'

'Yeah, please don't mind him too much, okay? He often sounds a tad bitter after he's had a few drinks.'

'I don't know what it was. I'm kind of worried he and I are gonna fall out really badly at some point.'

'No, don't worry, Elias. Henry gets like that after a few drinks. By the end of the summer, you two will be best friends, I am sure.' Lana paused and muttered to herself. 'He *has* actually turned out a little like his mother, now that I think about it.'

'What do you mean?'

'Some of those views he holds definitely came from his mother. People can be born under the same star sign, the same constellation, but the lottery of life will still mould them into completely different characters.'

As the pair continued to rest on the soft grass, Elias became aware of the peaceful summer sound of crickets, which chirped away among the trees. A rabbit suddenly emerged from the tall grass and stared at the peaceful couple, its eyes illuminated by the night sky. Then the hoot of a tawny owl grabbed the attention of its flinching ears. The rabbit twitched its face and swiftly scuttled back towards its burrow, jumping over Lana's legs. It must have been so liberating to be shoeless the whole time, Elias thought, and yet he did not follow suit.

With his gaze still fixed on the Milky Way, it was only another few minutes before a second shooting star flashed across his view. This one flew along the hills in a northerly direction—Elias knew this because the North Star was one of the few celestial bodies he was able to locate among all the constellations. It pointed towards his birthplace, and Elias's mind harked back to his childhood memories of the Northern Lights and his early wonder at the laws of physics.

'To me, light was a real miracle when I was growing up,' he told Lana.

'But light *is* a miracle. Even within the laws of physics, light is still a miracle.'

'When I was a child, I used to believe in things like miracles, but not any more. There is so much chaos and brutality everywhere—the word *miracle* has just lost its meaning on me.'

'Traditional laws of physics don't allow celestial bodies to emit any light,' said Lana. 'Without any magic in the stars, there wouldn't be any light out there or any life down here. You *were* right as a child, Elias. Light *is* a miracle. The technical term for it is quantum tunnelling, by the way.'

'Quantum tunnelling? What's that?' Elias was an academic himself but had to admit that his knowledge outside the life sciences was probably fairly limited, and the term *quantum tunnelling* gave off the connotation that it lay at the very edge of what humans could comprehend.

'All the light that reaches us from the stars consists of little energy particles, which are released when nuclear fusion occurs,' Lana said. 'The sun is a huge mass of hydrogen atoms, which pull each other together because of their gravity. Every time two hydrogen atoms fuse into helium, they lose a little energy, and we see this energy as light.'

'I know that, of course.'

'Hold on a sec. The problem is, as you know, protons are positively charged and should normally repel each other, not fuse together.'

'I thought the gravity between the atoms pulls them close enough for nuclear fusion.'

'Even with all the gravity in the sun,' Lana continued, 'there simply isn't enough energy to push protons past this repulsive barrier. It's like running against a brick wall and hoping the universe will blink at exactly the right moment so you pass through to the other side.'

'Is that what happens between the protons, then?'

'People used to think there was a fixed reality for everything. But in the 1920s, they found that reality is actually more like a probability wave; it's like nothing has a fixed location until it's observed. In everyday life, it hardly matters, because the probability wave is so tiny. But when it comes to things that are very tiny themselves, it's like the proton has no fixed location. And when it runs against a barrier, there's a tiny probability that, at the right moment, the universe *blinks*, and the proton miraculously appears beyond the repulsive boundary. The chances of that happening are like winning the lottery six times in a row, so virtually zero. But because of the mathematical law of truly large numbers, and the gigantic mass of atoms in the sun, it occurs every single second. It's like the universe is saying, "I know protons don't have enough energy to cross the barrier, but screw it, let there be light." And so there is light.'

'Does this mean the universe is constantly blinking in order to allow the impossible to occur?'

'Kind of, yeah. My mum used to compare the probability wave of atoms with everyday reality. Atoms have to be observed to be defined. She used to say the reality we collectively observe is like a probability wave that responds to our thoughts. And every time we think a thought or indulge in a feeling, it's like sending a signal to the universe and pushing reality, ever so slightly, in one direction or another.'

Elias wasn't sure he understood everything Lana was saying about light and miracles, especially in this tipsy state, but he remembered the odd occasion when he had felt as though his laptop had slowed down whenever anger or frustration had boiled up in him. He now wondered whether this was what she might be referring to. 'Did your mum tell you how we can use all this to our advantage?' he asked.

'Mum always said to think positive thoughts—it could be gratitude, it could be love or it could just be enjoying the moment: it's like sending a signal to the universe and pushing the fabric of our collective reality in a slightly better direction. Most of the time, our thoughts can only push the fabric of reality very little. We can't make two protons fuse into helium. But Mum said if someone hopes or prays with all their willpower—as in completely selflessly and indefatigably, the universe might blink and allow a spontaneous miracle to occur. A bit like allowing a paralysed human to move for a second, or something like that.' Lana turned her head in Elias's direction and beamed another playful smile.

'To be honest, I'm not sure I follow everything you said about quantum tunnelling and consciousness,' Elias admitted. It all had such a romantic smack to it, and even though he was delightfully indulging in Lana's talk of light and miracles, his inner sceptic struggled to piece together the science behind transmitting consciousness.

Lana turned her head back towards the stars. 'Growing up, I always thought there was nothing more wondrous than the stars that light up the cosmos, but when it comes to influencing reality, humans are far more powerful than the largest star. Stars will just burn out one day. They have no choice; it's their destiny. But *we* have consciousness and free will. We can decide our actions and how to shape the fabric of reality around us. We're more powerful than the brightest star in the cosmos. Stephen Hawking may have said, "We are just an advanced breed of monkeys on a minor planet of a very average star." He didn't tell us these monkeys have souls that are more powerful than the star they orbit. The stars light up the sky, but our souls light up the way to a more perfect reality.'

This made Elias recall the afternoon when he'd set off to chase after the aurora borealis with Sophia and then found something more wondrous than physical light.

It must have been past midnight when the tired pair finally sauntered back to the hopper hut to rest for the night. This rural area at the foot of the Malvern Hills was the perfect hiding spot from the Russians, but Elias had a vague sense that these few weeks on Windmill Farm might turn out to be more than just a game of hide-and-seek, that somehow it would be a pivotal time in his adult life. There was the surreal familiarity he felt around Henry, even though he had come across so very awkward that evening. Then there was enigmatic Lana, the first girl who was evidently attracted to him and did not even try to hide it. This whole place was so different from anything he'd ever been used to up in the Arctic Circle.

The Hop Festival

The month of August turned out to be some of the most therapeutic time in Elias's life. The manual labour in the orchard, blended with the fresh rural air of the hill region, lulled him into a near-meditative relaxation he had not felt since childhood. He had been on apple-picking duty as well as hop-processing, though he preferred the work with the apples, as it gave him more chances to move about the open fields. After three weeks in this place, there were days when Elias almost forgot that he'd come here to go into hiding for the rest of the summer, and that some Russians might still be looking for him back in Oxfordshire.

The more time he spent with Lana, the less nervous he felt, but the closer they bonded, the guiltier Elias felt for using her uncle's farm as a hiding place. Lana told him all about her joyous childhood, growing up in Worcestershire, and how her ancestors had lived around here for centuries. Elias told Lana all the stories from his own adolescence in Rayakoski and Nikel, though he would never bring up the incident with the Internal Troops. Every weekend, Lana would invite him for a morning run on her uncle's orchard, which she would always round off with a short meditation exercise.

The only person Elias subconsciously avoided on the farm was Henry. They hadn't fallen out yet, but neither had they become best friends, as Lana had predicted. It wasn't that Henry was particularly confrontational with him, but he would always nitpick over minute details surrounding Elias's work. Whether it was tiny bruises on apples he'd picked or a single fruit that had landed in the wrong basket, Henry would never shy away from putting him in his place, always with glowering, narrowed eyes. Elias had stopped asking Henry anything at all and would simply defer to Lana as his main supervisor. But for some reason, this seemed to incense Henry even more.

Today was Friday, 23 August 2019, and the day of the long-anticipated Hop Festival. Most farms were inclined to hold their harvest festivities towards the end of the season, but tradition and custom meant that Windmill Farm always celebrated well before the conclusion. It was a festival well known in the local community, and it gave old acquaintances a chance to commune or welcome newcomers to this part of the shire.

Dawn was breaking over the Malvern Hills, and a red twilight gleamed over the pastures of the farm as golden sunbeams shone over the summits. A rooster crowed from the distant barn, while little sparrows awoke, twittering in the treetops—soothing morning sounds that filtered through to the hopper hut. Lana was dressed in blue running shorts, a white top that loosely covered her chest, and a little anklet. Sipping a glass of tap water, she was ready to go for another daybreak run with Elias. He was dressed in brown shorts, a sleeveless blue tartan shirt and synthetic trainers.

The unpolluted morning air greeted the pair as they ventured onto the soft grass and stepped through the cool summer mist that rose from the moist field. But today it wasn't just the ground that was emitting this morning brume, Lana noticed, looking across to the crepuscular rays over the hills. The top of the spine she could see, but halfway to the summit sat a nebulous mist that shrouded the hills like a low cloud and very slowly flowed in a westerly direction. It extended over the entire farm and veiled the oast house like a dense fog.

'Ready to go?' Lana asked.

Elias nodded with an exhausted yawn, as though he were still half-asleep. Then the two dashed off for a run around the hop field, jumping over rabbit burrows and loose hop bines while a red sun gradually appeared from behind to warm the soil. The pair had already run over a mile when Elias started to lag behind, as though his energy was depleted, and he gestured for Lana to slow down. He was a slower runner than Henry, with whom Lana hadn't jogged at all this summer, but he was also less competitive. Lana came to a halt and put her hand on Elias's back.

'Everything all right?'

Elias nodded, gasping for the fresh air.

Lana projected her view towards the deserted oast house and noticed how, even now, it was shrouded in the nebulous mist, as though it had been swallowed by soaring mountain clouds. Pointing at this remote building, she gave Elias another pat on the back. 'Come on, one more run this morning. Make it a race.' She nudged him.

Elias gave her a somewhat tepid thumbs-up, and Lana darted off like a flash. A very brief race it was, and in under sixty seconds, they'd reached the foggy patch in giggles and high-fived. An exhausted Elias dropped to the ground and took off his shoes.

There was a peaceful silence around here, which complemented the humid breeze that swept from the hills. It was the very peace that drew Lana back to Windmill Farm year after year. She stretched out her legs and crossed them in a Siddhasana meditation pose, feeling her heartbeat slowly steadying after a power run. Those few minutes of mindfulness were her weekend routine, but Elias never seemed to fully relax, Lana had been quick to notice, always flinching at little sounds with those tense muscles on his handsome face. In fact, the two had been resting for over five minutes when Elias suddenly looked all around himself as though someone had fired a Taser at him. Swiftly, he snapped his eyes to Lana's.

She had heard it as well, the noise that had frightened him. It had come from inside the oast house, and it had sounded as though someone had dropped a chair on the floor. There was definitely somebody inside the building, even though the place was supposed to be deserted.

'What was that?' Elias whispered, his eyes bulging at Lana.

Lana slowly rose to her feet and lent a helping hand to him. 'I don't know. But I don't think we're alone.'

'Should we go and call Sam?'

'Wait. Not yet. It might just have been an animal or something. Let's go and take a closer look. Come on.'

The dense fog near the soil was sweeping in a fresh breeze as the pair ambled around to the timber door. Lana pressed down on the metal handle, but it was firmly locked, just as she'd expected it to be. She gave the arched door a feel with the back of her hand and then moved her view towards the Gothic windows above. She tugged Elias by the sleeve, and the pair wandered off to check them out, stepping over hop bines that must have been blown over by gusts of wind. Elias and Lana stretched out their arms and gave all the windows a gentle push, but none of them would open.

Suddenly there was this tapping sound again, emanating from within. It could have come from a trapped animal, or there could be someone inside.

Elias became aware of a slight wobbling sensation in his legs, and he looked at Lana for reassurance. She did not seem to share his anxiety at all. Instead, it was as if curiosity propelled her on as she motioned him to go around and check the back. Here a small wooden shed was attached to the oast house, and Lana immediately attempted to crack open the old door. Naturally, her attempts came to no avail, but when she pushed on the old windows, one of them gave way, almost as though someone had tampered with it.

'Shall we go inside and take a look?' she smiled.

Was she being serious? *I'd rather call Sam!* Elias wanted to reply, but then he settled for 'Yeah. Why not? Let's take a look,' seeing how fearless Lana was by his side.

The pair clambered inside the oast house, and looked around the building where Lana had stayed with her uncle during her teens, except now, it was a deserted, ramshackle place with worthless old objects cluttered around broken furniture on a dusty wooden floor. After looking inside the rickety bathroom and disused kitchen, Elias was led into Lana's old bedroom, where the two concluded there couldn't have been anyone around. This building did not feel as though anybody was hiding in it, and nor did they hear another beat of that odd thumping noise. It was strange, because just a few minutes ago, they had clearly heard something coming from this place.

The longer the pair stood around, the more Elias noticed Lana's face dropping into a soft, puffy melancholy as she traced every corner and object with her gaze. Maybe it was wistful nostalgia, or maybe it was the sorrow of seeing this place so neglected over the years. There stood a disused Denver record player from the 1960s, some empty baroque-style picture frames and even a golden grandfather clock that had broken into three pieces, scattered on the dusty floor. By the Gothic window rested a Georgian coffee table with a large open jar on it.

Looking out towards the sunbeams that emerged from the hills, Elias noted how the mist was starting to thin out and even appeared to flow a little faster. The luminous sunrays shone into the oast house and brought a little glint inside the open jar. Elias glanced down and sighted a selection of antique coins whose metal reflected those morning beams. Lana's uncle must have collected them on his travels and just deposited them in this derelict place. There lay US dollar coins from the 1970s, old Deutschmarks from before the unification, Spanish pesetas, and even British shillings from the 1960s. Then there was a coin that stood out from all the others. It looked a lot older, maybe even a few centuries in age, and it was much larger, as though it used to be a medallion that had lost its chain sometime through the years.

Elias could have sworn he'd seen this very object before, perhaps many years ago, though the exact recollection of it eluded him. It drew him like a powerful magnet of the past. Curious, he took a closer look at this rusty metal disc. The object was slightly larger than two inches in diameter, and it depicted a black man in a loincloth, kneeling in chains and facing to the right. Over him were embossed the words AM I NOT A MAN AND A BROTHER?

Elias knew deep down that his path had crossed that of the medallion before, though he could not remember where or when. When he gave the old medal a smooth stroke with the palm of his right hand, it oddly felt as though he'd just been reunited with an object he'd first seen a very long time ago but had never been able to physically touch—until now. It felt a little eerie, but also very empowering.

'What is this one here? This is not a coin, is it?' Elias asked.

Lana shifted her view towards the object and instantly dropped her jaw as she beamed with a glowing smile. She stroked and tenderly cupped the medallion in her palms. 'Oh my God! I thought I had lost this, like, seven years ago!' she exclaimed. 'Mum gave it to me shortly before she passed away, but I thought I'd lost it when we moved out of the oast house.'

'Maybe because it looked like a coin, your uncle kept it with his money collection.'

'We still have the chain somewhere, but I thought the medallion was gone for good,' Lana said, wiping the grimy dust from the bottom of the medal. 'This was so valuable to Mum, and I was so sure I'd lost it.'

'How did your mum get this, if you don't mind me asking? It looks super old.'

'My great-grandmother had it first,' Lana replied. 'She'd lost both of her parents, but someone around here had founded an orphanage and took in children from the workhouses and—'

'What's a workhouse?'

'It was a place where poor people were sent in Victorian Britain—mostly orphaned children. Anyway, there was this lady. She'd come back from America, but when her husband left her, she wasn't able to get a divorce. There's a legend that because she wanted more children, she founded the orphanage and took in all those poor kids. When she grew old, there was nobody to look after her, except one of the orphans she'd taken in. That was my great-grandmother in her early twenties. So just before the lady died, she decided to give this medal to her rather than her own child.'

To this story, Elias listened in awe. 'What does this mean? "Am I not a man and a brother?"'

'It was part of the abolition movement in Britain—as in the abolition of slavery. The woman who founded the orphanage took the necklace from England to America and back again.'

'Interesting… What was her name?'

'Rachel Jones.' Lana smiled. 'Why? Do you think you might have heard of—?'

She had not even completed her sentence when the strange knocking sound came once again, and this time, it seemed to emanate from the disused kiln upstairs.

For a second, Lana looked up with a kind of fright she'd not shown before, her mouth almost falling open. She quickly reached into her empty pockets. 'Do you have your phone on you?' she whispered to Elias.

'No,' he whispered back, shaking his head. 'Let's get out of here. Quickly!'

'Hang on a sec. If anybody wanted to attack us, they would have done it by now.' Lana gently tugged on Elias's shirt and gingerly led him towards the arched oak door that led to the stairwell. She leaned her ear against the door and whispered, 'I'd be surprised if anyone was up there. It's just one narrow cone and a tiny storage space.' Lana knocked a few times on the antique wood and listened out as the sounds reverberated into the hollow space upstairs. 'Is anybody up there?' she asked.

There came no reply, and Lana cracked open the arched door with an eerie creak, motioning Elias to follow her into the dark, dusty stairwell of the kiln. She slid the abolitionist medallion in the pocket of her shorts and started to walk up the grimy spiral. Elias followed close by and intuitively went on tiptoes, something that seemed to draw a little giggle from Lana. She obviously still didn't believe there was any real danger.

At the top of the stairs, there was one more door to be opened. Lana gave it a single knock, pushed down on the copper handle, and inside this disused furnace lay a coffee can and a human leg, which was swiftly disappearing behind a shabby Victorian sofa, dragging the dust along with it.

'Charlie?' Lana shouted at the man. 'What are you doing here?'

On all fours, the man crawled out from behind the couch and turned towards the staring pair, his tightening face marked with doubt while he seemingly gazed into the distance.

'Charlie, it's just Elias and me,' Lana reassured him. 'What are you doing in the oast house? Why aren't you in your caravan?'

'Because they're looking for me there,' he slurred.

'Who? Who is looking for you there?' Lana asked the tormented man.

'Frederick and Gavin.'

'Who are Frederick and Gavin?' Elias asked.

Together with Lana and her distant relative, he sat down on the ragged, old sofa as Charlie told them all about his debt problems and how two drug dealers were after him for the money he owed. Last time, they'd managed to break into his caravan, so this time he'd gone into hiding inside the oast house. The shed window was easily opened, so he'd spent the last two nights sleeping on the old sofa inside the kiln.

'How much do you owe these people?' Lana asked.

'One hundred and fifty quid.'

'Listen, I can lend you the money straight away, so you don't have to hide around here,' Lana said without hesitation. 'And then you can just pay me back in instalments. How does that sound?'

At this, Charlie's face of doubt eased into a faint smile, and he accepted her offer with alacrity.

'Just be mindful not to use the money on any drugs, okay?' Lana warned him.

'I promise I'll pay you back. I promise you will get the money before the end of the year.'

At that, Lana vented a single snicker before she led the men out of the oast house, carefully closing the tall window behind them. From the grass outside, Elias glanced up at the window on the kiln that still stood slightly ajar. He concluded it must have been Charlie's thumping the coffee can on the timber floor that had caused the noise. And yet, he was doubtful. The top of the kiln was so high up; the noise below had been so clear. How could this sound have travelled so unimpeded? Whatever it was they'd heard, it had brought Elias to an object that had triggered a very powerful episode of déjà vu.

By now, the sun had risen a little further, but for some reason, the morning mist hadn't been dispelled, even though the sky above it was clear. It might be one of those rare times when the entire day was gripped by a summer advection fog, making the farm look as though it stood on a mountain summit. Other harvest workers were already out and about, because the preparations for the Hop Festival required all to pull their weight from early in the morning.

Elias and Lana accompanied Charlie to his caravan, but when he attempted to open the door, the lock on the outside was stuck, almost as if somebody might have attempted to break in already, then messed up the lock and given up. The windows were still intact, though, so at least they hadn't tried to burgle the place by force, probably seeing how close the caravan was to other amenities on the farm.

'I think they've been here already,' Charlie said.

'Henry might know how to fix this,' Lana suggested. 'He's a very handy kind of guy.' After shouting over to some other harvest workers, she asked Sylvia to give Henry a quick call, wake him up if he was still asleep and tell him to make himself useful on the caravan door.

When the rooster crowed again, it was nearly time to open this year's Hop Festival and make a success of it. Gradually, myriad fruit stalls were set up around the field, dedicated to promoting the farm's early harvest, maturing Royal Galas and apple juice. Lana seemed so appreciative of her uncle's work, and Elias was determined to pull his weight and show Lana she'd picked the right candidate, despite his ulterior motive for being here.

Lana showed him all the booths that proudly displayed this year's hops in rows of wicker baskets, while festivalgoers would be able to obtain a free sample or try some of the beer. All stands were staffed by men and women wearing wreaths of hops or white daisies, and Lana laid one of the garlands on Elias's head too, smiling at him winsomely. In addition, a range of games had been prepared around the premises, ranging from trampolines to swingboats, and from face painting to water-walking bubbles. In the late afternoon, local musicians would give performances by the apple orchard, and Lana would be one of the singers. Apparently, last year, the farm had grappled with workers running between stalls like headless chickens. So this time, they would try out a mapping app; all employees would register their phones for the next eight hours and trace one another's whereabouts, requesting help with the click of a button.

It was only eleven o'clock now, but the farm was already teeming with festivalgoers from the hilly region. Most of them had arrived by car, some on bicycle; five or so had ridden on horseback and tethered the horses around the water trough.

Elias and Henry had been assigned the task of putting the finishing touches on the beer tent, which was the first time they'd worked together on a project. Being a farm senior, Henry had also been charged with the role of security and thus walked around with a fluorescent vest, which seemed to really boost his confidence. He walked around with wider strides, tilting his chin up a little and jutting out his chest. He was one of very few staff who weren't wearing a wreath, and he even appeared to let out a smirk from time to time at the garland on Elias that had drawn such a playful smile from Lana. The tent became very warm now, or at least that was what it felt like in those humid conditions. But Elias was feeling another kind of awkward heat, one that came from the inside and was accompanied by a light tingling in his arms. He attributed it to light anxiety, for ever since Henry had seen him in his running shoes next to Lana that morning, he had been wearing a sullen yet tense look on his face. There was an awkward silence that dragged on throughout the assembly works.

What could Lana possibly like about this bumbling, incompetent foreigner? Henry kept musing. When he watched Elias working alongside him, all he could do was shake his head at this man who wielded his hands as though they were foreign objects. Elias was supposed to be a research associate at Oxford University, but the way he went about manual labour—it was such a clumsy, inexperienced way of working. So inefficient! Dropping things on the ground awkwardly, faffing about between simple work tools, as if he couldn't tell one from another. He gave the impression that he'd never held a manual job in his life. He was probably pampered as a child or raised with a silver spoon and never had to help out with any chores. Elias was certainly an extremely inept, ungainly worker in this field. Just then, one of the upright poles was about to loosen itself and fall upon the clumsy man.

'Watch out, mate!' Henry shouted, and he quickly shoved Elias out of harm's way. That had been a close one.

He quickly readjusted the metal rod and secured it with an additional rope.

'Thanks for that,' Elias sighed.

Henry gave the man a thumbs-up and helped himself to another glass of water. As if by common accord, the two took a short break from their work.

'Actually, Can I ask you a quick question?' Henry asked.

'Sure. Go ahead.'

'Excuse my curiosity, but what did you do before, I mean job-wise?'

'Well, I work as an admin assistant at St Anne's College during term time—in Oxford.'

'And in Russia? What did you do in Russia?'

'In Russia… I never had a job in Russia, to be honest. I've only ever worked in the UK,' Elias replied.

'Hmm… I take it you're here on a student visa, then?'

Elias shook his head and wavered, as though he didn't completely trust Henry. 'I am a refugee, actually,' he eventually admitted. 'I've lived in Britain for three years now.'

'Them Russians are looking for you?'

Elias nodded hesitantly.

'You did something bad in Russia and then came hiding here?'

Elias shook his head.

'You did nothing bad?'

'I did bad only in *their* eyes. I broke the law, but the law is unjust.'

'Well, apparently, it's getting harder and harder to claim asylum here,' Henry commented. 'Everyone is leaving their own country. Everyone is heading for places like Britain and America. For some reason, nobody wants to stay in their own country these days.' He became aware of a mild breeze that swept in from the summer fog and brought momentary relief from the heat. Closing the top button of his shirt again, he inhaled the fresh air.

'How do you define *my country* and *your country* anyw——?' Elias blurted out, but he'd not even finished the last word when he suddenly stopped himself and looked away, as though he regretted broaching this subject.

'Well, my country is where I was born, of course,' replied Henry. 'Britain is my country. You were born in Russia. Russia is your country. Why are you asking me this?'

'I'm sorry I brought this topic up. I don't really like talking about politics,' Elias muttered pathetically.

'Well, go on, then, mate.' Henry nudged him. 'You brought it up. I finally get to hear about this subject from someone on the other side, and now you're cutting it short. Go on, then. How do you define *your country* and *my country*?'

Silence filled the tent.

'No comment at all?'

Elias let out a long sigh. 'Property is such a difficult thing to define morally,' he eventually said. 'Most people would agree that if you've truly worked for something, you can claim it. If you've grafted day and night to earn money for a house, it's yours. But nationality at birth is not something anyone's ever worked for. It's a lottery. It's sheer luck. You've won the lottery of birth, Henry; I'll give you that. But it was luck nonetheless. Neither your own labour nor your own achievement.'

Henry let those arguments sink in for a few moments,

wiping some more sweat from his cheeks, and then protested. 'Yeah, but I was born here, mate. You weren't.'

'I do get you. But being born into a wealthy country is *not* something anyone's ever worked for before their birth. It is not an achievement born of your own efforts.'

It was a feeble comment that made Henry frown, and he found himself swallowing behind a clenched jaw. 'I'm starting to find your remarks a little offensive, to be honest. I may not have done anything myself, but my ancestors have fought for this country and built this place; yours haven't. Or have they?'

'I am sorry. I really don't like talking about politics and—'

'Well, you started it, mate. Now I want to hear what you think. My ancestors have fought for this place. Yours haven't.'

At this, Elias took a deep breath and gently dropped his screwdriver into the plastic toolbox before he replied. 'Suppose you found out your ancestors had been involved in the ransacking of a particular place. Would you take responsibility and dedicate your life to rebuilding it? Would you take responsibility for something other people had done and you had no control over?'

'Like in North Korea? That's what North Korea does. When someone commits treason over there, three generations are punished. Even if none of them had any involvement in it.'

'So, if you found out your ancestors had left you a legacy of guilt, you would assert your individuality and the idea that people can't be held accountable for things outside their control. But if you found out your ancestors had left you a land of milk and honey, you'd lay claim to it? In other words, winning the initial lottery of birth gives you the right to exclude all others in sharing your fortune, even if you have never worked for that fortune yourself? What did you do before you were born that I didn't? I mean, fair enough—'

'Hold on there,' Henry interrupted him. 'Are you saying countries should open up their borders to anyone and everyone? Are you saying anyone who wants to come to Britain can come here? Are you actually mad? Do you know how much chaos that would cause? *That* would cause ransacking, mate! That would cause looting and overpopulation. That would cause mass unemployment.'

'I didn't quite say that.'

'Yes, you did, mate. You did!'

'I did not. Of course, no country can open up its borders to everyone at once—'

'But that is what you just said! Let in everyone; abolish all borders.'

'No, Henry. I was more… coming from a philosophical, long-term perspective, and—'

At this point, Henry's phone beeped, and he quickly reached for the device. He set it on speaker, and it was Ian who asked, 'Henry, can you hear me?'

'Yes. What's up?'

'Someone has spotted two men behaving disruptively in the apple orchard. Can you go and have a look?'

'Whereabouts in the apple orchard?'

'In the north-east, near the entrance. I will send you a signal on the tracing map.'

'What are they doing?'

'Just swearing and shouting at people. They're probably drunk. Can you go and take a look?'

'On my way.' Immediately he slid his phone back in his pocket and took his leave of Elias. 'You heard the message; I've got to go. Think there might be trouble around the corner.'

He stepped out of the beer tent and headed straight towards the apple orchard. If he was seen confronting troublemakers and keeping people safe on the farm, it would boost his standing in the community. His fluorescent vest made him stand out from the crowd and bestowed upon him an importance he'd rarely felt before. He was special, respected and looked up to. He was a supervisor, a prefect and a farm elder, and he would make use of this status today. Striking up conversations with people felt so much easier if you were that much more important.

Suddenly Henry caught a glimpse of a classmate he had not seen in five years. It was Emily, the first girl he'd ever dated, back in his GCSE years. She'd moved on to study acting in London and was now married to Abigail, a fellow actress, originally from Alabama. From the accent of the girl Emily was with, Henry knew she had to be her wife.

'Hermia, in *A Midsummer Night's Dream,* was my favourite to play,' Emily said, 'except for these grand jetes I had to perform halfway through. You have to leap from the ground, and while you're in the air, you're preparing to do the splits. When you've reached the highest point, your legs have to fully stretched…'

As Henry listened in, he stepped a little closer to the pair and readied himself to welcome them as the farm senior. 'Ho ho ho!' he said, all smiles. 'People all over the place are talking about ballet these days. I am getting full-on scared now, methinks.'

For a couple of seconds, Abigail beamed an angry stare at this stranger, then she drew her eyebrows together. 'Well, go and stand somewhere else, then!' she shouted. 'It's not like we're forcing you to stand around here, is it? Emily, do you know this man?'

'We went to school together…'

'Well, what's the point in standing here, telling us you're scared of us, if all you have to do is move a little. Nobody forced you to stand here, did they? What a weirdo. Come on, Emily. Let's go.'

Henry's ex-girlfriend seemed as though she was about to greet him, but her irritated wife was faster and swiftly nudged her on.

'But, girls, I'm this year's security guard!' shot through Henry's mind, then he realised he had spoken his thoughts out loud when Abigail replied.

'How did they make you security if you are even scared of ballet? Just go and annoy someone else. Look there! There's a man with a rucksack. He might be hiding drugs. Check his bag. Keep us safe. Come on!'

It felt as though they'd ripped his confidence from his heart and plunged it into an abyss. This fluorescent vest wasn't a miracle generator after all. *Very funny, girls!*

Emily turned around and gave him a friendly, melancholy wave. Henry waved back and then remembered the reason he was out here in the first place. He still had to find those disorderly men somewhere. He wandered further into the apple orchard and eventually caught a glimpse of Jill, his second girlfriend, from Year 11. Ever so placid and easy-going, she was clad in a navy-blue dress and black flats, strolling over the grass with her head tipped slightly back. Alongside her sauntered Catherine, her third cousin, whom he'd not seen since Year 6, when she had changed schools.

'How did it go this time?' asked Jill.

'It was a success,' replied her cousin. 'The lump was quite big, actually. But they got it removed in the end…'

Listening in attentively, Henry reminded himself to join in appreciatively this time, going with the flow of the conversation, not cutting them off. 'Hello, hello!' he started as he approached the pair. 'Long time no see. That's so funny. Hilarious! The big bump… or was it lump?!'

Catherine looked at Henry, slightly confused, and enquired, 'What is so funny? What could possibly be funny?'

'She got the lump removed. I like that.'

The cousins regarded each other with flinching eyes and half-open mouths. Then Catherine turned to Henry. 'Excuse me. What could possibly be funny about someone getting a tumour removed? My aunt survived two weeks of intensive care. What could possibly be funny about that?'

'Er… sorry. It's just, the way you were speaking about it. I just thought that sounded funny. I'm sorry.'

'Well, maybe you should listen a bit more carefully before you barge into other people's conversations,' said Catherine. She appeared to be nudging Jill forward and glanced back at Henry with indifference.

Henry attempted to laugh light-heartedly, pretending it was just a funny misunderstanding. 'Yeah, I guess I'll catch you guys later, then!'

'Yeah, *catch* us later!' replied Catherine. 'Come and *catch* us if you can!'

Today was clearly getting better and better as the day dragged on. By now, the sun had moved away from its highest point, but the heat of the humid air still weighed Henry down when he resumed his search for the disorderly men. He was still dwelling on Elias's offensive remarks when sweat covered his face and even dripped down onto his trainers. It just seemed such a long way to walk, especially inside these strange hill clouds. No sooner had he reached the Royal Gala lanes than he let himself drop to the soil and take a few moments' respite under the shade of a tree. Maybe he could close his eyes, too, and doze off just for a few seconds. Nobody would notice, after all. He quickly switched off his phone. Brushing a small spider from his shirt, he crossed his legs in the shade and was about to lower his eyelids. Then his attention was grabbed by language that even *he* abhorred as utterly vile when two men suddenly passed him by down the central aisle of the orchard.

'Fuck these hippies. We'll find the fucker eventually,' one of them muttered to himself, spitting on the grass.

These must be the two disorderly men. They both had their backs to Henry as they strolled towards the entrance, about fifteen metres from him, and yet there was something familiar about them. Henry had seen them before somewhere—it had only been a few months ago. He couldn't remember who they were, though he knew they meant trouble.

He leapt to his feet and followed them towards the front gate, heat lethargy weighing down on him like a mountain. One of them was short with a balding head; the other was tall and sturdy, but both of them wore heavy leather jackets despite the heat. The pair just left through the metal fence and mounted their ape-hanger motorbikes, revving their engines as they drove off. Henry could not pursue them beyond the premises, but he was told to spend the remainder of the day showing a presence on the farm and watching out for potential trouble.

A few hours later came the next distress call, and finally he was presented with the opportunity to shine as a hero. A young girl had climbed up to the mezzanine of the old barn where she remained stuck between wooden pillars when a built-in ladder had collapsed, leaving her trapped several metres off the ground. And all that because she'd been chasing after her helium balloon. This would finally be *his* opportunity to prove himself and *shine*.

Luckily, the weather had cooled down a little, but Henry still arrived panting for air. The area around the barn had been converted into a small playground for children, with swings and plastic slides, but this girl had managed to scale right up to the top of the building. Up on the mezzanine, a small group of people had just ascended before him: Elias, Lana, Emily and Abigail could be heard up there, trying to reassure the girl they would help her down. Everywhere lingered the smell of fresh hay.

Quickly, the hero of the hour climbed up the bamboo ladder——it seemed a little frail, as though it were not meant to be mounted at all. He arrived on the entresol with his fluorescent security vest and gave everyone a buoyant wave, but for some reason, the others present only glanced at him for a single second before they turned their heads straight back to the girl.

'So, where are your parents, then?' Lana asked her.

'In the beer tent,' the little one replied timidly.

'Can you guys lift me up, and I'll hold on to the girl?' Lana asked. She kept maintaining eye contact with the young child.

'Guys, *I'm* here now,' Henry protested. 'I'll handle it from here. I'll bring her down.'

'You sure?' Lana asked.

'Course!' Henry nodded. 'This is my job.'

The girls and Elias regarded each other quietly, then nodded tentatively. They seemed anything but convinced.

'Are you guys worried about my weight?' Henry blurted out.

Once again, a few seconds of silence filled the mezzanine. 'Right. Go on, then. Climb up,' Abigail replied.

On a set of shaking, unsteady arms, Henry balanced himself and cautiously lifted his torso towards the girl. She actually appeared a little frightened now that Henry was reaching for her, and she instinctively leaned away from him. For a second, Henry glanced down at the people holding him below, and suddenly his mind was thrown back to the scene in Year 3, when the ladder had gone missing from the old tree house. Immediately he felt his own balance tilting away from the arms underneath him, and the next second, he came tumbling down, rolling on the mezzanine.

'Are you all right, Henry?' Lana asked.

He nodded, feeling his cheeks going red, but he was otherwise unhurt.

'Right. I think maybe someone lighter should go next time, like Abigail,' Emily proposed, helping Henry to his feet.

'It's fine, guys. I'm fine,' Henry protested. 'Honestly,

don't worry about me. I almost managed it.'

The team looked at one another somewhat hesitantly before the hero of the day stepped back up on their arms. Cautiously, he edged forward and leaned towards the tall pillar. This time, he would take extra care and make sure not to disturb the balance below.

'Are you all right there?' Lana asked him.

'Yeah. This time, I'll be fine! Don't worry!'

He glanced down at his old schoolmate for just a few seconds but instantly found himself distracted once more. Lustful and randy as he was, the temptation of looking at a woman's glistening chest was too much for this young man to resist. He snapped himself out of it, but the moment he moved his gaze upwards, there was another distraction on Lana's neck that gripped his attention, and the very next second, Henry came tumbling down once again. He rolled away towards the edge and abruptly stopped himself from dropping off the open mezzanine. *That was close!* He swiftly rose to his feet, but as soon as he took his first step, his left foot became entangled in a landing net, sending a surge of adrenaline through his body. Immediately he slipped from the edge and was now left dangling from the mezzanine by just his hands.

Rushing to his aid, Emily and Lana scrambled to hold on to him while Henry gripped the wood. Suddenly the outermost beam snapped, and a moment of panic saw Lana pulling Henry towards herself when he let go of the falling timber. No sooner had he managed to grab the mezzanine floor than he felt his strength wane as he grappled to climb up, or even hold on. Panting, he was still being pulled by two people, but without his own strength, the more they strained to lift him, the heavier he felt.

'Bring the ladder over here!' Emily shouted. 'Quickly, before he falls!'

Hastily, Abigail and Elias shifted the ladder towards the dangling man. Henry stared at the ground, buzzing with adrenaline, then gradually felt his baggy trousers slipping away from him. Now the bamboo ladder was right next to him, and all he had to do was step over and hold on.

'Swing across!' he heard Abigail shout.

He finally placed one foot on the edge of a rung, let go of the mezzanine with his left hand and gingerly swung his torso towards the ladder. His trousers began to fall. Almost instantly, he grabbed them with his left hand as though they were vital to his survival. Then, before he could even react, the fragile bamboo ladder tilted sideways, and the frame snapped, leaving him hanging from the mezzanine by just one hand.

'Give us your other hand! Quick!' shouted Lana.

'Oh God, please, don't let me fall,' uttered Henry, quivering as he watched his jeans drop away with the ladder.

'Yeah, hold on!' shouted Lana. 'Just hold on to our hands!' But Lana and Emily themselves seemed to be tilting over with Henry's weight now, and Elias quickly braced Lana from behind as Emily let go of Henry's arm. He noticed there must have been half a dozen people on the ground by now, emitting a frightful commotion while they shouted things up to the entresol. Henry was straining to hold on, but as his strength gradually drained away, he sensed his fingers loosening and his arm muscles tiring. He knew he had to drop.

Lana nodded down towards someone else, as though

communicating a secret code.

'It's all right now!' he heard Sylvia shout from below. Then Lana let go of his arms and allowed him to tumble towards the ground.

His fall was suddenly broken by what turned out to be a stack of hay piled on the ground as Henry landed softly and unscathed, setting heaps of hay into motion upon impact. Immediately he frantically searched the dried grass for his lost jeans, which he slipped back over his torn underwear.

'Are you all right?'

'Are you hurt?'

People kept shouting at him. He nodded and sat in humiliation until everybody started to clap for someone: Henry turned his head up towards the entresol where the young girl was being carried on Elias's shoulders, holding on to the lost helium balloon. He shifted his gaze to the people on the ground and felt his face contracting into a frown. 'What are you guys smirking for? What are you looking at me like that for?' he griped.

'We're relieved you made it, Henry, and that you are unhurt,' replied Ian. 'Everybody was very worried.'

Quickly, a substitute ladder was fetched, and people cautiously climbed down as they congratulated one another for saving the little child and the big man.

'Henry, are you all right?' Lana asked, and she slowly extended her hand towards him. Her question was followed by a moment of respectful, almost reverent, silence.

Henry regarded Lana in shame and gratitude, and then noticed this distraction on her neck again, the thing that had caused him to lose his balance. The object was a round medallion that depicted a black slave in a loincloth. The man was shackled and facing to the right. Over him were embossed the words AM I NOT A MAN AND A BROTHER? Henry had never paid much attention in history class, yet this pendant on Lana's neck plunged him into a recollection hidden in the deepest chambers of his memory.

'Where did you get that medallion from?' he asked. 'I'm sure I've seen it before somewhere.'

'My great-grandmother had it first. She passed it on until it reached me. Are you hurt, Henry? Are you feeling all right?'

Still resting his gaze upon Lana's old pendant, Henry probed all the compartments of his memory.

'I thought I'd lost it, like, seven years ago,' Lana said. 'But Elias helped me find it in the oast house today. How are you feeling?'

Henry involuntarily caught a glimpse of the annoying asylum seeker—smirking to himself ever so complacently—and he instantly snapped out of this hypnotic reverie. 'Yes, I am fine, Lana. Thank you for saving me.'

'Don't thank me,' Lana said softly, pointing over at Elias. 'He braced me at the last second; otherwise, both of us would have fallen. In fact, he also saved the girl. Elias is the real hero of the day.'

A few people started to smile, then everyone clapped again. The scene was getting more and more unbearable. Henry had arrived the hero of the day, and now he'd turned into the laughing stock of the farm.

'Can you tell us if you're all right, Henry?' Lana asked him softly. 'Do you want to take the rest of the day off? You did drop from quite a height.'

Henry felt a sickening sensation tightening around his stomach, as though he was going to puke at any moment. The world started to spin around him. 'I am fine, Lana, really. Thank you,' he responded, glancing away from her.

'Okay. Let me know if you need anything. I am here for you,' Lana assured him. Henry gave his schoolmate a forced thumbs-up and made a humbled exit from the old barn.

Those strange hill clouds still sat upon the farm, but at least a fresh westerly breeze sailed over the fields now, and hopefully, it would stay for the rest of this humiliating day. Henry needed to be on his own for a few minutes, shut off from everyone else. Suddenly the word *beer* chimed sweetly in his head. Alcohol was exactly what he needed on a day like this. And off to the beer tent he marched, unclenching his fists. There was, after all, free beer to be enjoyed by all the harvest team.

Inside, the atmosphere was merry, a little too merry for Henry's taste. The festivalgoers had relaxed smiles on their faces while they patted each other on the back, saying how great it was to know one another. Hop bines abounded everywhere, and the bar was manned by people wearing the plants as wreaths on their heads.

'You're finished already for today?' Nora asked when she handed him his pint from the wooden cask.

'Just... let that be my concern,' Henry replied, grabbing the glass from her. Nora's face dropped somewhat, but for some reason, she didn't look that surprised either.

Henry sipped away at the refreshing homemade beverage and lowered himself onto the grass from where he watched the musical performances in the distance when they finally started. The sun was in the final quarter of its daily journey, shining towards the hills and into the summer fog. The sky began to glow a glimmering red.

One gig passed after another, and one pint followed the last. Tipsiness clouded Henry's senses and slowly turned into drunkenness. He knew it was a state in which his emotional balance could be tilted either way. An elderly couple ambled by and chuckled at the man wearing a fluorescent security vest while indulging himself into intoxication, burping into the air.

Then, at around eight o'clock, Lana appeared on the stage. She was clad in a floral summer dress that hung down to her thighs and so elegantly fluttered in the breeze. The only other things Henry could see she wore from this distance were a garland of hops and the curious medallion he could have sworn he'd seen before. The metal glittered in the setting sun. Then the music started. Singing from the stage, Lana's voice sounded like that of an angel. She was singing this hippy song Henry could not remember the title of, the old 1970s one by John Lennon about peace and brotherhood.

Frenzied cheers and applause followed from the crowd. Everyone loved the singer for whom Henry had come to Windmill Farm this summer, and yet he had no place in her heart, save as an old, unemployable school friend. Raising his hands high to clap, Henry dropped the remainder of his seventh pint on the grass and wiped his jeans with a soft tissue.

Soon the next song followed, and this time, Lana sang an old English folk song about love and nature, 'Greensleeves'.

Alas my love you do me wrong
To cast me off discourteously.
For I have loved you yes so long,
Delighting in your company.

Greensleeves was my delight,
Greensleeves was my heart of gold.
Greensleeves was my heart of joy,
And who but my lady Greensleeves.

I have been ready at your hand
To grant whatever thou wouldst crave.
I have waged both life and land,
Your love and goodwill for to have.

An even bigger applause followed when Lana hopped from the stage, seemingly impromptu, still clinging on to the microphone, and started ambling towards the audience. She sang those angelic words again.

I have been ready at your hand
To grant whatever thou wouldst crave.
I have waged both life and land,
Your love and goodwill for to have.

Lana strolled into the audience and stopped by one of the spectators, who gently rose from his seat and was greeted by a kiss on the cheek. It was Elias! Henry swiftly reached for his pint of beer, only to recall he'd spilled it all and there was none left. Dropping the glass on the ground, he sat motionless as he felt the alcohol thumping in his veins. For someone as talented as Lana to fall for this naive, clumsy refugee she'd only properly met three weeks before—it was unfathomable.

Why do I turn out so inadequate at everything I do? Henry reprimanded himself.

For a very brief moment, he caught himself toying with the thought of making up some fake stories about Elias so UK immigration would deport him, or even better, he could help Russian officials find the man here. Instantly he dismissed the idea. Then a near indifference slowly came over him while he watched people merrily passing him by, holding hands and kissing one another ever so affectionately. Time was flowing, but for Henry, everything was now like watching a movie he'd decided to separate himself from.

Almost nothing that was unfolding before his eyes affected him anymore, until he focused a little more closely on a middle-aged man about seventy metres from him, who was barrelling forward as though he was being chased. *That man is Charlie!* He was frantically racing towards the hop field, looking around himself fearfully, as though he was running for his life. Then two others suddenly came into view, about fifty metres behind, chasing the drug addict. They were the same two men Henry had seen that afternoon, and now that they were in Charlie's presence, Henry recognised them: they were Gavin and Frederick, the two drug dealers who had ruined his life. And now they were using the Hop Festival to track down their debtor. Henry had to do something immediately, for he was, after all, still on duty as a security guard.

No sooner had he risen to his feet than he dropped to the ground again, the excessive alcohol still pounding in his veins with every heartbeat. He was overcome by a light-headedness that pinned his body down and made the world twirl around him. Still, an effort had to be made to ward off those dealers from the premises and save the middle-aged junkie.

Taking a few deep breaths, he slowly arose once more and began to march after the two predators. They followed the paranoid man into the dark hop forest, gleefully rubbing their hands together and showing off some twisted martial arts moves. Henry could feel his heartbeat racing as his legs became limp, but whether it was the excessive alcohol in his blood that lowered his inhibitions or whether he was giving in to the need to vent his anger at the world, his focus remained fixed on the two beasts that had entered the hop forest.

Apart from the rustling of the hop bines in a mild breeze, this part of the farm was filled with near silence, and it was easy to let one's imagination run wild. Shadows and bines easily took on strange forms of their own in this glimmering twilight mist. Suddenly there was a rustling sound of an animal close by. Henry turned to his right, and next to him stood an adult red fox, staring him down with its pointed teeth exposed. The drunk man almost froze, then stamped his feet on the ground, setting a twirl of soil into motion. The animal closed its jaws and backed off a little until it turned around. Henry looked up from his feet and realised he'd now lost his sense of direction, no longer aware of where he stood or where the others were headed. Still, there had to be a way to listen for the commotion, Henry reminded himself, marching forward.

The hop bines grew a little denser, and Henry's own rustling against their leaves became more pronounced.

Dizziness and motion blur overwhelmed him just when he was about to sit down for a moment, almost tripping on a fallen hop bine. Then followed the screaming of a middle-aged man about thirty metres to the right, whining with a high, nasal pitch.

'We've got him! We've got the bastard!' quickly followed.

Henry swiftly turned in the direction of the voices, and he barrelled towards the scene. In front of him, the two drug dealers were pinning down the terrified, whining man and searching his wallet for banknotes.

'One hundred and fifty is not enough!' the balding man yelled at him.

'What do you two think you are doing here?' Henry suddenly shouted from behind. He noticed he was slurring his words, and he was aware of how comical this demand must have sounded. Still, he was wearing a fluorescent security vest—a garment that must surely command respect. The tall, sturdy man turned around and smiled. This was Frederick, and now he was reaching into his pocket, almost as though searching for a knife.

'Henry! Help! Help me!' Charlie wailed from his prone position.

'Leave this farm at once, you two!' Henry bellowed.

Frederick loosened his grip on his victim and started to approach the security man, while Gavin continued to press down on Charlie.

'You want trouble, do you? You want a beating? Come on!' Frederick challenged the young man.

Henry clenched his fists tightly and marched towards the drug dealer. 'Clear off out of here!' he demanded again. 'I am security!'

Frederick stepped a little closer to him, and when he was less than a metre from his face, Henry lifted his right fist, which he swung towards the man's stomach, belching as he did. It was caught by a much firmer grip as Frederick intercepted the punch, then twisted around Henry's body. He tightened his squeeze on his neck until Henry found himself trapped in a stranglehold. His muffled, suffocating cries were drowned out by Charlie's prolonged screams of panic. As Henry attempted to loosen Frederick's grip on his throat, he thrust his elbow backwards at the strangler. It had no effect, and now he was slowly running out of air, feeling more light-headed with every second that passed. Desperation took over. Instinctively, Henry imagined he was dealing with Elias, the queue-jumping refugee, and with all his might, he rammed his elbow into Frederick's torso, finally pushing the man away in a burst of fury.

'Elias, you piece of filth!' Henry screamed. 'Elias! You bastard!' He laid into the man with both fists. But his luck was short-lived, for no sooner had the tables turned than intoxication caught up with him once more and collapsed him to the ground.

Henry fell on his back, and the next second, he found himself being strangled once again. Lying on the soil, he struggled for air, and this time, he lacked the strength to push the drug dealer aside. Henry felt the effects of a lack of oxygen to his brain as his vision started to fade. Then Frederick stopped to pin him down and repeatedly punched him in the torso.

'This is what you get, you drunken git!' the brute snarled while Charlie continued to cry out for help.

A weakened Henry remained lying on the ground, surrendering to those incessant blows to his stomach. He felt he was going to be sick at any moment. Then, from the edge of his vision, he suddenly sighted a tall blonde man emerging from behind one of the hop trees and pacing towards the scene. Henry had never seen him before, but this man swung his arm around Frederick, yanked him off his body and wrestled the drug dealer to the ground with a force Henry had not reckoned on.

Gavin immediately let go of Charlie and rose to his feet, his fight-or-flight instincts seemingly activated. This blonde man was definitely not someone to mess with.

'Who are you?' Frederick asked.

'Get out of here right now,' said the blonde man, 'or you'll see what's coming!' The stranger was speaking with a foreign accent, perhaps a Russian accent, Henry realised.

Gavin and Frederick turned their eyes to the notes they had ripped from Charlie, then started to back off, heading for the west exit of the farm. There was a single screech from a night owl, then silence.

'Thank you! Who *are* you, man?' Henry asked his rescuer in his slurred voice.

The blonde man stared him down as Henry slowly rose to his feet.

'You shouted "Elias" earlier,' he said gravely. 'The man that beat you up is called Elias?' He pointed over at Frederick, who was slowly receding from their view.

Henry was startled and began to waver. His thinking was very slow but still logical. Those druggies were obviously not the only ones who'd managed to sneak into the festival. He recalled Elias was still wanted by the Russians. This man had a Russian accent. But surely, if he really was after Elias, he'd know what Elias looked like and that Frederick wasn't the person he was searching for. *Or could he be asking because he wants some kind of reassurance that there really is a man called Elias on the farm and that he's got the right place?*

Now, if there was going to be any opportunity to get rid of Elias, it would be now. All Henry had to do was tell the truth and confirm the Russian's suspicions: *The real Elias has gone to bed already. But yes, Elias still works here,* Henry wanted to say. *But no… hold on…* This would turn him into an antihero. This, he could not do to himself, for the sake of his own conscience.

'Yes, that man over there was Elias,' he eventually replied.

What a bad liar he was. Too late now, for after such a long moment of hesitation, the blonde man must have sensed Henry was fibbing, and deep down, Henry knew it. With cold, piercing eyes, this blonde Russian gave a death stare to the intoxicated liar and the confused drug addict. He radiated a vibe of absolute authority. The man turned around and then wandered forth nonchalantly.

Charlie leaned up from the ground and cast a blank stare into the hop forest, fumbling with his fingertips, his mouth half-open. Henry helped him up to his feet and supported him towards his caravan. It seemed such a long trek.

'They took more than what Lana gave me. They said it was interest,' Charlie slurred. 'They took one hundred fifty and another fifty. I'll have no money for a while. Can you lend me some?'

Henry immediately shook his head. 'Why did you keep all that money in your pocket, anyway?' he asked.

'Because they can break in.'

'I thought I'd fixed your lock this morning. Why else

do you think I did that?'

Charlie looked at the ground sheepishly.

'I guess I could lend you fifty,' Henry eventually offered.

'Please!'

'You must pay me back by Sunday.'

'That's too soon.'

'Fine. Make it payday next week, then.'

'I promise I will. I promise I'll pay you back, man.'

Henry opened his wallet and handed his co-worker five ten-pound notes, feeling his fingers pinch them when Charlie reached for the money.

In a strange daze, Henry wandered back towards the Hop Festival. Music was still being performed. People were merrily dancing away at the ceilidh and barbecuing fresh salmon in the glimmering twilight. But despite Henry's heroic efforts for Charlie, something niggled at his conscience that he was not able to explain—at least, not in this drunken state of mind. There was something he'd said, and not said quickly enough, that had put someone else in danger.

The Incident at the Quarry

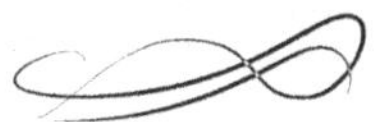

Faint crepuscular sunrays glimmered in from the edge of the ether as sparrows and meadow pipits sailed from black poplar trees. A light mountain mist swept over the farm field while the rooster crowed to announce a new day. Some timid rabbits hopped out of their burrows and started grazing on the pasture. It was half past five in the morning on the day after the Hop Festival, and some harvest workers were woken by the radio from the communal room. The device was tuned to the BBC, and a reporter announced, 'Prime Minister Boris Johnson has reaffirmed his commitment to see Brexit through by the thirty-first of October, with or without a deal. The new prime minister reassured the country that measures *were* being taken for the contingency of a no-deal, though his government remains optimistic an agreement can still be reached by the deadline. Commentators have predicted there will be a Brexit extension past the thirty-first of October to allow for an orderly withdrawal agreement...'

An invigorated Lana skipped across to turn off the radio and looked out the window towards the windmill. It was going to be a beautiful, sunny day, and she was feeling the usual early-morning buzz in her veins. With an old corn broom, she swept aside a few patches of soil, which harvest workers must have brought in on their soles last night. Stealing a glance over at Elias, who was sleepily finishing his morning tea, she was filled with a euphoric sense of anticipation for the day. Lana wanted to take him for his first horse ride and show him a special place at the foot of the hills. She also wanted Elias to finally open up to her, and perhaps she could find out more about all those anxieties he harboured deep down.

It was actually the first time she'd ever invited any other harvest worker to the stables. Located at the very far end of the hop field, it was separated by a wooden fence, and normally, the area was out of bounds to temporary workers. Lana pushed open the creaky oak door as morning rays shone in from the entrance. The scent of fresh hay filled the building and blended with the clean air from the farm pasture. Right away, a few horses neighed at the sight of their beloved carer, and Lana greeted every single stallion, shire horse and colt individually, giving them a light stroke on the head. She stopped at a sturdy brown steed with a little white mark on his face and gently caressed him.

'This one here is Hoss,' she told Elias. 'He is my favourite horse. I've been riding him every year since I was ten years old.'

Hoss greeted Lana with an affectionate neigh and rested his heavy head on her shoulder, letting Lana kiss him on the forehead before she fed him some fresh hay.

'Do you want to have a go?' she asked.

Elias appeared to waver while his gaze lingered on the horse's chewing jaws; his face cringed a little. 'What if he mistakes my hand for food?'

Lana giggled to herself. 'Horses are smart creatures, Elias. A lot smarter than we think. Here, keep your hand flat and your fingers together. Like this.'

Edging forward cautiously, Elias shifted his gaze from the animal's teeth to his eyes, and then stretched out his hand full of straw. From his tensely pressed cheeks dropped a half-suppressed smile as the horse's lips tickled away at his palm.

'Are you ready to go?' Lana asked.

Elias nodded and was shown his horse for the day: a slightly younger colt, Peter, would be his companion and riding mate. The two mounted their horses and set a course for the Malvern Hills. Riding through the orchard, Lana noticed Elias looked a little tense on the colt, barely making any movements, as though he feared Peter might shake him off at any moment. But as they ventured onto the bridle path, he gradually appeared to ease up a little and looked more trusting of the animal—it must have been his calm energy that put the boy at ease, and from time to time, Elias patted him.

It was half past six in the morning; there was no other soul on the green hills, and the pair were preparing for one of the hottest days forecast for the month. From the western slopes, they made their way to Worcestershire Beacon, snapped a few pictures from the summit and then continued towards British Camp. Up here, the fresh smell of wild, unpolluted grassland abounded alluringly and was so very therapeutic. Already, the temperature was rising quite fast, and the mercury must have climbed up to nearly thirty degrees when the pair approached the ancient hill fort. On horseback, they ascended the sloping Shire Ditch until they found themselves above British Camp. Here the solitary riders dismounted and gave their horses a little respite.

Lana took a few sips of water and doused her steed with some more. Just then, her phone beeped with an incoming text message from Henry: *Hey, what are you up to today? Do you want to meet up? I am biking to Ledbury after lunch. Let me know if you're heading this way.*

A few colourful butterflies took off from the dry grass as Lana laid her phone on the ground and wavered pensively.

'How did you get on with Henry yesterday?' she asked. 'I mean, in the beer tent.'

'Yeah, I guess it was okay. He's a very efficient worker. He knows his tools and things…'

'And?'

'We talked a little about politics. Then he got called away because of those two disorderly men.'

A short silence followed.

'Would you mind if Henry joined us briefly this afternoon?' Lana asked. 'Just for a little while, that is.'

Elias shrugged his shoulders, and with somewhat drooping eyelids, he cast a stare into the distance, rubbing his neck. 'No, I don't mind. The more the merrier, right?' he replied, dousing his colt with some cool spring water.

A soaring, fluttery sensation throbbed in Lana's

stomach as she rested her eyes on Elias. Then she looked back at her phone. *OK, meet us at the pub by the quarry. Around two!* she texted back, overcoming a moment of hesitation before she eventually clicked on the send icon. Lana slid her phone back into her jeans and crossed her legs in a meditative yoga position. She viewed the scenic landscape over the eastern slope of the hills and suddenly remembered something that was still in the back of her mind.

'Elias, can I ask you a quick question?'

'Is it really embarrassing, to the extent that I would fall off a horse?'

'Don't be daft!' Lana smiled. 'You don't have to answer, of course, but I *am* curious. And I *am* your friend.'

'Yeah. Go on, then.'

'Yesterday, when we were meditating in the field, you were quite shaken when you heard that knocking noise from the oast house. And to be honest, it wasn't the first time I've seen you like this. Something has happened to you, right? Something scary? I mean, you don't have to tell me, of course, but I *would* really be interested to hear the story. What actually happened?'

Elias sat there, pondering. He'd never opened up about this to anybody, and though he had suppressed those recollections for years, he'd always longed to tell someone. Maybe this would be the moment. After all, Lana was certainly a wonderful human being he felt he could confide in.

'Or would you rather not talk about it?' Lana asked softly.

'When I was fifteen, my elder brother, Mikhail, was

drafted into the Russian army,' Elias began. 'We knew he'd be sent to Chechnya to fight, and we were trying to help him flee the country. It almost worked. On the day he was going to escape, the Internal Troops turned up and took him. They fired a Taser at me and took our family savings. When Mikhail arrived at the barracks near Murmansk, his comrades subjected him to such brutal hazing—he ended up dislocating his knee. And still, they sent him to Chechnya to fight. He wanted to be a neuroscientist and cure people, not shoot at them. But Russia didn't allow that.

'One day, he had this strange premonition that he'd die in Chechnya and that *I* would be next. He sent an email to me, saying, "Elias, one day, they will come for you too. They will hurt you. You will find yourself in a hospital, and you will flatline." It was the last email he ever sent. His battalion was fighting insurgents near Bratskoye, in the north of Chechnya. One of the insurgents threw a grenade at the troops; Mikhail was the closest to the explosion and died instantly. The army just sent him home to us in a body bag… and I will never forget that mangled look on his pale, dead face. My brother had wanted to be a neuroscientist and cure people, but Russia hadn't allowed that. The government wanted otherwise…'

Leaning into Lana's comforting arms, he tried to stop himself from shaking at those recollections. A few weeks ago, when Elias had just met his new boss, such scenes would have been unthinkable, but he still worried about what Lana might say if she found out he was on her uncle's farm in order to hide from the authorities.

'Is this why you applied for asylum in Britain?' she asked him.

'Not quite. I became so obsessed with abolishing conscription. I joined pressure groups, ran campaigns at uni, wrote letters. First, I got a deferral myself, but my parents weren't happy about all the activism. They thought sooner or later it would get me into trouble. Then, in my second year—my parents had just gotten a pay raise, and I was on a trip to Tunisia with Mum. Someone from the town hall in Nikel tipped Dad off. He said there was a plan to arrest me for all my campaigning, that I'd be sent to a re-education camp in Siberia, and then to fight in Syria.'

'And that's when you came to Britain?'

'On the way back from Tunisia, we had a stopover at London Heathrow. That's when I said goodbye to Mum and applied for asylum. Mum got on the next flight to St Petersburg. That was the last time I saw her.'

'Oh… your parents are still living in Nikel?'

'They are. The first few years, I always felt so guilty for leaving her behind. I guess all this kind of turned me into the anxious, jumpy person you see today.'

Lana let a seven-spot ladybird crawl from her jeans onto her finger. She gently placed it back into the soft grass of the little mountain before she turned to Elias again with wide, gleaming eyes. He looked over from the summit of British Camp, drew in the clear air of the rolling pastures and viewed the green fields of Worcestershire. This whole nightmare was over now, he reminded himself, and then he remembered that wasn't quite true yet.

'You are safe in Britain now,' Lana said. 'Just keep reminding yourself of that.'

Elias shook his head. 'No, Lana. Things are not quite over. Even here.'

'What do you mean by that?'

Elias hesitated, but Lana had been such a good friend over the last few weeks—he couldn't keep it from her indefinitely. 'I continued campaigning online. From England. I encouraged people to flee the country, and I've helped conscripts defect to Norway. Then, last month, the same guy who tipped us off about Syria warned Mum again. He said there was somebody who was trying to track me down around Oxford and extradite me. Mum said I should go into hiding for the next few weeks. That's when I applied for the job you gave me… I am sorry, Lana. The reason I am here is to hide.'

Lana drew her eyebrows together, then put her hand on Elias's shoulder. 'Have you told the police about this?' she asked softly.

Elias shook his head. 'There's no evidence. What are they supposed to do? They already know I'm in Britain as a refugee.'

His answer was followed by a few seconds of silence while Lana seemed deeply engrossed in thought. 'It's very rare for foreign officials to just extradite people from England,' she mused. 'Although maybe I wouldn't put it past Russian authorities… especially if it was all unofficial. Or maybe it is someone who's got a personal grudge against you for helping conscripts escape… Anyway, regardless of what made you apply for the job, I'm still glad you did.'

The two lingered on the solitary summit a little longer, viewing the rolling pastures that extended from this hill fort. The white sun almost shone down on the pair vertically as the day became hotter by the hour. Yet Elias was basking in a sensation of lightness.

Slowly, the two mounted their horses again and rode further south along the Shire Ditch. They headed towards Gloucestershire and gradually climbed down from this little mountain. Even though Elias had learned to trust his horse, riding on those steep slopes was still nerve-racking at times, especially when the horse tilted forward as they descended. Instinctively, Elias would give the colt a few strokes on the shoulder every few minutes, reminding him there was still a friendly human sitting on his back. He kept glancing at Lana, who was sometimes leading the way slightly ahead of him. And whatever she did, she always looked as though she had been born for it. Whether it was harvesting apples from the orchard, operating the conveyer belt for the hop bines or riding barefoot upon English hills, she was a pro at everything.

Back in the hopper hut, a hungover Henry was charging the battery of his electric bike when he reread Lana's message: *OK, meet us at the pub by the quarry.*

Who was 'us'? If Lana was spending the weekend with that conceited Elias, then—was there any point in him joining them at all? he wondered. Who knew what such a brave girl saw in such a needy, pitiful asylum seeker like him? He was a stranger in this country, but he always behaved as if he were a peer… as though he were just like everyone else.

At the Hop Festival, Elias had stolen his thunder and left him utterly humiliated. Henry was still dwelling on last night as he felt a residual pain in his stomach, and now he recalled he'd been punched. He had been playing the hero, saving Charlie from two drug dealers in the hop field, but then, he had also spoken with a Russian he could no longer remember. Who on the harvest team had a Russian accent? It couldn't have been Gregorios, for he clearly spoke with a Greek one. It couldn't have been Elias either—he had a light Scandinavian twang, and the Russian residues in his speech were minute, although Henry *did* recall the imagination of punching him. It also couldn't have been Sylvia, for the person that had turned up had clearly been a man.

Henry brushed his teeth and got dressed, putting on a pair of jeans and a short-sleeved shirt for this hot summer day. *If only the hopper hut could have some proper air con!* He gulped down a bowl of cereal and then set off on his electric bike, picturing the intimate moments that Lana and Elias were probably sharing right now.

On the wild hill meadows, Lana and her special friend were riding on a rather narrow path that led southwards toward Gloucestershire, a sloping route very remote from the nearest town. Gradually, Elias found this place a little uncanny, if not slightly fear-inspiring. They hadn't run into anybody for hours, and now more shrubs and greenery were closing in on them. It was all part of the long Shire Ditch, and now the two found themselves surrounded by several Romney sheep on both sides, grazing on the ryegrass. The pair dismounted their horses to lead them through the field by the bridle. Most of the sheep scattered at the sight of the mighty stallion and the colt, but one rather adventurous sheep remained standing, curious, as if its job were to observe humans on their track. Suddenly it set off from the brush and gingerly wandered towards Elias before it gave him a nudge in the waist. Elias was trying not to show it, but he realised he must be cringing in fear when Lana giggled to herself at this sight. It was only a sheep, after all, a very common occurrence in the countryside. But there was something out there that presented a greater threat than just the sheep, something the pair were not even aware of. Half a kilometre behind them, the two horse riders were being tailed by a blonde man on a mountain bike. He was slowly reducing the distance between them as he observed the pair through his binoculars. At the same time, Henry was also starting to catch up.

Steadily, Elias and Lana descended from the hills on horseback and approached a little section of woodland, the fresh smell of the forest wafting across from the near distance.

'So, how many people did you help escape to Norway, then?' Lana asked.

'At least a dozen. All of them were conscripts fleeing from the barracks. Some of them were about to be sent to war zones; others just couldn't take the hazing anymore. I have an uncle who lives in Bjørnevatn. And two of my relatives live by the border river. We plan the escape. They pick them up at night and arrange for wetsuits and snorkels, then take them into Norway.'

'A bit like an international underground movement.'

'Kind of. Yes.'

Lana beamed with a cheerful smile and flourished the old medallion that adorned her neck again—this abolitionist pendant they'd found in the oast house yesterday. 'The woman who gave this medallion to my great-grandmother was part of an underground movement,' she said. 'It was called the Underground Railroad in North America. She helped fugitive slaves escape from their plantations. At one point, she even met Harriet Tubman.'

Elias was awestruck. 'Harriet Tubman? She was the former slave that helped others escape to Canada, right? I've heard about her in history lessons.'

Lana nodded, and Elias asked if he could take another look at the medallion and maybe hold it for a moment.

'Sure,' Lana replied.

The two horse riders edged a little closer as Lana handed the necklace to Elias. When he touched this old metal, it brought about the same déjà vu he'd felt yesterday, as though he were holding something he'd first caught a glimpse of a couple of centuries ago, and now he found himself physically reunited with an object from another lifetime. The familiarity of the medallion was so profound that Elias searched in all compartments of his childhood memories, and yet the recollection of this artefact *still* eluded him.

'Who did you say made these medallions again?' he asked.

'Josiah Wedgwood. He was the grandfather of Charles Darwin, actually. Mum gave it to me shortly before she died. I was so sure I'd lost it at one of the Hop Festivals.'

Elias handed back the pendant, one of the last surviving specimens of this seal, and Lana tucked it back around her neck, lovingly and tenderly.

The two horse riders were hemmed in by shrubs and thickets on both sides as they rode on.

'Some countries still practise slavery today,' Elias commented. 'And my brother died from it.'

Lana's face winced slightly, as though she wasn't totally convinced. She remained pensive, looking forward along the winding Shire Ditch. 'A few centuries ago, certain countries imported people from other continents and worked them as slaves,' she remarked, 'on plantations and farms. They were owned by their masters… I mean, don't get me wrong, Elias. I totally disagree with conscription and what they did to your poor brother, but is that really the same as slavery?'

Elias unscrewed the cap on his bottle to take a refreshing gulp of water as he considered her question. 'So, where do we draw the dividing line between mandatory national service and slavery? Is it the length of time you're made to serve, or is it simply whether you hold the same nationality as your master or not?'

'What do you mean?'

'I mean, let's take North Korea, for example. People are barred from leaving the country, and they are conscripted for a whole *ten years*. Take Eritrea. Thousands of people are locked into national service *indefinitely*. There are no plans to release them from the army, and even the UN has condemned this as slavery. What's the difference in years between national service and involuntary servitude? If a country sends slave catchers to remote continents and imports foreign people as human property, there is international outrage about slavery. But if a country sends its own troops to kidnap innocent students within its borders and sends them into war zones, everyone turns a blind eye. Now it's no longer slavery: the students hold the same passports as the masters. Now it's national service and acceptable. Lana, my brother did not choose to be born in Russia, and neither did I. The UN condemns

Eritrea for practising slavery, so I always ask, how many years does it take for acceptable national service to turn into unacceptable slavery? Why are countries forbidden from kidnapping foreigners as slaves but free to do anything they like to people they've forced their own passports on?' Every time Elias brought up this subject, it set his heart to pounding, and he took a few gasps of fresh air.

'And you don't think people owe a debt to the society in which they grow up and are nurtured?' Lana asked.

Elias turned his head to her and sensed she was playing the devil's advocate now, as she would sometimes do at the Oxford Union. He cleared his throat. 'If someone wants to live in a country, they should contribute. They should look for a job, and they should be made to pay taxes. But they should always be free to leave. That's how a free society works. The moment the border is closed to you, you become the property of the state. Besides, no government should be telling you what *your* country is simply by closing the border to you.'

'This reminds me of an exchange at the Oxford Union… back in March,' Lana suddenly seemed to recall. 'You also spoke in that debate. You were throwing arguments against—what was his name again?'

'I think it was Sergej.'

'Yes. Sergej. It was the debate on free societies. And your side won that one.' Suddenly Lana tensed up a little. 'By the way, keep away from that Sergej guy,' she said. 'I've always had a really bad feeling around that man, and… You look surprised, Elias.'

'I *am* surprised, Lana. You don't normally judge people like that.'

'No, I try not to. But that Sergej gives off a very unpleasant vibe.'

'Well, I think he was only there for one semester, anyway,' Elias said. 'Somebody mentioned the Russian government was sponsoring his time in the UK.'

'Yes, and from what I've heard, he's now applying for a job with the Russian security service. I would just advise you to keep your distance from him.'

Lana tucked her medallion underneath her T-shirt as the pair rode down a curving, earthy slope. 'Until now, I've always thought of this necklace as a symbol of triumph over a dark institution,' Lana said. 'A past institution which we have defeated for good. I was not aware of what was happening in North Korea, Eritrea… or even Russia. Maybe you are right, Elias. Maybe this battle isn't completely won yet.'

By now, the clandestine cyclist had caught up a little more with the unsuspecting fugitive and his hippy friend. He was carrying his bike less than one hundred metres behind. He briefly hid inside some bracken, then came out again, tailing the pair silently.

The horse riders snaked along a somewhat dark, narrow path that led them towards an old, forlorn quarry, white sunbeams shining upon the lake. A fine mist hovered up from the surface, glimmering over the water. In a field of wild vegetation, Precambrian rock rose like a hill on one side and towered over the basin of clear azure water. It mirrored the sun and reflected the nature around it. There was nobody else about, and Lana playfully cried an echoing 'Hello!' against the rock. Her voice reverberated and repeated itself across the distance.

'This is Gullet Quarry,' she said. 'It's one of the most special landmarks in the Malvern Hills.'

Indeed, it was one of the most beautiful spots Elias had visited. He really hadn't expected there to be a little lake tucked away at the foot of a few English hills.

'Shall we go for a swim?' Lana asked cheerfully, leading her steed a little closer to the fresh water.

Is she for real? 'You mean right here?'

'Of course! Why not? We're only round the corner from where we're meeting Henry. Let's take a little dip. Come on. It's so hot.'

'You didn't tell me we were coming to a lake. I didn't bring any swimwear,' Elias lamented.

'Neither did I,' said Lana. 'Have you ever swum in the wild before? Naked?'

'Are you serious? Really?'

'I mean, if you want, you can keep your briefs on, but you could also come with me in your birthday suit.'

'How do you even know I wear briefs?'

'Well, you do have a habit of kicking off your duvet when you're hot… and you're on my way to the bathroom. I've seen your briefs plenty of times, and so has everyone else, probably. Come on, let's go! There is nobody else around.'

Lana removed her medallion and started to undress as though clothes had always been optional. Naked, she stood in front of a nervous Elias and encouraged him to give it a try.

A fluttery sensation hovered around Elias's stomach,

and he felt his pulse racing at the sight of Lana. It was incredible. The sight of pure bare skin, the firm muscles that glinted with her sweat and bunched tensely in her bottom—her firm, strong chest and the natural hair…

Dipping her toes in the water, she waded into the lake from where she splashed Elias playfully. 'Are you coming in or not?' she shouted over.

Elias's heart was still racing. The prospect of his first-ever skinny-dip sent a buzzing adrenaline rush through his veins—If only he could feel a little less shy. It was only today that he'd broken one layer of ice between himself and Lana, and now she was already tearing down the next barrier.

Anxiously, he undressed, took off his briefs and ran towards the water as quickly as he could. The wet soil right in front of the quarry felt a little softer, he noticed, as he almost slipped on a marshy patch of earth.

Once he was inside the clear lake, he was gripped by a sudden urge to pant, and he took huge gasps of air. It must have been the cool temperature of the water, for his heart began to labour and his muscles shook. For the first time, he was standing completely naked in a lake, and now a naked girl was swimming towards him and affectionately grasping on to his arm. It was nerve-racking but so exhilarating at the same time.

The two swam around the quarry while their bodies slowly warmed up, and very gradually Elias was shedding his inhibitions around his nakedness. It actually felt quite liberating, for there was no other person about, except for this wonderful, eccentric hippy, who gently tugged him down for a dive below. Here the water was translucent enough for the pair to see down to the lakebed and take in the mesmerising scenery of this underwater basin. A small fish emerged from below; it floated between the two and glanced at Elias flinchingly before it hastily wiggled itself forward. Lana turned her head to Elias, smiling, and blew him bubbles of air, like a water kiss. Hand in hand, the two swam back to the surface and gulped the fresh, unpolluted air of this landmark. A few sparrows twittered in the shrubs as they rummaged for food, while carrion birds glided up the Precambrian rock of the quarry. It was the happiest, most exhilarating hour of Elias's life, and nothing did the pair suspect of the two parties that were watching them by now.

Henry had caught up on his electric bike but was taken aback by what he saw. She was naked? Should he call or not? Then, like a peeping Tom, he remained hidden behind some shrubs. But there was also somebody out there not even Henry was aware of, though this other man was hiding on the same side of the lake.

Suddenly Hoss neighed with a terrifying frenzy that froze Elias in the water, and instantly sent shudders of horror through Lana. From one moment to the next, she was put on high alert. There was something, or *someone*, hiding in the shrubs, and it had scared the stallion, which came running towards the lake.

'Stop!' Lana cried, stretching out her hand towards the horse. Too late, she quickly found. For Hoss had sunk his front legs into the water, while his hind legs had remained stuck in the soft soil. So soft and moist, it was like a little patch of marshland, which was dragging him in.

'Quick, quick, help him!' Lana shouted across to Elias

as she scrambled out of the water, tearful.

At that moment, two men emerged from shrubs on the lake edge. A tall blonde male climbed onto his mountain bike and nonchalantly left the scene as though nothing had happened. Lana knew he was the man who had scared the stallion. Then there was Henry, of course. A somewhat more innocent peeping Tom, he dropped his flushing face towards his chest, even trying to cover it with his hands for a second. Edging around nervously, he almost gave off the impression he was about to flee the scene in shame.

'Henry, wait!' Lana shouted, dashing towards him. 'Henry, please wait. We need your help. We can't do this alone.'

Henry gushed, 'Lana, I swear it's not what it looks like. You have to believe me. I wanted to say hi to you, and then… you were like…'

'Henry, it doesn't matter what it looks like—I won't judge you. We just need your help!' Lana pleaded. She gripped Henry's arms while he instinctively kept jerking away from her.

Suddenly the surreal nature of this scene dawned on Lana, and she saw herself pinning down an old schoolmate over whom she was crouching stark naked. She looked Henry in the eyes and then changed her mind. 'Actually, go and hurry to the pub,' she instructed. 'Get reinforcements and send for people. And cars. Quick! Quick!'

Henry nodded as Lana loosened her grip on him. He rose from the ground and swiftly ran forth, leaving his soiled, mud-covered bicycle on this awkward marshy terrain.

By now, Elias was back in his briefs and was holding

on to the sinking horse under his belly. Lana swiftly slipped on her own underwear and ran back towards her beloved animal, reaching for the horse from below to stop him from sinking any further. She cuddled him devotedly. The stallion was diagonally tilting into the water and neighing in panic. With Elias, Lana was straining in pain to support the horse, pushing him upwards with all her might. And yet there was no sign of any reinforcements, not even after fifteen minutes. *We should really have called 999 instead of relying on Henry,* went through Lana's mind. She eyed her phone, which was lying by the shrubs along with her clothes, but if she eased her support on the horse, he might slump down a little further. She could not let go.

'Shall I go and check on Henry?' Elias asked.

'I can't do this on my own, Elias. Hoss will slip down completely'. Lana gasped and thought, then she suddenly remembered the time of day and realised why Henry hadn't found any reinforcements yet: it was a Saturday afternoon, and the pub didn't open until the evening. Who knew where Henry had run off to now?

Elias's clothes were lying a little closer to the lake edge than her own, so maybe *he* could rush to his device and dial for help. 'Quickly, get your phone and call 999 and Sam. Bring your phone over here. Do it quickly!' she said.

'From Great Malvern? Will fire services from Great Malvern get here in time?' Elias blurted out. He sprinted over to grab his phone, but the second he let go of the horse, Lana felt the animal sinking a little further. She squirmed, straining to push up the poor animal by herself.

'The fire service is on the way. Sam's also on the way,' Elias reassured her in a tepid voice and with a guilty look, which betrayed his fears that Lana's hopes were too high, and time was running out too fast.

Peter was standing by and watching. Even he seemed utterly exhausted, neighing in full frenzy. Suddenly, the mud under Hoss's legs gave way a little further, and the stallion found himself swallowed almost down to his chest. It would only be a matter of minutes until his head would be underwater.

'Elias! Get Henry's bike! Quick!' Lana shouted.

Elias understood straight away. He hastily dashed off to fetch the electric bicycle from the bushes and planted it underneath Hoss's belly. But the bicycle only added more weight to the already subsiding mud, and less than three minutes later, it gave way and swallowed the horse down to his stomach. Lana continued to cling on to the wailing animal; she was absolutely determined that Hoss should survive beyond the next hour.

Suddenly a rustling sound emanated again from the shrubs, and Lana cautiously turned her head to the side. This time, a man in his forties emerged from the woodland, along with his pregnant wife. They sprinted towards the pair and immediately rushed to the horse.

'Are you guys all right?' asked the woman.

Her husband added, 'A guy stopped us and said two people are in trouble here.'

It must have been Henry!

The couple lost no time in offering to hoist the steed out with their van. They rushed back to the vehicle. A small barrier had to be broken before they could drive it closer to the lake and tie a towrope around the sinking horse. Then the man hastened back into the van and slammed the door shut.

So exhausting had the last five minutes been that

Lana knew she had no strength left to hold the horse any longer. Elias, too, seemed enervated of his stamina. But now it was all set and ready; only the accelerator had to be pressed. She heard the engine revving, and the exhausted pair eased their support on the horse. Just then, the mud underneath him gave way one more time so that the water completely engulfed Hoss's head.

'Come on! Please start the van now!' Lana shouted over.

Finally, the van began to roll forward, and the half-tonne stallion was dragged out of the water, out of the mud, and out of the jaws of his nightmare.

Lana and Elias sighed in relief. Finally, it was all over.

But hardly had the animal started to rise than his weight must have taken its toll on the weak van engine, and it stalled. The van rolled backwards, and within seconds, Hoss had sunk back into the mud and back into the lake, his legs flailing. He stood about a quarter of a metre from where he'd stuck previously, but within seconds, his head was about to be submerged once again. It was all beyond belief.

'What's going on there?' Lana shouted.

'The motor! The engine's stopped!' the driver yelled back.

Lana listened on as he tried to restart the vehicle, but every time he fired up the engine, it died down again. The motor simply refused to jump back on.

Lana knew her horse was going to die within seconds if they didn't restart the motor immediately, and she sensed her heart palpitating as the struggle dragged on. It was the first time she'd ever been gripped in such panic, her entire body trembling. She looked at Hoss's head and assessed its position. His mouth and nostrils were about to go under, but if they could lift his front legs just a little bit, they might be able to buy themselves some time. Eyeing Henry's electric bike, she asked, 'Elias, do you have a belt or anything sharp on you?'

Elias flapped his arms and swiftly shook his head, his restless gaze jumping between Lana and the horse.

'Does anyone have something sharp, like a belt or a knife? Quickly!' she shouted out. The woman narrowed her eyes for a second, her head flinching back a little, then she hastily handed Lana her Chinese-style hairpin from her plait. Just at that moment, the mud gave way yet another time, and Hoss's mouth went into the lake once more. Lana grabbed Henry's bike and jumped into the quarry, swimming to meet Hoss's front legs. She knew those limbs only had to be lifted a couple of centimetres to clear the horse's airway, and with all the strength in her arms, Lana scrambled to push them up. She strained to hold her breath underwater.

The next moment, she knew she was probably doing the naivest thing she'd ever attempted, but an endeavour still had to be made. Keeping the bicycle in place by propping it on her leg, Lana tilted the front tyre towards her face and pierced the rubber with the hairpin. She tried to breathe the air that surged outward with a jolt, but the air rapidly gushed out of the tyre and dissipated straight into the water. Still, there was a small but sizeable fraction of the air she was able to catch, and she bought herself just a little time. At least, Hoss was able to breathe above once she thrust his front legs back up.

Time and again, the van driver attempted to restart the engine, and time after time, he failed.

Now the oxygen was slowly running out, and Lana hastily pierced the back wheel. She pressed her mouth against the hole, knowing this would be her last chance. More air dissipated, and if the van didn't start in the next half-minute, it would all be over.

The next second, Hoss tilted forward into the water, while his hind legs were still stuck in the mud. By now, pushing up the horse was becoming too exhausting for Lana, and she reluctantly let go of Hoss's front legs and swam to meet his head. It was fully submerged underwater, and the animal was jerking about in panic. His eyes were wide open and looked frightened, but sad and soft at the same time. Yet saying goodbye to her horse was something Lana simply could not do.

Maybe out of instinct, maybe out of intuition, she pressed her hands against the animal's muzzle, stopping Hoss from inhaling the lake water, still naively hoping he would be hoisted from the quarry somehow. But gradually, she was being starved of oxygen herself, and she knew she had to swim up soon. It was the moment she would finally have to give up. Bracing on to Hoss's head one more time, she looked into his beautiful, kind eyes and remembered all the rides they'd had. She wanted to project one last message to him, 'I love you. Thank you for all the fun we've had. I'm sorry I couldn't save you today. I will miss you.'

Hoss regarded Lana devotedly, and it was as if he were returning his own thanks and now bidding her farewell.

Then Lana tightly hugged the steed one more time and spontaneously said a little prayer. 'I'm not willing to let this horse go today. If anyone can hear me, please help us. And help us quick!'

Just at that moment, the driver intuitively raised the

clutch a little before he turned the ignition and found that the engine started up.

The next thing Lana saw was her horse being pulled away from her arms as he seemingly soared out of the water and above the lake. Immediately she rose back to the surface and gasped for air. It was the sweetest, most delicious oxygen she had breathed in her life, while she basked in the sensation of a little miracle. It felt as though death had already taken the horse from this world but then released him when it had changed its mind and deferred to the wishes of mortals.

Cheered on by the pregnant woman and Elias, she swam back to land and gave each a heartfelt hug. The woman introduced herself as Mrs Wright, and when her husband stepped out of the van, Lana strode over to her favourite animal, fell onto him in an embrace and vented her tears.

'I thought I was going to lose you today!' she wailed. 'I thought I would never see you again!' Holding tightly to the muddy animal, she caressed his head tenderly. She thanked the Wrights for their relentless efforts and then put on her clothes.

It wasn't long before the fire service arrived, and Samuel turned up with his horse trailer. He thanked the Wrights for their indefatigable help and invited them for dinner that evening. The horses were loaded into the trailer and, along with the two university friends, were driven back to Windmill Farm. By now, Lana and Elias had almost forgotten about the blonde stalker who had watched them from the bushes.

It was now past seven in the evening, and Henry had locked himself into his private room, his heart pounding with shame and anxiety, for he did not even know whether it had been himself or the stranger that Hoss had recoiled from. Nor did he know whether Hoss had made it. He cleared his throat as a hot, tingling sensation rose to his face. Every time Henry padded past his mirror, he avoided it, for he simply could not accept this ridiculous person he saw in it, this voyeur he must have become in Lana's eyes.

Every time someone entered the cottage, his heart would start racing, his face would sweat, and Henry would fear he was about to be reprimanded or even sacked. Eventually, he could no longer bear the suspense, and he opened the door into the communal dormitory.

'Gregorios!' he called out.

'What do you need, Henry?' came the humble reply.

'Have you seen Elias or Lana anywhere?'

'Yes, I saw Lana in the cottage.'

'In the cottage? When?'

'This morning, I think.'

'Oh, come on. I mean *recently*, of course, not this morning. Sylvia, have you seen Elias or Lana anywhere recently? In the last few hours?'

'No, sorry. Haven't seen them since early morning,' she replied.

'I've seen both of them,' volunteered Nora.

'You have? Where?'

'They drove back through the main gate.'

'They *drove* back?'

'Yes, about three hours ago or more.'

'They weren't riding on horseback?'

'No. The horses were on the… what do you call this

again? The pulling car?'

'How many horses were there?'

'Two—a clean one and a muddy one.'

An immediate lightness came over Henry's body, and he exhaled with a long sigh. 'Thank you, Nora. Did you also see where they went?'

'I think straight to the windmill,' she responded.

Oh, thank God! Both horses were fine, after all. Henry would now summon up enough courage to head to the windmill and apologise. And if all went well, Lana might accept the apology and move on. And he would get to keep his job. In fact, if all went *really* well, she might even acknowledge him as a friend once again and forgive him.

Henry opened the door and looked across to the old mill. There was the usual smell of wild grass in the air while sunset began to glimmer over the farm. Part of him still couldn't believe he'd been downgraded from an eligible suitor to a cowardly voyeur grovelling for forgiveness. But he would muster the courage and make a move.

Inside the windmill, tapered candles had been lit as the Wrights shared a celebratory dinner with Lana, Elias, Samuel and his wife, Dorothy. They'd prepared some grilled salmon with home-grown spinach, which they were serving with King Edward potatoes and champagne. A toast was said, glasses were raised, and the diners dug into their food.

Lana apologised for losing Mrs Wright's hairpin and produced a new one she'd bought in town that afternoon. It was another Chinese-style metal pin, quite expensive actually, even though she'd acquired it from a charity shop.

'I'm sorry. I did look everywhere. That's the closest I found to the one I lost,' she said, offering the thin piece to Mrs Wright.

Mrs Wright held the piece of jewellery in her hands but then returned the gift to Lana. She seemed touched. 'That's completely fine, my dear,' she said. 'We're so glad we could help you guys today. Keep it for yourself. I think it would look pretty on you.'

'Speaking of jewellery,' Samuel suddenly said, 'I did manage to find the original chain for your medallion, Lana. We still had it in the storage chamber.' Her uncle cracked open an old tin adorned with fine gold and produced the original metal chain to which her amulet had been attached.

'You've kept it all these years! Thank you.'

'You *asked* me to keep hold of it, Lana. I remember how upset you were when you lost the medallion part. That must have been almost ten years ago now, I think.'

Dorothy added, 'Elias found her pendant recently—in our oast house. Without the chain, it looked like an old coin, so I kept it in Sam's money collection. Heaven knows where I thought it came from.'

'This is one of the last surviving examples of Josiah Wedgwood's anti-slavery medallion.' Lana beamed. 'My great-grandmother had it first, and I lost it one August, like seven summers ago—almost to the day.'

'Almost to the day!' uttered Mr Wright. 'That is almost eerie.' He dug into his potatoes and took another sip of the champagne.

'Eerie? But do you know what is *really* eerie, Lana?' uncle asked. 'Did Mum or Grandma ever tell you about the summer of 1853?'

'That's when the owner of the chain met Harriet Tubman, right?'

'More than that. One night in 1853,' Samuel commenced, 'the lady who owned this necklace was hiding eight fugitives in her coal cellar, in Maryland. A couple of slave catchers searched her house but didn't find them, even though all they had to do was raise the trapdoor. When they left, the woman dropped the medallion, and as she reached for it, she felt as though there was *another* hand trying to touch it. She thought it was only her imagination, but then she heard the child of the group telling her mum the same thing, that she'd *also* sensed the presence of two ghosts while they were hiding in the cellar and that they were even trying to communicate with them. That was the night she said this medallion was blessed by two friendly spirits— Elias is suddenly looking very intrigued there. Are you all right, son?'

'Er… yes… I just had one of those really strange moments of déjà vu. I am all right, thank you,' Elias replied.

At that moment, Dorothy glanced out the window again. 'Sam, Henry has walked around the windmill, like, twenty times. Do you want to check he's all right?'

'I'll go and check on him,' Lana volunteered, and she immediately made her way down the spiral staircase.

Outside, a few crickets were chirping in the fields, and the harvest workers had lit a small campfire by the old hopper hut. Henry had his back to the door, but as soon as he turned around, he froze at once, as if glued to the soil.

'Henry, are you all right?' Lana shouted out.

His hand shaking a little, Henry gingerly approached her and, at one point, even appeared to bow his head. He vented half a dozen pleas for forgiveness, reassured Lana that he was not a voyeur and begged her to overlook his actions and move on.

'No problem, Henry. I said I would not judge you at the quarry, and I won't judge you now. You have nothing to worry about at all.'

At this, Henry's jaw muscles suddenly loosened, and he gaped at Lana with a relieved sigh. For a few seconds, he stood in front of her, speechless. 'Really? So, you will just forgive me?'

'Yes, of course, but I do have a question, though. Why did you not come back to us? Or reclaim your bike? Why did you just run away?'

Henry wavered for a moment. 'I was ashamed, Lana. And I was worried you'd blame me if your horse died.'

'I don't actually think you were the man he was scared of.'

'Really?'

'Yes, really.'

'Anyway, that pub was closed, so I just ran and tried to find other people. Then I saw this couple in the van, and–'

'Thank you so much for sending them. That was a lifesaver.'

'You're welcome.'

'How did you get home in the end?'

'Someone gave me a lift. I hitched a ride on a motor-bike.'

'I see. I'm sorry, I had to use your bicycle to save Hoss. It's gone now. But I will pay for a new one.'

'Ah, don't worry about it. It's fine.'

'I promise. I will give you the money for a new electric bicycle.'

'Thank you.'

'I do have another question, though. Who was the other man, that tall blonde guy that was watching us at the quarry today? Do you know him?'

Henry shook his head. 'No. I didn't even know he was there until he suddenly came out of the bushes.'

Lana looked into his steady eyes and sensed he was telling the truth. Light-heartedly, she smiled. 'Come on, buddy. Do you want to come in and help yourself to some grilled salmon and spinach? There is plenty for everyone. I am sure Sam, Dorothy and Elias would also love to have you.'

For a few seconds, Henry dropped his head towards the grass, all dejected, as though part of his energy had just been drained out of his body. 'Elias… You really like Elias, don't you?' he eventually asked.

As soon as Henry posed this question, he noticed Lana regarded him with widening, empathetic eyes, as though it was the first time she'd sensed his sadness over her relationship with Elias. How could someone be as smart as Lana, excelling at everything they did, but not even spot such emotions around their own friends?

'Oh, Henry, but I like you too,' she said. 'You are one of the only classmates I'm still in touch with. Did you know that?'

Henry shook his head. 'And did you know they offered me a job at an exhibition event, but I came back just to see you?'

'I appreciate that. Otherwise, we would have missed you this time.'

'What do you like so much about Elias, then?' Henry

asked. *I mean, strictly speaking, he's not even one of us.* Of course, Henry only *pondered* this addition, which he kept from Lana's attention.

'Well, Elias is a very kind person. He's brave—although he doesn't show it. He's funny and he's very intelligent.'

'Unlike me. I am just the simple boy with no degree, the simple boy with no skills.'

'Come on. You know that is not true. Everyone knows how hard you work. That's why we keep giving you a job here.'

Henry mulled over the dinner offer but gratefully declined it. Lana embraced him before he went off to the thatched country pub, a man unburdened and forgiven, yet overcome with inadequacy.

After his third pint, his mood shifted, and reality dawned on him once more: he was sitting in the pub, *alone*, while his childhood sweetheart was spending the night with a conceited foreigner she'd known for less than a month. *He* had to apologise for catching a glimpse of Lana's voluptuous, naked body, while Elias had gone skinny-dipping with her. He'd been told how Lana still valued their *school friendship*, while a cowardly Russian had bonded with her more closely in three weeks than he had in two decades. Elias and Lana would return to the City of Dreaming Spires and advance mankind through their academia, while *he* would hop to another temping job or pick apples on the next fruit farm, just so that some poor sod could get pissed on a little cider.

Henry drank until he puked and then headed home, the broken man he'd been the night before.

Frozen in Time

It was Wednesday, 28 August, and the harvest was over halfway complete. The year 2019 had brought the island nation some of the hottest summer days in a decade, and today the mercury climbed up to thirty-six degrees under a clear sky. The scorching sun had baked the grass to a crisp brown, while the arid and heavy air weighed down the industrious fruit pickers, who gradually felt lethargic. For most, the hot summer days of 2019 were a dream interval, but a few were starting to wish for rain, or better yet, a thunderstorm.

It was quarter past four in the afternoon. The apple pickers had already finished their shift for the day and had ventured out to enjoy the blessing of the sunny hours. The hop pickers were still in the final fifteen minutes of their stint but were slowly starting to finish up. Inside an open shed, a group of five had been processing piles of hop bines reaped from the field and brought in by a carrier tractor. They had to be unloaded from the cart and hung onto a conveyer belt, then the hops had to be separated from their bines. Gradually, it was getting to that time of the afternoon when the machines would be switched off and the foreman would call it a day.

This foreman, Henry, turned around and peeked behind the shed. Very good—neither Bob nor Samuel was anywhere to be seen. It was the perfect time to open his first can of lager and start sipping away, for the heat of the last few days had made him unusually irritable and fractious. The beer tasted fresh and ever so crisp. Henry was dressed in a white vest, brown jeans and his signature leather shoes. These made him feel special, if not superior, for he was not just a worker like everyone else. At least unofficially, he was their foreman, and everyone would defer to his senior knowledge on the farm. And today was the time to teach one of them a little lesson about gratitude and punctuality.

Stealing a glance across at Charlie, Henry immediately noticed he was trying to avoid his line of sight—maybe he could sense Henry's intentions already. He started to look very uncomfortable now, looking down at the ground and clumsily fidgeting with his hands while he discreetly prepared to make a move. *What a cheek!*

'Hey, Charlie!' Henry shouted from behind. The middle-aged man halted for a moment and then kept on again.

'Hey, Charlie! Are you deaf, mate?' the foreman shouted again. 'Charlie, I'm talking to you. Don't just walk away from me like this!'

Charlie probably realised how futile it was, carrying on this pretence, and he stopped to feign a friendly smile as he faced his creditor. 'Ah! Hi, Henry. Nice to see you again. How are you?'

'Yeah, come on, knock it off. We've been seeing each other all afternoon,' Henry replied. He walked to a distance of four inches from him and delivered his lecture. 'You promised to pay me back on payday. You got your pay at lunchtime, and since then, all I've seen is you buying more ciggies for yourself. Do you have any intention of keeping your promises, mate? Today is the second time.'

The two workers ambled towards the apple orchard while Charlie made one excuse after the other. All of them fell on deaf ears this time, for Henry needed money himself now.

'Henry, please, I ain't got the money,' Charlie whined. 'I've got real debt to pay to Fred and Gav. If I don't pay *them*, they'll beat me and…'

'Why do you even keep buying from those thugs after the way they treated you? And what do you mean, you've got *real* debt to pay?' Henry asked. He frowned in indignation. 'Are you saying your debt to me is *not* real because I don't swipe you across the head from time to time? Is that it?'

'I didn't say that!' the debtor protested. The palms of his hands were glistening in the sun as he sweated out his predicament.

'I'm too kind to you, aren't I?' Henry lamented. 'And now you're taking advantage of my kindness. You're exploiting my generosity. It's not on, mate.'

'I am not exploding your generosity. I know you're a very generous friend. Please!'

'I didn't say "explode". I said "exploit". You're exploiting my kindness.'

By now, the pair had reached the lanes of Fuji apples, where Henry spotted Sylvia relaxing underneath the branches of an apple tree, seeking shade from the scorching sun. She was leaning against the trunk, cross-legged and reading some kind of illustrated adventure novel. As soon as Charlie and Henry came into view, her head winced back, and she dropped her jaw at Henry's pugnacious, near-violent demeanour. Immediately she lowered her gaze to her book, pretending she hadn't seen a thing.

Henry instinctively swung his arm around Charlie's shoulders and began to laugh. *Let's pretend it's all friendly banter here.* Charlie seemed aware of Henry's pretence and went along with it; he obviously knew he had to appease the loan shark.

But only twenty metres later, Henry felt his own smile fading away as he confronted his debtor once again, whispering, 'So what have you got to say to that, then?'

'Henry, why are you so angry today? Please, two more weeks!'

'You did agree to pay today, didn't you, mate?' Henry challenged him.

Charlie nodded and dropped his gaze towards the soil as the two continued wandering along the orchard. Henry thought back to the last time his co-worker had been beaten by violent thugs. He had tried to save the drug addict in the nick of time, and he knew if he took Charlie's money now, he might find himself in the same predicament all too soon. Still, he'd made a promise to settle his debts today, and he hadn't.

Retracting his arm from Charlie's shoulders, Henry noticed how his co-worker cast a pensive stare into the orchard. His mind was clearly elsewhere now, Henry could sense. Charlie cautiously edged away from him as he continued to stare into the distance. Then he suddenly clenched his fists, and the very next moment, he began to compete with the former cross-country sprinter and just ran and ran through the orchard.

It wasn't long before he must have regretted his impulse, for no sooner had he sprinted the first thirty metres than he tripped on his own sandal and fell face down on the soft soil, his wallet dropping from his jeans. With a quivering chin, he rose to his knees as Henry stood beside him, staring him down. He crouched by Charlie's side and reached for his tattered wallet, then searched for notes. For a few seconds, Henry caught his own hand shaking when he grabbed the money. Something really didn't feel right. Tightly scrunching up his face, he took five ten-pound notes from his wallet and was about to stash them in his pocket. Then he dithered for a few moments as he glared down into Charlie's pleading, vulnerable eyes, almost as though he felt a tug or a pinch on his arm.

The foreman slid three banknotes into his own pocket and then held back, brandishing the remaining notes in front of his debtor's nose. 'All right, mate. Because it's you, I won't take everything today. You can keep these ones, but next time, you have to keep your promises. Is that understood?'

'Yes, Henry. Thank you!' Charlie gasped, taking the notes out of Henry's limp hand.

Henry was aware there were two tormentors out there who meant Charlie genuine harm. But if he had known the precise consequences of his own actions, who knew whether he would still have taken the money that day? At least he'd let him off with a sizeable fraction of his debt, he consoled himself.

Charlie deposited the wallet back in his tattered pocket, rose from the orchard ground and wandered off toward his caravan.

The foreman watched him disappear and then sullenly regarded the thirty pounds he'd bagged from the drug addict. For some reason, those notes didn't fill him with the happiness he'd imagined. Neither was he the Robin Hood he'd always aspired to be, helping the poor in times of need, nor did he have enough money to buy himself a new phone. Both glasses were half-empty. In fact, he'd acted in the same way Gavin and Frederick had some days ago. This relentless heat really had made him nasty this afternoon. What would Lana say if she found out about this episode from today? Where was Lana, anyway? Henry wondered. Where had she suddenly disappeared to on this boiling afternoon?

A few miles from Gullet Quarry, at the foot of the Malvern Hills, there lies a little animal park in which herds of deer graze pleasantly on the rural pastures while holidaymakers camp in the tranquillity of the surrounding fields. A little further afield stands a Gothic Revival castle from the early nineteenth century, which towers over a quiet lake, in whose blue waters its imposing architecture is reflected like a painting. Near one of the most secluded parts of the mere grazed two horses, Hoss and Peter, who were waiting on their riders to return from a swim.

Today was the second time Lana had taken Elias for a wild splash, but seeing Lana undress so nonchalantly brought the same fluttery sensation to his stomach again. *How can someone always look so relaxed, as though everything will always work out in the end?* Elias glanced at the horses, as though they might be observing him, swiftly looked all around himself, and disrobed. He let Lana usher him toward the lake, where he dropped into the clear water and basked in its mild temperature.

Apart from a single middle-aged woman on the other side of the water, the pair had the entire mere to themselves. This time, there was no cold shock because the warmth on the surface seemed to run deep into the basin. Lana tenderly grabbed Elias by the hand and tugged him down to the scenic view underwater while white sunbeams shone through the lake's surface and diverged to illuminate the space below. There were more fish here than in the quarry lake. Some freshwater roach were gliding towards the pondweed on the lakebed, probably in search of food. Lana pointed at one of them and playfully motioned Elias to come with her and follow the little fish.

As they floated through the lake, the still water massaged their naked bodies, and they dipped further down towards the bottom. The roach swam into the pondweed, where it disappeared among its leaves. The human followers glided their feet over the underwater plant and rested their soles on the sandy lakebed. The texture felt soft and refined. Floating even nearer to the lakebed, Lana reached for a rusty tin box that was meshed in between the pondweed. She unearthed it from its leaves and playfully brandished the metal at Elias. It was an old reddish-golden case that displayed a faded picture of a young Queen Elizabeth II. Underneath it was inscribed a phrase, mostly washed off by the water but still showing the year 1953. It was just visible underwater. Maybe someone had been celebrating the Queen's coronation seventy years ago and then dropped this object into the lake. Lana let the rusty tin gravitate back to the bottom, and the pair rose to the surface to gasp for air.

'That was amazing! How long can you hold your breath for?' Elias asked.

'My record is two and a half minutes,' Lana replied.

Inadvertently, the pair had swum a little closer to the castle, where an elderly tourist caught a glimpse of the naked girl and her male companion from the rooftop. Immediately he winced back his grimacing head, as if he was questioning his own sanity—as though he had somehow spotted a mermaid. And now this shameless, mischievous fairy-tale creature was waving at him as if to say, 'No, I am not a mermaid after all. I am human, like you!' The elderly man lifted his arm and waved limply. It looked as though his hand were somehow detached from his body, but when he eventually seemed to realise what his hand was doing, he swiftly retracted it before he turned around, disappearing from the Gothic castle top.

Lana laughed winsomely and tugged Elias back down with her for another dive. With *her* stamina for holding her breath, she might be able to set a national record, Elias kept thinking. Hand in hand, they attempted to somersault underwater and then spontaneously went for a little race under the surface. Lana won that one. They rose back up, gulped down air, then locked together in an embrace and kissed. It was the most blissful day in Elias's life.

Lana turned her head towards the hills and pointed at a single dark cloud moving in from the east. It looked quite low and heavy, maybe even a little foreboding. In fact, before long, they might be caught in a heavy thunderstorm. At this, the pair climbed out of the water and got dressed again, preparing to make a move.

'I was thinking…' Lana said. 'You know how you told me your mum warned you to go into hiding for the rest of the summer—and that some Russians are trying to track you down in Oxford…'

Elias nodded, drying his hair with his tartan towel.

'I was just thinking,' Lana continued. 'What if that blonde man a few days ago—I mean the creepy one that was watching us by the quarry—what if that man was linked to this gang, and they already know you're here?'

'I thought the same thing, but then, why wouldn't he just grab me instead of watching us like that?'

'I don't know. It's just a thought… maybe he was waiting for an opportune moment, and maybe he wasn't even the only person out there…'

Elias pondered this. 'When I first came to the UK, I'd never have thought Russian officials would hurt people on British soil, but after the Skripal poisoning last year, it wouldn't surprise me anymore. I still have this feeling—whoever's out to get me has a personal grudge or special interest in my capture.'

Lana slipped on her jeans and rolled up the legs, shaking off the grass inside. 'Just be careful now, Elias, okay?' she advised.

Soon the pair were on horseback again and riding north towards the farm, winding past Gullet Quarry and onto the old Shire Ditch. Nearly all the Malvern Hills had to be traversed now, and Elias doubted they'd manage to get back before the storm broke. Maybe they should have taken the less scenic, more direct route after all. Gradually, the air was growing heavier and felt a lot more humid, so the pair gently spurred on their horses. A flock of over two dozen birds suddenly chirped in the sky, sailing southward, away from the rain clouds. The whole area started to feel more deserted now, more solitary.

'If only we could fly on these horses,' Lana suddenly muttered.

'Fly? My brother and I always talked about that— would you rather have the power of flight or invisibility?'

'What was your answer?'

'Flight, of course. I wanted to be like the Northern Lights, crossing international borders just like that. My brother always wanted to be invisible, especially during his later years.'

'And these days, would you still choose the power of flight?'

'These days… I don't know. If I could have any superpower, maybe I would choose the gift of healing.'

'As in the field you're studying for your research thesis?'

'Yes—If only I could afford to progress to a doctorate… But if you could have one magical power, which one would *you* choose?'

Lana was pensive for a moment. 'We have a superpower already,' she said. 'We have the unique gift of shaping the fabric of reality around us with our thoughts. That is magical.'

'And you'd never wish for anything else at all?'

'Hmm… The power of healing is a good one. Maybe a time machine would also be interesting.'

'You'd go forward to the future and see what becomes of you?'

'No. The future has not been written yet. I'd go back in time and observe *history*. I'd observe the work of my ancestors and see how the past and the present have tied together. I'd go back to the turn of the nineteenth century and visit my orphaned great-grandmother—or the lady that gave this necklace to her. Or I'd go back to that summer night of 1853—the one that Sam talked about—and see if there really were any ghosts in that Maryland house.'

Just at that moment, a very faint drizzle began to fall; the heavier clouds had moved in to cover the entire sky. The pair were still riding on the southern side of the hills when a few strokes of lightning suddenly flashed up in the far distance. They illuminated the area so brightly that the horses nearly stopped in their tracks, hypnotised by the flashes. A few rabbits scurried about aimlessly, looking for some shelter from the impending storm. Two of them hopped into a little burrow and squeezed themselves into the dry tunnel; a third one hastened into the shrubs and lingered between the branches. The animal watched the two humans with curious eyes as they drew past on their mighty horses. Above, the clouds were moving ever faster now.

Elias listened out for the rumbling sounds of a storm, but so far, it was strangely quiet, though the sky was growing darker by the minute.

'This is gonna be quite a big one!' Lana commented, gazing up at the low, heavy clouds. 'It's quite rare, actually, for a thunderstorm like this around here.' She stroked her abolitionist pendant and tugged it underneath her white T-shirt, protecting it from the unpredictable weather.

One of the strangest qualities of this storm was the temperature on the ground, for even though rain clouds had completely darkened the summer sky, the humid air remained unusually balmy and kept the grass on the soil surprisingly warm. Elias sensed it was going to be a rare hot storm.

A little later, the pair started to climb down the western slope and emerged alongside the hills, riding north, parallel to the spine.

'That's not quite where we came from, is it?' Elias observed.

'No. It's a slightly different route,' Lana replied. 'Do you remember that abandoned chapel you asked me about on your very first day?'

'Yes.' Elias nodded, beaming with a twinge of excitement.

'We might just about reach it before it's raining like a monsoon, and take shelter around there. We might just be in time, actually.'

Elias was intrigued. He'd never been to an abandoned chapel before and had wanted to visit that mysterious place ever since he'd laid eyes on it; now fortuitous circumstances were forcing the pair directly towards that deserted Victorian building.

Gradually, the distant lightning increased and moved closer to the two horse riders. Every minute or so, a new flash illuminated the towering green hills and the pastures at the foot of them. Looking towards the horizon, Elias was now able to make out a spired building of neglected, brittle masonry, about two hundred metres afield. That had to be the place they were heading for, he concluded. From this distance, it looked even older than it did on Dawson Road.

Soon, the drizzle became heavier and gradually turned into a light rain. Worms hastily wiggled themselves out of the soil as the earth was flooded with moisture. Just when light rain was transforming into an outright shower, the horse riders arrived at the deserted chapel and dismounted. Drawing in the refreshing, humid country air, Elias gazed at this historic building at the foot of the hills. The chapel had been in a state of neglect for decades but, just like the entire area here, exuded a rustic charm as though it were frozen in time. When lightning struck and illuminated the pastures around it, there was something truly eerie about the place, and yet it seemed to radiate very benevolent, very welcoming energy.

Elias and Lana led the horses underneath a vaulted porch, where they sheltered them from the pending cloudburst. It was a relatively narrow place on one side of the chapel, but just broad enough to cover the two animals. The pair walked across to the main entrance while lightning continued to strike from the distance. They gave the arched wooden door a solid push, but it was firmly bolted and refused to give way to their efforts.

'I guess we could go back to the horses and wait for the storm to pass,' Elias suggested. 'How long do you reckon it'll last?'

'Come on, let's try around the back,' said Lana. 'Last time I came here, the back hatch was unlocked.'

Tugging Elias by the arm, she led him to a somewhat secluded, almost hidden door that was only half the height of an average adult. In fact, it gave the impression that it went down to a lower floor, maybe a secret cellar of some sort.

'You've been here before, then?' Elias asked.

'Last time I came here was, like, five years ago, and this door could be opened,' Lana replied, pulling the black iron bar from its lock. She pushed the little hatch, which produced an uncanny creak as though nobody had touched it in half a century. The opening revealed a short drop to a somewhat lower level, and the pair had to duck in order to hop into the little space below. Only a little space it was indeed, and Elias wondered what this tiny chamber could ever have been used for.

'Okay. Last time, this is where we went… I think… here…' Lana mumbled, removing the wooden flap on a hidden tunnel. She pointed toward a long, narrow shaft and climbed into it.

Elias went down onto his knees and began to crawl behind her. Another flap had to be removed at the other end of this dark passageway, and the pair finally emerged by the altar of this frozen-in-time, forlorn chapel.
It was eerily beautiful. And yet the atmosphere inside was a kind one, very inviting. It was like a portal into the past, a doorway to a time long gone by. The place seemingly lay in ruins and yet radiated a mystical beauty from all its interior features. The stone floor was black from the grime that had accumulated over decades. The pews were broken and in a state of ruin. Some of them looked burned, even. Cobwebs had attached themselves to all corners of the nave, while pieces of debris and dead foliage lay scattered on the broken floor. Old pillar-candle stubs stood alongside disused lanterns and were towered over by angel statues that watched over a place long abandoned by man. The features on the stone statues had faded over the course of centuries. Their faces had grown pale and less marked; some of the wings were chipped. Out of the three angel bases near the altar, only two of them still supported those divine messengers. The third statue had gone missing,

leaving its base unoccupied and covered in dust. Time had stood still in this hall of worship as decades of change, war and peace had swept over the globe and taken mankind into 2019.

Lightning continued to strike outside as Lana and Elias beheld this rare building. One of the most peculiar features of the interior was its windows, Elias noticed, for although it was stormy and relatively dark outside, faint, ethereal light beams shone into the chapel like diverging rays of white. They almost made the place look like a time portal at the gates of heaven.

'What an incredible place,' Elias uttered.

His friend smiled. 'Hello!' she shouted a few times, and she blissfully tittered at her reverberating echo.

Elias followed with his own reverberating 'Hello!' only to recoil in a jump when an old rat screeched past his feet, heading for the rear tunnel.

Lana chuckled again and joyfully motioned her friend to follow. 'Come on. Let's take a look around,' she said.

By now, the thudding of pelting rain on the roof had grown louder and seemed to be reaching its peak. Thunder roared from the distance while lightning continued to illuminate the nave every minute or so. Each time lightning struck to brighten the chamber, Elias noticed more and more of those fine, hidden details that otherwise remained obscured in the dark. It was exceedingly beautiful.

Hand in hand, the pair walked along the central aisle as they carefully trod over crisp foliage and loose pieces of wood. Lana noticed some of them looked rather sharp, so she had to take a few wider strides to avoid stepping into them with her naked soles. This was her second visit to this mysterious chapel—or rather, her second trespass. Five years ago, she had been here with a friend from school, but he had been so freaked out by everything inside that he'd urged her to leave at once. Today she had more time to explore this deserted place.

All the pews were empty and bare, covered in dust, but they reached a small oak cabinet on the side of the nave whose door stood slightly ajar. Wiping some heavy dust off the wood, Lana gingerly cracked open the fragile cupboard; of course, no contents were left within, except for one torn-up piece of paper with faded musical notes at the bottom. Maybe this closet had once stored hymn books, documents or Bibles. Lana stroked the old wood on the inside and was about to retract her hand just when she realised there was yet another layer to this cupboard: behind a second sheath of broken timber were concealed the antiques of decades gone by.

'Wow, look, Elias!' she exclaimed. 'Someone forgot to throw these away. Let's see what we can find.'

By now, the few light rays that shone into the chapel were fast fading as the world outside became engulfed in a cloudburst, the raindrops pelting against the roof like little bullets. Yet the atmosphere inside remained tranquil, very peaceful.

Rummaging in the dust, Lana delightfully smiled at each item behind the cabinet. All of them looked as though they'd been forgotten by their owner. 'What have we got here?' she mused. She had found a leather wallet and a hairbrush, both of which harked back to the early twentieth century, an old Bible with half the pages missing and even a little diary, in which most of the ink had faded away. 'That's a shame,' Lana muttered. 'There is, like… almost nothing left to read.'

'Let's see if we can find a date somewhere,' Elias suggested, reaching for the little book.

'No way!' exclaimed Lana. 'There's even a nineteenth-century cigar box!' Opening the tin straight away, she found a box of matches and even an old candlesnuffer inside. 'Do you think these matches will still work?'

'As long as they haven't touched any water. Shall we try to light some candles?' Elias replied, pointing at the century-old brass holders. 'It's getting pitch-black in here.'

Lana removed one of the matches and playfully struck it against the box. A tiny flame flared into life, a fire that had probably been waiting to be lit for over a century, and just as soon as it came alive, it died down again. 'Let's also light some of the lanterns,' she suggested, 'so we might even be able to read the diary.' She noticed the wicks on the candles had been lit before, and the wax had greatly diminished, but maybe they could still manage to light a few short-lived flames. She handed Elias the small artefacts she'd found, but she kept hold of the matches, then the pair ambled across to the tall lantern stands. On her tiptoes, Lana reached for one of the old wicks.

'Do you need any help up there?' Elias asked.

'I am fine. I'll manage. Thank you, though!'

'Your feet are getting grimy on those flagstones,' Elias commented.

Lana glanced down at her soles and then, with a shrug, back at the fire she was cautiously lighting.

Between the two of them, they lit five candles and two lanterns. The third lantern had too small a wick, not enough wax, and the pair gave up. They lowered themselves onto the stone floor and leaned against the chapel wall. As Elias took off his rain-soaked shoes, Lana crossed her outstretched legs and began to examine the little diary. By now, it was pitch-black outside so that the pair were relying solely on the glimmering flames for their light.

Well, it was not quite pitch-black, for lightning continued to brighten the chamber every minute or so. And whenever the chamber was illuminated by a strike, Lana sighted more and more of those fine details that otherwise remained obscure. But there was something else to those moments that Lana simply could not put her finger on. Something otherworldly that kept reoccurring and yet was indescribable. 'Did you just see that as well?' she asked.

Elias nodded, his mouth half-open.

Not only did there appear refined details with every flash of light, but every time lightning illuminated the nave, the pair spotted additional features around the place, which, as soon as the flash passed, simply weren't there. Those seconds were truly eerie but at the same time stunningly beautiful, and always accompanied by a benign sense that there was nothing to fear here. Neither Lana nor Elias could make out any of these additional details, for as soon as they focused, the flash ceased. It almost felt as though the light were opening a portal into another dimension, maybe a past time. In the end, the two friends decided to put it down to an optical illusion, for their eyes were probably playing tricks on their brains in those exceedingly bright moments.

Lana browsed through the dusty diary and eventually lamented its condition again. 'I don't think we'll be able to find anything here… Virtually all the ink is gone.' The only thing they could decipher was the name of the author, Winston Adam, but everything else had vanished. Lana was about to close the little book just when she noticed a small brown envelope that was stuck to the very last page.

'Wait! There's a letter here,' Elias exclaimed. 'Let's see

if we can read this one.'

Carefully, Lana opened the torn envelope and drew out the brown paper inside. 'Yay, we can still see the words,' she exclaimed. The ink had faded, but the writing was just legible.

'How old do you think this letter is?' Elias asked.

'A hundred years at least, maybe older, going by the texture of this paper.'

'Hey, look, there's a date at the top,' Elias observed.

'The twenty-fourth of December 1914. I was right. It's almost one hundred and five years old.'

'Let's read the letter,' Elias nudged.

Lana focused on the faded writing and began to read it aloud:

24 December 1914

Dear Dad,

A little miracle took place in the trenches near Ypres today. You will never believe what happed to our division this night. I think it was about half past ten or so. I was on watch duty, and suddenly the trenches opposite filled with fir trees. Then somebody lit candles on them, and the Germans started carolling 'Silent Night'.

At those words, Lana stopped and solemnly looked up from the paper. 'No way! This man's describing the Christmas Truce!' she exclaimed.

'The what?'

'The Christmas Truce of 1914. German and British troops spontaneously fraternised on Christmas Eve and laid their arms aside. We covered all this in GCSE. Did you never hear about it in school?'

Her special friend appeared to search his memories but then shook his head, looking intrigued.

'It happened one hundred and five years ago,' Lana went on. 'They even gave each other little presents and souvenirs.' She focused back on the letter again:

We sang along, and there was a harmony between our sides. Then the Germans invited us over to their own trenches. There was a strange feeling that accompanied me. It is difficult to put this feeling into words, but it felt as though a spirit or two guided me to a man who introduced himself as Jens Altmann. There was something strange he told me. He said his great-grandfather was of Irish descent and migrated from Herefordshire around the time Great-Grandfather left from there. I know we never speak about my Irish great-grandfather, but can you tell me if his name was Seamus? Jens Altmann gave me a shiny candle extinguisher. He said it was a 'Kerzenlöscher' in German. I'm enclosing the object with the letter. Keep it as a souvenir!

'Oh my God! That must be the rusty candlesnuffer we found in the cabinet!' Lana concluded.

Elias shifted his gaze to the thin brass handle he was holding. 'One of my distant ancestors was also Irish, and my great-great-grandfather fought in World War One.'

'Do you know their names?'

Elias shook his head solemnly as Lana focused back on the paper and continued to read:

I so wish this bloody war was finally over, because nobody wants to fight it. Not me, not Jens, nobody! So why are millions dying for a few disillusioned leaders (wherever those leaders may be)? Because governments have an unlimited supply of warriors. If our world were a truly free place, if no government had the ability to force people into war against their will, there would never be a handful of leaders subjecting millions of humans to this bloodshed. We're in such a vicious circle! Once a single country conscripts their people, all others follow. If one citizen has a gun, all need one, until there comes a ban on arms.

I may never see you again, and I pray that you will receive this letter safely and that it will be kept in our family's legacy.

Stay safe.

James Adam.

'James Adam—What an old-fashioned way to sign a letter to your father,' Elias remarked.

Lana pointed at the name on the diary cover, Winston Adam. 'This must have been his dad. Maybe he worked as a vicar in this chapel and used this letter as a peace sermon.' Folding the piece of paper back into the envelope, she shook her head gravely. 'I never thought I'd find a real object from the Christmas Truce one day. Have they genuinely never covered this event in Russian schools?'

Elias shook his head and admitted he'd never heard of it, although the entire event in the letter rang true with him. In fact, as Lana had read the letter, he'd visualised the entire scene so vividly that for a moment he'd felt as though he'd been there himself, in those narrow trenches, one hundred and five years ago. Even the object he was holding right now, the little candlesnuffer, seemed to trigger a strange déjà vu. Indeed, ever since he'd arrived on Windmill Farm, a series of otherworldly flashbacks had come to pass—eerie recollections that he simply couldn't place anywhere.

This was the second time in one summer that Lana had led him into a historic building and produced relics of an apparent past life. Elias had never believed in the supernatural, the scientifically unexplainable or anything suggesting destiny, but now he almost felt guilty for toying with the idea that perhaps certain intersections in a person's life may be ordained by fate—thoughts that a scientist should not entertain. He wondered whether he would draw the same kind of past-life energy from Lana's abolition medallion as he felt from the candlesnuffer, so he asked to see it again. He held the candlesnuffer in his hand along with the anti-slavery pendant.

'There was a time black people could be turned into white men's possessions,' he said. 'Humans were held responsible for things outside their own control—like a lottery of birth. But what if one government can turn *their own* people into possessions and send them to their deaths? Like they did to the people in this letter. Or my brother. Or the people in North Korea and Eritrea. *They* did not choose to be born in Eritrea, Lana. The lottery of birth still exists today. Like you said, this fight is not won yet.'

Elias returned the medallion to Lana, and he listened out for the pelting rain that still came down on the roof like water bullets. One of the candles flickered and then ceased forever, the wax being depleted, and the wick burned out. Still, the pair had four left, and two rather tall lanterns.

Inside the hopper hut, the harvest workers were gathered around the communal table and glued to the television, waiting for the storm to pass. There were wine bottles and beer cans lying everywhere, and Gregorios was switching from one channel to the next until they found a Bollywood movie on the BBC.

'This one. Leave it on!' Nora said. 'It's a good film.'

A spontaneous vote was taken, and the Bollywood movie it was. Gregorios tucked into a bag of crisps and sipped at his beer, looking forward to a cosy evening in the storm.

Another coffee table stood slightly away from the 1990s cathode-ray TV set and quite close to the main entrance. Around this piece of furniture sat Ian and Sylvia, who were playing a round of draw poker with miniature coins. Next to them, the door suddenly opened, and a tired Henry stepped out of his bedroom, holding a pack of European cigarettes in his hand.

'How long's this storm been going on for?' he asked.

'About an hour or so. Did you have a nice nap, mate?' Ian replied.

'Wow, I slept for more than two hours,' Henry said, staring at the relentless rain outside. Slowly, he felt the circulation in his body waking up after a long rest. 'Guys, who's on cat-feeding duty today?' he asked.

Nobody answered him.

'No one? Really?' He walked across to the roster, only

to find his own name against today's date, and he recalled Elias had asked to swap with him that afternoon.

'Well, who is it, then?' Ian asked his old schoolmate.

'It's me. I completely forgot about it. Damn! Barcelona must be starving.'

Henry put on a pair of wellington boots and a cagoule raincoat, then ventured out of the cottage to light a cigarette on the field. He'd only walked about fifteen metres when the blast of the storm overwhelmed him, battering his face with liquid pellets, and he swiftly halted. 'What on earth is this?' he muttered to himself. 'This isn't real!' *I'm gonna wait at least half an hour!* he decided, lumbering back into the communal area with his boots muddy from the storm. He joined the others in front of the Bollywood movie but noticed some were avoiding his gaze, while others seemed to tense up just a little.

It had now gone past seven in the evening, and the thudding on the chapel roof was slowly diminishing. Elias and Lana were still leaning against the wall and waiting for the rain to pass by. A small part of Elias wished the thunderstorm would go on forever, so the pair could linger in this peaceful space for eternity. Distant lightning continued to illuminate the interior, albeit less frequently now. But whenever it did, it was the same: hidden, invisible features appeared for a brief instant, but as soon as the flash receded, so did these additional facets. Those moments reminded Elias of Lana's talk on light and miracles on the night he'd come to this area.

'Remember a month ago, when we were viewing the Milky Way from the farm, and you told me about quantum tunnelling?' he asked.

'Yeah, of course,' Lana replied softly.

'And you said if someone prays with all their heart and all their willpower, the universe might just blink to allow a spontaneous miracle to occur, like allowing a paralysed person to move one more time.'

'Yes…'

'Do you genuinely believe that as a scientist? Can science really prove that there is another *dimension* to all we can see?'

Lana wiped some dust from her trousers and shrugged her shoulders. 'Scientists have never claimed to be able to expound all we can see, and definitely not quantum scientists. There is something about the nature of consciousness that has remained a mystery since time immemorial. Normally we rely on proof. But certain things we can't prove yet, and maybe we just have to go by intuition for now until we know more.'

'I still don't believe in the supernatural or in miracles,' Elias said. 'And nor can I make myself believe in a white-bearded god who sits on a cloud and watches over the chaos that engulfs whole countries every day—a god who allows governments to maim and kill ordinary people as if they owned them. I would love to believe in miracles, but they contradict the reality we live in. It's just too chaotic here, full stop.'

Lana nodded. 'But then, the other day, when it looked certain that Hoss was going to drown in that quarry, I said a quick prayer, and the very next second, Mr Wright restarted the van and saved him.'

'Yeah, but that could just have been a coincidence.

You do remember he said he lifted the clutch a little just before he started the engine, right?'

'I do remember that; yes, it could all have been a very lucky coincidence. But one way or another, I just don't think we're completely on our own, Elias.'

By now, the shower had diminished into a light drizzle, and lightning was only striking every three minutes or so. Very soon, it would be time to set off again, so the pair rose to their feet, preparing to make a move. Elias felt the inside of his grey plimsolls—they were almost completely dry now—and he slipped on his right shoe, tying his lace in a double bow.

At that moment, Lana suddenly put her hand on his shoulder and said, 'I will say one prayer with you here, Elias. After all, we might never return to this place.'

'Who are you praying to?'

'God, the universe, the higher power, whoever might spare a second to listen.'

At this, the pair lowered themselves onto the flagstones again as Lana reached out to Elias and held on to his hand. They closed their eyes, and Elias listened to Lana intone.

'God, universe, thank you for bringing me and my friend Elias to this beautiful place today. Please bless this kind soul and show him some order or give him a sign of encouragement so he can let go and move on. Thank you for leading us to this letter from the Christmas Truce. Bless everyone. Amen.'

Elias mumbled an amen. Then the pair hugged and rose to make a move.

'We'd better set off now, before the storm starts again,' Lana said. She patted Elias on the shoulder and started to lead the way towards the narrow passageway. While she carefully trod past dusty debris and loose pieces of wood, Elias bent down to tie a double knot on his other plimsoll, and then followed his friend a few seconds later. Lana had just strolled past the two angel stands and the one empty base… then a single strike of lightning suddenly illuminated the chapel so brightly that it enthralled Elias's entire being almost beyond his physical vessel. For a brief instant, he had caught a glimpse of another world. There were the two crumbling angel statues, but for a single second, there had stood a third, ethereal figure, towering over the empty base, a being of light and indescribable beauty. Elias had blinked his eye, and just as the flash had passed, the being of light had disappeared again, leaving Elias with his jaw dropped. Staring into the distance, he tried to make sense of the last few seconds.

'Are you all right? What's the matter?' Lana asked.

'There was something beside you,' Elias replied. 'For just one second. It was like a figure of light!'

Lana shifted her view towards the angel statues. 'There are two decaying angels and one empty base. Did you see something else?'

'There was definitely a third being. It looked a bit like… very refined light, slightly blue… it was standing on the empty plinth, and it was *nydelig*.'

'*Nydelig?*'

'Sorry—that was Norwegian. I mean, just gorgeous.'

Lana concentrated her gaze on the vacant angel plinth and then shrugged her shoulders. She did not look incredulous, though she'd obviously completely missed the bright, otherworldly moment just then.

'Well, there you go, Elias. Maybe there *is* something out there after all,' she uttered. Along with Elias, she stood quietly and pensively regarded the statues for a few more moments. Then the old rat screeched past again, shooting past Elias's feet before it scurried into one of the dilapidated pews.

'I think we should head out now,' Lana said again, gesturing for Elias to make a move.

The two laid the antique items back in the oak cabinet and headed for the underfloor tunnel, clambered out of the cellar and back onto the green pasture. Underneath the vaulted porch, the horses looked virtually dry, and they immediately neighed at the sight of their owners. Elias mounted his steed. Then Lana turned her head towards the flickering light inside and remarked, 'Someone had better put those candles out, in case something bad happens.'

Elias offered to go inside one more time, but Lana took on the task herself. She climbed back through the tunnel, leaving her friend to watch as, little by little, the light inside the chapel dwindled and then disappeared for good. She emerged from the back again, gave her horse a stroke, and the pair set off for Windmill Farm.

As they progressed along, it was only a very light drizzle that accompanied the horse riders on their route home, although the evening sky was still fully obscured by rain clouds, while a fresh, grassy smell permeated the humid air of the countryside. To the right of the pair towered the green Malvern Hills; to the left, fields of ryegrass and the occasional fruit orchard. A few rabbits emerged from their burrows and took a few cautious steps towards the stallion and the colt. When their curious eyes were illuminated by distant lightning, they scurried off into wild shrubs or back down their warren.

What could it possibly have been that Elias had sighted that evening? It was a question he kept pondering. Whether it was a divine angel, a deceased relative or just an optical illusion created by effulgent light, a little hope had been enkindled in him that day, as though an old void had been filled with a little ball of light.

Of course, Elias did not know he'd stumbled across a letter that afternoon that he himself had inspired the author to pen one hundred and five years ago, though he was still dwelling on his own vivid imagination of those faintly lit trenches in 1914.

Lana fumbled in her right pocket as though something was irritating her, and then she produced a thin brass handle with a bell-like piece at the tip. 'Oh dear, I forgot to put this one back,' she said, looking at the old candlesnuffer from the Christmas Truce.

'Is that what you used to extinguish the last candles?' Elias asked.

Lana nodded and shrugged her shoulders. 'Oh well, I guess nobody would mind if we kept it as a souvenir.' She slid the artefact back into her pocket. 'It's quite a beautiful thing, actually—I'm almost glad I took it.'

The drizzle had almost ceased completely, although lightning continued to strike and illuminate the deserted route back to the farm. Illuminated also were the eyes of red foxes that lurked inside wild shrubs, probably waiting for the occasional stray rabbit or mole. They fixed their gazes on the two mighty horses and held back inside the bushes, watching the humans as they rode past on this solitary route.

Gradually, Windmill Farm came into view. The pair were less than two hundred metres from the premises when Lana suddenly covered her mouth with her hand, her face dropping in shock. Elias looked towards the farm in the distance and then saw it too: smoke was rising from the centre like an evil-spirited predator. The old windmill had been set on fire! Her face almost turning pale with worry, Lana gently spurred on her stallion. She stretched out her hand to Peter's bridle and nudged Elias's horse forward.

'Lana, Sam and Dorothy aren't on-site this evening. Nobody will be hurt in there.' Elias sought to reassure her, but Lana's unflinching gaze remained firmly fixed on the windmill as the suffocating smell of smoke slowly filled the air and grew ever more pungent. Could it be that lightning had struck the windmill? Elias wondered.

When the pair reached the farm, they headed straight for the mill and climbed off their horses. Lana beheld the fire that was consuming the lower rear portion of this century-old construction and slowly spreading upwards. Her head was racing with so many different scenarios. Outside, Nora and Ian were standing by the building and aiming their fire extinguishers at the blaze. The viscous foam quenched the flames like ocean waves reclaiming land, but very soon, the fire reignited from the inside, and the orange flames began to spread once more—flames that would soon sweep around the entire building like an inferno.

All the harvesters were standing around the mill, and Sylvia assured Lana that the fire service had been called and would arrive in less than fifteen minutes.

'Do we know what happened in there? Did lightning strike it or something?' Lana asked.

'We think it was Henry,' Sylvia replied.

'What? Oh my God! Are you saying Henry's *in* there?'

Ian rushed to Lana's side. 'Henry was on cat-feeding duty,' he reminded her. 'He was holding cigarettes when he walked to the mill. We think he may have lit one; then lightning must have triggered his epilepsy inside.'

'Oh, yes, of course. Henry has seizures from flashing lights,' Lana remembered. 'You think he then lost control of himself somehow?

'Maybe… yes… then locked himself inside and dropped the ciggy somewhere.'

'Poor guy!'

'But the cat's definitely run outside. We saw her,' Ian assured her.

Lana took in the havoc of the fire and sighed. It would probably only be a matter of ten or fifteen minutes before the entire building was engulfed in flames. And with Henry inside it. That was something she would *not* allow to happen. 'Elias, come with me, please. I think I know what to do,' she said, motioning him to follow.

As she led the way towards the cat flap, Ian accompanied the pair towards the rear, all coughing from the fine soot particles that twirled around the building. The right-hand side around the back door was fully ablaze and spitting sparks of burning debris onto the soil. Cautiously stepping around those embers, Lana covered her mouth with both hands as she scrambled to reach the entrance. It got hotter the closer they stood to the cat flap, the air full of soot particles and smoke. She noticed everyone's breathing becoming heavier and more strained.

Wiping the sweat from her forehead, Lana peeked through the cat flap. Smoke had taken possession of the inside, and the wall opposite was completely engulfed in fire. She tried to turn her head to the left and catch a glimpse of the narrow corridor, but her view from this small opening was blocked. She stepped back from the cat flap and rose to her feet, her eyes stinging from the smoke.

The three started banging on the timber at the back of the mill with clenched fists, then a glowing spark of wood crossed Lana's sight and blew into her hair. Quickly, Elias reached for the burning piece and wrenched it away from her singed tress.

'Are you all right, Lana?' he asked.

'Thank you so much!' Lana panted. She quickly tied her hair in a bun and then turned to Ian, who observed an oil can at the far end of the wall. He bent down to grip the overfilled bucket by the handle and hefted it away from the flames, spilling a few oil drops on Lana's jeans as she offered to help.

She returned to the cat flap. 'Henry, are you in there? Can you hear us?' Lana kept on shouting while the three continued to pound on the timber. But there came no reply.

Ian screamed, 'Henry, can you say something, please, so we know you are still here? Do you have the keys?'

Lana put her ear to the entrance, but the only sound that came her way was the crackling of burning wood. A diabolical inferno must be spreading inside.

The three of them took a few steps back, and on the count of five, they sprinted to kick in the stubborn entrance, running past burning debris. But however hard they tried, the door remained firmly shut.

'Let's do it again!' Lana said, wiping more sweat from her sooty face.

The trio paced backwards once more, and this time, they jumped onto the door. But still, it remained stubbornly locked.

Lana turned her head towards the tiny window over the cat flap and took a moment to reflect. There were a couple of these glazed apertures around the spiral staircase, and maybe they could smash one of them to climb inside—but then… no, it would be too narrow a gap for anyone to squeeze through. The only other way into the hollow cavity was through the main gate.

Elias opened the small cat flap below to stick his head into the narrow passage and shouted, 'Henry, do you have the key with you?'

They did not know it, but Henry had kicked open the interior passage door as soon as the inferno had begun to spread, and he had long been sitting on the spiral staircase, covering his chest with his arms and swinging his torso to and fro. He was reeling from his seizure and confounded by the growing flames that had engulfed the ground floor and were now working their way up the myriad bookshelves. They were the only pieces of furniture inside this dark cavity, and now they crumpled like paper as they collapsed to the burning floorboards. Every time Henry scrambled to move, a sensation of near weightlessness overpowered him, his muscles still limp from the epileptic fit. Suddenly he became aware of repeated bangs against the back door and somebody shouting, 'Henry, do you have the key with you?' It sounded a bit like that refugee. Yes, that arrogant Russian boy from the Arctic. What was his name again? Elias! It was Elias.

'I am here! I am here!' he shouted out.

'I think I just heard something!' Elias said, wiping the smoke from his eyes.

'Is he there?' Ian asked. 'Did he respond?' Thumping on the door with his clamped hands, Ian shouted, 'Henry, where are you? Can you hear us? Are you all right? Do you have the key? Where is the key? Say something!'

His old schoolmate strained to recollect where he'd last left the key before he shifted his view towards the narrow passageway leading to the cat flap. It stood fully ablaze, and the key was probably somewhere in there, possibly melted or fully deformed by now. Slowly, Henry started to feel more lucid as the blurriness dwindled away. The haze in Henry's vision disappeared, and gradually he was able to think and recall more clearly. 'I… I… I don't have the key! I am sorry!' he shouted out. The haziness in his mind was now replaced with adrenaline. *My God!* The fact that he was sitting in the middle of an inferno that would soon engulf everything in the building resurfaced in his mind. And he screamed.

'Hold on! Hold on! We'll get you out, mate!' Ian shouted. The two men were flanking Lana on each side as the trio continued to bang against the door with their fists.

Suddenly Lana stopped. 'Let's get to the front door!

Come on!' she urged, gesturing for the men to follow her. 'It sounds like Henry's sitting somewhere closer to the main entrance.'

She led the short walk to the front, which felt like a brief respite from the suffocating flames, but no sooner had they arrived at the main door than the full extent of the inferno became apparent to them. It extended from the left-hand side of the door all the way to the rear entrance, and nearly all the oxygen around it was being consumed by the fire. Panting for air, the three started to bang on the fortified front door with their fists, then Ian began to kick it with his rubber boots.

'Henry, we are still here!' Lana shouted, coughing. 'Can you climb up the tower and jump out a window?' She waited for some kind of response, but none came. Instead, sparks of debris shot out of the building and blew onto the open field. The trio moved back from the front entrance, drew in a few breaths of somewhat cleaner air, then rammed their bodies against the front door, jumping on arrival. Again and again. Sooner or later, the door just had to give way. Or so they thought.

Henry kept his gaze focused on the front entrance, hoping it would be breached any second. Then followed a moment when he simply could no longer trust his eyes; panic seized him, and he screamed again.

'Henry, what's happening in there?' he heard Lana shout from outside. She was battering on the stubborn timber.

'What's happening, Henry? Talk to us!' Ian yelled into the mill.

'Lana! Oh my God! It is too hot in here!' Henry

wailed from the inferno. 'The stairs are burning! I can't get away from them!'

'Move away from the stairs! Crawl up them!' Lana shouted from below.

Kneeling, Henry curled his fingers around the railing while he strained to lift his body. He faced the upper floor and pushed himself against the banister, then he slipped and fell back a few steps. He clung back onto the balustrade and glanced down at the rising inferno below. Within a few seconds, he would be inside it himself.

'Henry, are you managing?' he heard Lana shout from outside.

His legs felt as limp as jelly, but he seemed to be able to move his arms and close his hands—just about. Clamping his fingers around the banister again, he scrambled up the spiral staircase, only metres away from the mounting flames, until he let himself drop onto the carpet of the upper floor. But the fire was still following him.

'I'm upstairs now!' he shouted.

'What the hell is taking those firemen so long?' Lana uttered to Ian. She rubbed away more soot from her cheeks.

'I don't know,' he replied. 'They said they'd be here in ten to fifteen minutes.'

Just then, a deafening crashing noise roared from within and hit the front entrance like a grenade. It was so loud, Lana sensed it must have been the spiral staircase. Maybe it had split into two with the lower part separating from the top and collapsing against the inner facade. And still, the front door had remained unbroken.

'That must have been the staircase!' Lana uttered. She

took a few steps back from the building and stole a glance at Elias, who was eying the sails of the windmill, toward which he raised his hand and pointed.

'What about the external staircase?' he said. 'Can we rescue Henry from the *top* floor?'

Lana moved her view towards the storage chamber and then turned to her old schoolmate. 'Ian, can you go into the hut with some others and bring out the sofa, please?'

'The sofa?'

'Yes. Get some others to go with you. Bring the sofa over.'

Ian seemed to understand straight away and nodded. 'Okay! Whatever you need, Lana!' Immediately, he dashed forth with three other harvest workers.

Lana granted herself a few seconds' respite. She turned to Elias with an empty, weightless sensation in her stomach. 'Elias, we have to climb up the external staircase. There is a chance it will catch fire while we're on it, so I don't want to make you come with me, but will you?'

His eyes blinking rapidly, Elias took a sudden gasp of air. Then, something seemed to stir up inside him. With a gleam in his wide-open eyes, he stretched out his hand, and Lana took it in her sooty fingers, then led the way towards the winding staircase outside. Within seconds, they'd climbed up the wooden steps and reached the storage chamber whose inside Lana had never caught a glimpse of, during all her years on the farm. 'Ready again?' she asked.

Elias nodded. Then the pair took a few steps back and rammed their fast-tiring bodies against the fortified door. They jumped on approach. Sometimes they kicked.

Sometimes they turned sideways. Whatever they did, the door remained stubbornly locked, just as it had been designed to. Hope started to dwindle.

Looking upwards, Lana suddenly became aware of a few embers that loosened themselves from one of the sails, blowing in their direction. They were relatively small pieces of debris but were glowing red-hot and twirling in the air. She turned her head back to the stubborn door just before she realised one of the pieces had landed on her jeans, which were partly oil-stained.

The next thing she knew, her body was gripped by the fiercest heat she'd ever experienced as her trousers burst into flames, and the fire burned through the fabric of her jeans down to the skin on her left thigh. She let out the loudest, most piercing screams she'd ever made in her life, screeching at the top of her lungs. Grabbing the banister, she dropped and scrambled to quench the heat on the top of the stairs. But the oil quickly spread onto the wood, and as soon as the flames went out, they reignited on her.

'Oh God! I can't do this! I can't do this!' she wailed, staring at the unrelenting fire on her burning leg.

Elias hastened towards her and quickly started hitting the flames with his palms until he could cup his hands over the fire and smother it. He thumped on her jeans a little more, probably making sure nothing would reignite, then warmly looked into her moist eyes.

'I am so sorry. Are you okay, Lana?' he asked.

'Thank you, Elias! Thank you!' Lana wailed. She panted for air and felt her voice quiver as the wave of pain persisted. She let out one more piercing scream, as though the flames were still on her, then her consciousness waned for a few seconds.

'Are you okay?' her friend asked again.

'Elias, show me your hands, please!' Lana asked.

'Why?'

'Please show me your hands. Quickly!' She reached

out to grab them, held them by her fingertips, and sighted the blisters that were forming on Elias's palms. The entire epidermis on both had turned red with first- and second-degree burns.

Only now did she look at her own legs and become aware of the hole in her jeans. It was relatively small, fortunately, maybe less than six square centimetres, but it was still smoking from within. Underneath, there was blistering black skin. The upper part of her left trouser leg had turned into a dark, sooty mess.

The pair could only grant themselves a few seconds' respite, for the very next moment, the bottom of the external staircase caught fire, the flames rapidly sweeping upwards. This time, there was nowhere to escape to, nowhere to hide. The storage chamber was still locked. It just seemed beyond belief.

Elias had never thought Lana's warning would actually prove to be well-founded. Things like this just didn't happen. But now it had. And it was virtually impossible to think under such pressure.

Lana rose to her feet while Elias was still taking in the scene in front of him. They rushed upwards again.

'Elias, do you see that small window right there?' Lana asked, pointing at a very narrow rectangular window about two and a half metres from the top of the stairs. It was on the same side of the building but slightly inset and somewhat difficult to make out in the thick smoke.

'Yes, I think I do.'

'We jump!' said Lana. 'We've got to jump!' She began to wail again from her pain.

At this, Elias felt his muscles going limp. He knew

this jump was one he could not make. The window was so far away, and the ledge only narrowly protruded from the wall. He only had one go, and the leap would require acrobatic precision. But behind him, the flames were now rising higher by the second, and another option, he could not think of.

'Elias!' Lana urged him. 'When you jump, stretch out your right leg first. Get a grip on the ledge with your foot. Brake. Then lean towards the wall. Can you do this?'

Elias nodded, then realised he was telling a lie. Lana would go first, so she'd grab onto him on the other side. She squeezed his arm tightly, and off she leapt. Elias's heart was racing. Lana landed so elegantly and with such a firm grip, but her left foot had missed the ledge. She wobbled and was about to tilt off. It was so nerve-racking to watch. Swiftly, Lana knelt down and projected herself forward onto the ledge until she braced herself to a halt on the window frame. Then she looked back at Elias and gestured for him to follow with a leap, as if to say, 'Now you! You can do it!'

Elias wished he'd had a dozen practice runs and could have afforded a few fails before the real thing—the feat just looked too frightening to perform.

'Jump now, Elias!' Lana shouted.

The heat behind him was virtually unbearable now, the flames almost licking at his legs; it would only be a matter of seconds before he was inside them. Hastily, Elias clambered up the banister and just leapt off, trying to recall Lana's instructions: *Land on your right foot. Grip the ledge. Brake. Lean towards the wall… My God!* There were just too many details at once. A moment of confusion followed in mid-air. And the next thing he knew, his right foot had landed on the sill, but his left one slipped, and so did his entire body, which was now being supported solely by his palms, pressing against the window ledge.

Immediately Lana gripped on to his arms, scrambling to pull him up. But the space around the windowsill was so narrow; it must have been virtually impossible for her to keep her own balance, lest she tumble down herself and drag Elias with her. Panting in the smoke, Elias scrambled to push himself up, but the burns on his palms exerted such pressure on his skin; he longed to let go and free himself. He looked into Lana's soft, glistening eyes, which radiated so much empathy for him. Then a commotion roared up from below.

'Let go, Elias! Let go now!' Lana uttered a few times. She retracted her arms and let him fall towards the debris-strewn ryegrass.

A painful impact was going to follow any moment now, then Elias felt a set of arms closing in on his thighs as he dropped to the ground with them. A tight circle of harvesters had formed below, and just as the young man was about to crash, they had trapped him in their protective arms.

Elias looked up at Lana, now left up there on her own. She did not speak a single word, but she nodded warmly, as if to say, 'Thank you so much, Elias! And wish me luck!' Then she rammed her naked elbow into the window, smashed the glass, and climbed into the mysterious storage chamber.

Never would Lana have thought that her first visit to this room would come about by breaking through the glass. Inside, the shiny metal and polished gold contrasted with the dusty, dilapidated walls of this small rectangular place. She now understood why it was always locked—to the family, it was like a gold bank in which they had stored a not-too-insignificant portion of their savings over the past decades.

Now one last hurdle had to be overcome before all was over: the internal door had to be broken, and then this mission would end in success. All the doors inside could be kicked open in emergencies, but this storage chamber could only be accessed with a key.

'Henry, can you hear me?' Lana yelled as she started to bang on the timber. Her strength was waning, and the pain in her thigh kept returning in waves. It felt as though her skin were being ripped apart every few seconds. 'Henry, can you hear me?' she shouted again.

'Lanaaaa! I can't move my legs,' came the frantic reply from within.

Screams of panic streamed in from outside—the inferno was obviously fast engulfing the external facade.

'Lana, hurry!' Henry cried. 'Everything's on fire. I can't move.'

'Pull the door towards you! I will push!' Lana yelled. She strode backwards and rammed her injured body against the fortified door with all her might. And again. And once more. Still, nothing happened.

'Henry, are you pulling?' she shouted.

'I am trying!'

'Where's the fire now?'

The next thing she heard from inside the mill was the most spine-chilling scream a human could imagine. It was like one prolonged, frantic screech of sheer panic and fright. Lana knew she had very little time left. She took a few steps backwards again, visualised breaking through this barrier as though nothing in this world could stop her this time, and started to sprint. Leaping into the air, she tilted her body sideways against the door and slammed into it with all her strength, only to bounce off and drop to the floor the next second. Then she examined the lock a little more carefully, and her heart sank to rock bottom: the bolt of the lock was visible on *her* side. It was *she* who needed to pull, and Henry who had to push. In the heat of the moment, they had mixed up the basic mechanics of a door. There was no way she'd have the strength to *pull* the door open, and so long as Henry was reeling from his seizure, he would not have enough force to push the door in, and now time was up.

Finally, she reluctantly concluded that this door could not be forced in time, and she resigned herself to the fact that she would lose a valued schoolmate and friend today.

Now the windmill was gripped in one prolonged scream of frenzied panic coming from the top of Henry's lungs. Then Lana suddenly heard a strange metallic clanging noise sounding from the floor, and she glanced down: it was the little candlesnuffer from the Christmas Truce that she'd left in her pocket. All the ramming and pushing had finally caused it to drop, and now it lay there next to her ashy feet. Lana picked it up and examined the narrow brass handle. The door was firmly secured to the outside, but surely, if she was able to see the bolt on *her* side, maybe she could try to slide it open with a thin piece of metal, she pondered.

She moved the old candlesnuffer towards the door, inserted the narrow handle inside the lock, and the door finally gave way. With only seconds to spare, she grabbed Henry by the hand and hastily dragged him towards the narrow window. He was sooty, pale and sweating. Outside, Ian and a few helpers had hauled the sofa just below the chamber, and they motioned the pair to jump.

'Jump!' Lana cried. She grabbed the shaking man by the arm, and together they leapt from the inferno. It felt like another miracle within just a few days.

A few minutes later, two fire engines arrived at the scene and put out the flames to salvage whatever was left of this beautiful century-old mill.

Lana, Elias and Henry were taken to hospital along with Ian and treated for their injuries and smoke inhalation. All of them were discharged the following night, except Henry—he had inhaled so much smoke and carbon monoxide that he had to remain for two days. It was only Friday evening that he was given a lift back to the farm to face those he'd put in such danger. Of course, he could have gone home first and called Samuel from his mother's phone, but Samuel would only have advised him to rest with his parents, and maybe he would not have invited him back to work for the rest of the summer.

Returning to the farm after setting fire to the windmill was frightening. Part of him felt as though he was now an unwelcome guest as he very slowly padded towards the hopper hut, not knowing what to expect. Anxiously, he flinched at little noises around him, his face tingling with shame. The area around the mill was now cordoned off, and a temporary door had been installed on the storage chamber. In fact, right now, a few repair workers were testing a lock on it.

Henry finally caught a glimpse of Samuel, who immediately broke the news to him that he would never work on his farm again, for he'd admitted to lighting a cigarette in a no-smoking zone and almost killed his niece, recklessly endangering the lives of a dozen harvest workers and almost destroying the crown jewel of the property. Henry had not spoken to Lana since they had been taken to the hospital by separate ambulances, and neither was he aware of the extent to which Elias had gone to save him that night. Nor did he know that Lana had pleaded with her uncle to let him keep his job. But her wishes had been ignored this time, for the insurers had to be shown that the owner was taking the correct measures. Henry was allowed to stay until tomorrow afternoon. His co-workers would be told he'd left of his own accord, but then he would be banned from the property forever. His heart sank, though he knew deep down it was all justified.

Speaking to other harvest workers and responding to their concerns seemed such a chore. He knocked on Lana's door to check on her, but she did not seem to be inside. He left his own door slightly ajar so that he might keep a check on whoever was entering the hopper hut. Then he wallowed in bed and listened to the chatter from the communal dormitory. The whole atmosphere was different now. People were closer and more tightly knit, as though they had been welded together by the catastrophe he had unleashed. And yet, he himself had no more room in that community.

As he waited for Lana to return, his guilt gave way to another feeling. Maybe it was always easier to blame unfortunate circumstances for mishaps than to blame oneself. After all, his epilepsy should really have been treated as a disability he could not have controlled. But now he had been unfairly blamed for a mere accident, an act of God!

Henry's heart was sinking fast, but alcohol was always close by. *Thank God for that.* He opened a chilled bottle of Sauvignon Blanc and began to gulp it down, drowning his sorrows, as was his custom. He dwelled on the close-knit community outside again, and another realisation suddenly surfaced: he'd wanted to make his dad proud of him for securing a permanent job before it was all too late, and now he'd been fired from the one temp role he'd held ever since he was sixteen. Every year, he had come to this farm, not infrequently hoping something might happen between himself and Lana. And every year, it was the same. Then it suddenly dawned on him that he might never meet Lana again after this summer, the realisation sinking in like a thorn into his soul. Why would such a bright postgraduate, so knowledgeable in all fields, hang out with an underqualified jobseeker such as himself if they weren't even working together? As he continued drinking, for a fraction of a second, he caught himself wishing he'd perished in the flames rather than gliding down this emotional abyss.

It was already eleven o'clock when Lana's voice suddenly became audible from the neighbouring room. Henry couldn't even remember when he'd shut the door to his own quarters, or had someone else closed it for him? But now he leaned his inquisitive ear against the wall, for there was another person with her. It was Elias! The Russian boy would normally keep to the communal dorm, but tonight he had intruded into Lana's private bedroom.

Elias was the man who'd turned his entire farm stay

upside down, from start to finish. If it hadn't been for this one foreigner, he would have greeted Lana in high spirits when she had arrived. They would have gone jogging around the orchard together. They would have worked alongside each other at the Hop Festival, just like last year. Henry could have been the one to go swimming at the quarry and dine with her in the windmill. He would have been Lana's closest friend and team-mate on the farm, and he would not have been degraded to a grovelling voyeur. He would not have been on cat-feeding duty that day, and he would not have set the windmill on fire. He would not have lost the summer job he'd held ever since he was sixteen, and Lana would not have been burned.

Elias and Lana chatted. Elias and Lana laughed. Henry had lost his job, and Elias and Lana were merrily laughing among themselves. Then carnal desire overcame them both. It was the first time Henry had heard Lana in the act of pleasure, and he almost froze. He did not know whether he should recoil at this monstrous scene or leave his nosy ear pressed against the wall. *Better grab some more alcohol now.*

Another realisation suddenly hit him like a poisoned arrow. His own actions had caused the calamity that had united the community and welded everyone together. Like an ignorant Cupid, he had been the catalyst that had fused the pair closer together at his own expense. And now he would be expelled from the farm and Lana's life forever, welding her and Elias even closer. It was a causal cycle that Henry pondered over and over again, and it was as though every time he traced it around, he deepened the grooves of the spiral until he was buried inside it, seeing no way out, save for his bottle of Sauvignon Blanc. *Why can I not just be grateful to people for saving me?* he kept asking himself.

But on that night, which would certainly be his last one on the farm, he could not. Every summer, there would always be one or two harvest workers who got on his nerves. But never before had he detested anyone as much as this conceited, queue-jumping asylum seeker who'd come out of nowhere and stolen his thunder. He had taken other people's jobs in Oxford and was training at one of England's most prestigious universities, while a native like Henry hopped from one temp job to the next. Elias was always in the right place at the right time. Elias had won the lottery of life. More than that, he had *cheated* in the lottery of life by stealing other people's fortunes.

Henry reached for his wine and drank and drank into the night.

Betrayal

It was Saturday, 31 August 2019, the day after Henry's return. At half past five in the morning, the sky was still dark, but a very faint twilight was gleaming on the horizon, shining over the slopes of the hills. The rooster crowed at those first sunrays, while a faint breeze swept over the pastures of the farm. Henry was still sitting on the floor of his room, awake, having consumed three bottles of French wine, and he was dozing in and out of sleep. He gulped and burped. Then his phone rang again. It was the eleventh time his mum had tried to contact him that night, but he'd ignored every call.

That morning, whether it was still from the commotion of Wednesday's blaze or whether it was from the first sex she'd had in a long time, Lana awoke with a buzzing sense of energy she'd not felt in months. Immediately the thought of a morning run chimed sweetly in her head, although with her burn, it would have to be a morning *walk* this time. She glanced at Elias and wanted to wake him up with a nudge but then held back. He looked so exhausted, still fast asleep. *Better let him rest a few more hours*, she decided. She quietly padded out of the room and ambled to the fields.

By quarter to six, Lana was out and almost jogging, taking in the fresh, unpolluted country air. She was dressed in running shorts and a sleeveless top while a large bandage covered her flame burn. Her feet thumped on the mushy ryegrass of the soft soil that grounded her in nature. A morning mist hovered over the farm again, the same type that had enshrouded the fields on the day of the Hop Festival, except that it was a low brume this time, and it was seemingly rising from the ground. But in this twilight, it made everything look a touch more mysterious.

Trotting past the burned windmill, Lana glanced to her left, and the extent of the devastation sank in once again. It would probably take many months before this crown jewel was fully restored. It was so badly damaged; there was still some rubble lying on the ground, and… *Hang on a second.* Was that a man standing there, about fifty metres away? For a couple of seconds, she sighted a male figure of slender physique. Then the mist enveloped him, or he entered the mist. It had only been for a brief moment, and the instant she had focused, he was gone. She took a little detour, trotting south towards the oast house, but now the figure was nowhere to be seen. There were only a few rabbits, which hopped out of underground burrows and darted off into the distance. It might just have been her imagination, she hoped. After all, it was still relatively dark; morning was still breaking. Lana turned around and started to jog into the hop field.

Very quickly, the strain of the movement took its toll on Lana's partial-thickness burn, prompting her to slow down and eventually come to a halt. She'd completely underestimated the stress of repeatedly stretching her broken skin. Lana unwound the dressing and inspected the affected area. A few remaining blisters were cracking under the pressure of the jog and had started to ooze. She gently wound the bandage back on her leg and continued walking, strolling between fragrant hop plants and dipping her toes into the soft, fertile soil of her uncle's land. The freshest, most pristine air would always sweep over the fields in the early morning and trigger a surge of endorphins. It was like meditation in motion.

Suddenly she spotted a rather familiar and yet unexpected figure strolling in front of her. He looked as though he'd been jogging himself and was now slowing down to take a break. It was Gregorios, whom Lana had always thought was more an afternoon person. Seeing him out and about at the crack of dawn was certainly a surprise. She sped up a little to catch up and then projected her voice. 'Gregorios!' she shouted, waving at him.

Gregorios stopped and turned around.

'Good morning!' Lana called out, drawing a little nearer to the young man. 'What brings you here at *this* time of day?'

Gregorios beamed with an enthusiastic smile, almost as though he'd just won a little fortune, looking at her with an unblinking gaze, as if he was in awe of something. Ever since Lana had rescued Henry from the fire, everyone had been treating her like some kind of superhero, and the privilege of spending a few private moments with her was a cherished one.

'Good morning, Lana. How are you? How's your burn?' Gregorios asked in his Greek accent. 'What did the doctors say?'

'Ah, it seemed so much worse than it really was. My trousers got the worst of the fire. The only bit where the flame burned through the dermis was here. It's not that big an area. But thank you for asking.'

Gregorios looked somewhat squeamish with his grimacing face, and he quickly shifted his glance away from her leg and the bandage. Then, as the two continued to amble between two lanes of green hop plants, the last visible night stars were slowly eclipsed by the faint, emerging light shining in from the hills.

'So, tell me,' Lana asked again, 'what brings you here at this time of the day? I've never seen you up this early.'

Gregorios told her he'd had difficulty sleeping because his mind was gripped in worries. 'Sometimes I just worry far too much,' he confessed.

'What is it you're worried about?'

'The future. My family's future. Your uncle has a very beautiful farm in England. In Greece, my parents also have a farm. We grow clementines and grapefruit near Thessaloniki. Every winter, we pick the fruit, and we sell so much to the UK. Then, in summer, I love to come to the UK and pick fruit here. This is my third time on this farm, and I'm worried this will be my last. I am worried my family can no longer sell the fruit to England next year. I worry England, or the UK, will put… will put… How do you call this again?'

'Do you mean import duties?'

Gregorios nodded. 'I am worried the UK will put import duties on Greek fruit because of Brexit. We sell so much to England. But in the last three years, my parents earned very little. And next year, everything will be even harder.'

'But you will always be welcome on my uncle's farm, Gregorios. And by the way, the EU withdrawal agreement specifically mentions seasonal agricultural workers in the political declaration.'

'Thank you—I mean for always welcoming me.'

'Besides, nobody wants to impose import tariffs on any products. All these intentions are written into the withdrawal agreement.'

'There won't be any more withdrawal agreement now!' Gregorios retorted.

'Why do you say that?'

'It was on the BBC news. Your new prime minister—Boris Johnson… How do you call this again? It's like *suspend*, but for much longer…'

'Do you mean *prorogue*?'

'Yes, prorogue! The new prime minister has prorogued Parliament, and now he wants to force through a no-deal Brexit. Do you think he will succeed?'

Lana shook her head at once. 'I am not really an expert on politics, but remember, even the prime minister has to act within the unwritten constitution. If Boris Johnson tries to prorogue Parliament and force through a no-deal Brexit on the thirty-first of October, there will be a challenge in the Supreme Court in London. And I'm sure the Supreme Court will rule this kind of prorogation interferes with Parliament's constitutional duties and is therefore void.'

'Well, I hope you are right,' Gregorios muttered, kicking away a few fallen hop bines with his sturdy trainers.

Above, the sky was glowing a deep red as twilight turned into daylight and the first daylight rays emerged from behind the hills to warm the summer air. Little did Lana know that by the time the last sunrays were to shine today, nothing would ever be the same again.

The pair had reached the westerly edge of the premises, where they greeted a few locals that drew by beyond the fence. They turned around and headed back towards the hopper hut, facing the tall hills whence the lambent sunrays glimmered through the morning mist. Lana picked up a clump of grass that was stuck to her left sole and let it drop to the ground as Gregorios stepped over some thorny twigs with his sturdy trainers. He turned his head towards Lana, and his face writhed for a second.

'Your feet are always bare. Do you never worry they will get hurt?' he asked.

'It's still summer and warm. My feet hardly ever get hurt. I feel a lot freer. And connected to the earth.'

'And you're not worried that you'll step on a bee or a nettle? Or maybe some animal or stranger attacks you? For example, today I saw another man on the farm, and…'

At those words, a sudden shudder swept over Lana's body, and she immediately tensed up. *So there really was another man on the farm this morning!* Now she knew it hadn't just been her imagination after all.

'What did this man look like?' she asked, intuitively lowering her voice a little, as though this intruder could still be within earshot.

'I only saw him for, like, five seconds and only from the back. He was… maybe in his forties or fifties, and he had a checked shirt. Blue and white squares. And blue jeans.'

'Was he blonde and tall?'

Gregorios shook his head.

'He was not blonde and tall?'

'He was medium height, like me. Hair was dark, I think.'

'Gregorios, can you do me a favour?'

'Of course!'

'If you see any other intruders today, please call Bob or me. You have our numbers, right?'

Gregorios nodded. 'Do you really think it was a burglar?'

'I don't know. But please let someone know if you see that man, or anyone else that shouldn't be here,' Lana pleaded.

Henry had almost finished his last bottle of wine and was about to pass out. The world felt so heavy, and everything was in a daze now that exhaustion was gradually overcoming him. Tugging at the curtains, he peeked out the window towards the hills and realised that morning had already broken. Then he slowly lowered his eyelids. Suddenly another beep sounded from his phone and brought him right back to consciousness. Once again, it was his mother. He'd been ignoring her all night, but now he would take a look at his device and see why she'd been pestering him for so long.

Henry, can you quickly call me, please? the message read. *Dad has passed away.*

The next ten seconds were a blur of incomprehension and outright denial. *This just can't be real! This can't be happening all at once!* The meaning of the message gradually sank in, and the blur gave way to a paralysing shock that numbed his senses like a protective wall. He barely felt able to move, let alone stand up. Such was the overwhelming sense of disbelief that Henry read the message over and over again, and when the tentacles of reality eventually pierced his emotional wall, a bitterness and grief overwhelmed him in a way that he could only compare to the inferno inside the mill. A weak, weightless sensation overpowered him while he slowly imploded. Then his grief gave way to anger and fury. It was a wrath that he projected onto everything and everyone. This farm, his mother, his father—and even himself.

How could the reality everyone lived in be so messy and chaotic? There was an abject randomness to this world that rendered life, every person, and every thing, futile and senseless. How could NASA send a man to the moon and robots to Mars, but doctors in the twenty-first century were still unable to cure a few abnormal cells? His mum had been so right all along: the National Health Service really was cracking under the pressure of all the queue-jumping foreigners.

At that thought, he took a deep gulp of wine, rushed to the sink and puked. He collapsed onto the floor and was ready to fade into sleep. For the next hour, Henry would drift in and out of consciousness, sometimes believing it was all a horrific nightmare. Then the tentacles of reality would pierce his mind once more.

It had already gone seven o'clock, and Lana was eating a bowl of cereal in the communal area when the rooster crowed from the distant barn. She had to quickly call her uncle and report the sightings of the curious intruder today. After the windmill fire, Samuel and his wife had relocated to a relative's house in nearby Worcester, where they would stay for the next few weeks.

'Oh, no, don't worry, Lana,' he reassured her. 'It was probably just Paul you saw. We took most of the stuff out, but there were a few old banknotes I forgot about, locked up in a hidden safe. How's your burn, by the way?'

'Really? Are you sure it was Paul?'

'Yes, it had to be him. He always gets up at the crack of dawn, this old farm boy. I'll give him a ring later. How is your burn this morning?'

'It's all right. Well, as long as you're confident it was Paul…'

'Yes, it had to be him. I'll call him in a bit. I'll check on everyone in two hours.'

Lana poured some more soy milk onto her cornflakes and finished her breakfast somewhat reassured. *Well, I guess if it wasn't Paul, Uncle Sam will probably phone me straight away*, she told herself, glancing out the window. There was no more mist above the ground, and the weather forecast had predicted another scorching day. Maybe this was the right time for a quick horse ride in the fresh air, before the heat became too intense again.

Lana trotted back to her room and checked on Elias. She was about to give him a quick nudge but then faltered once more. Even now, he still looked fast asleep, completely motionless and oblivious to her presence, as though the last few days had finally drained him of his energy. *I'll just send him a text later*, she decided, and she put on a little anklet before she headed for the stables.

Lana mounted her favourite stallion and rode towards the side entrance. By now, some other harvest workers were out and about, and even though it had been a few days since the fire, one or two still looked around the mill with mouths slack, as if the reality of last Wednesday still hadn't completely sunk in. Every one of them greeted Lana with such courtesy and respect, treating her like a celebrated hero. And Lana thanked each of them for their hard work and help during the fire. Then there was a middle-aged man who did *not* greet, or even acknowledge her. In fact, as soon as this man glimpsed her, he seemed to recoil at once and immediately turned his head around, as though he somehow feared her presence.

Near the side gate of the farm stood Charlie, dressed in a pair of ripped blue jeans and a sleeveless vest, and despite the slightly cooler temperature in the morning, there was a glistening on his skin. Something was different about him today. He looked quite sleep-deprived, with a pallid face and dark circles under his eyes. He was unusually dishevelled, and he did his best to avoid Lana's line of vision, even though she was virtually standing in front of him now.

'Charlie! Charlie, it's me, Lana. Are you all right?' she softly asked from up on her horse. 'Are you all right today? How are you feeling?' she repeated herself.

Charlie looked up a little to meet her gaze but slid his glistening hands in his trouser pockets. 'I'm fine. Thank you, Lana,' he replied in a tepid, subdued voice.

'You sure?'

Charlie nodded, then swallowed.

'A hundred per cent?'

Charlie nodded again.

There lingered a few seconds' silence between the two as Lana rode a little closer to her distant relative. 'So, what are you standing here all alone for, then, looking all worried?' she asked.

Charlie hesitated. 'The windmill… the windmill burned down this week,' he stammered. 'Everybody was worried, very worried and…'

'Oh, Charlie. We *have* talked about this. You don't have to worry about your job. The harvest will continue until the end. And I'm sure Sam can find little bits and pieces for you to do afterwards to keep you employed. Like always, okay? You like painting and tidying the barn, right?'

Charlie nodded, then cautiously edged away from Lana and her stallion. Normally, he loved to be in her presence, but today he seemed agitated and in a hurry to leave.

'Charlie, is there anything else I can help you with?' Lana asked.

'Honestly, Lana, I'm fine. I'm just a little messed up after the fire. Just do whatever you were gonna do, all right?' he slurred. His words sounded strained and stilted, and the more Lana lingered, the more fidgety he became.

'All right. I'm gonna go for a ride now,' Lana eventually responded. 'If there's anything you need, or you want to talk, just let me know, okay?'

'Honestly, don't worry about me.'

'Okay, Charlie. Take care of yourself.'

Lana ventured out of the premises, giving Charlie another glance around her shoulder as she rode off on the bridle path. There was definitely something different about Charlie this morning. *I'd better go and check on him as soon as I return.*

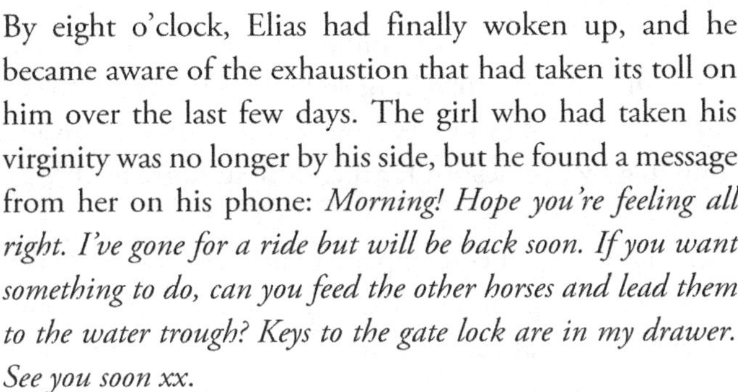

By eight o'clock, Elias had finally woken up, and he became aware of the exhaustion that had taken its toll on him over the last few days. The girl who had taken his virginity was no longer by his side, but he found a message from her on his phone: *Morning! Hope you're feeling all right. I've gone for a ride but will be back soon. If you want something to do, can you feed the other horses and lead them to the water trough? Keys to the gate lock are in my drawer. See you soon xx.*

Elias dressed himself in a short-sleeved lumberjack shirt, blue jeans and grey summer plimsolls. He made himself a cup of Columbian coffee and had a slice of toast with baked beans for breakfast, then headed for the stables. As he strolled past the ravaged windmill, the traumatising events of the blaze came back to him in flashbacks. The damage still looked gruesome, but the building itself also appeared more resilient than he'd imagined; it was restorable, even if it might take many months. Bob was standing inside the cordoned-off area, taking pictures of the damage and chatting to someone on the phone. Elias could only make out brief fragments of their conversation, but the tone of his voice was an unsettling one.

'Paul came and went… He didn't find those notes… Really?… But, Sam, what time…? Yes… the makeshift door was definitely damaged… The door was broken and also the banknotes were stolen! Paul said… What clothes did Lana say he was wearing?… Sorry? This is… A checked shirt… and… Someone on the farm… or… definitely broke into the mill either… or very early this morning… and… Sam, so Gregorios said to Lana a checked shirt?'

It all sounded very ominous, and Elias got a vague sense that someone had burgled the windmill and stolen a sizeable amount of money from it. He passed the ravaged building by and headed for the spacious horse field.

Bob hung up and contemplated the crime that had taken place on the premises. The burglar was either a poor wretch from outside or a thieving, opportunistic harvest worker who had tried their luck before the crack of dawn and made away with nearly one thousand quid.

Wait a sec. That man over there is wearing a white-and-blue checked shirt with blue jeans. Exactly what Gregorios described to Lana. He's of medium height with dark hair. Just like the intruder. What was his name again? Elias! Where is he heading? Let's see what he's up to!

Immediately he started to tail Elias, sometimes hiding behind trees, other times even crouching on his knees.

The boy was wandering towards the stables on the western side of the farm. Those were out of bounds to harvest workers, so what could Elias possibly want from there? Anyway, he wouldn't have the keys to the fence. But his clothes definitely fitted the description of the burglar's. The young man had reached the oak fence and was trying out various keys on an old iron ring. *Where did he get those from?* Well, there were only two places on the farm where they kept keys for the horse enclosure: the cottage, where he worked, and the windmill. So Elias must have been the man who'd burgled the windmill today, and now he was trying his luck at the horse enclosure. Indeed, the boy had managed to unlock the oak gate and was now gingerly heading for the stables.

'Hold it right there, young man!' Bob roared from behind, his words freezing the boy to the soil in fright. He turned around and looked timidly into his eyes as Bob raised his index finger like a schoolteacher.

'Hold it right there!' Bob repeated, striding a little closer.

'What have I done?' Elias called out.

'Where did you get those keys from?'

'Why?'

'Because the stables are out of bounds for you guys. Now, this morning someone broke into the windmill and stole nearly a thousand pounds.'

'It wasn't me, Bob. I only just got up.'

'Excuse me, there are only two places where we keep keys for the gate. My office and the windmill. So where did you get the keys from?'

'Lana gave them to me. She's got a spare set. She asked me to feed the horses today.'

'She asked you to feed the horses?! So where is Lana herself, then?'

'She's gone riding.'

'She's gone riding while you are to feed her horses? I'm sorry. How can Lana go riding if *you're* holding her keys? How did *she* get in, then?'

Elias wavered pathetically. 'Well, she must have *two* sets of keys, then.'

At this, Bob let out a sarcastic laugh and grabbed Elias by the arm, shaking his head as he wrested the keys off the boy. 'I think you're just making things up as you go along. Now, come with me.'

'Bob, I'm telling you, I did not steal anything. Call

Sam. Call Lana. Phone them. Ask them. I am Lana's friend.'

'Well, what do you think I'm doing right now, kid?' Bob retorted as he dragged Elias towards the hopper hut. He dialled for Lana and Samuel, but neither of them picked up. Bob led Elias into the hopper hut and knocked on Lana's door, tightly holding on to his suspect.

'Lana, are you in?' he shouted. 'Are you in?'

There came no response from her room, so Bob stepped a little closer to Henry's door, whereupon he thumped with his clenched hand. Bob had briefly spoken to Henry the previous evening and knew about his involvement in the fire but had no idea about his dismissal yet, for Henry was a long-standing and respected colleague whom Samuel had given the chance to explain he was leaving of his own accord, whenever he felt ready. As far as Bob was concerned, Henry was still a farm senior, at least informally.

'Henry, are you there?' he shouted again, thumping on the door. 'It's important!' He lingered a few more seconds; then the door slowly opened and revealed a haggard, pale foreman, obviously sleep-deprived and reeking of alcohol. What a rare sight.

'Henry, how are you feeling this morning?' Bob asked, a little baffled.

It seemed to take Henry a good few seconds to process this simple question before he eventually replied, 'All right, I guess… How can I help you?' His words came slow and flat.

What was going on with him today? It obviously wasn't a good idea to ask anything at all of Henry in this state. Bob decided he had better take Elias into his office and keep him there until Samuel came back. He was about to tell Henry he was sorry for bothering him.

'Well, how can I help, Bob? What do you need?' the farm senior suddenly volunteered.

Bob remained hesitant. 'Er… Henry… Somebody broke into the windmill this morning. We don't know for sure if it was Elias, but he had the only other keys to the stables. Can you keep an eye on him until Sam comes back?'

Henry's pale face relaxed into a mild smile, and he nodded. 'You bet I can,' he said. 'I'll take care of him, make sure he doesn't flee.'

'Are you sure you're feeling all right this morning?' Bob asked.

'I am. Don't worry,' Henry reassured the manager.

An unpleasant fluttery sensation quivered in Bob's stomach, as though his mind was torn between two actions. But then, who was he to judge in the end? After all, he'd known Henry as a reliable worker for years now, and there was a reason they considered him the farm senior. Any other action would be a breach of the trust Samuel had placed in this man. He would now step back and wait for the owner in the admin cottage.

No sooner had Bob vanished out of sight than Henry grabbed the foreigner by the wrist and yanked him out of the hopper hut. He knew he would regret this one: Henry knew as soon as he did this, he would repent and bemoan his own actions, but now was not the time to set the future right. What he needed right now was one act of cathartic revenge, and dragging Elias over the grass, he led the young Russian towards the wooden side gate. It was completely harmless but felt so good.

'Henry, what are you doing?' Elias protested pathetically. 'Bob said to keep me in the hut until Sam comes.'

'You and me, outside! Now!' Henry demanded.

'What are you talking about?' Elias whined.

Henry wrenched open the timber gate of the side entrance and shoved Elias out onto the bridle path, where he awkwardly tripped and fell to his knees. Watching this delightful scene, Henry imagined himself a border official who was finally expelling a queue-jumping foreign invader from his own land.

'Now, listen, Elias! Listen to me, you Russian twat!' Henry lectured him. 'You've come into my land. You've come into my country. You've stolen our jobs so that us natives are begging on the fucking dole. You've invaded our universities. You've overcrowded our hospitals—'

'Henry, please. I did not steal any money,' Elias interjected.

'I haven't finished yet, you Russian bastard!' shouted Henry. 'You've come into my country as if you were born here, just because you didn't like your own country –'

'Henry, please, what are you talking about?'

'Do not interrupt me again!' Henry bellowed as he pointed his forefinger at the cowardly boy. 'I haven't finished yet. You've come into my country as if you were born here. You've overcrowded our hospitals, and now you've killed my dad! Now, leave and never return! Do you understand, you spoiled Russian twat?'

Sparrows and meadow pipits fluttered off tree branches as Henry strode towards a silent Elias and pushed the refugee away with one heavy jolt.

Nearly tripping on a set of small rocks as he fell backwards, Elias scrambled to regain his balance and then looked in the eyes of the man he'd helped rescue a few nights before. He was absolutely unrecognisable today. Instinctively, Elias turned his back on him and began to walk away in panic and confusion. A light-headedness clouded his mind, and yet he felt as though pangs of pain were stinging from all directions.

'Yes, walk away, man!' Henry shouted from behind. 'Go away, you entitled monster! Wander off and never come back! Russian twat!'

What a strange day this was. Swiftly, Elias pulled out his phone and called Lana. She picked up straight away, but the connection was unreliable, as they were quite used to around the hills. The fact that he should really have shown Lana's text message to Bob suddenly went through his mind. He hung up and texted: *Where are you? Someone's broken into the windmill and they're blaming me. Henry's just thrown me out!*

A little later, his phone beeped and brought the reply: *Oh my God! I knew Charlie had done something this morning. He looked too nervous around me. Where are you now? Walk west along the bridle path. I am less than ten minutes from the farm. I'll catch you in a bit!*

Elias dropped his phone back in his pocket and continued to trudge along the narrow country road. A mild breeze was blowing in his direction. Then, from the distance, Lana emerged on her mighty stallion. She raised her hand and waved at him ever so reassuringly.

He was probably less than seventy metres away from her when the noise of a small car suddenly emanated from behind, gravel crunching under its tyres. There was clearly a motor-powered vehicle on a public bridleway! Elias turned his head around, and from behind emerged a red Nissan, driving past and skidding to a halt in front of him. Out of the car stepped two men in stylish business attire, staring in his direction. There was one man of medium height with brown hair, and there was a tall blonde figure, who was hiding his face under a pair of sunglasses and a black bowler hat. The two men marched towards Elias until they were standing less than thirty centimetres in front of him, blocking his way forward.

'Excuse me, young man,' said the tall blonde one. 'We were on our way to Cowleigh Park but got lost near the bridleway. Do you happen to have a map, or could you kindly point us in the right direction?' He had a slight tinge of Russian in his speech and towered over Elias ominously, edging sideways as Elias was trying to find a way out. Every single cell in his body was screaming for him to flee.

The moment he began to run, the two businessmen pounced upon him and wrestled him to the ground.

'Elias!' he could hear Lana shout from the distance. The sound of her stallion's hooves became faster and more powerful. 'Elias!' she yelled again.

Elias's screams of panic resounded across the public bridle path. He managed to free his left leg and attempted to plant a foot in the attacker's stomach. But it immediately backfired when the sturdy man intercepted the kick, twisted around Elias's leg and forced a black hood over his face, blocking his vision. Handcuffs were rammed onto his wrists. Then Elias was dragged into the red Nissan and thrust onto the back seat. He heard the locks pop. The ignition came on, and the engine was revving. A muffled, tantalisingly close cry of 'Elias!' and the noise of mighty horse hooves were the last sounds he heard before the car accelerated away.

It was the most surreal, unbelievable scene Lana had ever witnessed—such incidents would only occur in action or spy movies, but now one was manifesting right in front of her. She scrambled to gallop after the receding Nissan, but her stallion soon tired of the pursuit and began to slow down. Swiftly, she fetched her phone and snapped a picture of the rear number plate just before the vehicle disappeared into the distance. Out of breath, she brought her horse to a complete halt and examined the photo she'd taken. It was quite small and a little blurred, but the authorities might just be able to use it.

For Elias, the next ten minutes passed as a ride in silence. He dared not speak a single word as he leaned towards the window as far as he could. He was fully blindfolded, and occasionally, a firm hand grasped his arm. It was probably the medium-height man with brown hair, while the blonde one was driving the car.

The vehicle slowed down again and then stopped in the middle of the road. Elias could feel his heart starting to race once more.

'Where are you taking me?' he suddenly blurted out.

Silence filled the car. Then someone grabbed his head and yanked off the black hood that covered his eyes. It was the tall blonde man. He took off his dark spectacles and finally revealed his face.

'You do speak Russian, Elias. So speak Russian with us,' he said in Russian. 'Or do you think that just because you're a swine in a stable, you've turned into a horse, you lousy rat?'

My God! The man in front of him was Sergej Andropovitch. The man who'd spent a term at St Anne's College and attended debates at the Oxford Union. Had he always been a spy, or was he doing all this *after* he'd applied to the Russian security service? Elias wondered. Was he maybe doing all this to show commitment to the job? This whole mission was probably completely under the radar.

'Do you now recognise me, you little traitor?' he asked in Russian.

Elias faltered and then nodded anxiously. 'You're Sergej from the Oxford Union,' he replied in English.

'*Was!* I *was!* But I am a member of Oxford University no longer. I am going back to Russia today, and you're coming with me.'

'Sergej, why are you doing this to me?' Elias blurted out.

His captor stared at him with cold, piercing eyes and frowned in indignation, probably at his continued use of English. 'The government sponsored my semester here, and I stayed loyal to them. My own brother was killed in service, so when I heard you boast in front of everybody how *you* got away from it all and continued to help soldiers flee to Norway, that's when I knew one day, I'd get you. You are the most selfish piece of vermin I have ever met. All you think of is yourself, never your parents or country. And I knew I would make this my first mission in the job.' Those were words that sent a cold shudder down Elias's back, and he instinctively leaned into the backrest as hard as he could.

'Do you think that just because you send your emails from a university account, nobody else can read them?' Sergej continued to rant. 'The only trouble we had was that you applied to a dozen different farms. But we still found the right one. All we had to do was wait for the right moment.'

It all felt like an impossible nightmare that had somehow escaped the confines of improbability and penetrated through to this reality. Even in the UK, he was still Russian state property. If these men succeeded in his extradition, Russian authorities would send him to a re-education camp before deploying him to fight in Syria, as a conscript. Suddenly, Elias remembered the angel of light he'd sighted a few days ago, and a little hope glowed inside him. He wanted to scream and maybe catch the attention of someone nearby. But no. There was nobody around here. Nobody would hear him. That would only invite more trouble.

Sergej stepped out of the vehicle and shoved open a little gate to what seemed like a private country road. But just as Elias strained to focus ahead and get a sense of their location, the quiet sidekick forced the hood back over his face to cover his eyes. The driver marched back into the Nissan and continued to steer it at least half a mile down the private lane, a few bumps on the old asphalt bringing the vehicle to a rattle.

Eventually, they parked the car, and the sidekick gave Elias a full pat-down on his body. His wallet and phone were wrested off him; it sounded as though the device was chucked onto the lane, cracking as it hit the asphalt. Finally, he was yanked out of the red Nissan, fully blindfolded, and led into another place.

The air outside was hot and dry; the smell was reminiscent of farm pastures. Beneath Elias's feet, there was soft soil and the occasional fruit, maybe an apple or a peach. Someone opened the mortice lock to a creaking door, and Elias was led into a spacious, open hall. The floor could have been made of tiles or concrete, but it was definitely a tall, damp building, their footsteps reverberating on the walls. The inside smelled of freshly harvested fruit and farm grass. It could have been a shed, a warehouse or a storage facility for farm produce.

Elias felt one agonising impact of glass on his head, as though someone were shattering a glazed tabletop on his skull, and the next second, the world went black.

It had now gone one o'clock in the afternoon, and the atmosphere on Windmill Farm was more heated than ever before. Official reports had been made to the Great Malvern police, who'd promised a full investigation and commissioned a search team. Lana was resting her legs on a coffee table as she watched Bob defend himself.

'Sam, I'm so sorry. I swear, I honestly thought Elias was the thief. You should've seen the way he walked to the stables. He wore exactly what Lana had mentioned. Everything was pointing to——'

'And you didn't think to ask Lana before you accused the poor kid?' Samuel shouted. It was the first time Lana had heard her uncle so agitated, and rightly so, she thought.

'I did call her, but she didn't pick up. Sam, you have to believe me. You should've seen how he was sneaking to the stables. You never told me Lana kept her own keys. I thought the office and the windmill were the only places that had a set. You've always said the stables are out of bounds for harvest workers and—'

'Elias is not only a harvest worker,' Samuel interrupted him. 'He's Lana's friend. And my friend. And you should've known that.'

'Honestly, Sam, if he'd mentioned Lana had given him the keys and that you were happy with it, I wouldn't have… I really wouldn't have—'

'Well, where did he say he got the keys from, then?'

'Well, he was, like… like…'

'Like what, Robert? Like what?'

'Sam, honestly, I admit I made a mistake. I'm sorry. Someone stole nearly a thousand quid from the mill, and I just—'

'Oh, for God's sake, Robert! I don't care about a petty burglary and a thousand quid. I care about our workers — and what you do to them. You handed an innocent kid to an obviously sleep-deprived, intoxicated man who'd just lost his dad. Obviously, none of the signs rang alarm bells with you. Instead, you—'

Just at that moment, the landline rang, and Samuel immediately strode to his phone. 'It's the police,' he said, gesturing for Bob to remain and listen quietly. 'Windmill Farm. Samuel Watson speaking,' he answered. After a moment, he whispered across, 'Lana, they had a look at the number plate.'

Lana felt her face light up as she listened.

'I see… I understand… Do you think so?… And how long do you think it's gonna take?… I mean, we'll certainly continue to… Yes, we fully understand… Do let us know if you need anything else… Thank you. Goodbye.' Putting down the receiver, Samuel slowly turned his head towards Lana.

'Any news?' she asked.

'Lana, please don't be too disappointed,' he uttered.

Lana could feel her face dropping already.

'They said the photo you took was too blurred. They weren't able to read the numbers from it. I am sorry.'

Lana sighed, examining the shot on her phone again. How naive she had been, assuming they could make anything out on it. She was about to drop the device back in her pocket, but then she suddenly recalled there was something else on her phone that could still lead to Elias. For it was only recently that they'd all installed the tracking app for the Hop Festival, and Lana browsed her phone to see if Elias still had it. The app had only been meant for one working day, but a few of the harvest team hadn't delinked themselves yet. Elias's phone was showing as off, but the location of the last trace pointed to a place called Hillside Farm Road, a private lane about a fifteen-minute drive from Windmill Farm.

Lana showed the exact coordinates to her uncle and told him to pass them on to the police. Maybe they could investigate the area around the lane and find something. Of course, there was only a slim chance of it, but an effort still had to be made before it was all too late. For now, all she could do was wait for more news.

Now was probably the right time to check on Henry, Lana decided, to see how he was coping.

Everyone was out enjoying the afternoon sun, leaving the hopper hut in an awkward silence when Lana stepped in. She leaned her ear against Henry's door and listened, but his room seemed quiet as well. 'Henry, can I come in?' she asked. 'It's me.'

There came no reply from inside.

'Henry, I'm coming in now. Is that okay?' she said again. Gingerly, she pushed open the door to step into his quarters.

A pale, feeble Henry was sitting on the timber floor in torn grey pyjamas, bracing on to his head, which was firmly pressed against the wall. He appeared more awake than he had been this morning when Lana had given him a heavy dose of righteous anger, and maybe even a little contrite.

'I didn't do it, Lana. I didn't do it. Are they still on the farm?' Henry muttered.

'You didn't do what? And is who still on the farm?' Lana asked. She was half whispering in a calm, soothing voice.

'The cops. The police. Are they still here?'

'No. The police left several hours ago. They did not come for you.'

'I really didn't do it. I didn't know Elias would be taken,' Henry uttered. 'I was drunk. I was completely out of it. I just wanted to push him a little. That's it. Just push him. It was harmless. I had no idea.' It was difficult to tell whether Henry felt genuine remorse or simply feared repercussions from the police.

Lana gently took him by the hand and led him back to his bed. 'Get some rest. I'll drive you to Worcester in an hour,' she said. She fetched a small bucket from the corner of his room and placed it by Henry's head, in case he was going to be sick again. Then she pulled the curtains closed for him, made sure he was lying on his side, facing the bucket, and retreated to her own room.

Opening her drawers, Lana dug out a pair of flip-flops, the first time she'd put on any shoes since the start of the month. She searched her wooden cupboard and adorned her bun with the hairpin Mrs Wright had left her a week ago. All she could do now was linger and wait for some news from the police.

By half past six, a few light clouds were shifting over the sky; they moved over the fervent sun and brought a moment of relief from the mid-summer heat. Lana helped Henry load two suitcases into the trunk of Samuel's Mini and watched him step into the passenger seat.

When she commenced the drive to Worcester, an awkward silence lingered in the car, as though both of them were dwelling on a deed of shame neither of them felt comfortable broaching. Lana started to feel guilty about leaving Elias alone that morning and had so many questions she wanted to ask Henry, but now was not the right time, she felt. Why had Henry acted this way? What had he hoped to achieve? And how deep-seated had his jealousy been of her boyfriend? She did not know where to start. Lana recalled how much Henry had always doted on his dad, even though he had never openly shown it, and she granted him some time out of respect.

A scorching air weighed on the car's inside, but at least the refreshing smell of the countryside permeated the vehicle. 'Would you like the windows to stay open? Or would you like the air con on?' Lana eventually asked. To her, it almost felt as though she was speaking for the sake of saying anything at all, to break the silence.

'Just leave the windows open,' Henry replied. 'Thank you.'

About half an hour later, they were exiting the country road around Worcester and turning into the village of Fernhill Heath. Just then, Lana's phone suddenly rang, and the dashboard screen showed *Uncle S.* She answered straight away.

'Lana, my dear. Is everything all right?'

'Yes, we're fine. We've just passed Worcester. Should be with Henry's mum in, like, the next five minutes. Do you have any news?'

'I do, actually. But don't get your hopes up too high. Apparently, they searched the area on Hillside Farm Road and questioned one suspect. But he came away all clean.'

'What did they suspect him of?'

'I don't know. I think he had a previous record or something like that. But there was nothing they could find this time, so they had to let him go.'

'And he was the only one they questioned?'

'Apparently so. Are you guys all right, though?'

Lana sighed. 'Yes. Thank you. Thank you for letting me know.'

It was not long before Henry finally saw his parents' house sliding into view. Lana double-parked her car right in front of it and switched off the engine. He suddenly started to feel very uneasy, as though the prospect of mourning with his mum had begun to haunt him.

'Shall I come in with you and say a few words to your mother?' she offered, regarding him with warm, sympathetic eyes. It was the same look of compassion she'd radiated ever since she was a child, and Henry's mind harked back to the first time he'd seen her face. They had grown into young adults now. She had remained the kind soul she always had been, saving him from the burning windmill, while *he* had caused her heartache and sorrow. And all because of one impulsive act. There was that look of compassion on her again, but today would surely be the last time she'd bless him like this. From this moment on, their life paths would separate forever.

'Do you want me to come in with you?' Lana asked once more.

Henry faltered and shook his head.

'Are you sure?'

Henry nodded. And then he loitered on. He felt as though he was protected from the future so long as he could stay inside this vehicle.

'Right, so is there anything else I can do for you today?' Lana offered, tapping her foot on the carpet.

Henry shook his head again, and Lana began to look a little confused, fumbling for a response.

'Henry, speak to me, please! What do you need?'

Just then, a little shiver swept over Henry's body as he looked up from the floor and finally admitted, 'I'm… I'm just not ready to face all this. I'm not ready to go in there today, and—'

'But Henry, please—'

'Look, Lana,' he continued. 'I am so sorry for what I did. I was pissed and messed up today. I'm sorry. You'll probably never speak to me again, and—'

'I never said that.'

'—I know what I did is unforgivable. If I leave this car, and Elias is never found, and you never speak to me again, and—'

'Henry, please,' Lana interrupted. 'Today, just worry about yourself and your mum. She needs you now. And I promise I will keep in touch, whatever happens.'

'No!' Henry roared. Then he immediately covered his mouth with his trembling hands. 'I am sorry. I'm sorry I just shouted, Lana. I just can't face it in there today. I knew I would regret it. I know I act impulsively sometimes… and if Elias is never found again… and you never speak to me again… I just don't want to have a part in that. Please…'

'So what else do you want to do, then?' Lana challenged him.

Henry swallowed and then stammered. 'I know you aren't just gonna go back to the farm and let the police do the search. I know you can't resist, and you'll go and check out that Hillside Farm Road place tonight. Once I leave the car, you'll head straight there, right?'

Lana shrugged her shoulders and sighed. 'Maybe.'

'Then let me come with you,' Henry pleaded. 'Let me help you. Let me try at least, please!'

'This is not your concern right now! Right now, you should go to your mum and be with her. She needs you. I need you to be with her.'

'But, Lana, please,' Henry pressed. Whatever arguments he came up with, Lana would order him to step out of the car and console his bereaved mother. On this one occasion, however, Henry would not give way in. 'Lana?' he asked.

'What do you need?' she shouted back. And a heavy moment of silence followed.

'Back in our primary years,' Henry said, 'do you remember that day you rescued me from the tree house in Year Three? And then you owned up to something you hadn't even done?'

Lana nodded, flinching back a little as Henry continued softly.

'I felt so stupid that day. I thought I'd get into so much trouble for trespassing. Then, out of nowhere, you turned up and saved me, and you even supported me on the ladder. Nobody had ever been that kind to me. I fancied myself a superhero but didn't even have the guts to face up to those bullies or admit to Mr Anders what had happened. On that day, I wanted to be just like you. You were like… a *real* superhero to me, brave and fearless and all. I knew I was nothing like that, but I also knew one day I'd show Dad there is a real hero in me. And now he's died with a coward for a son—I don't want to be this coward, Lana. I've let everybody down now.'

Henry stopped to take a few gasps of air and then remembered something else. 'My grandparents have often told me about my Vietnamese aunt. She was only a child when she was blown away by a grenade. But my grandparents say that just after she died, they saw her spirit going to heaven. They say there were two strange lights around her soul. If they're right—I mean, if there's a heaven out there, and if Dad is watching us, I want to show him there is still some hero in me—even if it's the last thing I do in this life. I can come back and console Mum later. But please take me with you one more time. And let me help you. I promise I will not let you down this time.'

Lana's features softened somewhat, and eventually, she let out a long sigh. 'Put your seat belt back on,' she said, switching on her GPS. 'Let's see if we can find this place: Hillside Farm Road… Look. It says fifty-one minutes. Do you think we can do that?'

'Thank you so much, Lana! Thank you!' Henry uttered. He leaned into his backrest when Lana pressed the accelerator and commenced the journey back towards the Malvern Hills. Through the rear window, Henry stared at his mum's house until it disappeared out of sight. Somehow the sombre atmosphere in the car had lifted just a little, and a small glimmer of hope now lingered in the air, Henry liked to think.

By half past seven, the two had finally reached the private lane as a red sun was slowly setting for the day, gleaming towards the green slopes of the Malvern Hills. A rural lane this was—a narrow and peaceful stretch of road with family houses and gardens cluttered around farm fields. There was nothing menacing about this place, really, no sense of foreboding or any threat at all. It was an ordinary English country lane, similar to Dawson Road, except that it was equipped with two proper car lanes. *Is this really the right place?* Lana began to doubt it.

There were a couple of kids jumping on an outdoor trampoline. Another family were letting their children take a late dip in their paddling pool. Still a couple of fields further on, an extended family were barbecuing beef and mackerel under the sky to the beat of 1980s music. The delicious odours penetrated the Mini and made Lana crave her favourite Indian takeaway.

A little later, a much larger property followed and extended itself beyond a slope in the lane. It was some sort of hay farm, where three tractors stood idly by while the elderly proprietor gave his old Aston Martin a thorough handwash.

Lana went into second gear to climb the hill, and just as they went over the slope, a horse rider in his late sixties emerged from the opposite direction, riding towards the Mini. The bearded man was wearing a brown vest and black riding boots, and when he passed the car, he suddenly snapped his eyes to Lana's like a magnet. Lana gave him a friendly wave, which was a greeting he returned with a widely drawn stare, almost like a lascivious look, as if to say, 'I wish, girl! I wish!'

What a creep.

Driving swiftly on, Lana stole a glance at the side mirrors and noticed the man had stopped completely and was now shoulder-checking her, watching the car move on. A little shudder ran down her back, and Lana intuitively closed all the windows. She tried not to judge, but it wouldn't have surprised her if this creep was the man with the previous record.

'How are you feeling?' Lana asked her schoolmate, glancing in the back mirror. Henry gave her a thumbs-up and a very faint smile.

Soon one of the largest farms on the lane came into Lana's view on the left-hand side. Like Windmill Farm, it seemed dedicated to the harvest of Royal Galas, but another half of the orchard grew Williams pears. The place did look a little run-down, if not derelict, and this was the property from where Elias's phone had last transmitted a signal.

Lana slowed down the car and parked it about seventy metres from the main entrance. She turned off the engine and opened the door to a stretch of road that was filled with almost complete silence, save for the fluttering of leaves in the summer breeze.

'Okay, this is it. Let's see if we can find anything here,' she said, locking the doors behind her.

'What do we do if we see something?' Henry asked.

'We call the police, of course. Call the police straight away.'

Pretending to be a local couple on an evening stroll, the pair ambled alongside the property, looking out for anything that might give them a clue. They searched for Elias's phone on the asphalt but found nothing. They rang the doorbell on the wooden fence and loitered around, but nobody answered. Lana felt these premises did give off a different vibe from the other fields, but apart from the derelict nature, there just didn't seem to be anything special about the place. In fact, if those men this morning had come to extradite Elias to Russia, it seemed highly unlikely they owned a farm around this quiet area. But then again, they could always have paid someone to let them use their property for a day. This end of the road felt a lot more deserted than the southerly end, and apart from the evening breeze and the occasional twittering of meadow pipits, an almost eerie quiet lay over the place. After more than five minutes, the two were still strolling alongside the property, hoping something would grab their attention one way or another. Suddenly there was some activity. Behind a tall viburnum hedge, at least two people were carrying large crates into a white shed, and then they shouted something to some kind of foreman. From a distance, it was quite difficult to hear what they were saying. It might not even have been English—the vowels sounded softer, while the consonants carried a much harsher tone. Still, on its own, this activity was not a reason to call the police.

'If only we could see what they were up to,' Lana whispered to Henry.

As though her wish had just planted a new idea in his mind, Henry suddenly shifted his wide-open eyes towards the shed with a lifted chin, retracting his hands from his pockets, and the next thing Lana saw was her old school friend climbing over the fence and gingerly sneaking towards the hedge.

'Henry!' she called out, stretching her arms towards him. It was almost as though Henry was recklessly seizing this moment just to prove to her that he was not a coward.

There was a moment's silence, then the sound of metal hooves from a large steed approaching from the left. Lana turned her head, and from the bushes of a side road emerged the creepy horse rider from earlier on. Now he appeared to be riding directly towards her. Swiftly dropping her gaze towards the ground, Lana became acutely aware of her own vulnerability, which sent a spine-chilling shudder down her back. She sensed she was being watched. Instinctively, she stepped away from the wooden fence and began to walk forth, pretending there was nothing to see here, and she was merely a local on an evening stroll. Hopefully, the man would simply ignore her and leave her alone. She stole another glance in his direction, and now the man even appeared to be speeding up. A moment of panic gripped her. Speeding up herself, she tried to stroll towards her Mini as nonchalantly as she could. *Must not run. Just pretend you are out to get fresh air.*

But she had hardly walked thirty metres when the wet muzzle of the shire horse nudged against her right arm, and the bearded rider suddenly appeared by her side.

'Good evening, young lady,' he greeted her in a somewhat nasal voice. 'You look rather lost, my dear. What's the matter? Did something happen to you?'

'No, nothing, really… I'm just out for an evening stroll. I'm all right, thank you.'

'Are you sure you're all right? You don't seem it. What's the matter? Are you lost?'

'I am fine. Don't worry about me. I've just had a rough evening. That's all.'

The rider seemed reluctant to back off, and when Lana speeded up, so did he; when Lana slowed down, so did he, always remaining close by her side.

'Didn't you have a passenger in the car today?' he asked. 'Where is he gone? Surely, he can't just disappear, can he? You *did* have a man in the car, didn't you?'

'I did,' Lana replied hesitantly. 'We kind of had an argument, and he ran off. I tried to call him, but he's not answering his phone, so…'

'Well, if you want, you can come to my place and rest a little until your friend picks up his phone again,' offered the bearded man.

Lana turned to the horse rider and forced an artificial smile. 'Thank you, sir. That's very kind of you to offer. But I don't think it'll last that long, to be honest.'

Now Lana's follower suddenly put his hand on her shoulder and squeezed it, as though he wanted to halt her. 'Well, where could your friend possibly be, then? How far could he have walked in such a short time? Are you sure you don't want to come with me and take a rest? I've cooked the finest potato soup. So don't be shy. Feel free to come by!' At this, his horse released a pained-sounding bray.

'That's so very kind of you to offer, sir, but my boyfriend would probably kill me, knowing I ran off on him. He'd be so angry, you know?'

'Are you sure?'

'If my boyfriend… well, my boyfriend is a jealous

kind of guy. If he spots me chatting to another man, he'll go nuts. You don't want to see *him* going nuts, I assure you. He even went nuts at my dad once, and my dad is a police officer, so I'd better watch out.'

'Is he?' asked the man. 'Well, surely your boyfriend wouldn't think that an attractive young lady like yourself would be running off with a rough old local like me, would he?'

'My boyfriend is a jealous man.'

The horse rider cast a pensive stare into the distance before he finally picked up a bit of speed. Then he lagged once more and asked, 'What is your name, young lady?'

'Naomi.'

'Naomi. That is a very sweet name. I am David.'

'Thank you. Nice to meet you, David.'

'Well, since you insist on leaving me, I guess I must go now, mustn't I? It was a pleasure chatting with you, and you're always welcome to drop by at The Orchard by the Hill—if you change your mind. Yes, that's the name of my property.'

'Thank you, David. I really appreciate it.'

'My pleasure. Look after yourself, Naomi. Don't venture out too far. It's getting dark now. I can hear the bats already.'

David's shire horse neighed at Lana as its owner spurred it on. It was a friendly neigh, as if to say goodbye, and Lana waved at the creepy man when he finally rode on.

Now it was high time to sprint back and check on Henry. What on earth was he trying to prove, just clambering over the fence and sneaking towards that open warehouse? Indeed, the sun had completely set now, and save for a little dusk light glimmering on the rutilant horizon, darkness lay over the area.

Back here, Henry was nowhere to be seen, and neither was anyone else. Lana decided to call him but spontaneously held back. His phone probably hadn't been set to silent, so if there were people around him after all, her ringing would only alert them to Henry's presence. She climbed over the wooden fence and landed on the tall weeds, a small bee buzzing from the blades and circling around her legs. Lana felt her hands moistening as her pulse began to quicken. What had she got herself into today? Still, the prospect of losing Elias this evening spurred her on. She settled her gaze on the large open shed, whereto those men had hefted the wooden crates. It must have been the place Henry had sneaked towards. She listened out for any voices, but now it was completely silent around the shack. Lana looked all around herself, ducked down, and gingerly slunk into the mystery house.

A damp and faintly lit place, it seemed to be a storage shed for the summer harvest, but there was nobody here, not even Henry. Inside, crates of Royal Galas and Williams pears were stacked upon each other and lined the walls to the ceiling. They were probably waiting to be loaded into this tall freight truck that was parked towards the back of the shack, with the rear door wide open. It was about ten metres in length, with access to the freight compartment from the driver's seat.

Suddenly a pair of voices became audible from behind. Lana rapidly turned her head towards the door and prepared to sprint away, but stopped herself at the last second. Too late now, she realised, for they would certainly see her if she ran. Dashing further into the building, she quickly looked all around, trying to find a spot to conceal herself. But the crates were filled with fruit to the brim, and the space around the truck was completely hollow. There was no place for her to hide. The two men were fast approaching, their voices getting louder as Lana weighed up all possibilities. The ceiling was too high. The shed had no back door. And *under* the freight truck was too perilous to even contemplate. On a rare stroke of intuition, she hopped into the lorry, but what Lana saw next, she was not prepared for.

Wooden boxes of fruit filled the interior of the vehicle, while a pale, unconscious Elias was shackled to one of the crates, blood sticking to his forehead and lacerations showing on his skull. Lana gingerly padded towards him; then she became conscious of another person in the truck behind her, their tall shadow growing larger as it came closer. She'd been watched all along, and now she'd fallen for the trap. Anxiously, she turned her head around and eventually found herself locking eyes again with Henry.

'Quick! They're coming back!' he whispered, grabbing Lana by the hand. Henry led Lana towards a small, hollow space between the truck wall and some fruit crates, into which the pair swiftly clambered to cover themselves.

Now a tall blonde man stepped inside, along with his brown-haired assistant. They were discussing something in Russian. Lana took another sneak peek and immediately recognised the blonde one. It was Sergej, the exchange student from the Oxford Union and most likely the guy who'd stalked her at the quarry a week ago. He called the meeker-looking assistant Isaac, while he fastened the rear gate and secured it with a brass padlock. Then Sergej marched to the driver's seat like a soldier and made sure all doors were firmly locked. He fired up the engine and began to reverse the lorry out.

Now there could be no escape from this place until they'd reached their final destination, wherever that was. But most likely, it was Russia, for they were leaving under the guise of a freight truck, exporting commercial fruit from England. Elias would probably be concealed inside one of the fruit crates and then smuggled out of Great Britain.

Towards Dover

Save for the moonlight, it was growing very dark outside, and the lorry was taking advantage of the quiet evening traffic as it rolled along the dual carriageway. Neither Henry nor Lana understood any Russian, but whenever Elias's captors spoke, Sergej was definitely the dominant one, whereas Isaac almost seemed as though he'd been pressed into all this, as if he didn't really want to be there himself. Repeatedly, he was on the receiving end of Sergej's incessant anger.

'I called the police, but the connection cut out,' Henry whispered to Lana. He was shaking a little, and Lana softly laid her hand on his before she gingerly got out her own phone and checked for reception. Luckily, two bars were showing on the screen, so she typed: *SOS. We found Elias. We're stuck in a freight truck. Truck is driving from Hillside Farm Road. Call the police.* After reading the text back once, she sent it to Ian, Gregorios and Nora. If only Samuel and Dorothy finally got a mobile phone as well! Lana and Henry set their phones to vibrate, making sure incoming calls would not alert the two Russians.

At the front, Sergej and Isaac started to argue over

something again. While Isaac kept mentioning the name Elias with a tone of concern, almost worry, Sergej kept on hitting the steering wheel with his fist, sometimes causing the truck to swerve. The vehicle was suddenly picking up a lot of speed—maybe it had just entered a motorway— and now cruised along steadily.

On this fast route, two or three hours had passed, and the two Russians still seemed completely unaware of the intruders. Lana basked in a sense of *We just made it before Elias vanished forever!* But there was also a more sinister vibe inside the vehicle, as though somehow this ride would be something final. She noticed sleep deprivation was catching up with Henry once more as he repeatedly lowered his eyelids and kept forcing himself awake. She did not know where they were, but slowly a humid sea air started to enter the lorry, permeating the space inside. It was a fresh odour she always associated with the white cliffs of East Sussex and Kent.

The next thing Lana knew, Elias awoke from his coma and began to groan quietly. His voice sounded strained and panicked, as though he had no idea where he was or where they were heading. Sergej let out an angry sigh and quickly produced a syringe from the glovebox, which he shoved into Isaac's hands. It was obviously some sort of tranquiliser to anaesthetise Elias for the border checks at Dover.

Lana quickly hid her face behind the fruit crate when Sergej pivoted his head around to check behind him. She felt the vehicle gradually slowing down until it came to a complete halt. There was the clicking sound of seat belts being unfastened and then heavy footsteps making their way from the driver's seat.

'*Privet, Elias,*' Sergej said. The rest was a blur of incomeprehensible Russian, though the tone was a patronising one, almost as though Sergej was taking pleasure in ridiculing Elias.

'Where are we?' he mumbled in English, sounding drowsy and confused. Sergej slipped into his condescendding, half-humorous tone again, but then he abruptly stopped, and the whole vehicle was gripped by a sudden dead silence.

Lana knew exactly what it was: Gregorios had rung her phone, but with the lorry standing still, the vibration was now audible to the Russians. She'd swiftly cancelled the call, but it was too late now; their presence had already been noted. Henry was crouching motionless on the floor as low as he could, and he stared at Lana with his frozen face.

Sergej hastily asked Isaac something in Russian, his rising tone carrying an obvious tinge of panic.

'*Net,*' replied Isaac. '*Net.*'

Sergej repeated the exact question word for word but slightly more agitated and higher-pitched, only to have his assistant respond with another '*Net*'—*No.* Then footsteps slowly trudged towards the intruders, and the next thing Lana saw was Sergej hovering over the apple crate and glaring down at them with his piercing eyes. His lips quivered in fury.

'I know who you are!' he eventually said. 'You're the hippie librarian and skinny-dipper! How the hell did you get in here?' Taking a few steps away from her, he turned to Isaac and screamed in Russian, swinging his clenched fist into his pale visage so that it bounced off Isaac's nose. Isaac tumbled backwards against a crate of Williams pears and dropped to the ground. He wailed something in Russian but was ignored by his boss, who strode back to Lana and grabbed her shirt. He lifted his clenched fist over her face and then threatened them. 'Listen to me, you two! I know exactly who you are, girl! We'll get rid of you before we leave this country. If you guys make any sound, I will crush you under this truck. Is that understood?'

'Yes, we understand.' Lana nodded submissively. Then, with the back of his hand, Sergej swiped Lana across the cheek and watched with livid eyes as she felt her lips burst and wiped a drip of blood from her face. He reached into Lana's pocket and wrested her phone from her shirt. The more of her sent messages Sergej read, the more his face muscles tensed up in rage, until he stared Lana down like a general who was about to execute a rat. He crushed her phone in his fist and smashed the device against the metal wall of the lorry. Then he did the same to Henry's device.

'Isaaaac!'

'*Da*,' his assistant cried out.

'This is all your fault! Watch these Brits here. If they do anything, strangle them!' He spoke in English now, probably to make sure the Brits understood him while he grabbed them by their shirts and yanked them from their hiding place. 'Now, you watch Elias and these two rats. If they scream or do anything, take action!' he commanded.

'What do you want to do to them?' Isaac asked.

'Leave that to me. We'll dump them on a field somewhere before we cross over. They don't have their phones anymore. They can't call for help now. But if they do anything, take action! This is all your fault, and this will come out of your pay!'

While a panting Sergej marched back to the driver's seat to restart the engine, Lana took a quick peek out the front window and finally got their bearings: they had already passed Brighton and were now on the coastal route in East Sussex, heading in the direction of Dover. Lana turned her head towards Elias and regarded him tenderly. She padded over to the shackled man and swung her arms around his body to embrace him. Like this, they remained locked, and Lana whispered in his ear. 'Elias, I promise you, we will get out of this truck together. We will not leave you alone.'

But the next thing she knew, her arm had been pulled away by Isaac, who commanded, 'Sit on the floor, girl! Do not touch him! Sit with this man, there!'

Elias nodded at Lana, and Lana reluctantly let go to join Henry on the floor of the fruit truck.

The vehicle started to move more erratically, and other cars began to honk at them. Sergej tooted back and even appeared to accelerate further still, revving the engine as he went. He was obviously still gripped by rage. The truck sped over a large pothole, and the whole lorry was brought to a wobble. Sooner or later, such driving would surely cause a crash, Lana feared. She noticed sleep deprivation was catching up with Henry again, as he gently lowered his eyelids while the vehicle raced forward. *Just remain calm*, Lana kept reminding herself. In front of her, Isaac was typing up a message on his own mobile phone, which he laid right under her eyes, almost like bait. Lana looked away, pretending she hadn't seen, but Isaac stared in her face and discreetly pointed down at the device again. Gingerly, Lana stole a glance at the phone and skimmed the text.

My name is Isaac. I am sorry all this ended in violence. I have debt to pay and took on this job. I did not know Sergej would beat you. I am sorry.

A burst of righteous anger surged in Lana's mind at a man who'd agreed to a kidnapping simply to pay off his debt. For a second, she wanted to give him a death glare, but she held back. He did show remorse, after all, and now he had to be encouraged to switch sides. Lana slid the phone back towards Isaac, gently placed her hand on his and nodded discreetly.

The very next second, Henry was shaken awake by a forward jolt that sped up the truck to at least seventy miles an hour along the coastal road. From the side mirror appeared flashing blue lights, and a moment later, sirens sounded from behind. The truck was being chased.

Isaac had been so submissive to his boss throughout the operation, but he knew Sergej's worst-case scenario had come true, and giving up was not a possibility his boss would entertain; outpacing the police cars was the only option he saw in front of him, and Isaac had to do something before the lorry crashed.

'Sergej, what are you doing? Do you want to kill us all?' he shouted in Russian, quickly striding to the front. 'Sergej, please, what are you doing?'

'Shut up! This is all your fault!' yelled his boss. He went into fifth gear and pressed all the way down on the accelerator. 'Stay away from me! Stay where you are!'

The police car behind them tailgated the truck and approached ever faster. There was a little traffic in front of the lorry, but the lane to the right was almost clear. The next gap that came, Sergej steered the truck onto the opposite lane, and from there, he veered over onto the grass field, barely missing an oncoming Citroën. The police swiftly followed.

'Listen. If you try to grab the steering wheel from me now, I will kill you, Isaac!' he threatened. 'So stay away from me!'

Isaac glanced away from his leader and looked out the windscreen. It was such a dark field, and it was virtually impossible to see where the boundary lay and where the grassland turned into tumbling cliffs. Everything was moving so fast now. Suddenly a dead tree trunk emerged, lying in front of them.

'Watch out!' Isaac shouted, pointing at the fallen tree. Sergej tensed his grip on the steering wheel and turned it to the right, missing the deadly wood by a few inches. But in the next instant, the front tyres had shot over the cliffs as the lorry tilted downwards and began to tumble towards the English Channel.

The three hostages behind felt the truck listing in weightlessness as it accelerated towards the water. Bracing themselves for impact, they gripped on to crates of fruit as the sensation of free-fall overcame them all. They braced their panicked heads… then there was a brief moment of silence before the truck violently impacted the sea, apples and pears tumbling from their crates. Slowly, the vehicle sank into the water, where it came to a halt on the seabed.

A little later, Lana awoke to a continuous banging sound and opened her eyes. The lights in the vehicle flickered at times, and they gave the impression they could fade away at any moment. Water had begun to trickle in through the few cracks on the walls and was starting to flood the lorry from the rear.

Suddenly she became aware of an acute pain in her right forearm, as though the crash had fractured a bone. She tried moving her joints, but it swamped her brain with even more pain. Her two friends were lying motionless on the floor, Elias still handcuffed to the wooden crate. At the front, Sergej had bloody lacerations on his forehead and sat unmoving in the driver's seat, his mouth half-open. He appeared to have banged his skull on the windscreen and lost consciousness. Now Isaac stopped banging against the windscreen and reached for Sergej's wrist. As he felt for a pulse, Isaac's face dropped, and he shook his head, muttering something in Russian.

'Isaac, are you okay over there? Are you all right?' Lana shouted across. She waited for a response from the silent, mesmerised man, who was frantically pressing the window switches on the door panel, but apart from a repeated clicking sound, nothing came of it. Lana scrambled onto her own feet and leaned over an unconscious Henry. She brushed aside all the apples that had buried him, and then sighted his awfully pale face as he lay there completely motionless. Lana swiftly reached for his wrist only to find that his heartbeat was almost undetectable; Henry's ribcage was barely moving at all.

'Isaac, please help us!' she shouted across.

Only at that point did the young man finally take his gaze from the window switches and stagger towards her.

Lana waded across to Elias and stroked his pale, motionless face. He was breathing fine, but he seemed to have lost consciousness from the impact. 'Elias, it's Lana. Can you hear me?' she asked, caressing his cheeks. 'Elias, can you hear me? If you can, can you give me a sign, please?'

Isaac towered over the two, his pale face marked with shock, his eyes blinking more rapidly. 'I am so, so sorry,' he muttered in his Russian accent. 'I really did not want—'

'This is not the time to apologise. Do you have the keys for these cuffs? Please!'

At once, Isaac reached into his pockets, then pointed over at Sergej's dead body. 'He's got them,' the man replied. His fearful eyes swayed down to the truck floor, which was gradually flooding with cold water, and he uttered, 'Let's get out of here. Quickly!'

'Isaac, please, bring the keys over here. We need to free Elias,' Lana implored. With a single nod, he darted to the front again and searched Sergej's clothes. By now, their feet were already fully immersed, and the water continued to rise.

'Come on, Elias, please, say something to me!' Lana pleaded. She leaned over her boyfriend and tried rubbing Elias's hands, her good-luck medallion dangling above his chest. Intuitively, she took off the abolitionist pendant and tucked it around Elias's neck. It was almost as though she wanted to make sure if their paths were to separate, part of her would still remain with him.

'Have you found the keys?' she yelled across.

'Wait. Wait! They are here somewhere… I think,' Isaac stammered. 'Yeah, I got them. I found them!'

'Quick, bring them here!'

Isaac hurried back to hand her the key ring. He was panting for air and almost dropped the precious keys from his wet hand when he reached her. 'Help me break the window. All the doors are jammed. We have to try together!' He was trembling.

Lana inserted the key, freed Elias from the cuffs and then granted herself a moment's respite. She noticed the tiny cracks around the vehicle were widening, and water began to trickle in a little faster now, slowly climbing up towards the knees. But there was something else happening in this truck that Lana had only just realised, though it frightened her more than the water: the oxygen level was falling. The air in this confined space was slowly diminishing and would probably vanish completely in the next five minutes or so. She stretched her arms under Elias's body and attempted to lift him. But no sooner had she exercised any force than her fractured arm bone swamped her brain with pain signals once again. Almost dropping her unconscious friend on the floor, she fell back and wailed, gasping for air.

'Are you all right?' Isaac asked.

'Can you help me carry the guys to the front? We'll try to break the windscreen. Quickly!'

Isaac nodded, and Lana waded towards the front seats, the bulbs flickering about every thirty seconds. She put her palm on the solid glass and repeatedly rammed her elbow against the windscreen. Then she tried her fist. But the windscreen resisted both. *Damn safety glass!* she lamented.

From the rear of the truck, Isaac was carrying both of Lana's friends on his able body, wobbling towards her through the rising water. At one point, he appeared close to stumbling; then something else suddenly caught Lana's attention. The more she stared, the more she became aware of it, for it just didn't look right: one of the fruit crates was shaking of its own accord, as though it were caught in an earthquake or a tremor, except this tremor was rattling but a single box, while everything else remained unaffected. It was an uncanny and surreal sight to behold, almost as though a poltergeist or some other entity were haunting this vehicle. The shaking suddenly stopped, and Lana quickly helped lower her two friends onto the front seats. Henry looked more pallid than before.

'What were you looking at?' Isaac asked, a little baffled.

'Nothing, really… I mean… what's in that crate over there? Do you know?'

Isaac rapidly glanced behind him and then back at Lana. 'Apples. It's only apples or pears,' he replied.

Lana dwelled on this uncanny motion a little longer, shook her head and focused back on the windscreen.

'Ready?' she asked.

Isaac gave an emphatic nod, and the two took a few steps back to throw themselves against the windscreen, leaping on approach. After a while, the pair were stood in water up to their knees, but the windscreen still remained stubborn, and so did the side windows.

'This must be safety glass, right?' Lana asked.

Isaac fixed his eyes on the glass and nodded. Then he suddenly winced his head back with raised eyebrows and took a few rapid gasps of air. Whatever it was that frightened him thus, it made him shudder until he leapt from the ground, throwing his body weight against the windscreen to smash his skull against the glass.

'What are you doing?' Lana uttered. 'Stop that!'

'Air is running out. We're so dead!' Isaac whimpered. 'I'd rather die from concussion than drown. I really don't want to drown. I am sorry!'

Lana grabbed his shaking hand and looked him firmly in the eyes. 'Isaac!' she barked, catching his attention. 'I genuinely believe you're a good person. You just got mixed up with the wrong crowd. I promise you, all of us will make it out of here. But we have to keep calm, keep our breathing to a minimum. Otherwise, we *will* run out of air, okay?' She gave Isaac a few more seconds until his breathing became somewhat less strained and he stopped flailing about.

'There has to be another way out,' Lana muttered, looking towards the back. 'I take it that door's also jammed?'

At this, Isaac shook his head. 'I don't think so. But the underfloor locker *is* jammed, and that's where Sergej hid the key.'

Hastily, the two bent over the underfloor locker, and with all their strength, they yanked on the metal lever, only to see it detach itself from the base, Lana almost falling backwards with her own momentum. She now stood immersed in water up to her thighs, and she trembled with the cold of the English Channel. Soon the two would start to float. Time was quickly running out.

'Quickly, put the boys on top of the rear crates. Otherwise, they'll drown,' Lana whispered.

'The boys? What about us?'

'We'll get out of here, I promise. But we have to help the boys. Please!'

Quivering with cold, Isaac waded to rescue Lana's friends from the front seats while the water was rapidly rising.

Lana stared towards the back door again and examined the keyring for Elias's handcuffs. Maybe one of these keys could open the padlock on the door, she wondered. There were two keys on the ring, and they looked roughly the right size for this kind of lock. It might just work.

'I'm gonna try out the handcuff keys,' Lana uttered. She took a deep breath before diving down as the bulbs flickered on the ceiling.

The water had fully engulfed the padlock near the floor of the truck, and when Lana reached it, the hole appeared too small, not even the right shape. Yet, an attempt still had to be made. After all, this key was their last hope. She inserted it in the lock and began to turn, slowly and steadily, and the lock rotated with it. In a few seconds, they might all be out of this lethal prison and breathing fresh air again. Lana had managed about three-quarters of the revolution; then the key suddenly stuck. It was almost beyond belief: just a tiny bit more, and the lock would open. Scrambling to thrust the key a little further in, she began to jiggle the piece of metal. There just had to be a way to complete the whole revolution and force it. The lights above guttered again; then her broken bone swamped her brain with pain messages once more. And Lana exhaled her remaining oxygen supply in a moment of exhaustion. Yet there were only a few millimetres to go, and with all her remaining energy, she forced the little metal to turn. Instantly, the key snapped inside the lock, and all she was left with was the metal head. Air hunger overcame her, and it was high time to rise to the surface and gasp for oxygen. Even up here, there was little left of it. In fact, Lana could no longer even rest her feet on the floor; she was now floating within the cool sea. The whole truck seemed smaller now, very confined. *Wait! Where is*

Isaac? He was here a minute ago!

'Isaac! Are you all right?' she shouted a few times, looking all around herself. Her two friends were up on the fruit crates, but surely Isaac couldn't just dissolve into thin air. Unless he had dived under or found a way out?

The lights quivered again, and the water continued to push her higher up. They probably had less than three minutes before everything was completely submerged. Suddenly bubbles rose in front of Lana, and with them emerged the only other conscious person.

'Isaac! My God! Where were you? I was looking for you,' Lana exclaimed.

'I was looking for you too,' Isaac mumbled. He was shaking with cold. 'I thought maybe you were in trouble. Can we open the door? Did you manage to open the lock?'

Thereupon, Lana let out a long, exhausted sigh and showed him the remains of the severed key. 'I'm sorry. It just broke on me.'

The next second, a roaring '*NET!*' sounded inside the truck and reverberated against the shrinking walls.

'Isaac, please! I promise you! We still have some time. Please! You're using up all the oxygen!'

'What do you want to do now?' he cried. 'I'm going to smash my skull open!'

'Don't do that, please! Look, we still have one more key. Let me pull out the blade and try the other one.'

'But…'

Immediately Lana inhaled a lungful and dived back under. The water felt colder than before, and her entire body shuddered, but Lana knew the whole mission had to be completed in the next two minutes. Holding on to the padlock, she attempted to yank out the stubborn blade that had been left from the first key. But her trembling left arm lacked the strength, while her broken right one was almost left immobile from the pain. Yet that piece of brass had to be wrenched out at all costs, and Lana kept struggling.

Amid the turmoil, a hand suddenly placed itself on Lana's shoulder, and she turned around. Isaac was floating next to her, gesturing to let him have a try, as the lights above guttered again. Lana nudged herself away from the door and watched as the young man tackled the metal blade with his teeth and eventually wrenched it out with the force of his jaws. He gave her a thumbs-up, and the pair immediately swam up to gasp for the thin air that was left within this shrinking space.

Up here, Isaac's face softened into a light smile, and he handed Lana the little splinter from the stubborn padlock. Lana reached out for it, stretching her arm towards Isaac. But such had been the exhaustion of the last five minutes that the second she did so, she let go of the vital keyring in her right hand, which floated away from her like a fish.

'Oh, watch out!' she said, grasping for that life-saving ring. She hastily dived under once more to follow it with the faint current, but the moment she stretched out her hand, the bulbs above faltered again; it was impossible to keep her orientation in such flickering light so that the ring eventually slipped away from her sight and disappeared in the deluge. It was all beyond belief.

Up she came to the surface empty-handed, the water almost reaching up to the ceiling. There was less than half a metre left now.

'Did you find the ring?' Isaac asked.

Lana shook her head, exhausted and trembling. 'I am sorry, Isaac! I am so sorry!' Even she realised this one sounded so final and absolute, as though she had finally given up this time.

Isaac appeared to be inhaling the air for one final scream before they embraced their certain deaths. Those moments in the English Channel would certainly be their last seconds on earth, and…

'Hold on!' Lana suddenly exclaimed. 'Do you have anything sharp, like a needle or a paper clip or anything at all?' (It had only been a week ago that Henry had shown her how to pick the lock on Charlie's caravan.)

Isaac hastily shook his head, but then his right hand spontaneously moved towards his closed shirt pocket, from which he produced a Russian passport. In it were paper-clipped a residency document and a registration certificate. He yanked the clips off the little booklet and flourished them at Lana, as if even the most hopeless effort was now better than facing the next few seconds of suffocation.

'Quick, grab the guys,' Lana said. 'Prepare to make a move. This really *is* our last chance.'

The bulbs flickered once more and then went out for good. Just before the freight truck was completely filled up with sea water, Lana inhaled another lungful and dived down, ready to utilise her record in breath-holding. She floated nearer to the truck bottom and felt her way towards the brass padlock, armed with two pieces of sharp wire. She inserted the first paper clip in the bottom of the lock and pushed down. So far, so good, and she still had enough air in her lungs. Then she stuck the second wire into the little barrel and began to jiggle it up the plug; it felt a lot stiffer as Lana strove to line up all the pins so the padlock could pop open. Everything just seemed so fiddly and hectic, the whole thing taking place underwater and in the dark. At least the pins in the lock felt as though they were moving while the paper clip slowly glided through the barrel until it hit the top. Now the top wire had to be removed so the bottom clip could be given a little twist. This was the last move that needed to be done, and then they would all be out of there.

Right then, a crushing pain suddenly possessed Lana's broken arm—it was probably Isaac who'd just managed to knock over a whole fruit crate onto her fractured bone, and she flinched. In a single second's agony, she let go of both paper clips, which instantly disappeared into the flooded truck. Reaching out into the dark, Lana realised there was no hope in the world of finding them in time, and she put her palm over her head to say a quick final prayer for all in this doomed vehicle. At that moment, Lana suddenly remembered she had a new hairpin stuck in her bun, an ornament with a little metal not much larger than a thin piece of wire. With one renewed burst of energy, she wrenched it out, pushed it through the bottom of the padlock, then twisted it in the barrel. Finally, the padlock popped open, and Lana immediately pushed down the handle. The door swung into the sea as four souls, masses of wooden boxes and tonnes of commercial fruit were unleashed into the English Channel.

Diving out of the freight truck, Lana could see Isaac escaping above her, holding two bodies. He was saving her friends, but then one of them suddenly dropped and tumbled towards her. Such must have been the combined weight of the two men on an exhausted Isaac. The falling body was that of her boyfriend, Elias, now dropping towards her in this freezing, moonlit water. The crushing pain in Lana's arm almost paralysed her muscles, and the hunger for air was now unbearable. Yet the thought of losing him in the English Channel filled her with one final burst of energy, and with the last bit of strength she had in her exhausted body, Lana caught the boy and pushed herself up through the tidal water towards the life-saving surface.

Her consciousness started to wane, and for a fraction of a second, the world went black. The next thing she knew, she had reached the surface, head above water, and she inhaled the most blissful, most delightful air she'd ever breathed in her life. It felt as though she had scaled the highest mountain on earth and then found herself elevated into the heavens above. Utter relief, pure bliss. Then she suddenly felt very light. *Wait a second...* Elias was no longer by her side! Had she dropped him at the very last second? For a moment, she panicked, swiftly looking all around.

Two lifeboats were floating in the sea now, and three of their team were swimming towards the casualties. Then an unconscious Elias suddenly emerged from the water, being carried in the arms of another diver from the team. 'I've got him! I've got your friend!' she shouted. 'Swim towards the boat!'

Just then, another female lifeguard grabbed the panting girl by her broken arm and dragged her towards the motor raft. Everything seemed in fast motion now. Lana climbed into the inflatable and let the team put an oxygen mask over her mouth, breathing into this life-saving device. She wanted to close her eyes for a few seconds, but then thought of her two friends. They were not out of the woods yet.

'Was anyone else in the truck?' a male lifeguard asked on the neighbouring boat.

'There was one. It was the driver. But he is a hundred per cent dead,' Isaac replied.

Soon the rafts landed on the shore, and paramedics helped the casualties into three ambulances. There were police cars and even a fire engine standing by. Isaac seemed to have only light lacerations and could be treated on the shore. But Henry still looked extremely pale, completely lifeless, as though he was dead already, and immediate resuscitation was started. Lana saw a paramedic place the electrodes of a defibrillator on his chest; his body was shocked. Then the doors of the ambulance closed, and the vehicle raced away.

Lana herself was in the same ambulance as Elias and now took off the oxygen mask. Her boyfriend looked awfully ashen by now, as though he'd been deprived of oxygen for too long, and he was quickly connected to a heart monitor. CPR and defibrillation commenced immediately.

The doors of their ambulance closed as well, and the vehicle accelerated. One of the paramedics held on to Lana's broken arm and put it into a sling. She wailed in pain throughout the ride.

Ten minutes later, they had reached Eastbourne University Hospital, and once inside, their paths separated. Lana was taken to A&E, while Elias was rushed straight to intensive care.

A team of seven doctors and nurses were attending to the unconscious man as tubes were fitted to Elias's body, filling it with life-saving fluids. A resuscitator lay over his mouth as the senior doctor gave the command for manual resuscitation. The heart monitor was showing a quivering signal, but it seemed to be gradually flattening. For the next five minutes, a succession of defibrillation and chest compressions was performed, but the heart monitor continued to display a flat, and only lightly quivering line.

Suddenly one of the doctors stopped, as if mesmerised, and turned towards the supervising doctor as though a ghost had just spoken to her. 'Daniel?' she asked. 'Is that definitely a crystalloid solution we're giving him? Did we remember to scan the bag before we opened it?'

'Yes, we did. We always do, Heather. Don't worry,' the senior doctor reassured her. 'Give him another thirty.'

Heather focused back on Elias and started another round of chest compressions.

Suddenly the heart monitor beeped, and the quivering signal flatlined, showing a continuous horizontal line across the centre of the screen. Still, the team kept on their resuscitation efforts for another ten minutes in which they battled to revive his heart. But eventually, the senior doctor came to the reluctant conclusion that they'd done everything in their power to save this young man, and that it was time to let go and accept what everyone knew already. He shook his head and motioned his team to stop. At 00.37, Elias Alexandersen was finally pronounced dead. A timeline on earth had come to a close.

In fact, it was just as Elias's brother, Mikhail, had

predicted shortly before his own death: *One day, they will come for you too. They will hurt you. You will find yourself in a hospital, and you will flatline.*

Between England and Another Dimension

There was a little traffic in front of the lorry, but the lane to the right was almost clear. The next gap that came, Sergej steered the truck onto the opposite lane, and from there, he veered over onto the grass field, barely missing an oncoming Citroën. The police swiftly followed.

'Listen. If you try to grab the steering wheel from me now, I will kill you, Isaac!' he threatened. 'So stay away from me!'

Isaac glanced away from his leader and looked out the windscreen. It was such a dark field, and it was virtually impossible to see where the boundary lay and where the grassland turned into tumbling cliffs. Everything was moving so fast now. Suddenly a dead tree trunk emerged, lying in front of them.

'Watch out!' Isaac shouted, pointing at the fallen tree. Sergej tensed his grip on the steering wheel and turned it to the right, missing the deadly wood by a few inches. But in the next instant, the front tyres had shot over the cliffs as the lorry tilted downwards and began to tumble towards the English Channel.

The three hostages behind felt the truck listing in weightlessness as it accelerated towards the water. Bracing themselves for impact, they gripped on to crates of fruit, as the sensation of free-fall overcame them all. They braced their panicked heads… then there was a brief moment of silence before the truck violently impacted the sea, apples and pears tumbling from their crates. Slowly, the vehicle sank into the water, where it came to a halt on the seabed.

Henry felt the force of the impact throw him forward, and he now stood nearer the front of the truck. He noticed water trickling in through the few cracks in the walls, and the vehicle was starting to flood. Every person in the lorry seemed to be unconscious, except for Isaac, who hastened to the front doors and frantically attempted to open them into the sea. When it didn't work, he desperately attempted to lift the door to the underfloor locker.

'Are you okay?' Henry asked him. 'Are you all right?'

But Isaac did not respond, as though he was so engrossed in his own survival that he had chosen to ignore everyone else. He strode towards the windscreen, which he started to bang with his clamped hands.

Now Lana woke from a few seconds of unconsciousness and tilted forward. She shouted across. 'Isaac, are you okay over there? Are you all right?'

'Lana, are *you* all right?' Henry responded. 'Are you hurt?'

Striding a little closer towards her, he noticed that

even Lana was ignoring him now, so engrossed did she seem in uncovering someone else from a pile of apples. Henry was a little confused. He knew there was Elias, Isaac and Sergej, but Lana was checking on another male figure he'd not been aware of. Had he been hiding inside a crate of fruit all along? Henry looked a little more closely at this other man and eventually realised that this body was his own. One way or another, he had died from the crash or somehow exited his body and was now watching everything as an observer within this doomed truck.

It was utterly surreal, and a little frightening. Only now did he become aware of how hypersensitive he was, feeling and seeing everything there was in the truck. He could feel Lana's crushing pain from her fractured ulna bone. He could hear Isaac's thoughts of panic and his desperate endeavours to keep them under control. He could see everything and every item in the truck. He could even hear people's exact thoughts.

As soon as he realised that he was merely a ghost, a brilliant white light appeared inside the lorry, and it seemed to beckon to him. It shone so luminously, and yet the others seemed completely oblivious to it. It was like a powerful magnet, so radiant and full of love that Henry wanted nothing more than to float inside and be carried away from this chaos. But he hesitated and held back: His whole sense of morality and responsibility appeared to be elevated. Water from the English Channel was trickling into the vehicle, and there were still three living humans trapped inside it. He glanced over at Elias and recalled he himself was partly to blame for this mess. Sergej was dead now, but Elias could still be rescued, and Henry could still keep his promise to Lana, even if that were the last thing he did in this world. The instant he decided to stay and help his friends, the ethereal light slowly faded away from this world, as though it respected Henry's wish to remain a little longer. Henry watched on as Lana put her palm on the windscreen and rammed her elbow against the glass.

'Lana, Isaac, listen!' Henry exclaimed. 'You won't break this glass with your elbows, no matter what you do!' Naturally, his words fell on deaf ears, and the two kept banging their bodies against the windscreen, regardless.

There was a little screwdriver stuck inside one of the fruit crates, and Henry knew if that tool was rammed into the corner of the glass, it might just give way. If only he could draw their attention to this tool. He floated over the box and attempted to reach for the screwdriver, but his hand went right through, reminding him that he was only observing this world from another dimension now.

'Lana! There is a screwdriver here!' he shouted. 'In the crate.' Helplessly, he watched on as his school friend, still a living human being, continued in her fruitless endeavours, trying to break the windscreen with her bare hand. It was heartbreaking to watch.

'Come on, please! There's a screwdriver here! Please, Lana! Isaac!' he screamed again, banging on the wooden fruit crate. But nothing grabbed their attention.

Suddenly all his rocking and rattling appeared to cause a very light disturbance on the wooden box. Henry was not moving it with any physical force, but it was as if he was projecting his emotions, or maybe his mind, as though somehow his intentions were causing a very light movement in the crate.

Lana had her gaze towards the rear of the truck and now seemed to notice it too. Yes, the more she stared, the more she became aware of it. One of the fruit crates was seemingly shaking of its own accord. To her, all this must have appeared like an earthquake of some sort, except that this tremor was rattling but a single box, while everything else remained unaffected. Like the activity of a poltergeist. For a second, Lana stepped forward as though she was about to check this crate, but then she wavered. In fact, now these movements even appeared to frighten her, so she refused to respond, and the moment Henry realised this, all the rattling stopped. But somehow it felt as though this was the last time that he would move anything in this three-dimensional world. He was like the dying tail of a vanishing comet, and if he were to stay in this dimension any longer, it would be merely as an observer.

'What were you looking at?' Isaac asked, a little baffled.

'Nothing, really… I mean… what's in that crate over there? Do you know?'

Isaac glanced behind him and then back at Lana. 'Apples. It's only apples or pears,' he replied.

The water continued to rise and was already near the ceiling when Lana let go of the last remaining key in a second of exhaustion. She dived under to follow it in the faint current, but it eventually slipped away from her sight. She rose up empty-handed. 'I am sorry, Isaac! I am so sorry!' she uttered.

Henry knew that for a brief moment, Lana had resigned herself to dying inside the lorry, and Isaac sensed it too, gripped by an immediate surge of panic spreading inside his body.

'Paper clips!' Henry suddenly screamed in Lana's ear. 'Isaac has got some in his passport! Open the lock like I showed you at the Hop Festival! On Charlie's caravan! Quick!'

Isaac was inhaling the air for one final scream before they embraced their certain deaths. Then, somehow, Lana seemed to have heard him.

'Hold on!' she suddenly exclaimed. 'Do you have anything sharp, like a needle or a paper clip or anything at all?'

Isaac instinctively shook his head, but then his right hand moved towards his closed shirt pocket, from which he produced a Russian passport. In it were paper-clipped a residency document and a registration certificate.

'Quick, grab the guys,' Lana said. 'Prepare to make a move. This really *is* our last chance.'

The bulbs flickered once more and then went out forever. Just before the freight truck was completely filled up with sea water, Lana inhaled another lungful and dived down towards the brass padlock, armed with two pieces of sharp wire.

She had managed to align all the pins in the padlock, just as Henry had shown her at the Hop Festival, and now she pulled out the second piece of wire from the barrel.

Just then, Isaac managed to recover Henry's and Elias's bodies from the top fruit crate, but as he did so, it toppled over and came tumbling towards Lana's fractured arm bone. In agony, she flinched, and she let go of both paper clips, which floated away in the deluge. Both Lana and even Henry reached out for it, but none of them managed to recover this vital piece of metal. At last, Lana put her palm over her head to say a final prayer for all in this doomed vehicle. It was from the heart, rather than words, only a single second long, but Henry could hear she was praying. 'Thank you, universe, for those twenty-three years. Bless everyone. Thank you for bringing me my hero friends. I love them!'

'Lana, I love you too!' Henry exclaimed. Then he added, 'Remember you still have a hairpin in your bun. Use it!'

As though her subconscious had heard Henry's words, Lana fumbled along her head and found that her new hairpin was still stuck in her tresses. With a renewed burst of energy, she yanked it out, inserted the piece into the barrel and twisted. It felt as though death had already clutched her in its claws, and once again, changed its mind at the very last moment, as if to say, 'Go on, then. One more chance. Make the most of it!'

Lana pushed against the door, and it finally swung into the sea as four souls, masses of boxes and tonnes of commercial fruit were unleashed into the English Channel.

Isaac was trying to carry Elias and Henry to the surface, but he soon found himself running out of strength.

'Oh, Isaac, let go of *my* body!' Henry said. 'I'm dead already! Hold on to Elias! Lana needs him!'

His words fell on deaf ears, and the next moment, Isaac let Elias fall, who came tumbling down towards the seabed. Henry knew the crushing pain in Lana's arm almost paralysed her muscles, and the hunger for air now became unbearable. It was so heartbreaking to watch, and naturally, Henry reached out to catch Elias's body, only to see him fall right through his ghostly fingers. Still, with one final burst of energy, and with the last bit of strength she had in her exhausted body, it was Lana who caught the boy and now pushed herself up through the moonlit water, towards the life-saving surface.

Henry could see her consciousness was starting to wane, and for a brief moment, the poor girl fainted. The next thing she knew, she had reached the surface, head above water, and she inhaled the most blissful, most delightful air she'd ever breathed in her life. But completely oblivious was she of her boyfriend below, who was tumbling back towards the seabed, inhaling water as he went. Then a few torchlights suddenly shone on the falling man, and one diving lifeguard hurried down to grasp him as he fell.

A little later, they were all on the inflatable boats, and surely they would all make it now, but Henry needed to stay until he could be certain—until he knew that Elias was definitely out of the woods and would survive to see the light of tomorrow. Then he would have kept his last promise to his hero school friend and would say goodbye to this world. Staring at his own pale, motionless body, he instinctively followed it into the ambulance and watched on while manual CPR was performed on him.

'Leave me, guys. Leave me,' he said to the paramedics. 'I'm dead already. Can you not see? Don't waste your time on me. It's not worth it.'

Suddenly the doors were locked, and the ambulance raced towards Eastbourne University Hospital. Henry had to stay in the vehicle until they reached the building so that he could rejoin Elias to check on him. Inside the ambulance, watching paramedics trying to resuscitate his own body was a surreal experience. Even here, it still felt as if human consciousness was transferrable, as though every human was somehow part of a single collective, and the vibrations of a single soul rippled through this entire pool of consciousness. There was one paramedic in her early thirties who was giving him a round of chest compressions and kept feeling his pulse. Henry knew her wrist was suffering from repetitive strain injury from all the CPR she had done, and yet all she cared about right now was bringing Henry back to life. The paramedic's name was Tora Bergssen, from Sweden.

'Tora, you're doing a great job,' Henry whispered to her. 'But please, you can give up now. Take care of your wrist. I won't come back. It's not worth it.'

For a single second, Tora stopped to look up, then she immediately went back to her resuscitation efforts, pressing down on Henry's chest.

In less than fifteen minutes, the ambulance reached the hospital, and the staff wheeled Henry's stretcher into the ICU. One minute later, Elias's ambulance followed, and Henry accompanied him into the intensive care ward. He had to keep his promise to Lana and make sure her boyfriend survived, even if he had no more power to touch or move things in this dimension. It was the last thing he would see to in this world, and then he would meet his father in the next.

Henry followed the entire resuscitation scene with the knowledge of the entire medical staff, but eventually sensed *Something just isn't right here. Elias's body should be responding to those shocks by now, but it still isn't.* He scanned every detail of every apparatus and device in the room; then he settled his gaze on the crystalloid solution inside the infusion bag.

'My God! This isn't crystalloid fluid!' he shouted. 'This is *clonidine*! This will kill him! Stop the IV immediately!' Both liquids were abbreviated as CID, but somewhere in the storage room, these chemicals must have been mixed up, so now they were dripping a lethal dose of clonidine into Elias's dying veins. No wonder his heart wasn't responding!

'Doctor! Heather! Guys!' Henry shouted frantically. 'You're giving him the wrong infusion! This man is dying! Disconnect the line, please! Stop the IV!'

Nobody in the ICU showed any reaction to him.

'Heather, give him another thirty chest compressions,' the senior doctor ordered. The junior doctor nodded and commenced manual CPR again.

Henry raced towards the IV line and battered it with his ghostly arms. It had to be disconnected at once. Otherwise, Elias would die in the next three minutes. He battered, thrashed, and thrust at this lethal tube, but nothing effected a change. His hand just went straight through, as though he was standing in a different dimension from everybody else. He soared over to the doctor and shouted, 'Daniel, please! If you can hear me, stop the infusion. It's the wrong fluid! We have to neutralise the clonidine. Otherwise, Elias will die!'

But Daniel appeared completely unfazed, so Henry swiftly floated a little closer to Heather, who was now shocking Elias's body with a defibrillator.

'Heather, please,' he shouted in her ear. 'If you can hear me, please tell the doctor you're giving him the wrong fluid. This is clonidine, not crystalloid! Please! Elias can still be saved!'

Suddenly Heather stopped, as if mesmerised, and looked up at the senior doctor as though a ghost had just spoken to her. 'Daniel?' she asked. 'Is that definitely a crystalloid solution we're giving him? Did we remember to scan the bag before we opened it?'

'Yes, we did. We always do, Heather. Don't worry,' the doctor reassured her. 'Give him another thirty.'

Heather focused back on Elias and started another round of chest compressions.

'No, you did not scan the bag!' Henry shouted. 'You mixed up the two. This is clonidine! Trust Heather! She is right! You're killing this man! Stop this infusion!'

Suddenly the heart monitor beeped, and the quivering pulse flatlined, showing a continuous horizontal line across the centre of the screen. Still, the team kept on their revival efforts for another ten minutes while Henry repeatedly tried to disconnect the infusion line. Then the senior doctor came to the reluctant conclusion that they'd done everything in their power to save this young man and that it was time to let go and accept what everyone knew already. He shook his head and gestured for his team to stop. At 00.37, Elias Alexandersen was finally pronounced dead.

'No! He is not dead yet!' cried Henry. 'We can still save him! Please, pull out the infusion line! Yank it out! Please!' He frantically battered the IV line with his ghostly hands, but every time he did, they would go straight through. If only he could borrow a single second of life from the universe. Just half a second would do. It all hinged on one millimetre of movement, and he would have kept his promise to Lana and absolved himself of what he'd done that morning. It was so utterly frustrating.

Weeping, he sank to his knees and said a prayer in desperation. It was the first time he'd prayed as an adult, and it would probably be the last. He emptied his soul to the universe, pleading for just one more moment of life.

And he would use it to save Elias's.

The next thing he knew, his attention was suddenly caught by a little medallion that was dangling from Elias's neck. It was the necklace Lana had tucked on him in the freight truck, and which the doctors had swung away from his torso for the revival efforts. The medallion was made of an old metal, over two inches in diameter, depicting a black man in a loincloth. He was shackled and in a kneeling position, facing to the right, his hands clasped in prayer. Over him were embossed the words AM I NOT A MAN AND A BROTHER?

As if a window had been thrown open to recollections of a distant past, memories suddenly came flooding in from another world. It was as though the medallion had opened a hidden gate to ghostly memories from another time, a time when the two souls had been eternal brothers, observing the history of humanity unfold, up to the point when they had descended to earth twenty-three years ago. The dying man in front of him was none other than his eternal brother and friend Elias. They had been separated for more than two decades and had then found each other in this world as a Russian refugee and a young Englishman.

If Henry could have, he would have thrown himself on Elias to embrace him. He was reliving the past as all the ghostly memories came flooding in from one hundred and seventy years ago. But as they did, it was as though time stood still in the hospital, the analogue clock on the wall seemingly frozen, as if somehow all these recollections reached him at once, and yet he made them out in chronological order.

Henry reached out for the medallion and recognised

it was the same one he'd beheld in 1853, when he and his eternal brother had been observing history in the making. He recalled trying to pick up this very same necklace from a timber floor in the newly created United States on a warm summer night. It was the first time he'd ever attempted to lift physical matter, and his hand had gone straight through, just as it did now. What an irony, he realised, the first and last times he had tried to touch physical matter were with this very medallion. He'd come full circle now. Back in 1853, his hand had gone through the metal because his time to affect humanity had not come yet. Now his hand was going right through because he'd used up all his time in this world and had become an observer once more. His powerlessness to touch this particular pendant, or any matter at all, meant he could no longer save Elias, for he had used up his entire timeline in this dimension. Never would he have guessed that he would end his existence on earth by running into his eternal brother, wearing this medallion of brotherhood around his neck.

Memories flooded back of their encounter with Harriet Tubman, Rachel and Seamus. They'd always known the timeline of this couple was likely to intertwine with their own lives as humans, in one form or another. Now Henry knew Rachel was his five-times-great-grandmother. 'One day, in the very distant future, there might even be a black president running the United States,' she had said to Harriet. How much inspiration they'd taken from this brave couple who fought against slavery, this epitome of the lottery of birth. Rachel would return to England, found an orphanage in Herefordshire and pass the abolitionist medallion to Lana's orphaned great-grandmother.

A few decades on from their encounter with Harriet Tubman, and the two eternal brothers had witnessed a spontaneous truce on the Western Front near Ypres. It was December 1914. Henry had learned about the Christmas Truce in Year Ten and now remembered he had been there himself when a few soldiers had hopped into no-man's-land on that frosty night one hundred and five years ago. It was the time his great-great-grandfather had met, on a strip of graveyard, his distant cousin, who would go on to become Elias's great-great-grandfather. In fact, he now remembered how he and Elias had whispered to Private James Adam, 'Write home. Make people remember this night so others will learn about it in school.' James had enclosed a little candlesnuffer that Jens had gifted him that same night. James had regarded this item as a reminder that little miracles could happen any day, like a token of hope. It was the same candlesnuffer that would save Henry's life in the windmill one hundred and five years later—as though there had been a helping hand in the clockwork of the universe that had helped to line up certain events in their lives.

A few decades on from the Christmas Truce, and the two brothers had watched history once again. This time, it had been Elias's great-grandfather, swimming against the current and saving an innocent soul from the violence of the Nazis.

Henry's memory leapt forward three decades, and he now recalled the final miracle as an observer. It was Vietnam, 23 March 1975. So often, his grandparents had told him of his golden-hearted Vietnamese aunt, who had died as a child, and now Henry remembered he had been there on the day it had happened. His grandparents had never found out that Anh Nguyen had sacrificed herself so they could live, but Henry now remembered those final moments of her life. She was paralysed from the waist down, unable to move her legs, but it was as if she projected every fibre of her soul, crying to God and the universe. It was absolutely sincere, indefatigable, final, absolute, all-powerful, utterly selfless and altruistic. It was like one final push, and the universe just blinked and allowed the girl to move her limb one more time. The next instant, the bomb detonation cord was miraculously cut.

Henry's grandparents had taken him to Vietnam on two of their pilgrimages and shown him the village lane where they'd sighted those ethereal lights after the explosion. Now Henry recalled *he* had been one of those lights, standing with Elias in the company of his future grandparents.

'Thank you, Mum and Dad, for the last three years. I am fine, and I'm going home now. You must try to have a child of your own. I love you, and I will see you again in a few decades,' their foster child had said. Then she had been drawn into the wonderful light that carried her to the Other Side. The following year, Henry's own grandparents would go on to found the Anh Nguyen Foundation for Neural Research.

It was events like these that had inspired Henry and Elias's journey to earth so that each could leave his own mark on humanity's timeline and be a hero in his own way. In the very long run, generations would always become kinder and build on the progress of the last, always loosening the shackles of the human condition and the lottery of birth. On their first excursion to earth, they had witnessed their future ancestors saving a group of fugitives from slavery. And now Henry had inadvertently betrayed his own brother into servitude himself and eventually brought him to his untimely demise. He had allowed the lottery of birth to defeat Elias and himself by giving in to bitterness and revenge.

What went wrong in those twenty-three years that I did not even recognise my own eternal brother in the end?

Henry was now reliving his final moments on the Other Side. He and Elias were about to descend as humans when a mischievous soul soared up to embrace him. It said 'Bring us back some of those funny-looking Spanish grapes! I'd like to taste one here.' The spirit had such a familiar energy around it. Henry had definitely met this soul on earth somewhere. He searched his memories and realised this soul was none other than Lana, who would descend only a few weeks after them and meet him again in primary school five years later. She was the girl who now owned the anti-slavery medallion they had first seen in 1853.

In the hospital ward, less than a single second had passed while time was seemingly frozen. Nobody moved, and the analogue clock stood still. Henry regarded his ashen brother and apologised that he'd failed him in this life. He had come so far and would have needed to borrow just one more second to save his eternal brother, just one more instant of life. But the arrow of time could not be broken. Any moment now, Elias's human brain would cease, and they would return home together. Maybe Lana had sensed that Elias would die that night, so she had given him the medallion as a final gift. In a way, there was even a strange beauty in the irony of those final moments, Henry tried to console himself. They'd come to earth on the same day, had been separated at birth, had found each other through the medallion of brotherhood and would now return to the Other Side again. Henry had learned his lesson now and was ready to let go. Just then, an ethereal light glowed up by the wall, signalling that Elias's soul would leave his body any moment now.

Time was still seemingly frozen when Henry let go of his recollections of the past, but for some reason, his visions didn't stop there. It was as if those visions fast-forwarded to the future, or maybe it was a possible future, or perhaps the likeliest future: the doctors would break the news of Elias's death to Lana, and the poor girl would collapse to the hospital floor, sobbing. All her pain, her air hunger, all her torturous efforts had come to nothing. For she had still been unable to save her boyfriend from the clutches of death.

More images started to appear: Lana would lock away her notebooks and stop writing stories completely. Her appetite for life would diminish for a while, and she would take medication to treat post-traumatic stress disorder and survivor's guilt. Lana would forever blame herself for dropping Elias into the water the moment she fainted. Elias's death would affect her for years to come.

No! Lana should not suffer like this! Henry pleaded. Lana had suffered so much already, battling to save him and Elias. She'd risked her life running into a burning windmill to rescue him. She had suffered a severe burn on her leg, a broken arm and near suffocation, all to save the eternal brothers. She had gone through hell on earth to help the two survive.

'Lana should not suffer from Elias's death!' Henry cried out. In one last prayer of desperation, Henry clasped his ghostly hands around the medallion and asked the Divine to intervene for her. Lana must be able to move on, become the author she'd always aspired to be, and reap the rewards of her kindness and bravery. 'She is the greatest hero in my heart. Help her move on and be happier than I've ever been! I love her!' he cried out. If there was any fibre in his soul he could have traded for Lana's happiness, he would have given it and then a thousand more.

It was absolutely sincere, indefatigable, final, absolute, all-powerful, utterly selfless and altruistic. It was like one final push; the universe seemingly blinked and allowed him to physically hold the medallion one more time. The sheer shock of touching solid matter once again made him retract his hand so that the medallion was now dangling across the infusion line. Henry had touched the necklace but for a single second, and yet its uncanny movement did not go unnoticed by the senior doctor. He stepped forward towards the medallion and inspected it. It was draped across the infusion lead, and he suddenly recalled a question Heather had asked him a few minutes before.

'Heather,' he said, 'when we get those infusion bags, do you guys scan them when we take them out of storage or just before we use them?'

'Just before we use them,' Heather replied.

'And did anyone scan this bag here?' Daniel asked.

The junior doctor looked at another colleague, and both shook their heads.

Daniel examined the reverse of the bag, which displayed the letters CID. But in small print below, he found $C_9H_9Cl_2N_3$. 'Clonidine! This is clonidine! Not crystalloid!' With eyes wide open, as if with a renewed sense of purpose, he wrenched out the infusion line and commanded, 'Give him two shots of naloxone. Neutralise the clonidine. Start chest compressions again. Defibrillate one more time. Do it now! Do it fast!'

Within seconds, the full hustle of a renewed resuscitation was underway again. Elias's soul was already glimmering out of his physical body when the team embarked on the final push to extricate him from the clutches of certain death. Then, as his spirit rose from his body, it soared towards the otherworldly light, which drew him like a powerful magnet.

But blocking his trajectory towards the radiance, Henry caught Elias' ghost in a tight emotional embrace and looked warmly into his eyes. 'Stay here. Don't go yet. Let them revive you,' he said. Both of them hovered under the hospital ceiling. Then the heart monitor beeped once more; the flat horizontal line began to quiver as oxygen was pumped into the dying man's brain. At 00.38, Elias's soul was flung back into his body, which was coming back to life once again.

For Henry, watching this scene was as surreal as it was otherworldly. It was as though he'd already failed his entire mission and then managed to rewrite reality in the very last moment. Indeed, Henry had managed to rescue his lost twin and had kept his promise to his hero school friend in the very end. Elias would stay on earth with her and most likely remain Lana's partner for life. Henry felt his work was accomplished now, and he was ready to leave this world. The ethereal light still shone in the ICU but now beckoned him alone.

'Thank you so much for taking care of Elias!' he said to all the doctors and nurses, and then he turned to Elias. 'Brother, I will leave you behind now. I am sorry I did not recognise you. I love you. Take good care of Lana, and I will see you in a few decades.' He did not know whether Elias would retain those few out-of-body seconds in his memory.

Henry gave everyone one last wave and then floated into the light, where he basked in the crystalline glow that shone from the other side of this ethereal tunnel. It felt like a sort of gravity, as though some kind of magnet was intensifying and drawing him towards an indescribable benevolent energy. It was pure and total bliss. The radiance from the energy was so welcoming and utterly loving. It was as if every single star in the galaxy and the cosmos rose to the occasion and lavished their thanks on a soul for their contribution to humanity's timeline, however small or insignificant it may have seemed.

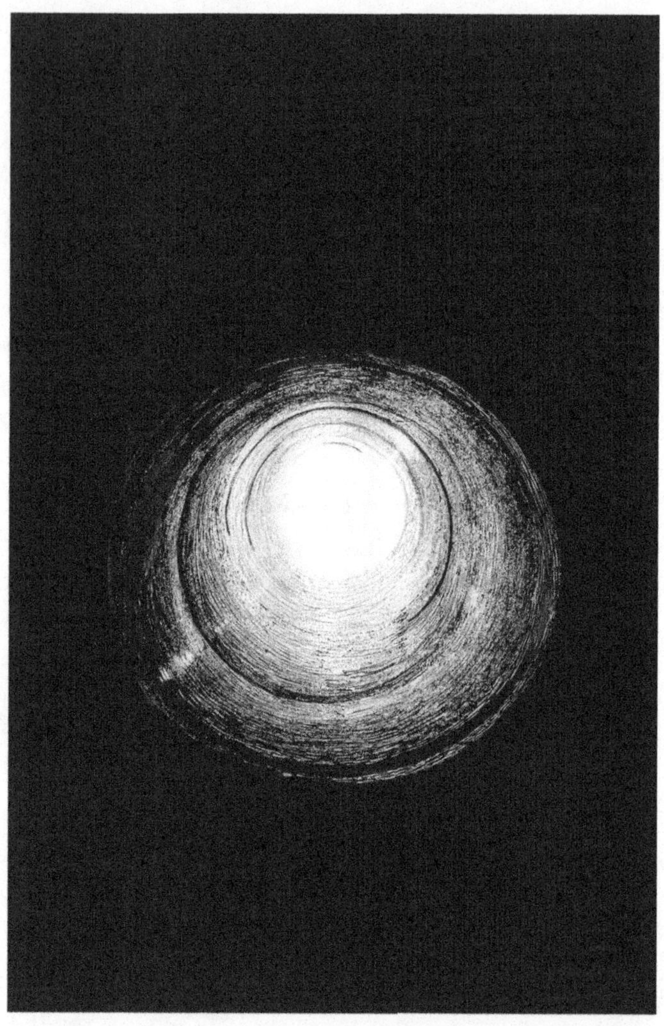

This most loving and ecstatic light greeted Henry as he exited the tunnel and basked in a radiance of love, as though euphoria were a blanket in which one could wrap oneself for eternity. Then a single vision appeared in front of him. He recognised it was himself as a baby, being cradled in his mother's arms just after he had been born. Like a movie of his human life, the pictures unfolded before his eyes, but this time, it was something more than just reliving the past. The review was panoramic, and he was able to see the ripple effects of every single action and thought of his twenty-three years on earth. It was brutally honest and yet felt so gentle and kind.

The first soul to greet him at the gates of this other world was his biological father, who'd only passed away the night before, yet his soul exuded a much longer presence from this realm, reminding Henry that time passed differently here. In fact, everything seemed like one continuous stream of eternity. In this altered sense of time, Henry stepped towards his father and embraced him. It was a hug of welcome, but to Henry, it was the one embrace he'd so longed for when his dad had suddenly passed away the previous night. The two had always doted on each other, although they had not always been on speaking terms. But up here, there was only love, and they opened up their hearts freely.

'I am sorry I put so much pressure on you,' his dad said. 'I always considered you a hero in my heart.' The two floated inside the crystalline radiance as though they were part of its luminous energy, then Henry's father suddenly stopped and put his hand on his son's shoulder. 'Listen, Henry!' he said. 'If you truly want to, you can still go back and be the hero one more time. You can still bid time return.'

'But I don't understand,' Henry objected. 'I'm brain-dead. Nobody can bring me back now. I'm probably already in the morgue down there.'

'Yes, that's what lots of people think who have these

near-death experiences,' his father replied.

'What do you mean, near death? Surely, I am dead, right?'

'Time flows differently here,' his dad reminded him. 'If you really want to, you can still return to the instant right after you entered the tunnel in the ICU.'

Henry was told he had been blocking his own resuscitation by longing to move into that light as soon as he had beheld it in the freight truck, but if he genuinely wanted to go back to his own body, he could still change his mind and allow the doctors to bring him back.

'Your mum still needs you, remember?' his dad said. 'She just lost me and can't afford to lose you too, son.'

The light up here was so peaceful and lovingly blissful that Henry wanted nothing more than to linger here for eternity. But then again, he would come back to this place anyway. Down there, he'd asked the universe for a single second of life, and now it was rewarding him with a second chance at life. If he went back, he would belong to a few select people who'd crossed to the Other Side and returned to tell the tale. He would bring back all the memories from heaven, and this time, he would really become the hero he'd always aspired to be. Sooner or later, he would head back home anyway. Going down to earth would be but a little detour to visit Lana, Elias, his mum and myriad other people he could touch with his actions. Throughout his life, Henry had made so many detours already, and now he could embark on the most meaningful detour in his existence and really make every second count.

At this, Henry made up his mind to go back to the physical dimension. There was one other soul his father wanted him to meet while he was visiting heaven. Then Henry hugged his dad goodbye and embarked on his second, and final, trip to earth as an active participant.

The next thing he knew, he woke up in the ICU of Eastbourne University Hospital, and he was back in the body of a twenty-three-year-old Englishman—the one he was very much accustomed to.

Somewhere Between Light and Time

OXFORD, 25 SEPTEMBER 2019

Just before sunset on this mild Wednesday evening, a tinge of crimson red glimmered from the western sky while a gentle wind sailed over the City of Dreaming Spires. It set into motion a heap of yellow-orange foliage that twirled around itself and signalled the start of the new season. The crisp smell of deciduous leaves lingered in the air. And after a long, hot summer, undergraduates were starting to trickle into this university city, ready for the Michaelmas term.

Little lights flickered on in stone buildings around the town as twilight gradually neared for the day. Inside one of the Victorian houses, Lana had found a new apartment for the academic year and was working on her master's paper in English literature. It was a relatively small apartment she lived in, not much larger than a studio flat, but that was all she could afford on her budget, being so close to Oxford's Iffley Road. It was an attic apartment in a building made of Kentish ragstone, and it boasted a brick fireplace for the winter months. On the wall above hung a picture of Lana with her favourite horse on one of their first rides, about a decade ago. A few cardboard boxes were scattered on the carpeted floor, still waiting to be unloaded by their owner. In the centre of the room lay a black yoga mat that was surrounded by Shakespeare's works and a selection of Lana's favourite novels.

Sipping away at a cup of Earl Grey tea, she lit a purple candle on her wooden desk and looked forward to a cosy evening. Lana was dressed in a sleeveless white shirt and blue jeans, while the abolitionist medallion on her neck reminded her that Elias had pulled through and made it. It had been more than three weeks now since the truck accident in East Sussex and those life-threatening moments of that 31 August. The summer of 2019 had certainly been the most memorable one in her life, with so many unforgettable moments and then her brush with death in that closed vehicle. Lana still vividly recalled those crucial minutes in that sunken lorry, when it had seemed as though the battle was lost and she would drown along with three other people. For a while, she had only remembered the pain, the suffocation, and her relentless travails to free everybody from that fortified vehicle. But as more time had passed, her mind also harked back to those otherworldly seconds when a curious fruit crate had suddenly shaken of its own accord, as though there had been another entity, another soul, in that truck with them.

Just then, Lana's doorbell finally rang, and she stepped over to the entrance to welcome her guest. She had not seen Henry since his ambulance had raced away from those Sussex cliffs, and she had worried about his health. He'd spent the last few weeks in a rehabilitation centre belonging to Eastbourne University Hospital, where he'd been learning to walk again, for his legs had fractured in two separate places. When Lana opened the door to welcome him, she was greeted by a beaming, youthful smile. And Henry was holding a bunch of fresh lilies for the host.

'Henry, come on in!' Lana exclaimed, giving her old school friend a tight embrace.

He was walking on a pair of crutches, and he limped in pain into Lana's new apartment. It was a strange sight to behold, but it wasn't just the crutches that made him seem different, Lana noted. Something else had changed. Henry seemed a lot more composed. His facial features had somehow softened, as though all the tension in them had been sucked out. In truth, there seemed to be a very light glow around him—an energy she'd only very rarely noticed around other people.

'How are you? Did you find the place all right?' Lana asked, giving him a kiss on the cheek.

'I'm certainly better than I look. I'm sorry I'm late— I just had some trouble finding this place.'

Henry supported himself on Lana's sofa and reached into a black satchel. 'Actually, I've brought you a little something as well today,' he said. 'Here, I got you some funny-looking Spanish grapes. They were on offer, and I thought you might like them.'

'Thank you! I love funny-looking Spanish grapes. How did you know?' She chuckled at his curious expression. *Who would ever use the term 'funny-looking Spanish grapes'?*

'Well, you might've told me that many years ago.'

'Thank you, Henry. Where did you find them?'

'Just at the Tesco down the road.'

Lana helped herself to some of the fruit and offered her old schoolmate some scones with tea.

Henry told Lana about his weeks in rehabilitation, and Lana told Henry about her plans to move in with Elias in 2020. Henry said he'd long suspected she would, and then he suddenly began to waver on the spot, as though he feared Lana's judgement about something important. On his lips, there was definitely something he dared not say to her.

'What's wrong?' Lana asked.

'Lana, there is… there is something else I really want to tell you,' Henry began to stutter. 'But you mustn't think I'm crazy or anything, okay?'

'I promise. You can tell me *anything* after what we've been through.' And yet, her old school friend still seemed shyly in doubt, cringing slightly.

'Lana, would you think I was crazy if I told you that when you thought I was unconscious in that truck, I actually floated out of my body and was watching everything—like, literally everything you did to save us, and then I crossed over to the Other Side?'

'You had what people call a near-death experience?'

Henry nodded. 'I didn't know what they were called, but apparently, a lot of people have had them.'

Henry recounted the events inside the lorry in such vivid detail, describing every action, every thought and prayer, that it left no doubt in Lana's mind that Henry *was* telling the truth. In fact, it would have been so out of character for him to lie on a topic such as this.

'So, when that fruit crate was suddenly shaking like

crazy, it was actually *you* wanting to get my attention?'

Henry nodded.

'And then, when that crate fell on my arm, and I lost both paper clips, you shouted into my ear and reminded me of that hairpin?'

Henry nodded again and told her the events leading up to the moment when he finally made the choice to go back to earth.

Though Lana knew of the notion of a near-death experience, this was the first time she'd heard about it from someone first-hand. She basked in a sense of reassurance, though she also felt there were a lot of details Henry did not feel comfortable sharing yet. Maybe he wasn't ready for this conversation so soon, Lana concluded, and she eventually allowed him to move on to other subjects. She made some more tea for both of them, and led Henry a little closer to her attic window. The last, rutilant, sunbeams of the day shimmered in from the edge of the sky.

'Did you hear the news yesterday?' she asked.

'Do you mean about Judge Hale?'

Lana nodded. 'The Supreme Court ruled that proroguing Parliament was void and that Boris Johnson never had the power to suspend Parliament for five weeks. The House of Commons met again today. It's gonna be a few exciting weeks in British politics now, don't you think?'

'Hmm,' Henry uttered, shrugging his shoulders. 'Yeah, probably. Everyone's still talking about Brexit and politics, even in the hospital.'

He seemed a little disinterested, Lana noticed, almost as though he'd started to move on from this world down here, as if he was just visiting this place. Then it dawned on her that to someone who'd really crossed over and returned, all humans must seem like temporary visitors who'd come from a common collective and were merely passing by on earth. Almost like tourists flying into a foreign country and trying to leave some mark before flying back.

Henry briefly glanced at Lana's master's paper, and then, on a single crutch, he limped over to his cotton satchel from which he produced a large amber envelope.

'Are you all right over there?' Lana asked.

'This reminds me,' he said. 'While I was in Eastbourne and learning to walk again, I had a lot of time to write, and—'

'Did you write an autobiography or something? Let's have a look!' As she impulsively reached for the envelope, Henry swiftly retracted his hand, wincing with flushing cheeks.

'It's not really an autobiography. It's more like—what's the word? Like a set of memoirs—like a diary, but not a complete one. And I was thinking, erm...' He wavered.

'What? You can tell me.'

'You know how you said you want to be an author and go into publishing one day, right?'

'Yes.'

'Well, I've never been good at writing myself, but after my trip to the Other Side, I thought maybe we could team up, you and me, and publish something together. This is, like, a draft of a mini memoir, but it's not complete yet, you know? It needs your input and your experience. It's only half-publishable, and—'

'Let me take a look,' Lana smiled, trying to snatch the paper from him once more.

'No, not yet. I wouldn't feel comfortable if you read it in front of me. My writing isn't very good, you know? Maybe you can wait until I'm gone and then email me what you think, okay?'

'It would be a privilege to read it,' Lana assured him. She laid the envelope on her wooden desk next to her master's paper.

It was getting dark earlier now, and a few more lights flickered on in the buildings across the street. A mild breeze from outside extinguished Lana's candle, and she swiftly relit it, closing the window.

'How is Elias doing these days? Is he still working on his master's thesis?' Henry wanted to know.

'Yes. And he's also working as an admin assistant again, until December. He couldn't afford to go on that doctoral course, so now he's looking for jobs outside academia. What about you? I suppose you haven't really had the time to apply for jobs from hospital, have you?'

'Actually, I have.'

'Really?'

Henry told her that he'd got to know a paramedic while he was at Eastbourne, who'd pointed him to a temporary admin job at the hospital, and with a little help from her, he'd got the role.

'Congratulations! So you'll be moving to Eastbourne soon? Are you still in touch with that paramedic, then?'

'We're very much in touch. Her name is Tora Bergssen. She's from Sweden. Wonderful person. It's not gonna be until November, and the job is only for six months, but they pretty much told me if I show I can do the job, they'll keep me on.'

'I'll keep my fingers crossed for you.'

'Do you think Elias would mind if I paid him a quick visit today? Just to say hello and apologise for everything I said and did on the farm.'

Lana sent Elias a quick text to ask. 'I'm sure he'll be fine,' she said. 'Trust me; I know Elias pretty well. He still sometimes helps us renovate the windmill, actually.' She moved a little closer to Henry and showed him the newest restoration photos on her phone. 'Isn't it amazing? However broken you think something is, it can always be fixed. Look at those walls inside. The old ones had to be demolished completely. These ones here are new, and—'

'Who's that woman with the baby in the picture?'

'Ah, do you remember Mrs Wright? The pregnant lady who helped us save Hoss? Right after you almost peed yourself seeing me naked at the quarry. Remember?'

Henry chuckled and felt his face flushing at the thought. *Lana, you've always been a little mischievous soul!* he wanted to tell her, but thought better of it. 'Yeah, I guess I remember her. And this is her baby? Time flies, huh?'

'I am actually driving to Windmill Farm today. I can give you a lift to Worcestershire tonight, if you want.'

'That would be great. So, you've got your own car now?'

'That silver Mini out there is my car. It's my first time owning a car.'

Just then, Lana's phone beeped, and she showed Henry an incoming text message from Elias.

'Look. Elias says it's completely fine if you go over there today. I told you so. Come on; I'm heading to Tesco myself. I'll point you in the right direction.'

Lana casually put on a light pair of slip-on shoes and

handed Henry his other crutch. He declined to be driven the short distance to Elias's flat, for he needed to exercise his broken legs and learn to walk independently again.

In pain, Henry carried on to a little side street where twentieth-century redbrick architecture contrasted with older, Victorian buildings, similar to the house Lana lived in. One of those buildings was the address that belonged to Elias. After holding back in front of the block, Henry eventually stepped inside when a fluttery, soaring feel around his abdomen was replaced with a buzz of anticipation. He had not been able to bring himself to tell Lana that he'd known Elias, and even her, from another dimension, a realm of light. So intimately connected did he feel with Elias that it oddly felt as though Henry knew a lot more about Lana's possible future husband than he should. One day, he would definitely tell both of them, but not today, he decided.

Inside his rectangular studio flat, Elias was studying the stem cell dedifferentiation of salamanders. On his desk were spread a range of well-wish cards from members of the faculty, his friends and family, and even one from his old neighbour Sophia. All cards from Russia had been forwarded via Norwegian relatives, making sure his address had remained hidden.

Dressed in a short-sleeved shirt and blue jeans, Elias was analysing a set of genetic graphs. They depicted the amphibians' power to continually renew themselves after losing body tissue, even if part of the head was missing. Salamanders could avail themselves of a virtually unlimited supply of stem cells, and Elias was pondering whether there was potentially a way that human progenitor cells could be reprogrammed to—

Right then, the doorbell rang, and Elias swiftly stepped towards the entrance to greet his old co-worker from Windmill Farm. Henry had contributed to a catastrophe that had almost got everyone killed. But he'd also appeared inside the freight truck in an attempt to rescue him, and Lana had assured him that Henry was coming in friendly spirits today. Gingerly, Elias opened the door behind which he sighted a feeble man supported by two crutches, limping into his humble flat.

'Elias, my old friend!' Henry uttered solemnly as he stepped inside.

The two never had been *normal* friends, and now he was calling him an *old* friend? Nevertheless, there was something different about Henry, Elias noticed. It was difficult to put his finger on it, for it was more than his physical appearance. Fair enough, his facial features looked more relaxed, but there was also something different about his aura. This old feeling of mutual repulsion was hardly there anymore. For some reason, it felt more comfortable to be standing in Henry's presence. In fact, there was a calmness around Henry today that he'd never shown on the farm.

'Would you like a cup of tea or something to drink?' Elias eventually offered.

His old team leader asked for some tap water and leaned his crutches against the legs of the dining table. He carefully lowered himself onto a cushioned chair and smiled blissfully. For some reason, he seemed unusually content despite his injuries. Henry sipped at his water and began to tell Elias about his rehab sessions in Eastbourne, the wonderful paramedic he'd met at the hospital, and the job he was starting in mid-autumn. The whole conversation sounded somewhat stilted or artificial, as though Henry was working towards some crux that he kept postponing. *Just get to the point.*

'Elias!' Henry finally exclaimed. 'I've actually come today to say sorry for everything I've said and done to you. I was horrible. And then, when my dad passed away, and Bob led you into my room, and I hadn't slept all night— oh my God, I just lost it completely. I am sorry! I've realised so many things since the accident. And I feel ashamed for what I've done. I've come to let you know if there's anything you ever need from me, you can text me, and I will do everything and more.'

Is that what he's come to say to me? Elias was stunned, but at the time, he no longer felt completely surprised. 'Thank you, Henry. That was certainly quite unexpected.'

Henry took another sip of water and then produced a brown envelope from his cotton bag, unsealing the flap from the pocket. 'You remember the evening when you and Lana risked your lives to save me from the burning windmill?'

'How could I forget that?'

Henry took a deep breath before he continued. 'I have never thanked you for saving my life that night. But this time, I really want to put things right. I understand you were applying for a DPhil in stem cell research. Is that correct?'

Elias nodded.

'And I also understand you've only been offered self-funded courses, so you can't afford to go on any.'

'That is also true.'

'Well, I still owe you a big favour,' Henry said. He handed Elias the envelope before continuing. 'Forty years ago, my grandparents worked as doctors in war-torn Vietnam. When they came back, they set up a foundation for neural research, and every year, they give out a few scholarships to gifted people. I've spoken to my grandparents, and they're very happy to give you this.'

Upon opening the envelope, Elias found a bursary application to the Anh Nguyen Foundation for Neural Research. It was already made out in his name and was worth eighteen thousand pounds.

Was this supposed to be a joke, or was Henry being sincere?

'Henry, is this for real?'

Elias's old team leader nodded sincerely. 'I owe you big time, brother. This time, I will start off right. My grandparents have spoken to the foundation, and all you have to do is fill in the details and send in your certificates. And the money is yours.'

'Henry! Oh my God! Why are you doing this for me?'

Henry repeated again that he'd become a different person and wanted to thank Elias for helping to save his life that evening when the mill stood in flames, and to apologise for the damage he'd inflicted on him. It was all only half-true, of course. One day, Henry would tell him that they'd travelled through history together like inseparable twins. One day maybe, but not today.

'Thank you so much, Henry…'

'My dad died of cancer. And you're doing research into regenerative medicine. He would've wanted it, Elias.

We're entering an era when scientists are collaborating globally, and each time a candle is lit in one place, a wave of knowledge will ripple through like a chain of connected lights.'

Somewhere, sometime, Elias had heard a very similar phrase, but the origin of that sentence eluded him.

'So, who's Anh Nguyen then?' Elias asked.

'They named the foundation after my Vietnamese aunt—'

'Your Vietnamese aunt? I never knew you had a Vietnamese aunt.'

'She died in an explosion when she was still a teenager, more than twenty years before you and I were born.'

'Before you and I were born?' Something about this sentence stirred up a few hidden recollections. 'Wait, were *you* the one in my vision just before I awoke from the coma? In Eastbourne?'

Henry opened his mouth as though he was about to announce something but then stopped himself. He slowly rose to his feet and cautiously stepped towards Elias, almost tripping without the aid of his crutches. Conscious of Henry's wobbling gait, Elias got up from his own chair and then caught the stumbling man in his arms. Henry embraced him, just as the man in the vision had hugged him shortly before he'd awoken in the ICU.

'Elias, I promise, one day I will tell you more. If there is ever something you need, just ask.'

'Thank you, Henry. I will never forget your help.'

Elias was intrigued to know more, but Henry was obviously reluctant to open up to him so soon.

When it was time for Henry to depart, he asked whether they could keep in touch from now on and whether he could note down Elias's new mobile number.

'Of course! After all, you've just funded my Doctor's degree. Let's see… Where did I leave my phone?'

'I can see a small black thing by your brother's photo. Is that it?' Henry asked.

Elias glanced at the dark object and then up at Mikhail's photo. 'How did you know this was my brother?'

Henry shrugged his shoulders. 'Well, he looks a bit like you, so…'

'Really? Everyone always used to say the very opposite—even our parents!'

Henry opened his mouth but then simply pulled off another light shrug. He produced his phone, and the two exchanged their numbers in friendly spirits. Henry obviously knew a lot more than he was letting on, and Elias watched him from the window as he struggled to limp forward and at times appeared close to falling. A female passer-by offered to help, but Henry gently touched the Good Samaritan's arm, declined her support, and staggered on. Elias closed the window and ambled back to the dining table. He researched the Anh Nguyen Foundation online and then filled in the precious bursary application. He was about to throw away the tattered envelope that had contained it, but then he spotted another piece of paper at the very bottom of it. Reaching down for it, Elias found a small note, written to him in blue ink, and he began to read:

My dear friend, there are so many things I want to tell you about that accident, and I promise you, one day I will. (I was not as unconscious as people thought I was). But there is one thing I want to tell you today. I want to tell you that your brother, Mikhail, sends his love. He is very happy on the Other Side, and he is waiting to see you in a few decades. He's very glad you did not join him so soon and that you are completing his work.

However moved Elias was by the DPhil funding, this piece of paper touched him even more. Fragments of a far bigger picture were now coming together.

By half past eleven, Lana had dropped Henry off near Worcester, and she was strolling to the hopper hut on Windmill Farm. The field was marked by the distinct beauty of autumn, and the fruit trees resembled ghostly shadows of a rich summer harvest, deciduous foliage sweeping about Lana's feet in a mild breeze. The refreshing smell of wild grass permeated the air and immediately grounded her back in nature. It was a crystal-clear night again, just like the night when she'd first brought Elias to this place at the beginning of August.

A bright shooting star sparkled from the hills and crossed Lana's vision in a northerly direction. It appeared to fly towards the North Star before it swiftly evaporated in the mesosphere. Lana's mind harked back to the time she had lain hand in hand with Elias in the orchard and gazed up at the Milky Way. She felt so lucky that Elias was still here, and they had decades of life to look forward to. In fact, as she ambled towards the stone cottage, every single object, every smell and every light reminded her of something in the summer of 2019.

When she reached the old hopper hut, Samuel and his wife were fast asleep, and Lana quickly helped herself to a bowl of cereal, took a shower and was ready to head to bed. She was just about to turn off the light when she remembered the large envelope that Henry had given her that day, and which she'd brought with her to the farm. It was lying on her old desk and appeared to beckon to her. *Let's give Henry's memoir a very quick skim*, she decided.

Lighting a little candle, she laid her hands on the paper and intuitively decided she would co-author this piece of work with Henry. She browsed through the pages to skim some of the text. There were so many gaps that needed filling in. So many places in the book said *To be written by Lana* or *Seeking Lana's side of the story*. Some passages even said *Seeking Elias's side eventually*. It seemed like a daunting task, and Lana turned to the very first page to view the preamble. It read:

Devoted to the victims of conscription and unfree labour worldwide, and written in the hope of contributing to a world where the lottery of birth loses its teeth. Dedicated to the institutions of learning and scientific research. Written in the belief in miracles, and drawn from my own near-death experience. I hereby dedicate a story featuring three protagonists of equal weight, this novel by the name Somewhere Between Light and Time.

About the Author

Aiden Leman lives in East Sussex, England, where he works in financial services for his day job. He studied International Relations in Scotland and was previously active in the teaching sector. He has worked in five different countries across three continents, although his dream job would probably be a firefighter.

Made in the USA
Las Vegas, NV
02 August 2022

52585465R00225